TANGLE OF TIME

TANGLE OF TIME

A Unique Historic
Time-Travel Adventure by

GIN WESTCOTT

Book One

BISCUIT TUESDAY PRESS · GLEN ELLEN · CALIFORNIA

BISCUIT TUESDAY PRESS · GLEN ELLEN · CALIFORNIA · USA

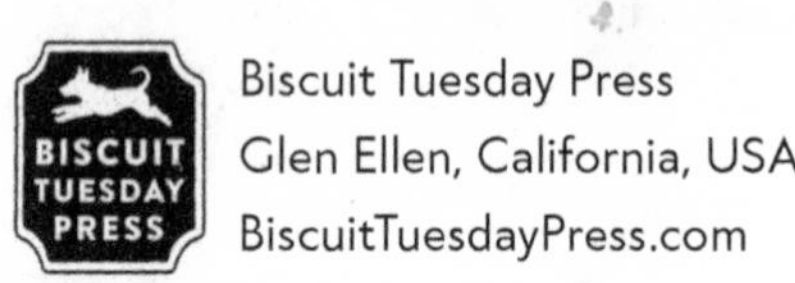

Biscuit Tuesday Press
Glen Ellen, California, USA
BiscuitTuesdayPress.com

Cover Illustration by Brian Edward Miller
Inside illustrations by Shelby Lestrange @sketchyshelby
Graphic Design and maps by Westcott Design

Tangle of Time / Gin Westcott — 1st ed. paperback

ISBN 978-1-952435-00-3

Library of Congress Control Number: 2020906613

Dedicated to my wonderful husband, Scott Callow who has inspired me from the very beginning with unique historical facts and being my first beta reader. And, my children, Trey and Hayley, who I snagged personality traits and quirks to weave into the characters of Toke and Mae.

Buried alive

with one way out.

You don't ask questions.

You survive.

PART ONE

Chapter One

She thrust her arm forward and clawed at the open water—reaching—reaching—grabbing handfuls of water and violently thrusting them behind her. Her entire body begged for oxygen—for one tiny breath—just one. *Where was the surface? Was she swimming down instead of up?* Panic stormed her heart, sending blood thundering through her ears. She kicked her legs into a wild thrashing hysteria until the deep, desperate ache in her lungs became unbearable.

The imprisoning blackness surrounding her began to soften and wrap her in a welcoming embrace. Her head felt pleasantly fuzzy. Insulated in peace. There was no more fighting, just a sleepy smile when she decided to give in to her body's demands and b r e a t h e…*breathe in the water.*

Six days earlier.

As if designed for the set of a TV show, the peaceful street preened gloriously in all its suburban harmony. Tidy monochromatic homes flaunted vibrant flower gardens that surrounded their plush, cushiony, dandelion-free lawns. Three happy chattering kids rode bicycles down the middle of the road without a care, waving to the mail carrier as he greeted each of them by name.

This beautiful summer morning continued its idyllic day until it was savagely murdered by the deafening revs of a furious car engine. No one heard the much-anticipated cheery jingle of the ice cream truck as it turned the corner and drove on by.

Mae sat in the driver's seat, unaware of the unpleasantness she was causing, singing without inhibition to the music in her earbuds. With her foot propped on the gas pedal, she awaited further instruction from her boyfriend, whose head was buried somewhere between the carburetor and the dark abyss.

"Got it!" Greg's greasy hands reached up and slammed down the hood. "You did good, babe—now get over here." He stepped back and grabbed at the empty air in front of him. Mae jumped out of the car, nearly tripping in her four-inch heels, and launched herself into his arms. Catching her mid-air, he swung her around, leaving dirty prints behind where he squeezed her butt. For anyone else, engine grease on Mae's favorite jeans would have been followed by a heated lecture. But with Greg, she adored everything he did and simply giggled, wrapping her hands around his neck for an inspirational kiss.

For the tenth time in the last half hour, her phone vibrated from her pocket, and she groaned. "Sorry, I've got to get home. My mom needs help with something," she said, following it with an exasperated eye roll.

"Not just yet," he said, deep and seductive. Weaving his dark brown fingers through her light brown ones, he led her into his parents' house.

"Um, don't you have class?" Mae didn't really expect an answer, nor wanted one, and shut the door of his bedroom behind them.

An hour later, Greg dropped Mae off in front of her cottage-sized house. Her mother had been busy that morning suffocating the tiny porch in even more hanging baskets and terracotta pots overflowing with pink and orange geraniums. Mae slipped off her heels to make it safely through the narrow path her mom remembered to leave to the door.

Dropping his arm out his car window, Greg slapped the metal. "Love you, babe. See you tomorrow." He pointed his finger. "Early." He added an exaggerated wink for clarity.

She leaned over the porch railing and blew him a kiss. "Wouldn't miss it." The warm breeze stole away a few wisps of her espresso-brown hair and lapped them against her rosy cheeks. Most people wouldn't consider Mae all that pretty, but what she lacked in looks, her body made up for in curves.

The budget was tight living with her mom, Carmen, a single mother without a steady job, and a lack of interest in getting one. Besides, right now, Carmen's career seemed to be finding the perfect husband. Mae had only been four when cancer took her father away and ever since had endured a lifetime of almost-stepdads, though each would eventually fizzle out for one reason or another.

Just before she could turn the knob, the front door opened and a heavyset man with the stench of stale cigarettes sidled past her while his eyes took a slow, uninvited walk up and down her body. Her startled expression shifted to disgust, and she aided his exit by quickly shutting the door behind her.

"So glad you're back, honey." Her mom rushed over and greeted Mae with her usual smothering hug as if it was a miracle her daughter had returned home once again.

Mae needed space when she got home, not asphyxiation in needy love. Yet, if she showed any negative feelings, her mom would launch into sobs, and she would need to comfort her even more.

"Hi, Mama," she said, hugging her back. "Who was that creep?"

"Oh, just the plumber," Carmen said, dismissing the subject, then went to clear two teacups and a small plate of cookie crumbs from the coffee table. Mae didn't want to further that particular discussion either, so she failed to point out that the "plumber" didn't have any tools with him. "I have lunch made so we can get to work right away."

"Work? It must be important then—calling every five minutes and leaving a message each time."

"You should try to keep your ringer on, honey." Carmen arranged the silverware on two floral placemats trimmed with ruffled lace. "What if something terrible happened? What if Nonna was in the hospital, or I got into a car accident—or *married*? Wouldn't you want to know?" She slid her laptop in between them and sat down, placing a napkin on Mae's lap and then her own.

Mae stared at the mountain of lettuce on her plate, topped with unappetizing cold cubed tofu. Carmen waved her own plate of roasted herb-crusted chicken under Mae's nose, trying to entice her to drop this silly vegetarian fad. After fifteen years of this, Mae learned it was best just to say, "Yum," or listen to her mom quoting an hour's worth of healthy reasons to eat meat that she found on some web page. After two small bites, Carmen pushed her dish to the side, hit a key on her computer, and the screen lit up opened to a dating website.

"Oh, really, Mom? *This* was the emergency? I thought you had some critical news or something."

"Now honey, you know how you need a father. I thought you should have some say in it too." Her mom continued opening an assortment of web pages, tapping keys with the tips of her perfectly manicured fingernails, which matched her perfectly made-up face and hair. She often reminded Mae to *always* be ready for Mr. Right. He could come knocking on your door any day, handing out brochures.

"For God's sake, Mom. I'll be a sophomore in college this fall. I don't need a father anymore. Especially not some creepy old man fumbling his way into my bedroom in the middle of the night." This particular vision of her future stepdad always made Mae cringe.

Carmen brushed Mae's comment off. "Anyway, I want you in on this decision."

"Find one who doesn't smoke. Please."

"Well, honey, my prospects aren't that plentiful anymore. Maybe if I were under fifty." She patted the loose skin under her chin. "Do you think I look forty? I'd have more opportunities if I was forty." She moved in closer to the screen and scrutinized her retouched profile picture—which was taken ten years before—when she was actually in her forties. "Yes. I'm going to say I'm forty."

"Do you really want to start off a new relationship with a lie?" Mae asked as her mom logged into one dating site after another, updating her new age. "Geez, how many singles sites do you belong to? Are you paying for all of these?" Carmen didn't seem to hear, so Mae sighed in surrender. "Okay, what *exactly* are you looking for in a man?"

"I'm thinking cinnamon-colored skin and a mustache. He doesn't need to be Latino like us, but I *do* like the dark meat."

"Yuck." Mae covered her ears. "Are you aware of the damage you can cause a child?"

"You're not a child anymore. We're like girlfriends now," Carmen said, contradicting her earlier statement while rearranging browser windows in order of preference.

"See? I don't need a father," Mae said to deaf ears. She picked up her cell phone to text Greg an assortment of heart emojis.

"Your father died when you were very young. You need the experience of having a father."

Mae had only been four when cancer took her father away and the few memories she had of him could never be replaced. "You're enough. You've done a good job at both." But her mother's mind was already set, so she conceded. "Okay. Let's find me a new father." Mae slammed her spirited fist on the table. "What else do you require of him?"

"Well, I know what I don't want. I don't want some over-baked potato that sits on the couch with caramel corn embedded in his backside. Someone that doesn't spend half the day on the toilet and the other half watching sports." Her list went on for some time, then slowed. Her eyes glazed over, and she looked wistful. "Oh, honey, your father was such a handsome man." Her hand pitter-pattered over her heart. "One hundred percent pure Mayan decent." Carmen touched Mae's cheek. "You look a lot like him. But you've definitely got my spunk."

Mae repeated the word "spunk" softly, not sure if it was truly a word she liked. "I sure do."

"Sass. That's another thing we've both got. Spunk and sass—"

"And a big fat ass," Mae added, causing them both to laugh.

After Carmen cleared away the plates, she handed them each a pen and paper. It was time to get to work. Mae stretched her arms and yawned, accepting the fact that this was just the beginning of a very long afternoon.

Chapter Two

Fridays meant live nude models in Toke's figure drawing class. He was even on time this morning, which was particularly challenging in the 105-degree heat for a single-unit summer semester course. Two years as a full-time freshman at Sacramento City College just wasn't impressing the ladies.

The air conditioner blasted him as he flung open the classroom door. Unpleasantly chilled in his sweat-soaked t-shirt, he sauntered across the room and dropped into the seat next to his friend, Greg. He flipped his sunglasses up on his windswept blond hair but groaned when he saw their model for the day. His eyes met Greg's, who mirrored his expression. Exhaling his disappointment a little too loudly, Toke grudgingly pulled out his art supplies.

Crossing his arms over his chest, he leaned back in his chair and studied the nude model perched on a stool in the center of the classroom. He held a contemplative pose, seeming perfectly comfortable having thirty pairs of eyes crawling over every inch of his tired, sagging body. In a curious sort of way, Toke found the old man intriguing. Where clothing usually covered, his skin remained baby smooth, not one wrinkle. A disturbing contrast to the armadillo-like leather on his arms, hands, and face.

Greg coughed, and said under his breath, "Nutsack," gesturing to the long, hairy pendulums spilling over the top of the stool and grazing the upper rung, overstretched from so many years of gravity. Toke let out a stifled gagging sound. This was beginning to feel more like a science course studying deformity in geriatrics than an art class.

Moments later, Toke sensed the teacher standing behind him. She spoke softly, like a yoga instructor strung out on chamomile tea. "May

I?" Her arm breezed over his shoulder and held out an open palm. Relinquishing his charcoal stick, she took it into her long fingers and sketched right over his feeble scratches with deliberate, confident lines. She leaned into his side a bit more to get the proper perspective, and that was all it took. His focus shifted from the charcoal pencil to this woman pressing against him. The heat of her body radiated, and he breathed deeply, letting his lungs fill with the honey musk of her sweet skin. His eyes sought more and slipped away unnoticed, meandering up her arm, and comfortably lounging on her chest. Her shy, plump cleavage peeked in and out from the top of her blouse with each stroke she drew, begging to escape their imprisonment. Maybe, if he fixated on it long enough, one would get the courage to break free, popping a button on its way out to embrace its new wild freedom. Then he'd have to catch it with his cupped hand, none of this being his fault, he was only helping. She would have to insist he stay after class to instruct him further…

"Now you try it on a clean piece." The teacher whipped her drawing to the back of the large sketchpad, jolting Toke back into reality. He picked up the charcoal and made a single long wavy stroke that started at the model's neck and finished at the bottom of his foot. This solitary line revealed the fundamental curves of a human body, allowing the viewer's subconscious brain to fill in the rest.

The instructor beamed enthusiastically. "That's it—you got it." She moved on to the next student, leaving Toke with not only more confidence but a slide show of images playing through his mind of their special time together. This was one of those days he was grateful he wore baggy jeans.

Leaning far out of his way, Greg's eyes followed the retreating teacher. "Damn. If she was the nude model, I could be so inspired."

An hour later, class was over, and Toke hurriedly packed up his drawing tools, not wanting to put in one more extra minute than he had to. Flipping his sketchpad closed, he stuffed it under his arm, and he and Greg walked out of the classroom.

Standing six feet tall, Greg was nearly the height of Toke, but half his girth. "So, where you off to this summer?"

Fingering the pack of cigarettes in his pocket, Toke squinted at the Five Years Smoke-Free and Proud sign securely fastened to the concrete partition. "My dickhead dad's been on my case about me getting a job. He said if I don't, I have to start some bullshit therapy," Toke rolled his eyes, "so I can be his younger clone."

Greg snorted. "I'm picturing you and your dad in matching jogging suits and new white tennis shoes. You're smiling at each other, drinking bright green smoothies. Then he makes a delightful G-rated joke, and you both laugh hysterically." He finished with a labored sigh and wiped a fake tear away. "It's just beautiful, man."

When they got to the bike racks, Toke bent down and spun a number combination into his lock. "So, what's up with you this summer?"

"I'm hooked up, on the weekends at least, starting tomorrow." Greg straddled one of the bikes pretending he was riding it over jumps. "Shit work, pulling rocks and crap, but they pay by the piece, and it promises to add up fast."

"What's he paying?" Toke yanked impatiently at the stubborn lock.

"The boss says each day we could come home with three hundred dollars in our pockets. Where else can you make that in a few hours, here in Sacramento?" Toke glanced at him sideways, so Greg added, "Legally, I mean. Dude says he's looking for more people. You down?"

Toke breathed out, "Yeah, sure," wiping the sweat from his forehead with his t-shirt. "Sounds hella better than bagging groceries at the market or handing burgers and fries to a screaming carload of wasted chicks through a drive-up window." Catching what he just said, he adjusted his words, "Okay, that last one wasn't really a good example of torture."

"Cool. Tomorrow morning, then. Pick you up a little past seven."

"Seven—like a.m.? What the hell, dude? It's summer." Toke unwound the cable, freeing his longboard, and stuffed the lock in his pack.

"Up to you, man. Gets frickin' hot by noon, so we cram it all into the morning, and you've still got your day left." Greg fished around in his pockets for his car keys. "My buddy Dex is picking me up. You'll get to meet Mae. She's pulling rocks, too. Trying to save money for school but keeps spending it on random shit, and then more shit." He eventually found the pocket with his keys and tossed them in the air. "But yeah, about a half hour southeast of Sacto. Still at that place off Third?"

"Yeah."

"K, see ya." They swiped hands and Greg jogged off to the parking lot, his glistening coils of black hair bounced rhythmically, doing their own style of spunky dance.

With a single swift motion, Toke flipped his board to the ground, lit a cigarette, and checked his messages in transit. Once past the city college sign, without slowing down in the least, he traded his cigarette for a half-smoked joint. Like being reunited with a long-departed lover, he engulfed the smoke, letting it meander slowly through his lungs before exhaling with a contented smile.

Under the blaze of the afternoon sun, heat rose in lazy waves off the roasting pavement. Toke peeled off his drenched t-shirt and tucked it in his belt, revealing a soft stomach that bounced like Jell-O over every bump, broadcasting his passion for chocolate Pop-Tarts.

With a wide swing, he pulled up to his dad's simple and tidy cookie cutter townhouse. No neighbor dared break the rules of the homeowner's association by exposing even the smallest hint of character, with his father getting an A+ in that contest. Even a potted rose bush or hanging musical chimes could unbalance the conformity of the complex and open themselves up to neighbors' judgments. Toke found their over-obedience entertaining, so occasionally brought home pieces of discarded art from the ceramics building's dumpster and thoughtfully displayed them in random neighbors' front yards. Just to stir things up.

Stepping off his board, he flicked it up with skater precision, swiped his hair back with his free hand and walked through the front door. His dad, Ron, stood, leaning against the kitchen counter, stabbing at an intensely green organic salad. "Hi, buddy," he said a little too cheerfully, attempting to hide his annoyance at his son's sloppy appearance.

"Hey," Toke breathed, flinging open the refrigerator. He bathed in the chilled air, examining its contents, then settled on a jar of peanut butter. "I told you I don't like it cold."

"Would you rather your body be infested with cancer-causing aflatoxins?" Ron put down his fork, ready to talk about any questions his son might have on the subject. Toke didn't answer, but dumped three packets of hot cocoa mix in with the peanut butter, found a spoon and stirred.

"Jeremy." His dad refused to call him by his nickname. "Your eyes…I see pain. You're only making it worse by feeding your hurt with calories." Stepping back, Ron held out his arms to display his fit physique. "Look at me. All this doesn't come easily." He waited for some kind of inspired nod from his son, but Toke was completely consumed peeling a banana, which also went into the peanut butter. After a short stir, he shoved a spoonful of the sticky sweet concoction into his mouth, left the kitchen, and walked down the hall to his room.

Ron called after him, "I'm here if you would like to process what's going on inside. I haven't been there, but I can listen and help you become the person you've always wanted to be. I know he's in there, lost somewhere inside of you." Then, as if being pulled by a strong magnet, Ron whisked down the hallway and wedged up against Toke's bedroom door. "Jer, I know you're in there," he said, tapping lightly with his knuckles.

"What?" Toke muttered.

"Can I come in?"

"No." Video game gunfire blasted in the background.

"I think this would be a good time to begin a session with you. We can work out some of the issues you're having. Whether it's about girls or your weight, it doesn't matter. I'm here to help." Ron considered himself a psychologist, having read a myriad of self-help books.

"I'm fine. No issues. Go away." More gunfire.

"Knock-knock," Ron said out loud while opening the door and walking in. His nostrils twitched as they picked up the offensive odors of a post-teenager's room: sweaty socks, spilled beer, and mildewing wet towels. He crunched a trail through the potato chips that littered the carpet to the unmade bed, smoothed out a spot, and sat. With his expression now adjusted to concern, Ron used his practiced, soft, "engaging" voice. "Jeremy, we need to talk about your actions lately—"

Toke handed his dad the controller, walked out of the room, peanut butter jar in hand and spoon hanging out of his mouth. In the living room, he grabbed the TV remote and launched himself over the back of the couch, landing flat onto the overstuffed cushions. The first thing that came on was a porn station, which his father had apparently been watching last, so Toke just sat there and let it play.

Finding his way to the living room, his dad was now standing behind the couch and continued talking where he left off, "...Because I understand, son. I've been there. Well, not to your extent. But, to be self-aware, we need to uncover your destructive patterns..."

The white noise of his father's wisdoms finally found their place, and Toke's eyelids grew heavy, fluttered twice, then closed.

Chapter Three

Groggy, lacking sleep, Mae filled her water bottles from the refrigerator door while a strong pot of coffee brewed. She gazed dreamily into the cold stream of water, imagining all the ways she could wake Greg up that morning.

Then like rude party crashers who let themselves in, images of gray-bearded men in sunglasses, sitting on their new mid-life crisis Harleys, speedboats, and convertible sports cars from her mom's dating sites flashed through her head, ruining all her romantic ideas.

She slid the plastic bottles into the elastic of her waist pack, stashed it all into her backpack, and poured herself a large steaming cup of coffee. She stared, half asleep, mesmerized with devoted affection as the french vanilla creamer transformed the bitter black into a caramel seduction. Then with a quick glance at the time, she downed what she could and dashed out the door at the ungodly hour of six a.m. Since her mom needed the car for the day, she trekked the five blocks to Greg's house on foot. He would just have to appreciate her "sporty" scent without complaints.

Under the discreetly brightening sky, Mae rounded the last corner and spotted Greg's house. She turned down the walkway and headed to the front door, preparing to slip silently inside. "Good morning, Mae!" Startled, Mae jumped, grabbing hold of a small trellis for balance as Greg's mom smiled and waved her pruning shears from behind a rose bush.

Taking a slow breath to calm her racing heart, Mae waved back. "Hey, Mrs. B.!" She couldn't help but wonder what drove Greg's mom to be up gardening at six a.m. on a Saturday. When Mae had the option, she could sleep well into the afternoon, snuggled deep into her four-inch memory foam topper, and block out an entire world.

Mae loved Greg's mom, even with all her oddities. She was eternally cheerful, patient and exceedingly kind. Just like a TV mom. In fact, they called her Mrs. B because of her obsession with the old 70s show, The *Brady Bunch.* As if that wasn't weird enough, she insisted they name their firstborn Greg, after the oldest Brady son on the show. They named their next son Peter, and the two girls, Marcia and Jan, following the Brady pattern. Greg's dad simply went along with it, shrugging a, "Why not?"

But Greg wanted no part of this weird Brady Bunch cult. And especially to be named after a fictitious suck-up white boy. "If you notice, I'm black. My whole family is black. So why would we want to be like a candy-coated white family? Why not some cool black family? There were plenty of those on TV."

All Mae could do was take his hand and pat it reassuringly. "They didn't *have* cool black families on television in the early 70s when your mom was young."

"Ha—what about *Good Times, The Jeffersons*, or *What's Happening*—Dy-no-mite!" He acted it out as anyone who knew it would.

"Those came in the late 70s. Your mom was in high school by then and had better things to do than sit in front of the TV at home while being verbally and physically abused by her strung-out parents."

By six-fifteen, Mae had finished complimenting each one of Mrs. B.'s rose bushes, and walked through the front door like she lived there. With a "hi" to Marsha and Jan, who were making breakfast popcorn balls out of cereal, she continued down the hall to Greg's room.

Saturday at Greg's house was TV day. Everyone, except Greg, was up as soon as the sun broke the horizon, then sat in front of the television where they ate all three meals—eyes glued to the set. It was like a Superbowl Sunday, but every Saturday and without the sports, favoring the nostalgic sitcoms. They sang all the show theme songs together with trained perfection and watched all the commercials for the rare chance there might be a jingle to sing. Dinners were much anticipated on TV day. Mrs. B. microwaved frozen meals and called them "TV dinners," which made them taste even more delicious. She didn't like how they stopped making them in the sectioned foil trays. "It's just not right," she said regularly, shaking her head.

For family dinners the rest of the week, they went around the table, and each person described their day as if it were an exciting adventure. By dessert, they'd be reenacting their favorite scenes from TV Saturday and laughing hysterically at jokes that were far from funny. Greg often tried to shock them with gruesome news stories of the real world, peppered with as many vulgar words as he could fit in. But they would only smile through their rose-colored blinders and say things like, "Thank goodness that didn't happen to us!"

By age fourteen, Greg had saved enough money to buy the electric guitar he had his eyes on since he was ten. Now it was his turn to give back and fill his family's bizarre utopian bubble. What he was unsuccessful at expressing with snide comments, he could now express through the sweet melodies of his soulful music. With pick in hand, he plowed through all six strings, releasing an ugly aberration of dismembered chords that devoured the peace like a screaming tantrum on steroids. He continued to play his guitar, at all hours of the day and night, letting it hatchet its way through the walls, dominating the house with blaring compositions of unhinged madness. He explained to his family that he was channeling Jimi Hendrix, and Jimi never slept. But, like everything else, they remained unfazed. Simply a note under his door suggesting he take guitar lessons, signed with a smiley face at the bottom.

Exhausted and defeated, Greg eventually stopped rebelling and gave up the guitar. Then he met Mae, who changed his world and took all his misery away. She helped him appreciate what he had, and whenever he would start up his frustrated rant, she would remind him, "You take your family for granted. Sure, they might be a little quirky, but your house is *so* full of love. Imagine what it's like for poor Dexter."

"Hey, little asshole—bring me a beer!" Dexter's father shouted from the couch, his bloodshot eyes glued to the TV. Dexter tossed over a can, which purposely landed on the rug a little out of his father's reach. "You're going to regret that one day, boy," he slurred, using his big toe in hopeless attempts to bring the can closer.

If he weren't transferring to USC on a full scholarship in the fall, Dexter would have been long gone from this shitty house and his shitty dad and into an apartment with his best friend, Greg. He spread a thick layer of peanut butter on two pieces of toast, while his phone pinged the latest texts, adding to the constant roll of messages from girls he had no serious interest in. Working as a barista across from the college gave him no shortage of new opportunities that he wasn't really looking for, and the less interest he showed, the more they wanted him.

He pulled an empty plastic soda bottle from the trash and filled it with tap water, then stuffed it into his backpack. Heading for the door, he checked his pocket for his keys and grabbed his sunglasses.

"Rent's due next week, so you better be on your goddamn way to work." Still reaching for the beer, his dad fell from the couch with a graceless thud. "You ungrateful, little piece of—" Dexter shut the front door behind him, distancing himself from his father's barking with every step.

And there she was, even more beautiful than the day before, patiently waiting just for him. As if on stage with the sun as her spotlight, she beamed brilliant crystals from her polished chrome and a glossy black finish. His 1969 Chevy Malibu, the most positive thing in his life. He rebuilt the engine twice, the carburetor three times, installed seat belts, air-conditioning, killer speakers, and the best stereo he could afford. She was perfect, inside and out, and the closest thing Dexter ever had to a girlfriend.

Circling her slowly, he buffed out a couple of blemishes with his sleeve, got in and turned the key. She purred with luxury, like a contented cat.

Dexter patted the dash. "Good girl." The years he spent under the hood provided the well-needed escape from his drunk, violent father and filled a void that could have, too easily, been packed with drugs and booze.

The front door of his house opened, and Dexter turned in time to see his father propped up in the doorway saying goodbye in his own special way. With a stream of urine, he watered the cracked dirt of the dried-up weedy lawn, that being so parched, thirstily soaked it up. He cackled bitterly and began waving it around, until he toppled backward through the open front door, landing flat on his back.

When Dexter was younger, he would run to his father and help him up, so full of his mother's goodwill and kindness. But now, there was no pity left for his dad. Only the harbored guilt of wishing one day he'd come home and find his father dead. Dexter hated himself for being capable of thinking such a selfish thing, especially of his own father. The feeling of worthlessness his father beat into him, and his own self-loathing, left him believing he didn't deserve anyone's love.

Dexter gunned the engine a few times until she was warmed up. After checking his hair in the mirror, he flicked a few pieces around, turned on his music, and drove off to pick up Greg and Mae.

Chapter Four

The silky down of Greg's comforter slid luxuriously across Mae's bare skin as she rolled onto her back. He pressed his body into hers, decorating every inch of her face with soft kisses that she imagined were tiny butterflies dancing on her skin. His lips wandered, teasing a trail down the side of her neck and she groaned in pleasure.

Suddenly, her eyes shot open in a panic. Why didn't she think of birth control before she left her house? She attempted to slide off the bed without being noticed, which was awkward in itself as if Greg couldn't tell she was squeezing out from *under* him. "I'm sorry, babe," she pleaded, covering herself with random pieces of clothing she found on the floor until she could duck into his bathroom.

"Why do you hide your deliciousness from me?" Greg pouted and groaned at the same time.

"I don't know, I always feel fat," she called from behind the closed door.

"Fat? Is that what people are calling perfection these days?" He threw a pillow at the door, growing impatient. "Why do you still use that diaphragm thing, anyway? Why not do the patch, or pill, or ring like the rest of the world? Hell, I can put on a condom."

Rustling noises came from the bathroom. "You know hormones wig me out and I'm actually *here* in the world because of a faulty condom. This is my way of being in control of my own destiny. *And* yours. It's a simple silicone cup I fill with spermicide—" She ceased talking before she totally destroyed the mood. Mae exhausted herself trying to squeeze the last tiny bit of spermicide gel out of the crumpled tube.

"Okay, whatever—just get back here." He threw the other pillow at the door right as Mae opened it, hitting her square on.

She pounced on the bed, straddling Greg, holding his arms over his head like a prisoner. Lowering her face to his, she stopped short and hovered in the sliver of pause between their lips.

Lingering just above the surface of his skin, her mouth laid a slow and torturous trail of whispery breaths and radiating heat. She breezed down the tendons of his neck, taking a moment to devour the masculine pheromones from his moistening skin before moving down to his shoulders and chest. Her face, so teasingly close, but just out of touch, *driving him wild.*

His dark brown eyes, fierce with lust, stared into hers. "I love you more than I've ever loved anyone." His voice resonated with such intensity, so deep and guttural, it stole her breath. "You are my everything." She sensed his muscles tighten, and he took possession, flipping her onto her back and pinning her under him. This stirred something raw and primal in Mae, and she never wanted anything more than she wanted him right now.

They startled awake to loud knocking on the bedroom door. "Hey Greg!" his little sister shouted, still pounding on his door. "Dexter's outside."

"Wha—?" Greg grabbed his phone and checked the time.

"Mom said to tell you to tell him not to honk at seven in the morning. She says it's not neighborly."

"Damn, why does he always have to be on time?" Greg dangled Mae's bra over her nose tickling her to get up then pulled his t-shirt over his head. "Good day for Jimi." He smoothed his hands over the front of his shirt, where an artistically altered photo of Jimi Hendrix stared out.

Before they could dash out the door, Greg's mother called to them. "Hang on a second." She finished setting up the last TV tray and hurried over. "I've packed your Captain Crunch breakfast balls to go." Then began fumbling through her pockets until she pulled out a small tube. "And be sure to wear sunscreen," she said, slipping it inside the paper bag along with their sugar coma. At the door, she waved a quick hello to Dexter, who sat in the car, drumming his hands on the steering wheel to some unheard music. He waved back, then leaned over to push open the passenger door revealing his favorite well-worn red plaid flannel button-up over a simple white t-shirt.

Dexter was, simply put, beautiful, but didn't seem to really notice this, so it never went to his head. Women couldn't stop staring, and men envied him. His masculine face was sculpted to pleasing perfection. Well-tanned skin defined natural muscles that rippled across every part of his body. He kept his sun-streaked brown hair long enough to pull back in a band with a few escaped pieces seductively hanging in his face, teasing to hide his sea green eyes. He was absolutely mesmerizing, and Mae caught herself, ashamedly, staring at him much too often.

Mrs. B. placed her hand on Greg's arm catching him on his way out. "Be sure to call me and let me know where you'll be. And don't forget that tonight's TV dinner night," she added, her eyes shining in anticipation. Greg planted a quick kiss on her cheek, threw his backpack over his shoulder, and tucked his shirt into his pants on the way to the car.

"Hey, man," Greg said, then offered the front seat to Mae.

"Sup?" Dexter gestured back.

"Hi." Mae got in, feeling self-conscious like she always did around Dexter. She started to put her unbrushed hair in a ponytail and flipped down the visor for a mirror.

"Sorry, no mirror in a '69." Dexter shrugged apologetically.

Greg buckled his seat belt. "I told my bud Toke he could catch a ride. He lives right on the way."

"Sure." Dexter looked back in the rearview mirror. "But what kind of name is Toke?"

"Toke *earned* his nickname. You'll see." Greg smiled, adding a slight cough.

Toke leaned against his dad's spotless champagne-colored SUV parked in the driveway, wearing a black t-shirt branded in bright faux-graffiti skater art. He stubbed out his cigarette once the old Chevy pulled up, but when he caught sight of a girl in the car, he also smoothed out his uncombed, pillow-flattened hair.

The front door of the condo opened, and Ron stepped outside, causing Toke to dive into Dexter's back seat immediately. "Let's go." Toke tapped the back of the seat impatiently.

"Hey, Toke's dad!" Greg leaned over Toke and waved through the open window.

"It's Ron! Call me Ron!" He waved energetically from the front porch and smiled, showing way too many compulsively flossed teeth.

Toke jabbed Greg. "Stop encouraging him." The only thing that could easily embarrass Toke was his father. His excessive cheeriness was excruciating to endure.

Ron's frantic waving "hello" morphed into waving "goodbye" as he cheerily proselytized his unwanted advice. "Today's a good day to believe in yourself! Exude bright rays of confidence and face your difficult situations with courage—" They drove away, completely unaware Ron was even talking at all.

Taking a deep breath once they had some distance, Toke eventually relaxed. Ron was a caring father, but all Toke saw was his father's obsession to change him and his inability to accept him for the man he'd grown up to be. His father wouldn't be happy until Toke was the ideal son he had always wanted. Someone he would brag about at the gym and proudly upload photo after photo to Facebook, Twitter, and Instagram, zealously tagging him along with his baseball, basketball, and football stats. Casually working into his posts Toke's genius GPA that semester, his enviable body mass index, and the university scholarships he was offered that fall. Ron would also tag himself in the photos, even if he weren't in them. Whether this was all true about his father or not, he didn't care. This was the picture he painted of him in his mind. Toke always felt shitty, like a complete failure every minute he was around his dad, and it made him try even less to better himself and his grades.

But now, Toke found something far more interesting to think about and began to stare, fixated on Mae. She squirmed uncomfortably as if she could feel him touching her with his eyes. Greg flapped around his hand, saying, "Toke, Mae and Dexter, Mae and Dex, Toke."

Toke gestured with his chin. "Hey."

Introductions, though a formal courtesy kids were forced to learn, had an unspoken purpose. They gave official permission for strangers to speak to each other, magically whisking the awkwardness away. Mae glanced back with a quick, "Hi," and her stiff body slowly relaxed.

For the first five minutes of the drive, Greg and Mae awkwardly held hands over the seats. Toke finally said, "Uh, we can switch places if you want," which he sprinkled with a touch of sarcasm. She took him up on it and crawled over the seat, scooting close to Greg to allow room for Toke to crawl through to the front.

Toke looked amused at their needy affection. "Nah, I'll stay here." Plus, where he sat now, he appeared to have a good view down Mae's shirt. "Chauffeur away, dude."

They found a deli in the gas station mini-mart and ordered sandwiches for lunch. Toke did a bit of shopping, then unloaded his second armful of snacks on the counter by the cashier. Greg walked over and curiously surveyed the growing mound. "Dude, you building a bomb shelter?"

"Nah, my Dad gave me a fifty for lunch and said to bring him the change." Greg understood perfectly and added a family-sized bag of peanut M&M's to Toke's pile of protein bars, breakfast bars, a five-pack of Snickers, Doritos, cheese puffs, energy drinks, and an endless variety of salted nuts.

Toke loaded his purchases into his backpack, having to pound them down to fit everything in. He groaned, slapped his forehead, and stared resentfully at his pack. “Fuck.”

“Smokes at the bottom?” Greg sympathized and patted his friend’s back.

Chapter Five

The prospect of wrestling rocks out of dirt under the sweltering summer sun versus spending a breezy July day in the city would seem insane to most. But a little physical torture in the morning could earn Mae a pedicure and the red ankle-strap sandals with the stiletto heel she'd had her eye on by late afternoon. This made it an easy choice.

Dexter turned off the main highway onto a narrow dusty road that went on for miles and miles. Scrawny signs, handwritten on torn cardboard and stapled to dilapidated fence posts, showed up every so often, leading the way. The punishing mess of turns on this desolate road was making Mae carsick, so she leaned against Greg's shoulder and gazed out the window. "Where are we anyway? Nothing's even out here. Can you imagine being stuck out here without a GPS to get us back out?"

"Wait! Turn around. Over there." Greg pointed to a grouping of trucks, cars, and a temporary trailer office, nearly hidden under the immense oak trees.

Soon they were out of the car, slapping on their packs, and discreetly merging in with their fellow rock pullers. Mae felt a little uncomfortable, seeing no other females but herself, so she stood close to Greg, trying to disappear.

Ignoring their late arrival, a man in his mid-sixties perched at the top metal stair of the trailer office continued with his instructions. "So, that's it for the rock wall, now for the well. If any of you bring in a size like this, that one'll land you five bucks. That one there"—he nodded to a larger rock—"*and* unbroken, could get you ten bucks. Anything bigger, well, there will be a generous tip in it for you." He held up a sizable clipboard in his large pink hand. "You keep tally here and make sure Roman signs off on it. We'll pay you in cash and your team will split the money equally at day's end." He removed his sunglasses and scanned the crew of about twenty men until his eyes rested on Mae. "So, you all better work equally as hard."

Mae's jaw dropped in indignation. "Did you see that? He looked right at me!"

"Bastard." Greg backed her in support. "He's just never seen you work before. You'll blow him away, Mae Bae."

Stepping forward from behind the boss, and without having to be asked, the assistant handed him a large white cowboy hat. In a well-polished move, knowing the exact angle which looked best, the boss carefully positioned the hat on his overly groomed salt and pepper hair. *Did he wear that same hat in the oil painting he surely had of himself hanging over his mantle at home?*

With a flick of his hand, indicating they were moving, the boss stomped down the steps, so the heels of his cowboy boots struck the metal rungs with an authoritative gong. He ambled over to the line of trucks, basking in his own self-importance as the subservient crowd followed closely behind. "I want groups of five or six. One group will have the abandoned well, and the rest will demolish the rock walls. The well goes down maybe twenty feet, and I want it all. This type of stone is extremely tough to come by, so don't waste any of it." He handed off his clipboard to his assistant without even a glance. "All right. Who still needs a group?" He proceeded to assign a short man with carrot-red hair, who reminded Mae of a little clown, to their own party of four.

"The rocks from the well are to go in these trucks according to size, and rocks from the walls go in these." The boss waved toward each truck like a bored game show hostess. "For the people going down inside the well, you are required to wear a harness." This was the same type of contraption Mae had worn on a zipline, where, for guys, it tied around their man parts and pushed them out in a neat little package to avoid a painful squeeze. She groaned when the boss gave a demonstration. She did not like seeing this old guy's genitals presented like this.

"This is a dangerous job and it's your responsibility to take care of yourself. If you forgot your gloves, there's plenty here," he said, motioning to a box filled with what could be taken for dead rodents. "Take the tools you need and return them when you're done for the day. Do not leave anything, including personal trash, at the worksite. And watch out for angry rattlers."

Mae squeezed Greg's hand tightly at the thought of running into a rattlesnake. He squeezed back. "I got you, baby."

"The well is located quite a ways out so you'll need to haul the stone back in this Caterpillar. Anyone know how to drive a Cat front loader?" Their new redheaded teammate was the only one who raised his hand. "Okay Red. You and your team are assigned to the well."

"Sweet," Greg said, and Mae wondered if it actually *was* sweet. But since those were the only instructions they heard, she agreed.

"I'm putting Roman in charge for the rest of the day, and I will see you again at seven-thirty a.m. tomorrow." The boss removed his hat and handed it to his assistant, Roman, then walked back to the office.

Mae relaxed somewhat knowing the boss was leaving. He was a bit intimidating and had too many rules. Besides, Roman looked like he'd been drinking since three this morning.

Gesturing with his chin and a half smile toward their new teammate, Toke said to Mae, "That guy's going to make *you* look good."

How many chauvinists did she have to meet in one day? Mae barely even knew Toke, and here he was already insulting her. Greg put a supportive arm around her shoulders. "Dude, you have no idea what this little fireball can do." She liked the fact he called her little. At five foot three inches and one hundred eighty pounds, people usually just referred to her as short.

"Yeah, okay." Toke rolled his eyes and resumed his "too cool for school" stance.

"What a jerk," Mae said under her breath while she and Greg walked over to the pile of gloves.

“Don’t worry about Toke,” Greg assured her. “He’s really a good guy. Sometimes speaks his mind without thinking. By the end of the day, you’ll love him.”

Toke left to go to the porta potty and waited for one to free up. A few feet away stood the redhead lighting up a cigarette. Toke patted his pocket then remembered his smokes were at the bottom of his backpack. “Mind if I bum one?”

“Sure.” The man’s voice was raspy but friendly. Probably only in his mid-forties but could pass for eighty. He coughed into his hand, then wiped it on his shirt. “Name’s Carny,” he said, holding out the same hand.

Toke coolly swiped the back of his hand instead, passing it off as intentional. “Carny?” He smiled, amused. “What kind of name is that?”

“Heh. A nickname that sort of stuck. My family always worked the fairs and carnivals.” He took another draw on his cigarette, and the creases around his mouth deepened, making his lips look like an anus.

“They call me Toke.” He exhaled, cocooning himself in smoke.

“Toke, heh, heh. I think I’m going to like you.” His laugh punished the air with scents of mint and budding lung cancer. A few puffs later, their new substitute boss, Roman, called Carny’s name, so Toke handed him back his lighter. “Nah, keep it.” Carny ran off but turned around after a few yards. “I’ve got something better for us later.” And with a sly wink, he dashed off.

Chapter Six

Mae put her small hand in one of the humongous, stiff gloves. "Gross. They're still wet from someone else—and that's from yesterday!" She bounced up and down, shivering in disgust.

After Carny let out a piercing whistle from the driver's seat of the giant Caterpillar, waving them over, the four of them headed his way. Dexter said, "I checked around, and there doesn't appear to be any waivers to sign for release of liability." Then added with a shrug, "Nothing."

Greg glanced back at the temporary office trailer suspiciously. "Guy must have one hell of an insurance policy."

"If he pays cash, who cares?" Toke shoved his hands in his jean's pockets and walked around the Caterpillar, sizing it up.

"So, do we just climb up the bulldozer?" Mae asked anyone who would answer.

"It's called a Caterpillar front loader," Carny haughtily corrected her while attempting to tame his puffy red hair into a ponytail. To Mae, this machine was a giant Tonka toy. Bright yellow with four enormous tires that were almost as tall as she was and a shovel in front that could hold a small car. Dexter climbed into the cab behind Carny while Toke, Greg, and Mae scrambled into the bucket. "That's not really safe," Carny said with little interest and drove off anyway.

After a dusty, bumpy ten-minute ride, and according to the hand-drawn map, they had arrived at their work site. There stood not a well, but a massive stack of gray rocks. It was the only thing around except for a grouping of low spindly trees, possessively bound together by the wandering vines of wild blackberries. If there had once been a house that used the well, it was long gone by now. All they could see for miles in each direction were expansive empty fields carpeted in dry brown grass, freckled with a variety of oaks.

Carny parked the Caterpillar twelve feet away for safety's sake, and they all scrambled out. Feeling filthy and coated in dust, Mae flipped her head over and thrashed her long silky hair around far more than necessary before tying it up in a ponytail. She brushed off her clothes and wasn't happy that her black Converse were already gray before they even started.

Planting his hands firmly on his hips, Toke scanned their surroundings. "So, where's this frickin' well?"

"Over here." Dexter was kneeling by a large pile of rocks on the far side and motioned them over. A few of the rocks had tumbled away revealing an immense slab of wood that was buried beneath them all. "I'm fairly sure these are covering the opening."

"This sucks, man." Toke glared at the stack. "We're not getting paid to move these shit rocks."

"The sooner we get started, the faster we're out of here," Greg said with his usual optimism, carrying away his first rock. Mae groaned, slipped on her sweaty gloves and joined in. What did she expect? The job was to move rocks.

It took about ten minutes to roll all the stones off the cover, which turned out to be two three-inch-thick solid wood doors butted side by side. "Check these out." Greg fingered the old rusty hinges still attached to the doors.

Dexter carefully picked the thick coating of dried mud off one of the metal hinges, revealing the shape of a long, curved fish-like creature. "Fascinating." When he tried to remove more of the dirt, a piece of the fish easily broke off, being completely rusted through.

Although the doors were extremely old and weathered, they were solid and thick, and it took every bit of strength from all of them to drag them off the well opening. They laboriously walked each door over to a nearby tree and dropped them in its shade, declaring it their lunchroom floor.

This well didn't look like any kind of well Mae was familiar with. Rather than the storybook well from "Jack and Jill" she had pictured in her head, these top stones had been removed, leaving the rest flush to the ground. She was now staring down into a dark, foreboding hole nearly five feet wide and smelling of old musty earth. And, as promised, it was lined with hand-cut green rectangular stones, each about four inches tall and varying in width. But what really made this well unique was the craftsmanship someone put into building it. The polished green stone walls looked more like she'd expect to see lining an elaborate city fountain designed for royalty.

"This ain't no local Sac rock. Never seen it 'round here before." Carny folded his arms across his chest. "Must be some fancy imported shit."

Picking up a chisel, Dexter tapped at the grout between two stones which crumbled away easily. "Not much holding these in." His finger traced the unique trails of vibrant blue marbling that ran throughout the stone, then passed it on to Mae.

So instantly entranced, her mouth dropped open in awe, and she breathed the words, "Just beautiful." She could almost see Mother Nature sitting behind her large stone canvas, gracefully painting each thread of blue with her finest brush.

Toke held out his hand and politely cleared his throat a couple of times until she reluctantly handed it over. He lifted the stone to catch the sun's light and inspected it suspiciously. "What idiot lines their underground well—that no one will ever see—with showy polished imported stone?" He turned the piece over as if expecting the answer to be on the other side. "Seems a bit extravagant, don't you think?" Then tossed it to Greg.

"Must've had money to burn," Greg said, studying it, before passing it over to Carny.

"Boss was saying this used to be some large private ranch or some shit way back. Only thing left is this here well and the rock walls surrounding the property." Carny stopped speaking to hack up something deep from within, chew it a couple of times, then spit it down the well.

A barely audible "Dear God" came from Mae, looking away a little too late.

"That sure as shit ain't no twenty feet, I can tell you that much." Carny coughed through a hoarse laugh, replacing his spent cigarette with a new one.

Mae stared down at the unnerving blackness, feeling a little anxious. "Something seems so shady about the whole operation. Like, look how unsafe this all is. We could so easily fall all the way to the bottom." She cautiously took a small step closer and cupped her hands around her mouth. "Helllоооо." But no echo came back. "Well, that is if there happens to be a bottom."

Resting his arm around her shoulders, Greg cooed, "Shhh, it's money, baby. Money for school." Or the sassy red stilettos she planned to model for him later that night. She leaned against his strong, able body feeling secure and protected, and her foreboding began to fade.

Chapter Seven

Grouped around the well, they strategized the best course of action for this suicidal operation. It took some time, but they nailed down a foolproof plan where Dexter and Toke would lower themselves into the well by a rope attached to their harnesses. Greg planned to hang from his own rope midway to work the pulley system he'd rig using the bucket he saw in the loader. Toke and Dexter would use the small crowbars to extract the stones and place them in the pail so Greg could raise it up to Mae who was waiting at the top. Her job entailed walking the stones to the Caterpillar's shovel and dumping them in. Once full enough, Carny would then drive the loader over to the office, get them all tallied by Roman and return where a new pile of stones would be ready to load.

Carny and Mae got to work, pushing aside the thick layer of gray rocks that had once covered the well and wooden doors, and not wanting to waste their energy, only cleared a narrow path from the well to the loader. In the meantime, Greg tied the ends of all the ropes to the thickest of the trees using a variety of knots until it looked like a tangled mess, but it was solid and firm. Mae sat to rest a moment, took a swig from a water bottle, and shared it with Greg. In her peripheral vision, she could see Carny reaching out for a sip, so she quickly shoved it back into the band of her waist pack and played busy. She reached over and snatched up the hard hat from inside the bucket then held it up. "Who gets this?"

Taking it off her hands, Toke examined it and looked in the bucket for more. "What—are they kidding? We get *one* hard hat?" He tossed it to Dexter, but Dexter tossed it back, insisting Toke wear it since he'd be the furthest down.

"Now that we got all that crap out of the way"—Greg picked up the green stone Dexter first removed—"the faster we work, the more money we make. We've lost a lot of time." He walked it over to the loader's bucket and dropped it in. "That's five bucks. Now I'm richer than all of you."

"Got that wrong, dude. We share that five. Now we're all rich," Toke said, sarcastically, adjusting the strap on his harness. "Hey, only two hundred and ninety-nine more to go."

Once Dexter and Toke finished fastening themselves to their ropes, they threw on their backpacks, which held their water supplies and Toke began lowering himself down. Once he made it down the first part of the well, he gave the thumbs up to Dexter who went next. It had always been drilled into men not to show fear, but Mae knew they both had to be petrified. Who wouldn't be? But soon Toke was comfortably blasting his metalcore, which, to Mae's frustration, funneled into a deafening level by the time it reached the top and her ears.

So far, the pulley system worked well and the first hour went by smoothly, though physically exhausting. The front loader's bucket filled fast, and Carny returned right away after unloading. But the last two times he took much longer to return and reeked of strong skunky weed. Mae shot him an icy look as he drove off. He was going to cause an accident in his state and was already lagging far behind.

Piles and piles of the ornate green stones were stacking up just waiting for Carny to return this time. It had been at least a half hour, so Mae took a little rest, had half a granola bar, a few gulps of water, and applied some fresh lip gloss. "Geez, Carny. It's about time," she said, scowling, as he finally pulled up.

To speed things up, Carny got the brilliant idea to lower the loader's bucket to the ground and use it like a shovel and simply scoop up the waiting stones. Unfortunately, this didn't work too well. Instead of sweeping the stones up, the Caterpillar's bucket only pushed them farther back toward the well opening along with all the other rocks. Mae waved her arms wildly yelling at him to stop. When he finally gave up, he jumped out of the Caterpillar, adjusted his earbuds, and walked around to the front of the bucket to load them in by hand.

If she weren't so angry at Carny, he'd be entertaining, reminding her of an old rusty robot in a factory assembly line, where they used tar to lubricate joints instead of machine oil. Then something caught her eye. Did the monster machine just move? She studied it for a few seconds and saw it move again. "Carny! Didn't you turn the engine off?"

"Shit," Carny growled but continued to stand there, just looking at it slowly move forward, pushing the stones in its path.

"Oh my God! Carny!" Mae cried. "Put the emergency brake on or something!" But he didn't move. He was still trying to size up the situation. She rushed over to him and yanked both his headphones out by the cord. "Listen to me. These rocks could kill them if they fall in the well!"

He tried to bat her off, annoyed. But then slowly his doped brain grasped the reality of the situation, and he started to make his way toward the machine. He lost his balance as the rocks pushed their way under him and he fell back. When his phone toppled out of his pocket and out of sight under the stones, he immediately dove for it, howling as the procession of rocks mangled his probing hands.

The machine continued to plow forward, greedily collecting all the green stones and gray rocks in its path. The piles turned to mountains as it forged ahead getting closer to Mae and the well. Out of sheer terror, she screamed at the top of her lungs, "Carny! Stop this thing!"

Twisting her body around, she shrieked down the hole, hysterical with fear for them inside, "Rocks! Move! Get out of the way!" When she turned back around, the mountain of rocks was much closer, with Carny in between, still digging for his phone.

"Hey, Babe, what's all the noise? Everything okay?" Greg called up, oblivious to the urgency, since Toke's music had drowned out all of her warnings.

"Get out of the way! Rocks!" she shouted, her voice shrill and frantic.

Suddenly Carny was right behind her yelling, "Shi-i-i-it!" as his body slammed into hers pushing her into the hole.

Chapter Eight

As if Mae were just an annoyance in their way, rocks pushed past her, over her, and at her while she clung desperately to the top edge of the well. She screamed as they crushed her fingers, so intent on stealing her grip until she couldn't tell if she was still holding on. Just then, Greg sprung toward her, snatched her up in one arm with such momentum, they slammed against the opposite wall, and away from the falling rocks.

Above, the front loader continued to move steadily forward with Toke's music blaring on as if in triumph. After wrapping a part of his rope around Mae, Greg used his belay to shimmy down to get them as far from the twenty-ton machine as possible.

Mae glanced down, searching for Dexter and Toke just as a stone whizzed by barely missing her head. "They're gone!" she shrieked. Then, out of nowhere, a hand reached out and grabbed hold of their rope. In a matter of seconds, Dexter had them both pulled into the small cavity he and Toke had frantically dug in the soft and gravely soil behind the grout.

Streaks of blood clung to Mae's shirt like grasping claw trails, and she braced herself in the tiny cramped cove. Everyone's limbs wrapped around each other wherever they would fit until they resembled a loaf of monkey bread.

The Caterpillar slowly crept over the top of the opening, slowly choking off their ambient light. Toke flicked on his flashlight in time to see a flash of red hair streak past followed by an avalanche of rocks. Mae listened carefully, waiting for it to continue on over the top, but it seemed to be caught on something and unable to move.

Now that the stones had stopped falling, they listened to the unsettling silence as their brains tried to process the last two minutes of hell.

"C'mon," Greg said breathlessly, tugging on his rope to test it. "We've got to climb back up before something worse happens." He held out his hand for Mae.

But before she had a chance to move, the machine commented from above with a heart shuddering creak. Mae clawed her nails into the dirt walls of their cove as the surrounding darkness began to rumble. Soft and low at first, then angry and agitated, causing the solid dirt underneath them to become loose and start to crumble away.

Now with nothing more to hold them up, they found themselves back inside the well shaft suspended by their ropes. Mae had her arms wrapped around Greg as tight as a tourniquet, afraid of what was coming next.

When the dust had settled, and they could see again, Dexter shined his light into the dark below. But Mae wasn't ready to look down just yet and tightened her grip.

Sounding as if he were being squeezed to death by a python, Greg choked out the words, "You…can let go…now. Look…down."

She had to muster up the nerves, but eventually looked down and felt a little embarrassed. Only a few feet of air separated their feet and the rocky bottom.

Once they all stood safely at the bottom, with ropes and harnesses hanging down from above like empty nooses, Greg pulled Mae in for a tight hug. "You okay, babe?" All she could do was nod uneasily and hug him back.

"This is so messed up," Toke said shining his light up, shaking his head in disapproval.

Without enough time to even agree with Toke, let alone catch a little rest, the rocks suddenly shifted under their feet and began to churn. Each realized a little too late that where they stood was not the bottom at all, but simply a bottleneck of rocks, as it gave way beneath them.

Clutching Mae in one arm, Greg hurtled off a sinking rock and seized one of the dangling ropes, nearly colliding with Toke, who barely clung to another. Dexter staggered like a drunk, trying to stay on top of the moving rocks, but at the last second, was able to snatch Greg's pant leg, though only by a few fingers.

Their bodies dangled in mid-air above the clacking of rock hitting rock and the thud of rock hitting wall, the sounds growing fainter as they descended further into the depths unknown. A few feet away Toke began flailing around on his rope and Mae could tell something was wrong, but when she looked over—he was gone.

Someone was screaming, and Mae opened her mouth to shout for Toke, but her mouth was already open—she was the one screaming.

The distant sounds of rocks were now replaced by the sickening thumps of Toke's body as it hit the walls where the shaft bent and kinked, this way and that. Mae sobbed quietly, knowing that Toke was just the first of them to go and now she was grieving for all of them.

No one wants to see how they're going to die before they do, but the black chasm that already fed on their friend teased them mercilessly with their impending death. "I can't hold on like this much longer," Greg said through gritted teeth. "Mae, can you climb over me to get a better hold?" Mae swallowed hard, dug her foot into Greg's pocket, and reached for the rope above him. She got it!

But she was too late. With an anguished cry, Greg lost his grip, and he and Dexter followed Toke, plummeting down the dark void, leaving a screaming Mae and their ropes far behind. She screamed for Greg, she screamed for Dexter and Toke, but now she screamed because her hands were slipping, too. If she could just reach the other rope…only a few feet away…her foot could reach it if she just stretched a little further—

Now it was she who was falling. Plunging deep into the dark snaking chasm that tossed her around indifferently like a discarded rag doll. Where the shaft narrowed, it batted her body against its damp clay walls like a pinball machine. This erratic pattern went on for a while, resembling a large intestine, but in the bowels of the earth.

She was beyond screaming now. Having her body ceaselessly tortured, and her mind numbed from terror, she wasn't even aware when her knee struck a protruding rock and tore her skin open. When the steep incline of the well curved slightly, it slowed her descent by painfully using her body as a brake. She felt relieved once she heard the dead echo of the bottom and knew her end was just seconds away. Suddenly a bright light flared in her eyes, and she felt someone's arms catch her—

Chapter Nine

The arms carried her down a large pile of rocks and quickly set her down. She was still adjusting to this surprise when Greg ran to her, and she sobbed loudly, so overcome with relief. But who had saved her? She turned around to see Toke and threw her arms around him and thanked him over and over as he tried to move them away from the well's open shaft where they stood far too long.

With only one flashlight left, they joined Dexter and hustled to the far side of the dark cavernous space until they reached a wall where they could go no farther. Mae listened to the sounds from the well as they settled until it was almost quiet. But was it done?

Dexter was first to speak. "Is everyone okay?"

It took a while, but Greg eventually answered, "We're all here, man. That's a start."

"Anyone seriously injured?" Toke asked, shining his light on each of them. "Broken bones, severed limbs, a missing eye, collapsed lung, you know."

Silence.

"Dude. We are some lucky people." Greg pulled Mae tight to him.

"Toke, you totally saved us, man. We owe you." Dexter pulled out his phone and checked the bars. Nothing, which didn't surprise him being this far under the surface.

"Damn, man, you rock, dude." Greg patted Toke's back.

"First you survived that fall yourself without any help, then you turned around and saved us. Who needs a superhero when we've got you?" The small pieces of gravel and sand that stuck in Mae's lip-gloss bounced with each of her words.

"No problem," Toke mumbled, wanting the attention off of him. He shined his flashlight around the subterranean cavity and began looking for the best way to climb back out.

"Let's talk about what just happened." Dexter stood, banging his head on the low ceiling. Having lost his flashlight, he used his phone and shined it around the cavernous dry bottom of the well. The walls and ceiling surrounding them were made up of layers of rock and dirt, without any recent signs of water. "What started this?"

Still shaking, Mae quickly explained a condensed version of her story, trying not to make it obvious that she was blaming it on Carny. But after all, it really was his fault, wasn't it? Could she have done something to stop it?

"Mae Bae, it's not your fault," Greg assured her. "You did what you could." Then he noticed the blood pooling around her leg. "Baby, you're bleeding!" Greg pulled off his t-shirt and pressed it to her knee to stop the bleeding. He then ripped a couple of strips off the bottom and tied them around her knee like a bandage. "Can you stand, baby?" She straightened out her leg, and he helped her to her feet. She tested her leg, which hurt, but she could walk on it. Greg put his torn bloody shirt back on, looking like he just murdered someone. "Sorry Jimi," he mumbled, patting it down.

Mae finally had a chance to look up at the foreboding hole they had fallen through. "Do you think we should wait here to be rescued or try to climb out somehow?"

"Let's just hope Carny ran for help." Dexter brushed the dirt off his clothes and shook it out of his hair.

"Carny, my man!" Greg said, then returned to peppering little healing kisses on Mae's face.

"Uh, I don't know about that…" Mae was feeling a little guilty for having forgotten all about him until now. "He was right behind me."

"No, he was actually *ahead* of you, Mae." Toke pointed his flashlight at the giant pile of rocks and dirt under the well shaft. "I think he's in there." Mae's hand shot to her mouth in horror while Greg and Dexter groaned.

Toke moved closer to the rock pile and wedged the flashlight between his teeth then picked up one of the rocks and moved it to the side. Then another. Dexter propped his phone up for light, and he and Greg joined in.

"Why are we doing this?" Mae exhaled, wearily. "He can't possibly still be alive under there."

"Yes, but what about the possibility that he *is*?" Dexter tossed a couple more rocks to the side. "This entire thing all happened in less than ten minutes."

When Greg lifted the next rock, he froze with the rock suspended in his hands. "Shit..." he said somberly, then dropped the rock at his feet.

Toke and Dexter rushed over, and Mae hobbled over, but she wished she hadn't. Peeking out from under a stack of rocks were the tips of three fingers. Toke hesitantly poked at them, and they all watched the fingers separate away from the rock, having been pinched off from the rest of the hand. They hurriedly moved more rocks away, calling his name loudly. Mae just watched, not being able to help much with her injured leg. She began to wonder if this digging was still hope or just morbid curiosity.

"Okay," Dexter said, battling the urge to recoil but kept his light shining on the place where Toke and Greg had just removed a large rock. "This might be the point where we stop."

The tone of his voice even got Mae to come back over. "Oh, dear God—" She covered her mouth and let out a dry heave. There he was. Like someone had painted a face on a plate. Flattened beyond recognition as not just Carny, but as a human. Drastically distorted features, areas where nose cartilage and skin were missing, only to find them still clinging to the rock they just removed. She had an impulse to take a picture with her phone, then totally disgusted with her own shallowness, she added, "I'm going to yell for help."

"Okay, you do that, baby," Greg said, not really listening, too preoccupied with staring at Carny. "Man, he's been utterly pulverized. His bones weren't just broken, they've been completely smashed. The insides of his head squeezed out any crevice they could possibly find." Putting what he saw into actual words, Greg turned away, gagging. But Toke kept going, pulling off rocks, where Carny's body should be if it were still attached to his head.

"What good is that doing?" Dexter said, still looking nauseated. "Carny's already *proved* he's dead."

"Real, real dead," Greg added, still not able to look, but Toke kept going, nonetheless.

"My pack! I see my pack!" Mae squealed as Toke's digging revealed a small piece of the blue plaid fabric. He yanked it out and tossed it to her and continued digging. Embracing it like a rescued puppy, she dusted off its new flattened form and reached in only to pull out the shattered mess that used to be her phone.

"So, we've just got the two packs then?" Greg looked around just to make sure.

"Looks that way." Dexter worked his way around to the dark spaces in the back of the cavern. "I can feel air coming in around here. Maybe there's another way out than climbing up."

"Whoa—do you feel that?" Greg steadied himself on a rock. Then they all started to feel it, coming up through the soles of their feet, low and deep like the earth below them was grumbling, getting angrier and angrier. Soon the intensity worked its way up through their bodies, and by the time it registered in their brains—Greg yelled, "The ground. It's falling!"

Chapter Ten

Like a slow-starting ignition, everything around them began to rumble and vibrate, then came a horrific pounding from above. Toke jumped out of the pile of rocks and hollered, "Move!" pushing Greg and Mae in front of him toward where Dexter was.

"There's a hole back here!" Dexter shouted as he clawed furiously at the rocks until the opening was large enough to fit a person.

Massive amounts of dirt, gravel, and sand came pouring down, filling the room. Mae's panicked heart pounded, and she couldn't find Greg. Then from the darkness in front of her, he yelled, "Mae! Follow my voice and grab my hand!"

One after the other, they scrambled through Dexter's hole, crawling blind, like scattering insects, creating as much distance as they could from the old collapsing well. The earth raked their exposed skin raw. Dirt and tiny rocks ground themselves into Mae's bloody bandage, but pain was the least of her worries.

Back in the cavern that they just left, Dexter's phone sat forgotten near Carny. It had fallen on its back but still offered a helpful amount of light—until it was crushed seconds later as chunks of concrete and stones came bashing down, followed by massive clumps of clay soil which slammed on top in a loud, sticky thud. The cavern walls crumbled violently inward, and then, with a loud crack, the floor gave way, taking the ceiling, rock pile and Carny down with it, disappearing into blackness.

They had only cleared ten yards when the deafening boom of the cavern's collapse reverberated through the walls, hastening their speed. Dexter led the way and Toke took up the rear. Then without warning, the earth shifted again and released a large rock above Toke, slamming heavily onto his head. With his hardhat taking most of the blow, he kept moving and pulled forward with his elbows.

With the fleeing-for-their-lives adrenaline that none of them knew they possessed, their bodies moved where they would fit, ducking the protrusions, hurtling through the wider parts, and slithering through the narrows. Their lungs were kept busy trying to sort the oxygen from the dirt, coughing up what they didn't like.

The damp earth had buckled, opening up a slim crawl space with almost enough room to sit up. Mae needed to rest, but could she? The dirt above teased ruthlessly, threatening to close her up in her own earthly coffin.

"Fuck," Toke groaned in agony. "My head hurts so bad." He reached up, and his fingertips found the sizable lump on the top of his head and sucked in sharply.

Catching his breath, Dexter shined the light over. "Looks like you hit your head on something pretty hard."

"Good thing you were still stylin' in this fine thing." Greg showed him his hard hat, which had split open like an egg.

"Cheap bastard." Toke grabbed it and flung it far away.

After resting for a few minutes, Mae could feel the ancient moist air of deep earth weighing heavy on her lungs. Distant thumps, skittering dirt and other small noises she couldn't place prevented any sense of calm. "This is really creepy." She shuddered.

"That's for sure." Greg blindly reached for Mae with one hand and checked his phone with the other.

"You get anything?" Dexter patted his pocket for his phone then dropped his head, remembering where he last saw it.

"Got nothing. But at least the screen still comes on."

"We need to save our batteries, or we'll be stuck in pitch blackness."

Mae watched the flashlight dim and flicker. "Our only flashlight's not long for this world either."

"And my phone battery, it's only at five percent—I'm powering down. It's all we've got." Greg took out the flat rectangular flashlight attached to his key ring and pushed the button. "Useless. Damn."

With the instinctual urge to keep moving, Dexter shined the dimming flashlight down a small, dark passage to their right. "I'm going to check something out. Be right back." And their eyes followed him as he crawled away.

Ten seconds later, his light went dark, and he seemed to disappear. "Dexter?" Mae felt for Greg to make sure he was still there, but he was already on his way to find his friend. Groping her way blindly in the dark to the last place she saw him, Mae called, "Where are you, Dex?"

"Dex! Where the hell are you, man?" Greg's hands scoured the ground in front of him like a metal detector.

"Shh," Toke said. "I heard something."

Then a faint, "Down here—ow."

Scrambling over to the voice, Mae stopped just in time before falling into the large hole that took Dexter, and called down, "Dex, are you okay?"

Greg cupped his hands around his mouth and shouted into the abyss, "Buddy, can you see us? How far down are you?"

"Can you reach my hand?" Toke extended it down as far as possible.

He didn't answer right away, which was unnerving. But after some rustling and a few grunts, he was back. "I'm okay. But it's too dark to see anything down here." They could hear him whacking the flashlight hard, then taking it apart and whacking it some more. Then a small, "Damn—the bulb's broken." Dexter let out a long sigh. "But…this is weird. I can actually *see* that the bulb's broken. And I can *see* Toke's helmet's down here too. How can I see anything without a light?"

"Yeah, *really* strange," Greg said, skeptically.

"This probably sounds a little crazy, but I think there's a source of light down here." Dexter gritted his teeth in pain, pushing himself up to his hands and knees. "But I can't tell where it's coming from."

"Hey, if you've got light, maybe we should go down there with you," Greg said, sounding hopeful. "It could be the way out."

Then with much effort, Dexter pulled himself to his feet. "And, I can stand without hitting my head."

"That's enough for us," Greg said as he and Toke handed Mae down the ten-foot drop where Dexter delivered her safely to the bottom. Toke and Greg followed soon after.

"Wait—the light—it's over there!" Toke pointed to the far end of the cavity.

"Somehow a determined stream of sunlight made it all the way down here," Dexter said, too relieved to question its validity any further.

"That's our way out, my friends. Let's get moving," Greg said optimistically, taking Mae's hand and walking toward the dim glow.

Chapter Eleven

So, there they were, faced with the choice of three tunnels, so they turned down the only one with the small stream of light. Being able to stand and walk on her feet gave peace to Mae's silently screaming knee.

After half an hour of trudging along in the dimly lit tunnel, they decided to stop to drink some water. Mae sat down and leaned against the uncomfortably curved dirt wall and tugged on Greg's arm to join her. He was her rock and she loved him so much. She could make it through anything as long as he was by her side.

Toke sucked hard on his water tube and burped when he was done. Mae pulled out her water bottle and handed it to Greg before taking a sip herself. "This is our last. The other one's empty." She made sure to say it loud enough so Toke could hear.

Catching the hint, Toke handed his tube and reservoir to Dexter, with the warning, "Dude, I'm creeped about backwash."

"Don't worry. I'm right there with you." He happily accepted it. They all really needed this rest. It was the first time they had a few minutes to relax and take some inventory of their situation.

"Dex, you got the time?" Greg patted his wrist. "I wonder how long we've been down here."

Pushing the button on his watch, Dexter's watch glowed bright, illuminating all their faces. "2:04 p.m."

"Duuude." Toke nodded approvingly at the light, barely hearing the time.

"If we lose the light, at least we've got your watch." Mae took a tiny swig of water.

"That light's our best bet for a way out."

"Just thinking," Greg said, "but does anyone back home *really* know where we went this morning?" He looked expectantly at each of their silent faces. "Okay, then, does anyone we know have the worksite address? Did the boss ever take our names?" He looked at Mae and shrugged. "The only thing I said was we'd be working with Dex and moving rocks."

"My mom only knows I went to Greg's to do some work with him. I have no doubt she'll report me as a missing person by midnight." Mae chewed on her fingernail, worrying more for her mom right now.

"Hell, I just left." Dexter locked his fingers behind his head and leaned back.

"Yeah, me too," Toke added. "My dad was just happy I was working, so didn't want to risk anything by asking questions. Just handed me money for lunch."

"Our story's getting even worse. No one's going to save us if they can't *find* us." Mae could physically feel the optimism leaving the group.

"They'll find Dexter's car." Greg rubbed his chin. "That's got to lead to something."

"The more I think about it, that whole operation of theirs seems highly illegal." Dexter squinted. "Probably the last thing they'll do is report an accident or anyone missing."

Toke started to count on his fingers. "Dude pays in cash, boss leaves the site, temporary trailer office, no paperwork at all. I bet they didn't even have fucking permission to dig up any of those rocks."

"Well, at least we don't have to worry about food." Greg smacked Toke's backpack a couple times. "Toke loaded up at the quick mart, remember?"

After dumping his pack out, they surveyed what he had. Toke snatched up his smashed cigarettes and checked inside, carefully placing the remaining three into his shirt pocket.

"We'll be able to stay down here for a hundred years with all the preservatives in that crap." Mae emptied her pack and poked around at the flattened contents. "I've got a couple of *smashed* raw organic granola bars coated in mashed cheese veggie sandwich. One bar's goji berry and chia sprout, the other's açai, ginger, and flax."

"Yum," Toke mumbled sarcastically, rummaging through his stash of sugar and salt. "Now, *this* is a granola bar."

Mae wrinkled her nose. "Those kinds are more like cookie candy bars. There's a huge difference. Just because it says granola doesn't mean it's healthy."

"None for you then." Toke downed the entire bar in two bites. "Other than that, just a turkey sandwich."

"Let's think about this a minute." Greg leaned back against the wall. "We've already established no one is going to come rescue us, so what if it's days before we get out of this dungeon? Maybe we should eat smaller amounts, so it lasts."

"Yeah, look around us, there aren't even any roots down here." Dexter shined his watch light around the walls and then above them. "We must be pretty deep—quite far from the surface. I'm beginning to think that light has nothing to do with the sun."

"And, has anyone noticed that it's been slowly turning blue?" Greg asked. "Since when is sunlight blue?"

"Well, then, maybe we should pool our food together and not make Toke carry it all," Mae offered. Toke looked at her, narrowing his eyes in distrust. "Okay, you carry it all. I don't care." She shrugged, annoyed.

"Let's plan on say, max, four or five days." Dexter pushed the pile of shiny packaged snacks around, counting in his head. "So, how about we eat enough just to stay alive."

"Yeah, but what if we're here even longer? They'll call off the searches at some point." Greg put a protective arm around Mae's shoulders. "Maybe we should plan for at least a week."

"Yeah, especially if they give up hope after finding Carny." Toke scrunched up his nose. "If they even dig that far." That shut everyone up for a while trying to imagine what the scene must look like from the surface.

Chapter Twelve

Starting with small portions from the sandwiches, they slowly chewed their meager meal. They divided the rest of the food up between the two backpacks, shoving it away, zipping it in, and closing it off from themselves.

With an enthusiastic slap to his thighs, Greg announced, "Well, we've got places to go and people to see." He bounced up, forcibly psyching out his body's pain. "Hi-ho Silver, away!"

"Oh man—it hurts to get up," Mae groaned, slowly standing, one leg at a time, holding onto Greg for support.

"I've got this." Greg threw Mae's pack on his back. "I'm just glad it's not pink with unicorns and kittens."

After one last drink of water, they continued down the dark passage trying to find the light again. "And, here she is." Mae smiled as if seeing a friend. "The little light was waiting for us, once again."

"She? You made her a chick?" Toke raised a brow. "Is she cute at least?"

Focused on getting out, Dexter and Greg stayed far ahead of the rest. Every once in a while, Greg tried his phone again. Still nothing. Toke hung in the back so he could have a smoke here and there. "I'll catch up."

After a few minutes, Mae walked back, waving the smoke away. "Put the butt in here please." She held out an empty candy wrapper, not hiding her disapproval of his smoking.

"It's gone." Toke walked around her to catch up to the others.

Mae hurried after him. "You just dropped it? You littered?"

"Really, Mae?" He stopped walking and turned to face her. "Look at us. Look where we are. Who the hell cares?"

"Still." She pushed past him and walked away, hoping his conscience would get the better of him.

They hadn't gotten much farther after she and Toke rejoined them when Greg stopped abruptly, causing Dexter to plow into him. "A warning would have been nice," Dexter said from the ground.

"Sorry, man," Greg said. "But where'd the light go? Anyone see it?"

Dexter flipped his watch light and groaned.

"What the hell?" Toke pushed his way to the front and stared in disbelief. "A dead end? A dead *fucking* end?" Then hit the wall, hurting his hand.

Mae flopped heavy against the side of the tunnel. "This just can't be. We have to go all the way back?" She banged her head a couple of times on the wall behind her and squeezing her eyes shut.

"Back? Back to what? Another dead end?" Toke walked toward a pool of dark still water that had collected at the base of the wall. "At least we have water."

For the next minute, Dexter aimed his watch above, below, and to their sides checking for any other way out. Unsuccessful, he knelt by the water and smelled it, trying to determine if it was safe to drink.

"Wait a second." Toke inched closer to the water and pointed. "Dude, do you see it?" Without waiting for a response, he took off his pack and kicked off his shoes.

After shifting his focus lower in the water, Dexter brightened. "Yes—there!"

"See what, man?" Greg got down on his knees for a better look and

Mae peered over his shoulder. Now they all saw the little blue light as it glowed invitingly from four feet below the surface of the water.

"She wants us to go down there?" Mae said with more frustration than fear.

"The she-light's probably suggesting that we give up our pointless crusade and drown ourselves before we suck up all the oxygen." Despite his pessimism, Toke tested the water with his foot and exhaled heavily. "We're dead either way, so I'll go check it out and let you know what I find." He lowered himself into the tepid water until he was completely under and out of sight.

The three sat in silence while the black pool stared back at them like a deep gaping wound. Feeling too anxious Mae had to stand. "I'm getting worried. How long's he been gone?"

"Long enough." Dexter began taking off his shoes. "I'm going in."

Just then, Toke's head burst out of the water, and he whipped his hair out of his eyes, flinging water onto everyone. In between breaths, he explained, "The tunnel continues past the water. Somehow, this part of the tunnel got filled with water and this is all that's left of it." Toke pulled himself out and picked up his shoes.

"Our shoes will be like lead weights if we wear them," Dexter said, struggling with the knot in his laces. "So just tie them to your belt like Toke's doing or just put them in your pack."

With his pack secured on his back, Toke lowered himself back in the water. "See you on the other side."

"Okay, makes sense." Greg kicked off his shoes and stuffed them into Mae's pack along with her own. Before going under, he pulled her face up into his hands and gave his girlfriend a long deep kiss before releasing her. "Let's go—I've gotta get my baby home!"

A short swim later, Mae popped her head out of the water on the other side and was greeted with lung fulls of dank muggy air. The ground rose gradually, and she and Greg were able to walk out of the water with ease. "Hey, that wasn't so bad." Mae squeezed out her long hair and tied it up into a ponytail.

The guys took off their shirts and wrung out the water. Greg held his tattered shirt up to Mae, which was now pink with blood instead of red. Mae knew how much he loved that shirt and said, "Jimi, I thank you with all my heart for your sacrifice."

Toke pulled his wet shirt over his head and stopped once his eyes took in Dexter and Greg shirtless from the back. "Wait…am I seeing this right?" he said with an embarrassed smile struggling to get his arms through his soggy sleeves. "Can those possibly be matching tats?" He stepped closer to survey the artistry, confining his laugh to a snort. "Is there something special you'd like to share?"

In answer, Greg flexed his muscles and moved in closer to Dexter, butting their shoulders together for the full effect of their masterpiece. Each tattoo consisted of two wolves emerging from blue flames, one howling at the moon and one at the sun. From the middle of the swirling flames, an amateurish logo, combining their two initials, DK and GS proudly rose, unscathed from the fire.

"Isn't that cool?" Mae said with admiration. "They designed it together when they were in third grade. They drew it on everything, and when they turned sixteen, they got it permanently inked."

"Still." Toke looked away, hiding a laugh.

Chapter Thirteen

Roman arrived at the abandoned well worksite and stared down at the enormous indentation in the ground, which looked like a meteor had landed and hiccupped a Caterpillar front loader. He let his bicycle fall to the side without care, and with beer in hand, he drunkenly staggered to the edge of the depression.

"Spoiled little rich college assholes," he slurred, glaring at the abandoned machine sticking halfway out of the ground in the center. "That's right, the boss is away so just leave everything for Roman to clean up," he said, sneering in contempt.

If it were up to Roman, he would only hire migrant workers who would never leave the worksite in such a holy mess. But this time the boss said to hire local brats only. The legal kind. If the boss got caught stealing exotic stones from private land, the fine wouldn't be so bad as hiring illegals on top of it.

After sucking down the rest of his beer, he tossed the empty can into the trees and started down toward the Caterpillar. He stumbled over one of the wood doors that lay sprawled on the ground, cussed at it, then reluctantly got to work. He dug around the front end of the loader, then piled rocks into the back end until it began to right itself. He wedged a few more rocks under the front wheels and then sat down, exhausted, and popped open another beer. "But, hell if I'm taking heat for what you little shits did. Boss won't never know the mess you left, but *I* do, and I'm taking this out of your pay. With interest." He inhaled the rest of his beer then stood and attempted to stomp the empty can under his foot. He missed, swayed a little, but managed to pull a new one from his pocket, without falling. "Can't wait to see your pimply faces cry tomorrow when I hand you your pennies." The muscles of his lips twitched and twisted into a vengeful smile.

He stood back and attempted to survey the scene with a clear head, like the foreman he was hired to be. Something just didn't seem right. But instead, for a little clarity on the situation, he leaned his head back and poured in the entire contents of his can, then followed it up with a deafening belch. "Heh, actually, you little shits just saved us a shitload of work. We was going to have to fill this empty well in with them rocks from the walls, but you did it for us. Then once the weeds grow in, no sign of anything." This lightened his mood significantly.

Remembering his bike, he threw it in the back of the front loader, crawled into the driver's seat, and started it up. With great effort, the loader crept forward until it was clear and gripped the hard ground beneath it. He put it in gear and drove the machine out of the large dent in the ground, leaving nothing to confess that it had once been a well.

Chapter Fourteen

After trudging on a few more hours, following the trail of the mysterious blue light, Mae couldn't ignore the worry gnawing at her. "There doesn't seem to be any turnouts, and we've been going downhill steadily with every step we take. I'm wondering if we are going in the completely wrong direction—*away* from the exit."

"Maybe we should just get some sleep." Greg yawned loudly, and he stopped walking. "I'm completely beat, anyone else?" He reached into his pocket for his phone and groaned while a fine stream of water drained out.

"Oh no, babe." Mae rubbed his back in sympathy. She knew how much Greg loved his old model iPhone. He had even named it Fender after Jimi's favorite guitar. "But it's supposed to be waterproof right?"

"Supposed to be. We better get paid for all that work we did." Greg stared dejected at his soggy phone. "Damn. Just damn."

"Sorry, bro," Toke said, feeling his pain. "You can have mine if you want to dig it out of that well. Probably still blasting tunes." He'd known Greg since their first day at city college and the two of them shared so many classes together, they made an instant bond. Just like with Toke, Greg was leisurely searching for something in his life to grab hold of. For most of his young life, his dream was to be a professional rock musician like his idol Jimi. He was so sure of himself, that when he finally took his first guitar lesson in high school, he got the rudest awakening. No matter how many different instructors Greg tried, nor styles of guitar, he did not possess the talent required for any string instrument. This left a huge hole in his life, so he started at the city college to figure out his next plan. When nothing sparked his interest enough, he just stayed in school, taking as few units as possible, passing the time. Just like Toke.

When it was time to eat dinner, they found a fairly flat part of the tunnel and shared a meal fit for a mouse. It was over in thirty seconds. Feigning satisfaction, like he had just finished his third Thanksgiving plateful, Toke patted his belly and burped.

Shifting to a more comfortable spot, Dexter leaned back, locking his fingers behind his head. "So, I've been thinking, trying to figure out what caused the well to collapse in the first place. I watched a documentary once where something similar happened." He paused for a moment, to order his thoughts. "I think the well must have been sitting over a sinkhole."

"Oh yeah…I saw a video with something like that." Toke stretched himself lengthwise on the ground. "There was a car or a house that was there one minute, and the next the ground underneath it just sucked it down into a giant hole."

"Yes, that's it." Dexter kicked off his shoes. "So, apparently, deep under the surface, a large pocket of water can collect. At this point, all's fine and good. But after a while, if the water leaks out or dries up, it leaves a big vacant space underground. Slowly, over time, dirt from above will sift down into the empty space, thinning the surface area above it. Then if objects get too heavy on top of this thinning ground, like houses or cars—"

"Boom!" Toke smacked the wall. "They're shit out of luck."

"Or, how about, instead"—Greg stretched out next to Mae, trying to share her small pack for a pillow—"it could have been an earthquake? It's not like California doesn't get one nearly every thirty minutes."

"Yeah, could be any of those things." Dexter yawned, trying to get comfortable on the lumpy, punishing ground. Mae had already given up searching for a place on her body without bruises to lay on, but luckily the exhaustion from the day took over, and she and everyone else were out in minutes.

They all woke with a start to someone shouting in their sleep. Dexter sat up and wiped the sweat from his face with his shirt. "Oh, man, sorry. I must have had a nightmare." He blinked a few times and rubbed his eyes uncomfortably.

"Damn, so we're all still in this corn hole." Toke got up and stumbled his way down the dark tunnel to pee and Greg followed. Mae stretched out her arms, yawned, then dug around in her pack to portion out breakfast.

Walking back, Greg said, "This waking up in pitch black is completely unnerving." He plopped down next to Mae to give her a kiss. "Is it still night? Did we even sleep?"

Dexter tapped his watch. "Ten a.m. We got about five hours sleep. Unless my vivid imagination kept you awake like it did me."

"We probably *all* had some pretty torturous dreams last night. Yours were just louder, Dex." When Mae turned to give him a smile, she just had to giggle.

Embarrassed, Dexter hastily pushed his glasses up on his head. "My contacts got stuck to my eyeballs. I could barely peel them off."

A smile twitched on Toke's lips. "Dude, those are some mighty thick lenses. What, are you blind?"

"They're glass. Lenses made of glass are always thicker. I scratch plastic lenses way too easily, so now I only get them in glass. Plus, they're a lot cheaper." Dexter shrugged. "My eyesight isn't *all* that bad, just a little near-sighted."

"Well, as fun as this is, we need to hit the dirt." Greg pulled himself to his feet and reached his hand out to pull Mae up. "C'mon and get yourself up, brush yourselves off, pee, and pack up. There's got to be a song in that." So, he made it one.

Feeling terribly stiff and sore, it took Mae a while to stop limping. But they still made good progress that morning, considering the tunnel floor wasn't really a floor at all, but the rounded bottom of a tube with scattered rocks. She gave up hope of her leg healing anytime soon since she just kept reopening the wound with hourly falls.

By afternoon, the tunnel began to narrow, uncomfortably, and the bottom became strewn with large rocks, increasing in number until it was completely blocked off where the tunnel must have collapsed. Pulling a few rocks aside, Dexter peered through a tiny opening into an extremely narrow tube. "I hope none of you are claustrophobic—this is going to be tight."

Feeling unnerved, Mae peeked in and felt her stomach muscles tighten, and her heartbeat rise. "Not me, I'm not," she said with faked cheeriness.

"Yeah, that sounds convincing." Toke smirked.

One by one, they each snaked through, waiting until the first person cleared the end until the other started. Last to go was Toke. Having such broad shoulders and a large body overall, he had to fold himself inward and twist to even fit through the small opening. Once inside, he pulled himself forward, squeezing through the tiny curving crevice, one inch at a time. Halfway through, he couldn't move forward, nor backward—he was wedged in tight and began to panic. Alternating, they each tried a different approach to pull him out, but his body wouldn't budge.

"Listen to me, Toke," Mae said calmly, poking her head into the hole. "You need to stay calm and think of something else. We'll get you out. Promise." Even though she had no idea how they were going to do that.

Finding a good-sized rock, all three of them traded off chipping away at the walls that blocked his shoulders. It was like moving a ten-foot haystack one piece of straw at a time, but it was working. "Try wiggling," Greg said, brushing away the loose chunks of stone. But all Toke could do was grunt and remained motionless.

His whole life, Toke had been larger than most kids his age. So, in junior high, he began to play football and got really good at it. But in order to play against kids his own age, he had to be in the same weight bracket. The kids in his weight category were much older and had played for many more years than he had. He grew tired of starving himself, taking diuretics and sweating out the water weight in a hot car just to be able to play against kids his own age. In the end, he just quit and became depressed, so he took up partying instead. His father gave him the ultimatum of going to school or getting a job, so he started at the city college. He planned to be a firefighter but changed his mind when he discovered he wouldn't be able to smoke weed. His ADHD made school so difficult, but he kept it up so he could live rent-free at home and not have to get a job.

Being crammed in such a tight, uncomfortable space, Toke's body seemed to swell from the heat, squeezing him in even tighter. A claustrophobe's nightmare, but he didn't have the luxury of being able to freak out. All he could do was close his eyes and wish he was anywhere but there.

After they worked away at the rock for nearly two hours, Dexter decided to try a different approach. "Just keep your eyes closed. This might hurt a little." He wedged one rock in like a spike just above Toke's shoulder, then drove it in with another, giving it everything he had with each blow. Suddenly, a loud crack resounded, and Dexter pulled on Toke as hard as he could, but his efforts only moved him a little.

"He's not going to make it!" Mae cried, nervously watching the widening crack above him.

"Hell yes, he's going to make it!" Greg corrected. Mae was always fascinated by his ability to stay optimistic even when things looked impossibly bleak.

Then, like the breaking of an iceberg, ten times louder than the first, the rock above broke apart with an ear-splitting crack, sending fractures splintering down its face like bolts of lightning.

In frantic desperation, Dexter grabbed what he could of Toke, and put everything he had into one final pull. Greg panicked and yanked Dexter out by his feet, and along with Mae, the three ran, escaping seconds before the mass slammed to the ground in a thunderous boom.

Chapter Fifteen

Afraid to move after another all too familiar catastrophe, they remained crouched a safe distance away. With their hands still covering their heads, they protected their hearts by delaying the reality they'd soon have to face with the devastating loss of their friend.

A sooty cough rose from the dust just a few yards away. Mae immediately raised her head, "Dear God. That's Toke!" And in mere seconds they were all at Toke's side hugging his scratched up and bleeding body.

Still in disbelief of his sheer luck, Toke couldn't stop smiling and gave Dexter a friendly whack on the back. "Oh, man. Thanks, dude. I wouldn't be here if it weren't for you. All of you."

"I guess now we're even." Dexter smiled, with a nod.

"I'm just glad we don't have to go back this way," Greg said, wrapping his arm around Mae. "No way anyone's getting back through that ton of wall." But deep down, Mae knew they could only *hope* they didn't have to go back this way.

While their heart rates returned to normal, Dexter shined his watch's light around the cavernous space where they stood.

They were all stunned to silence as their eyes swept over the most enchanting place they had ever seen. Marbleized limestone walls sparkled lustrously as if they had been sprayed with tiny diamonds. To the sides, majestic stalactites and stalagmites connected the ceiling to floor, remaining locked together in a forever kiss. Random human-sized swords of milky quartz thrust at them from all angles, as if defending their fragile crystal palace.

Mae spun around, wide-eyed, bathing in the cavern's dazzling brilliance. "This all looks so magical." Gazing up dreamily at the delicate webs of crystal lace draping from above, she sighed and rested her hands on her heart.

After poking around a bit, Greg asked, "Hey, did anyone see that thing on the internet where a while ago someone discovered like three hundred human skeletons in an underground cave? They had bizarre giant-sized heads with stalagmites growing up through their eye sockets." With his own memory spurring him on, he continued searching around, as if hoping to find a couple of them.

Seeming to be done with all the splendor, Toke sat and propped himself against a large smooth mound, white with calcification. He twisted his arm around and examined where the rock had clawed through his skin on his narrow escape. "Not to trump your creepy story or anything but, back in the water, I think I felt something brush past my leg, then my arm and none of you were anywhere around to do it."

Mae looked at him sideways. "Oh, haha, you're kidding—right?"

"No, wish I was. Totally freaked me out."

"You're just telling us now?" Mae's voice pitched high with annoyance.

"Yeah, I wish I had Dex's watch to see what was down there with us," Greg added. "But then, I sort of don't want to know. You know?"

The next day was filled with frustratingly long stretches of walking and swimming through marble tunnels, crawling through tubes, scrapes, and bangs, tired bodies, and sore feet. Around each turn, the only thing awaiting them was the little blue light ready to show them the way. Mae had to keep reminding herself not to be resentful of the light for the never-ending journey it was taking them on, but to be grateful for it. Think like Greg. Accept this strange phenomenon, and work with it, for lack of other options.

At one point, Greg's step started to slow. "Whoa." He grabbed his head between his hands and steadied himself against the side of the tunnel.

Walking just a few yards back, Mae preoccupied herself by picking off the gummy waterproof mascara that still partially clung to her lashes. "What, babe?" But seconds later, she was on her hands and knees with her head hanging. "I feel dizzy…like I'm going to be sick."

"I thought it was just me!" Dexter called back, about twenty feet ahead of them. "But I kept walking, and it stopped."

Straggling up from behind, completely lost in his thoughts, Toke looked strangely at Greg and Mae and tried to walk around them. Then it hit him too. "Ugh—I think I'm going to barf." He hurried forward to vomit away from them, then as fast as the dizziness came, it had left. "Hey, it's gone."

"It might be just happening right where you are." Dexter illuminated his watch. "Come where we are."

And he was right, once Mae and Greg caught up to them, they felt completely normal again. "You okay, babe?" Greg said, reaching for her and pulling her in.

"That was hella weird. Let's get the fuck away from this place." Toke's logic gave wings to all of their feet, and they quickly distanced themselves as far from that bizarre place as possible.

Two more days passed, and they still hadn't found a way out. Mae knew she had to start rationing the food better now, so for dinner, they each only got five peanut M&M's and two crackers.

Toke looked annoyed. "Are you kidding? That's all we get?"

With an exhausted expression, Mae replied sharply, "Would you rather risk having nothing to eat?"

Greg began licking one peanut M&M, counting like in the old Tootsie Pop commercial. "One, two, three—damn." Then he started on the next one.

They dragged dinner out as long as they possibly could. Mae sprawled out, smiling lazily at the sight of Dexter and Greg's hair. Rarely did anyone get to see either of them completely natural, without hair products. Greg's head seemed to grow larger each day. A puffy halo of frizz surrounded his face instead of the usual black lustrous curls. Dexter's hair lacked the shine and tussled locks Mae always thought came naturally for him, and now just hung limply. It was like they had stepped back into the seventies.

After Mae filled her water bottles back up, she snuggled up next to Greg. "I was just thinking," she said thoughtfully. "No matter how many wormholes we've crawled through and how many miles we've covered, has anyone wondered why there aren't any spider webs, bats or bugs? Nothing. Not even algae in the water or on the walls. Especially with how warm the water is."

"Yeah," Dexter said, tying his hair back. "I just figured since there's no light, it's hard for anything to live. Especially since most systems are made to react with the sun in some form or another." Dexter was always good for an answer, being quite fluent in most subjects that others dumped from their brains for lack of need or interest. This also made him lost in his head much of the time, working out a theory or figuring out a problem, which would frustrate people because he ignored them when they spoke. He wasn't being rude, he just wasn't aware anyone was even talking.

With a quick study of the water they were camped by, Toke asked, "So, if the water doesn't have the kind of stuff to make algae and whatever, what will our pee do to the water?"

No one said anything.

Toke squinted his eyes at them. "Oh, come on—you *know* you all pee in the water."

"Dude..." Greg shook his head. "We drink that water."

"Ack...bleah." Mae tried to spit. She swore she could taste his pee in her mouth now. "No, no more of that." She emptied out the bottles of water she had just filled.

"Okay, but just for the record, I only peed twice."

They weren't convinced.

"Or so."

"I'm never swimming behind you again, man," Greg said, scrunching his face in distaste.

Chapter Sixteen

"Argh!" Mae complained loudly when they came upon the next pool of water. "I'm so sick of swimming. I'm so sick of the dark, and I'm so, so, so sick of this stupid tunnel we've been stuck in for six days!" She let out a frustrated scream, which echoed up and down the tunnel.

"Feel better, baby?" Greg pulled her to him. Mae nodded, burying her face in his chest. She reluctantly took off her shoes and followed them into the dark pool, splashing water like a rebellious kid in frustration.

They swam until the tunnel opened up into a large cavern. Mae pulled herself up on a sizable ledge above the water for a little rest. Greg saw her excellent idea and was soon sitting right next to her.

"Can anyone see the light?" Dexter asked, breathing hard and treading water.

Squinting down into the dark water, Greg soon pointed. "Thar she glows!" He had spotted a small hole about ten to fifteen feet down the rock wall where the faint blue light was waiting.

Mae leaned forward to get a better view and braced her hand behind her against a neatly stacked pile of rocks. This caused a few of the rocks to tumble away and release a thread of small arm bones, followed by the skeletal remains of a tiny human hand. As if in slow motion, Mae's hand clutched over her open mouth in a silent scream. It wasn't just the sight of the child's bones that unnerved her so much—it was the sudden deep pain she felt in her heart.

Somehow she managed to reach out and shake Greg's arm, and he followed her gaze. "Holy hell."

This caught the attention of Toke and Dexter, who were up on the ledge in seconds. The four of them watched silently as Toke prodded the tiny bones dangling from the rocky grave.

"They're so small," Mae said softly.

"And definitely human," Dexter said, tugging at a small piece of fabric protruding from the rocks, which nearly turned to dust in his fingers.

Mae wanted answers and fought the urge to pull the rest of the rocks away. Feeling her distress, Greg reached out and gave her back a comforting rub, saying, "I think we should just leave it in its little grave and get the hell out of here." She eagerly agreed by jumping back into the water, anything to rid herself of the strange, eerie emotion that was invading her.

In less than a minute, they were all treading water next to the wall above the hole. This one was deep and required them to psych themselves up while also trying to rid their heads of the tiny bones. It wasn't working too well for Mae. She kept glancing back at the ledge, hoping they would not be there, but each time they still were.

Toke took an exploratory dive to check it out before they all committed. He soon returned, breathing hard. "This one is long. A very, very long tunnel. My ears hurt like hell. The pressure was killing me."

"This might help," Dexter said between breaths, grabbing hold of the wall for a little support. "It's similar to when you're in a plane or driving in the mountains, and you yawn to pop your ears. In the water you can't yawn, so you plug your nose and mouth then blow out but without releasing any air. It might take a few times, to release the pressure on the way down. Like this." He then demonstrated and popped back up. "Got it?"

They all seemed to understand, but Mae looked nervous. "I'm starting to feel claustrophobic already. I don't know if I can do this."

"Geez, get some balls," Toke said, and Mae shot daggers at him through her narrowed eyes. "I mean ovaries! Or, whatever you grow in there."

With rapid shallow breaths, Mae could feel herself beginning to panic and turned to swim back to the ledge. "Baby, please stay." Greg blocked her way. "We'll do this together. Plus, do you really want to stay here with the bones?"

Toke took a deep impatient breath. "Mae, do you have a dog or a cat?"

"A cat, Paul. Why?"

"Paul? Seriously?" he smirked.

"Yeah, why?"

"Okay whatever, so when you're in there, just think about nuzzling up to Paul, playing with him and petting him. Don't take your mind off Paul. Only think of Paul."

Greg squinted. "Paul's a mean son of a bitch."

"Okay. Your mom then." Toke just wanted to get his point across.

"Cuddling and petting her mom? In your dreams, bro." Greg winked, and Toke nodded back. Dexter turned away, not wanting to laugh.

"Okay. I got it. Thanks." Mae grimaced, still looking petrified.

"Just don't stop to think about where you are, okay?" Toke looked sternly into her eyes. "Keep swimming and only think about Paul, even if he claws your eyes out the entire length of the tunnel."

After sucking in a deep, noisy breath like it was his last, Toke slid below the surface and soon disappeared into the tunnel. Dexter gave a confident nod at Mae and Greg then dove under, his kick splashing the surface and temporarily blinding them. Mae hesitated for only a few seconds and looked at Greg. He smiled back reassuringly with a thumbs up. She clenched her fists, drew in a deep breath and swam under, right behind Dexter.

Ten feet down, the pressure inside her ears started to throb. She plugged her nose and blew air into her tightly closed mouth, popping her ears as Dexter had taught them. So far, so good. When she reached the dark hole, she grabbed the edge and pulled herself in.

This was far worse than she had ever imagined. The space was much too narrow to actually swim, so she kept her focus by grabbing the jagged protrusions in the walls and propelling herself forward. Realizing she was blocked in the front from Dexter far ahead and blocked from behind by Greg, the familiar claustrophobic panic she knew all too well was taking over. She shook her head—*no.* Think Paul. *Paul, where are you?* Her brain wasn't letting him in, and this never-ending tunnel seemed to be getting smaller…*air*…she really needed air—not Paul. Air! She desperately needed to breathe…

Finally ahead, she could see some light. Dexter must have cleared the end of the tunnel. Just a little bit further…frantically needing to breathe. She could see the end now only a few yards away—it was so close she could almost grab the edge. But she couldn't move. Something held her in place. Her pack—it was stuck from above—she wiggled and squirmed, but nothing loosened her. She was going to die right here. Greg nudged her feet from behind, and she wanted to tell him she was stuck, but he seemed to figure it out. He tugged her backward, which freed her to twist and maneuver around the rock, but she felt so weak and just needed air! With the help of Greg pushing from behind, she eventually reached the end and made a feeble attempt to launch herself toward the surface, fighting the debilitating throbbing in her head, deprived of oxygen way too long.

She thrust her arm forward and clawed at the open water——grabbing handfuls of water and violently thrusting them behind her. Her entire body begged for oxygen—for one tiny breath—just one. *Where was the surface? Was she swimming down instead of up?* Panic stormed her heart, sending blood thundering through her ears. She kicked her legs into a wild thrashing hysteria until the deep, desperate ache in her lungs became unbearable.

The imprisoning blackness surrounding her began to soften and wrap her in a welcoming embrace. Her head felt pleasantly fuzzy. Insulated in peace. There was no more fighting, just a sleepy smile when she decided to give in to her body's demands and b r e a t h e…*breathe in the water.*

Suddenly—she was ripped high out of the water with such force it shocked her conscious. She sucked in a body-bursting intake of oxygen, then gravity pulled her back under where she fought back so ferociously, she exploded onto the surface again, inhaling harsh and throaty lung fulls of air—delicious sweet air!

At that very moment, Toke and Dexter, still recovering themselves, yanked Greg up and out of the water in the same way as Mae. His lungs howled like a wind tunnel, furiously pulling in the beautiful oxygen.

The dark cavern resonated with Dexter's vomiting and their lusty breathing, sounding much like a sickly dragon's den. Slowly things calmed as they found footing. A short run of coughing took over, which led to sighs and an overwhelming feeling of relief. Greg reached out and pulled Mae tight to him. Her tears flowed fast and through quivering lips said, "I'm sorry. I'm so, so sorry. I got stuck and almost killed both of us."

"Baby, we're here. We made it. We all made it."

"I don't know what to do if we come across another tunnel like this. I can't do that again."

They responded with an assortment of mumbled agreements, no one knowing how to be optimistic at this point. *Were the tiny bones the beginning of the end for them too?*

Chapter Seventeen

They walked and continued walking, each day rolling into the next. Three days passed, then another two, grateful no other situations were as challenging as their near-death swim of pure hell.

Two more times they came across the strange, dizzying parts in the tunnel but recognized them early and speedily ran through, barely feeling its effects. No one attempted to make sense of these episodes since their senses were already on overload with the bizarre. Their hunger was now unbearable, but the thinner they got, the fewer calories their bodies seemed to require. They stopped questioning their dilemma and complaining about their circumstances and just kept plodding on with the velocity of a three-toed sloth giving birth.

By now, they had to sit and rest their weak, famished bodies nearly every hour. Mae rested her head on Greg's lap while he weakly stroked her hair. "Shit. You know what I just thought of? My little brother can get on my laptop."

"Oh no." Mae would have sat straight up if she had the strength. "Are *all* the photos on there?"

"Yup."

Mae covered her mouth. "You *so* suck."

"No, *you* do," Greg said flirtatiously.

"Just stop." Toke groaned loudly. "Think about where we are and what's happening. How can you feel the least bit romantic?" But that didn't deter Greg from leaning down and kissing Mae, causing Toke to groan again.

Toke emptied out both of the backpacks surveying what they had left of the food. Mae sat up and poked at the small precious morsels on the ground, hoping they would look bigger in a different position. "This is it. Our last meal. Fit for a minuscule rodent." She sighed. "Enjoy."

All of a sudden, Dexter flattened his hands against the ground, listening through them like ears. His body became stiff and alert, then Toke's. Mae and Greg sat up quickly, and everyone stared at each other, wide-eyed in pre-panic. What started as a small and distant vibration rapidly grew to a thunderous pounding that pulsed through their bodies, paralyzing them in terror.

The far-off whine had grown into an unearthly howl, fast-approaching at a perilous speed. With no place to hide, nor shelter to protect them, they took the only choice left and hunkered together, protecting their heads, with some massive praying going on.

Leading with a screaming wind, the angry river introduced itself by tearing through the tunnel and sweeping them up with the ease of fallen leaves. It worked them like a roller coaster, the kind without seat belts, dodging rocks and low ceilings with familiar finesse. Mae fiercely clenched hold of her backpack as the water tried to bully it away like it had her waist pack and bottle. An ill-placed rock nearly bashed Dexter's head open as the current whipped them past one of its many serpent-like turns.

"Watch out! Sharp turn ahead—" Greg shouted until something hit him in the leg. "Shi—" Then he went under.

"Greg!" Mae screamed until his head popped up.

"Mother fucker—" Greg managed to say before he went under again. He was hurt, and she needed to get to him. White peaks had now formed on the surface, and she fought hard just to keep her head above the water. She spotted Greg back about thirty feet, and she called out to him, but her voice got lost to the wind.

Dexter yelled back, "Watch out, there's a—" but the water abruptly pulled him under.

"What? What?" Mae frantically tried to see—then she did. The river was separating in two. "Fork!" she yelled as it yanked her down its left side. To her relief, she could see Dexter's bobbing head ahead and Toke not far behind, both on the same half of the fork. But where was—"Greg!" she screamed but could not see him anywhere. She called again, this time with more desperation, "Greg! Say something!"

Being furthest back, Toke started shouting Greg's name, scanning the surface for any signs of him, eventually turning back to Mae. "Nothing. Must've been pulled down the other side of the split."

"Nooo!" Mae screamed, trying to swim back.

With a swift jerk, the river ripped Dexter around a sharp turn, spinning him backward, followed right after by Mae and then Toke. It threw them downhill at breakneck speed, holding them underwater as long as it could, only occasionally gifting them with the rare chance of oxygen.

This battle went on for nearly half an hour, depleting them of what little energy their bodies had left. The river grew in strength, and its momentum became so powerful, it flew them up and over the next incline that was as steep as a wall. Then, as quickly as it came, the water receded, leaving behind their three emaciated lumps in a small pool of water on the other side.

Chapter Eighteen

Aware of their new circumstance, the three of them hastily crawled to the highest ground, creating as much distance from the water as possible. If another wave rolled over the top, it might pull them completely back the other way. If it hadn't been so terrifying and deadly, Mae would have seen it as another chance to go back and find Greg.

The sound of rushing water was far off by now so Mae leaned her head back, cupping her hands around her mouth and screamed as loud as she could, "Greg! Are you out there?" After a few more tries with no answer, Mae stopped before she made Dexter and Toke deaf.

With their brains motoring slowly on fading adrenaline, they stayed put for a while, taking a somber inventory of their injuries. Just a few cuts and bruises, but not too bad.

Leaning back and closing his eyes, Toke took a few moments, then grumbled, "I guess now we know where all the water in here comes from."

"The evil force ripped through the tunnel and stole what didn't belong to it," Mae said angrily through quivering lips.

"But lucky for us," Dexter added, "it leaves little bits of itself behind to drink."

"Not a fair trade." She sniffed and wiped her teary eyes and nose on the back of her hand.

"I know Greg, and I know he's going to be all right." Dexter put his hand over Mae's with a gentle squeeze. "But we really need to get out of here in case the water returns."

Queasy with emotions, Mae felt her empty stomach wanting to heave its nonexistent contents. "What if he's hurt and just right behind us? I can't abandon him like this."

Looking conflicted himself, Dexter suggested, "We could leave him signs so he'll know which direction to go. You still have the bag of trash, right? This would be a good time to litter." His stomach growled painfully, and he doubled over. "If we get out *first*, we'll send a rescue team in to get him."

"That sounds like a plan," Toke said, looking pale from his stomach acids eating him from the inside out. He eased himself forward, holding his head in his hands and gazed blurry-eyed down at the pool of water where the river had deposited them.

"Why did Greg have to go down the stupid other side?" Mae sobbed. "Why?"

Suddenly Toke's head lurched forward as something caught his eye from down below. "Holy fuck!" Fresh adrenaline shot through his depleted veins as he leaped to his feet and feverishly scrambled down from their ledge, sliding most of the way on his butt. His eyes probed the water, while his body remained perfectly still. "There. Look! There it is!" He waded in and stopped when the slimy thing brushed past his leg.

Once Mae and Dexter saw the movement in the water with Toke, they tore down the hill. Dexter stepped slowly into the water until he was next to Toke and they both stared down wide-eyed at the large creature swimming between their legs.

"What the hell is it?" Toke said with his face nearly touching the water.

As fast as a bullet, Dexter's hands shot into the water. He grabbed hold of whatever was swimming around, but it took both of them to carry it to dry ground where it flapped around madly. "Just what kind of fish is this thing?" Dexter said, whipping off his glasses to examine the thrashing fish up close.

Choppy scales covered its body, resembling little gray teeth in bad need of a brushing. They all swirled to a crooked point at its face like a budding tentacle. Toke poked it with his finger. "Freaky looking guy."

"Sort of prehistoric." Dexter rubbed his hand along its skin which was deceptively soft.

"*Pre*-prehistoric," Toke added.

Stepping closer, Mae squealed, "It's hideous. Throw it back. I'm going to get nightmares."

"Throw it back? Are you serious?" Toke pulled out his keychain knife and handed it to Dexter. "It's food!"

Flinching in disgust, Mae felt her skin prickle. She edged closer to the gasping thing and took a long look, feeling sorry for its suffering. After a while, she said, "It almost looks human. Wise eyes…like you can see its ancient soul." She moved around to its other side and let out a small screech. "Oh dear God. It has hands!"

Dexter assured her unconvincingly that they were fins. "I've seen this fish before." Then without a moment's notice, he sliced its throat and swiftly cut the body in three, handing each of them a third, letting them disembowel and skin their own.

He and Toke practically swallowed its still-pulsing body whole. And Mae, so delirious with hunger, feeling completely out of control of her body—only hesitated a second before she tore her teeth into its flesh like a wild animal. The meat was firm and chewy and tasted exactly like overly fertilized potting soil. But no one cared. It was finally food. *Food.*

Ahh, the wonderful feeling of a full belly. Mae felt her brain wake up and her body wanting to be useful again.

Out of nowhere, Dexter said, "Hinges. The door hinges over the well." He gestured to the two fish still swimming. "They looked like these fish." That thought was too convoluted to even think about so they set upon capturing the rest of the fish instead.

With fish stuffed in Toke's pack, his water reservoir filled, they found the little blue light and braced themselves for the new terrors it surely had in store for them.

They hobbled along for the next two days on feet painfully blistered in the vacancies between callouses. Mae had to stop often to beat the ground in fits of anguish, and her eyes stayed puffy and red all day and night. No one got much sleep.

Early on, Toke's water reservoir got punctured and slowly leaked its entire contents out without anyone noticing. Water that they desperately needed. And when his backpack became so saturated with the putrid smell of rotting fish, it was useless, so he left it at their last stop. "Unless Greg lost his nose, he won't be able to miss *that* marker." Which launched Mae into another bout of sobbing.

Once they used the last pieces of trash, they scratched directional arrows in the walls, stacked rocks, and Mae ripped pieces of her backpack off until it was gone.

By now their bodies had become so weak from dehydration that no one could run through the next dizzying spot they came to and had to suffer through the entire length of it. Toke was on his knees holding his stomach, and Dexter looked like he was going to vomit.

"It's not just us," Mae cried, agonizing her way through. "These things are getting stronger, too." She curled up in a fetal position once she was free and clear. She desperately needed water. They hadn't come across *any* since the river dumped them out.

After a few minutes of lying flat on his back, Toke slowly sat up and propped his back against the tunnel wall. Dexter moved next to Mae, who remained in her same curled position on the ground. "You okay, Mae?" She didn't feel okay, so she just mumbled a response to show him she was still alive. He took a deep breath, leaned against the wall and opened his watch. In a dry, parched voice he softly announced, "It says we've now been underground for two full weeks."

"And it's been two whole days since we last saw Greg." Lacking the moisture, Mae had a tearless cry. The sadness of losing him was almost too much for her to bear and the motivation to keep moving had been depleted.

"Mae," Dexter reached over and rubbed her shoulder, "we're going to find him. He's one of the most resilient guys I know. And I've known him most of my entire life."

"He was writing a song for me," she said, with a pained smile. "He'd call me each night and sing me the new lines." With her face still pressed into the dirt, she began to sing softly, "Maaaaae Baaaaae…Before Anyone Else…Mae Bae…Brown Angel Eyes…my heart beats for your love…my hands feel for your body…my lips taste for your…hum hmm hmmm…" Realizing she didn't remember the clean version, she continued humming without words.

"You know, if this were a TV show, right now, we'd have a montage of Mae and Greg's favorite gushy moments." Getting no response, Toke eventually added softly, "Sorry, Mae. I'm sure he's fine. I really am." He wrapped his hands around his knees and stared bleakly at the tiresome wall in front of him.

It still took a moment for Toke to register what he was looking at, so he scooted closer on his butt for a better look. "Dex, shine your watch over here a second!" Not buying into Toke's enthusiasm, Dexter listlessly aimed his watch and illuminated the wall where Toke was tugging at something until it broke off. "Got it."

Under the glow of the watch, Toke inspected what he held in his hand, and a little smile quirked his lips, then a broad smile drew his entire face. Dexter eyed him suspiciously until Toke handed it over.

In an instant, Dexter knew what he was holding, and his eyes lit up. He excitedly reached over and wiggled Mae's arm. "Mae." But she wished he would stop and just let her be. Then he shook her arm harder. "Mae. Look at the wall behind you."

"Geez. Mae!" Toke said impatiently.

Slowly, she blinked her eyes into focus. When she saw the pure elation on both of their faces, she felt her pulse quicken, and she pulled herself up. "What? What is it?"

Chapter Nineteen

Mae's fingers caressed a small tangled cluster that pushed through a crack as the fog lifted from her brain. "Are these…can they possibly be"—then she started tugging feverishly—"Roots! Trees!" The surface had to be close. This nightmare was finally coming to an end. For the first time in forever, Mae felt her adrenaline ramping up as joy bubbled inside of her, filling her once again with hope, and a newfound strength and energy.

Testing the root between his teeth Dexter smiled for the first time in two weeks. "Definitely a root." He leaned his head back and laughed silently.

"We did it." Toke beamed like a child looking at a stack of wrapped presents.

Dexter was standing now, examining the walls. "They say a tree's roots are as deep as the tree is tall."

"Let's just hope it's a little tree in case we have to dig our way out." Pulling herself to her feet, Mae's eyes followed the roots up the wall trying to read their story.

"Well?" Toke stood. "What the hell're we waiting for?" Then he sprinted as fast as his beat-up body would take him down the tunnel. It wasn't long before he called back with his first report. "There's a shitload more roots and they're getting denser. Even hanging down trying to block my way." His voice was giddy at this point, and it wasn't long until Dexter and Mae were on his trail. Just the thought that Greg might have found another way out and was *right now* looking for them, gave Mae a new burst of energy.

The walls of the tunnel were now half living with tree roots, forcing their way into every crack in the marbleized limestone, continually prying the rock open to fit the growing root's expanding girth. At this point, the path began to ascend, deforming the tunnel into something like a worm that tried to make it across a sidewalk on a hot day. They had to crawl and squeeze through twisting tight places, licking thirstily at anything wet. And the farther they got, the more the water leached from the stone and in some areas, it was even dripping.

"Up here it opens up and—holy shit!" Toke shouted, excitedly. "I just stepped in water!" He immediately stepped out and fell to his knees ready to drink the pool dry but caught himself just in time. A soft blue glow began to spread through the water and increase in intensity until the entire pool was bright with its phosphorescent light, totally illuminating the tunnel and everything around him.

Toke stood and backed away, utterly mesmerized by it all, and stuck his foot out to touch it. "Wha…what the hell?" Then a softer, disappointed, "Shit, man."

Mae stopped short when she saw the source of the light. A gorgeous Caribbean blue pool poised serenely in front of them, straight from a sci-fi fantasy movie. "This beats anything I've ever seen at Disneyland," she said to Dexter, then raced to its edge and knelt, ready to scoop up a handful of water.

"Stop!" Toke's arm shot out, grabbing her wrist. "Something's wrong with it." Then pointed down to his feet without needing words. The water had completely dissolved his shoes, socks and the bottom four inches of his pants, leaving only the ring of his upper sock where the water hadn't reached.

Stepping closer, Dexter examined Toke's feet, then the water, and back to his feet. "Did it hurt?"

"Not at all," Toke said, suspiciously, watching Dexter unbuckle his belt. "What, are you going to whip me or something?"

In answer, Dexter slowly lowered half his belt into the water. Mae watched anxiously, until finally pleading, "Pull it out." Predicting they'd just be looking at a slimy, corroded version of its former self, maybe even stripped of its black color, instead the whole bottom half of his belt was—*gone*.

"Hmm." Dexter frowned, mystified, studying the remaining half of his belt.

Not knowing how to make sense of it all, Mae shook her head slowly. "But then we look at Toke's feet, and they're perfectly fine."

"Won't be for long without shoes." Toke knelt down and sniffed the water, then bolted right back up. "Agh." He wiped his nose. "Smells like burnt hairy broccoli farts."

"Hey, do you see this?" Mae pointed. "The water's not as bright anymore."

"Let me see something." Dexter lowered more of his belt in, and the pool glowed brightly once again. This got them started on testing other things, including handfuls of dirt, rocks, and pieces of roots to see what disappeared and what remained unscathed. The results just baffled them more, so they sat silently for a while, letting the water settle and dim, not sure what to do anymore.

Moments later, the answer came on its own. At the far end of the darkened pool, about five feet below the surface a bright shaft of blue light shined through a jagged opening in the rocky wall. Not like their dim little guiding light, but a bright, radiant glow.

"What do you guys think?" Mae squinted skeptically down at the light. "Is that blue glow in there a *good* thing?"

"I've been working on that one myself." Dexter's brows knit into something beautiful on his handsome face. "The water appears to corrode whatever it wants but leaves our bodies alone—as far as we know, that is."

"Maybe the longer the water touches something, the deeper it can penetrate." Mae pressed her lips together. "So, if we want to swim through that blue hole, the faster we swim, the less time it will have to eat through us."

They all seemed to frown at the thought of emerging on the other side partially liquefied. This prompted Toke to backtrack down the tunnel they just came from looking for their own little blue light, hoping they just missed a turn. He came back shaking his head in defeat. "Can't find the light anywhere. We're going to have to decide what to do on our own this time." He planted his hands firmly on his hips. "So, our only choices are to swim through this ravenous liquid shit or dig thirty feet through solid dirt, roots, and rock. I vote going through the water. If we die, it might be faster."

"Well, I'm definitely into swimming." Mae kicked off her shoes. "Right now, none of us are strong enough even to dig *two* feet."

Squatting down next to the water, Dexter took off his glasses and chewed the plastic arm. "First, let's see what we're up against before we just jump in. I'd like to know if it's properties are chemical or organic."

Mae carefully dipped her cupped hands in the water, which only made the water glow like a soft whisper then fizzle out. She stood and brought the water up with her watching it leak out slowly and burn holes in her socks where it fell.

"So, I guess this means if you're hanging onto something special"—Dexter started fishing around in his pockets—"maybe put it in your mouth or someplace."

"Someplace?" Toke smirked.

Dexter just continued, "And whatever you do, keep your eyes and mouth fully shut. On the other side, make sure you're completely clear of the water before you try to breathe."

"If there is another side," Toke added.

Knowing she was being ridiculously sentimental, her diaphragm was all Mae had left of Greg right now, and she needed to move it from her pocket to a safe place. Privately. She worked her way toward the dark part of the tunnel without explanation and stashed it deep inside her, the area for where it was intended.

When she returned, Dexter was busy trying to shove his car keys in his mouth, but kept gagging and spitting them out. Toke looked on, amused.

"You'll get bigger tips if you can master that gag reflex."

"Dex." Mae put her hand on his shoulder. "We're nowhere near your car, and I'm sure it won't still be just sitting there after two weeks." He looked at her with pained eyes like he had never thought of that possibility before.

Not accepting anything other than his Chevy still being there waiting for him, Dexter hunted around for another way. Toke held up his hands. "Dude, don't look at me. Mine stays virgin." So, with slumped shoulders, Dexter resigned and slowly slid his keys back into his pocket, like he was breaking up with his girlfriend.

After a minute of rummaging around on the ground, Toke handed them each a few pebbles. "Find ones that fit and put them in your ears. Hell, maybe even in your nose."

It took a little while, but when they felt psyched up enough and ready to aim themselves blindly through a small hole ten feet away—and also be okay with something invisible nibbling away at their bodies—Dexter volunteered to go first.

With pebbles in place and glasses clenched tightly in his hand, he inhaled the biggest lungful he could and shot off the steep bank with a running dive. Toke and Mae both cringed until he cleared the sides of the opening with perfect aim.

"His watch!" Mae pointed. It had lifted away from his wrist, floating peacefully in his wake. Seconds later, it vanished before their eyes, leaving only the parts it had no taste for, that sunk into the depths and out of sight.

"I guess I'll go next," Mae said nervously. "He must have made it by now, don't you think?"

"Or he could be wedged inside the tunnel, gummy and spongy from being half-dissolved, corking up the tunnel."

She shivered at the all-too-real possibility and glared at him. But his nose pebbles looked so ridiculous, she started to laugh and almost lost her own, needing to repack them in tighter.

And now, it was time. She took a deep breath and sprinted forward, shooting through the water like a blind missile. In seconds, she made it through the opening and kicked furiously to propel herself forward. Unable to open her eyes, she depended on her hands to feel her way through. Sharp little nips, like microscopic piranhas, tasted her everywhere, eating only what they liked. Her eyes began to sting, and her nostrils burned a little where the water must have found its way past the pebbles.

Expecting the worst, Mae was blown away when, in less than a minute, she was clear of the tunnel and taking her first breath on the other side. With closed eyes, she was unsure which direction to start swimming. She plucked out her ear pebbles and called out, "Dexter?" Her sightless voice searched the room, answering itself over and over in an eerie echo.

CHAPTER TWENTY

Like a big hug of relief, Dexter's clear voice shot through to her ears before joining in the chorus of echoes. "Mae! Swim a couple yards toward my voice, then feel for the ledge under your feet."

Once she found footing, she vigorously shook out her hands to rid them of water before wiping her eyes. Then, without thinking, Mae opened her eyes and let out a small yelp of pain. They stung a little, and once they cleared, she could make out Dexter's silhouette standing up on a ledge just a few yards away.

Making her way over to him, she blew out her ornery nose pebbles, which felt stuck for a panicking second, and wiped her eyes one more time. She immediately wished she hadn't. There in front of her was Dexter's naked pelvis, only two feet away. Her instinct would have been to turn away out of embarrassment, but she couldn't, this was far more intriguing at the moment—he was completely hairless down *there*.

Then, an alarming thought occurred to her. If *he* were naked, then *she* undoubtedly had to be too—in fact, they would *all* be completely naked after being in that blue water. Dexter reached down to help her up, fumbling blindly until she grabbed his arm and with her other, self-consciously covered her breasts.

Toke took longer than they expected, but when he finally emerged, Dexter guided him over. In shy self-preservation, Mae quickly advised him to keep his eyes shut until they were fully dry. But, once he was up and over the cliff-like ledge, he immediately started to wipe his eyes. Mae stood there, naked and exposed, not realizing she was holding her breath, silently pleading for the water to hurry up and go dark. *Why was it taking so long?*

Then, as if the scene was directed for a movie, the water dimmed just as Toke opened his eyes. "Blechhh. That blue slurpy smells worse on this side. It's freaking rank."

"It'll probably stink until it finishes digesting all the stuff it got from us," Dexter said.

Attempting to move away from the stench of the water, Toke was immediately blocked by a thick layer of small objects lining the water's edge. "What the hell—are these...*bones*?"

"Dear God..." Mae gulped, trying to adjust her eyes to the dark, while her brain was adjusting to the reality of where they might be.

"And why so many?" Toke puzzled, reaching up to scratch his two-week-old beard. His fingers suddenly froze in place. "What the hell?" Then his hands shot to his head. "Holy shit! My hair."

With hesitance, Mae reached up to her own head, and let out a strangled gasp. She nervously probed every inch of her head, with the sobering discovery of not *one single hair*. After running her hands down her arms and legs, she found that they too were totally smooth and hairless as if she just shaved her entire body with one of those super expensive five-bladed razors.

The cave echoed with groans and whines, but not one of them were from Dexter. Mae knew the loss of his long hair, which seemed to identify him, must have really hit him hard. When he finally did speak, his voice was bleak in disbelief. "Man, it just ate everything. Even our eyelashes and brows. Everything...that..." he paused, searching for the right word, "that wasn't *living*."

"Let's just get the hell out of here," Toke said. To light their way, he tossed a couple of bones in the water, and it erupted in its shimmering radiance, painting everything a brilliant luminescent blue.

And there they all were. Absolutely, undoubtedly, completely buck-naked. Not a stitch of clothing nor a wisp of hair. Anywhere. Mae worked hard at convincing herself, that with everything they had just gone through together these past couple of weeks, being nude in front of them hardly seemed a priority. Geez, they happened upon her peeing in the tunnel far too often for her to even be mildly embarrassed anymore. But she was.

Eventually their surroundings revealed themselves, becoming open and spacious, where immense tree roots intertwined with boulders of all sizes, battling it out over many, many years of sharing the same desired space. Along the cavern's walls and ceiling, a dozen hopeful spider webs waited patiently, presenting their stitched artistry to the competition of life or death. All of these signs of activity, dead or alive, reinforced hope that this underground nightmare would soon be over.

Curious about the small bones, Mae picked one up and examined it closely. And that's when she saw what else the water had done. "Oh, God—my fingernails!" she screamed, then looked down. "My toenails! They're gone!" With a look of horror, she stared at her raw nail beds, barely protected by a thin pink membrane and they looked back, defenseless and trusting like a newborn baby.

"Just wait until we start walking on these." Dexter held up his foot showing where the water had munched off the thick layer of calloused skin, leaving the bottom of his foot vulnerable and sensitive. "I guess we never appreciate something till it's gone."

"Just think what it would have done to our teeth." Mae could almost feel her teeth eaten down to just the extremely sensitive, living nerve, and shivered, closing her mouth protectively.

So caught up in their own changes, at first no one noticed when a light breeze had made its way to them and forced back the vile stench of the decaying water to fill their lungs with the fresh scent of trees and magnificent summer air. Toke stopped his self-examination and, with a lift of his nose, took a single breath. After a loud whoop, he shouted, "We're home!"

It only took a second for Mae and Dexter to realize what he was shouting about. And with noses raised, taking in the scented air, the look on all their faces was pure and utter joy.

Following the source of the draft was not easy. The ground was painfully rough, and the dark had overtaken the cavern again. "These rocks are so sharp." Mae fiercely sucked in air through her teeth. "Each step is killing me."

Dexter tottered along behind her. "I know. Me too. It's like we're stepping on shards of glass."

"Can you see it?" The wild enthusiasm in Toke's voice immediately stole away their pain. "Up ahead. A light. A real light! It's faint. Probably just a small opening—" He let out another whoop and took a few quick steps forward. "Motherfucker. Mother, motherfucker—" he yelled, verbally bullying his pain away.

Finally, Mae saw it. A tiny trickle of light, so pure and white it froze her in her tracks. For a moment she just stood there, afraid. Afraid it would just be a trick, another false hope. Then the tears came, and she was overcome with weeping, which soon transformed to laughing as she fell to her knees, hands to her face. Like a protective brother, Dexter hung back with her until she was back on her feet.

They caught up to Toke on an incline, gingerly placing one foot in front of the other, carefully climbing over large boulders and dirt. The light grew brighter and glowed around Toke's large silhouette like a halo. "We are *so* almost there!"

Light streamed through a tiny opening where a single stone had fallen free from the deliberately stacked pile of stones walling off the exit. Seeing this simple act of human intervention filled Mae's being with such a joyful comfort her throat ached from trying not to cry.

With a grunt, Toke pulled himself up and over the highest point. Glancing back at Dexter, who gave him a thumbs up, and Mae, who held up crossed fingers, he took a preparatory breath, then poked his head through the opening. He immediately yanked his head back in and covered his stinging eyes. "Son-of-a-bitch!"

Mae strained her neck from below trying to see something. Anything. "What did you see? What's on the other side?"

"I'll tell you in a minute. Once I'm not blind." He gave his eyes a little rest, then attempted it again, but much slower this time, peeking between each finger a little at a time.

"C'mon, Toke. Give us a clue!" Mae begged, her heart pounding so hard, she thought it would hammer a hole through her chest. The wait was torturous, and she almost needed restraints while Toke leisurely adjusted his eyes to the brightness. "C'mon…"

The time had finally come, all Toke's fingers were down, and his hands fell to his side. He exhaled his pleasure, so loud and guttural it almost sounded sexual. "You need to see this for yourself."

PART TWO

Chapter Twenty-One

Mae gaped at the spectacular valley spread before her. Mountain after mountain of dark green forest rising under a cloudless blue sky that seemed to reach into forever. It looked like someone had painted a dream. A dream she could feel, that pulsed and breathed, sharing its sun-warmed earth like no painting ever could. She took a deep breath of the fresh pine-scented summer air and laughed, finding peace after their long and brutal battle. "I just can't believe it's finally over." Mae struggled guiltily with the bittersweet feelings of getting out but leaving Greg behind.

Dexter's eyes were last to adjust, and when he eventually lowered his hands, he groaned a pleasurable, "Oh, man…" Gazing out, he diligently surveyed the land and announced that they seemed to be on the side of a steep cliff, but the tree's roots appeared sturdy enough to aid them in climbing up.

Mae remained still, mesmerized by the sound of life surrounding her. Birds singing, squirrels chattering, and a breeze shuffling through the leafy trees above and below them. But it was time to stop gawking to join Toke and Dexter in tearing away the stones that blocked the exit. "I bet we've been all over the news—four missing Sacramento college students. We'll tell them about Greg, and they'll send a SWAT team in to rescue him. The press will probably swarm us for interviews."

"Buck naked interviews." Toke removed the last stone and brushed off his hands. He reached up and grabbed hold of a thick tree root tangling its way down the face of the cliff, then pulled himself out of the opening and onto a new perch above them. Wrapping his legs around the root, he reached down to help the next person up. Mae waved her hands, insisting on going last, and they seemed to understand without any explanation.

Successfully swinging her leg over the root above, Mae followed with the rest of her body. "How far do you think we're from home?"

"We were pretty much crawling the last few days, but who knows how far that demon river took us," Dexter said from a few yards above her. "If I had to guess though, I'd say we've gone maybe forty or fifty miles underground."

Toke reached up and tested the next root above him, releasing a small shower of dirt. "We'll find out soon enough."

"Can you imagine what the three of us must look like to another person?" Mae hoisted herself up to the next branch. "No one's going to help us. They'll be afraid of us."

It took nearly half an hour to reach the top—their weakened bodies making the climb as difficult as it was painful. Mae tried to haul herself up the very last part, but the muscles in her arms shook uncontrollably. She gratefully took Dexter's extended arm, which pulled her up and over the top of the cliff.

They each took a few quick steps away from the steep edge and scrutinized the densely packed trees and tall grasses that stood like armed guards in front of them. The sun beat down on them dehydrating them even more, making it difficult to swallow.

Toke moved forward. "The animals know where the water is." He began limping pitifully down a narrow deer trail, and they soon followed. Mae tried to take her mind off the tiny particles that seemed to pierce through the thin layer of skin on the soles of her feet, making each step complete agony.

They came across a ripe patch of blackberries and, without thinking, began shoving berries in their mouths at perilous speed. Soon they were howling in agony as the bush's thorny tentacles thrashed at them with razor sharp swords. Mae had never given thought to how many nerve endings resided just under her nails—until the nails were gone. Each berry came with the taste of blood and a small internal yelp of pain.

Looking like satiated vampires after a messy kill, they left the berry patch and continued their search for water. Toke had been right, and the path led them straight to a little stream that flowed clear and clean through the rocks and grasses. Dropping to their knees, they voraciously scooped handfuls of the fresh spring water to their mouths.

Eventually, Mae sat in the middle of the stream and dabbed at the bloody etchings the thorns carved in her skin and splashed the sticky berry juice off her face. Feeling a little sickened by the amount of water she drank, she leaned back, lying flat, and let the icy water run over her body.

They followed the brook to where it merged into a much larger creek and relieved their feet in the soft clay-like mud lining its banks. Mae scooped up a handful of it and self-consciously covered certain places with a mud bikini. Toke soon followed with a sculpted mud hairdo, and Dexter slapped some over his genitals.

Wandering upstream a short way, Dexter found shade under a large bay tree. He leaned back against its massive trunk and closed his eyes.

Toke trudged his way through the creek and plopped noisily down next to him. After waving Mae over, he held his hands out in front of him then flipped them over. "Damn, no fair. The blue water must have a distaste for warts."

Keeping his eyes still closed, Dexter answered softly, "Warts are living. If you've ever tried to cut one off, you'd know." His voice trailed off at the end, as he seemed to have fallen asleep.

"And your tat, it's only a little faded, but definitely still there." Toke leaned against the tree and closed his eyes next.

Anxious to get going, Mae stared down at the two, disappointed. She wasn't tired at all but what was she going to do? Limp on her own somewhere and get arrested for indecent exposure? With no other choice but to wait, she found a comfortable spot next to them and laid down.

Mae let out a startled scream that jolted Dexter and Toke unpleasantly from their nap. Above her stood a boy holding the stick he had used to poke her awake. She quickly sat up. "Oh my God—we are so happy to see you!" She grabbed the end of his stick and reached out with her other hand to touch him, to make sure he was real, but he jumped back.

Two kids, about twelve or so, both in costume, studied them suspiciously. The one with the stick wore a raccoon hat covering his blonde hair, which badly needed a cut, and a small spray of freckles over his tanned nose. Mae figured that he must be playing Daniel Boone. And, if his *real* fur hat wasn't roadkill, he was going to get a lecture. But later. After he helped them.

The other kid, who she thought looked Hispanic like her, stayed on his horse. He was dressed as a Native American, but instead of the typical costume headdress with a showy display of feathers, his head was wrapped in a roughly woven material with dried seed ornaments dangling from the folds. He must have made it himself, which would have been cute if he wasn't holding a bow with an arrow aimed right at them—and it wasn't a suction cup tipped toy arrow, either.

Mae held out her arms open in a pleading gesture. "We know we're a freakish sight, but, please. We'd like to talk to your parents."

Dexter attempted to get up onto his sore feet while trying to keep the mud covering his genitals. "Would you by chance have a cell phone on you?"

The kids looked at each other and spoke in some secret language of their own. Then the Boone kid finally spoke. "Where are your horses? Why are you with no clothes?"

"And hairs," his friend added with a slight accent.

"Kid, please. Do you have a cell phone we can use?" Toke stood as the dried mud on his head cracked and fell off. "It's an *emergency*."

Not feeling threatened, the kid on the ground continued, "Where are your horses?" This time he poked Dexter with the stick.

"Ow. Stop. It's such a long story. Can you just help us, and *then* we'll explain everything?"

"Where is your home?" He then turned to Mae. "Or tribe?"

She shook her head, confused. "We're from the Sacramento area."

The kid on the horse nodded. "Sacramento. The Great River."

"We're hungry and need food and clothes," Dexter said calmly.

"Please, we need to contact our parents." Mae held her hands together as if in prayer.

"Geez. Can you just tell us if you have a *freaking phone*?" Irritated, Toke yanked the stick out of the boy's hand and threw it in the trees.

"We'll pay you—anything!" Mae added.

Boldly reaching out a hesitant hand, Little Boone felt the top of Dexter's bald head. Then bent slightly to look closer at his face, touching the smooth skin where his eyebrows should be. He moved on to Mae, his eyes taking in her bloody scratches while Mae busied herself making sure her dried mud was fully intact. When he got to her fingers and toes, he sucked in some air, saying. "Ouch."

Curious now, the boy on the horse got down and walked over to them. He grimaced at the missing nails his friend pointed out. "Where are your clothes? White people always wear clothes."

Mae subconsciously covered herself more with her hands. "We don't have any. We lost them."

"Got any extra?" Dexter worked his winning smile.

Though nearly naked himself, only wearing a skimpy leather g-string with flaps, the Hispanic kid went to his horse and retrieved his saddle blanket for Mae. Little Boone took off his vest and handed it to Toke, and then unlaced his shirt and gave it to Dexter who tied it around his hips. Toke struggled with how to wear the small vest around his hips until the boy tossed him a piece of twine to hold it in place.

“Thanks, man, we’ll give these back or buy you new ones. I’m Dexter.” He held out his hand for a few seconds before putting it away. “That’s Toke, and she’s Mae.”

“This is Milok.” The blonde boy motioned to his friend. “I’m William.”

“Where are your horses?” was all Milok said.

Toke fumed, “We don’t have any.” He was exasperated by the same stupid question. “And no bicycles, no cars, and no giraffes either.”

The two boys talked in private for a moment, then Milok said, “Come with us.”

Once the horses turned around, they headed out slowly. The three of them followed behind at a crippling pace, braving the sting of the stickers that embedded themselves into the soft virgin bottoms of their feet.

Chapter Twenty-Two

It seemed like an eternity until they arrived at the creek where William and Milok had been fishing earlier. William tested his lines that were attached to floating oak galls and came up with a large fish. Dexter's eyes grew big, and Toke wiped the drool off his chin. Mae was unable to turn this down. She'd get back to her veggie life later.

While they waited for William to finish roasting the fish over the fire, Milok took a sharp piece of obsidian and sliced off a tubular plant growing near the water. One at a time, he gently squeezed a gel-like fluid onto each of their fingers where the nails had been, causing a cold torturing sensation that soon numbed. Toke howled in pain when Milok picked out an embedded thorn from his raw nail bed until the gel did its miraculous work.

Relief gushed over Mae's face as she leaned back against the tree, smiling with closed eyes. "Thank you, Milok, that feels so much better." She slowly sat up and opened her eyes. "What is that stuff anyway?" Milok gave her a quizzical look, then over to William with eyebrows raised. Mae was impressed with their maturity for such youngsters, even though they seemed a bit full of themselves.

"So, what's with the costumes?" Toke said with a smirk.

William stopped roasting the fish for a moment, looking confused. "Costumes?"

"You know." Toke gestured his hand up and down toward their clothing. "The Indian and Daniel Boone theme." Mae gave him a stern look for his politically incorrect use of the word "Indian" and opened her mouth to say something, but Toke quickly cut her off. "Okay, whatever. Enough talking. Back to cooking."

William and Milok found it amusing to watch them desperately suck every tiny bit off the fish bones, not wanting the experience to end. Mae sheepishly admitted, "We haven't had any real food for days. We were trapped underground for two weeks." Her eyes foraged the area for more fish, but that was it. "And the water, it ate our hair and all our clothes."

"And our horses." Toke couldn't help it. "The water ate our horses."

"We are also looking for a friend of ours," Mae said. "He's about our age, African-American and wearing a tattered Jimi Hendrix t-shirt."

"African, like slaves?" William asked innocently. Mae glanced at Toke and Dex who didn't know how to take this racist comment either. What they really needed was their help, so they chose to ignore it. "There's no Africans here. Milok's as dark as they get in these mountains." William pointed his thumb at Milok, who straightened himself proudly.

"So, back to the phones." Dexter stood up. "Do you think we could use your phone?"

William glanced at Milok for feedback, but he just shrugged. "Come with me, and you can ask my parents about a fone."

"Parents! He has parents!" Mae jumped to her feet, re-energized with hope. She couldn't stop imagining conversations with her mom over the phone, images of a hot shower, fresh, clean clothes, and a car ride home. *Home*. Her friends would be worried, and she would have to call them all from their phone, too. Maybe Greg would even answer his phone! So excited, she tried to help William pack the horses up but just got in the way.

"You two." Milok pointed to Mae and Dexter. "Ride together." He turned to Toke. "You ride mine." Toke, having never ridden a horse in his life, nervously held on, unwisely tugging on the rope and giving the animal confusing messages. Milok frowned disapprovingly, and to Toke's relief, took the rope and lead, walking in front like William was doing with Mae and Dexter's horse.

Fifteen minutes later, William pulled the horses to a stop. "Almost home." He and Milok split up their fish, rabbits, and ducks. "Milok leaves here for his home."

They thanked Milok profusely, making him a little uncomfortable, then he rode off between some trees and was gone. William took them a little farther, with Toke limping behind and parked behind a set of trees. "Stay here with Petey. I'll get my folks. But, stay out of sight until I come and get you."

Before William got five steps away, they were off the horse and running to a grove of trees heavily laden with apples like shiny Christmas ornaments. "Wait!" William called after them. "Those are my Pa's trees!" Then seeing how they didn't stop, added, "You can't pull them off like that. You have to twist them. No, not like that. One won't grow next year if you take the bud—" But they didn't listen and continued to yank apples off the tree letting the branches bounce wildly.

"Ack—sour!" Though they kept gorging on them like ravenous wolves.

A woman emerged, cautiously stepping into view. Her unsteady hands held a long shotgun aimed right at Dexter. She was thin with wispy blonde hair pulled back into a tight bun.

"Ma! No!" William ran over and put his hand over hers.

Not feeling threatened in the least, Toke peered past the nervous woman and fixated on her gun. Wanting a closer look, he took a few steps toward her, but she quickly raised the gun to his face. Still oblivious to her threat, Toke said excitedly, "Whoa—check this out!" He glanced back at Dexter and Mae, who didn't share his enthusiasm. "Lemme see that. You mind?" He held out his hand expectantly, still unfazed that it was pointed at him. She yanked the gun out of his reach and quickly stepped back, nearly tripping over her long brown skirt. "Holy shit. That's an original Flintlock. Carbine design…smoothbore barrel and caplock! Hey, how much you want for that? Do you still have the muzzle cap, entry pipe, and ramrod thimble?" Toke let out a low whistle of appreciation. "Sick."

"I think she's serious." Dexter pulled Toke back.

"Ma." William stepped in front of the woman. "Me and Milok found them back in Craggy Canyon. They're not going to hurt us."

Mae walked over while wiping the apple off her face with the saddle blanket. "We're so sorry to intrude, but we need to contact our parents. We got way lost and haven't seen another person for over two weeks." William's mother gave no hint of hearing her, so she went on, "I'm sorry we look so freakish. I guarantee we're not from another planet. We're normal people from Sacramento who just got super lost, and all we want is to use your phone and get home to our families."

The sound of hoofbeats gave all of them some relief as they watched a man ride up in a nicely preserved, antique wagon, driven by four wooden wagon wheels and pulled slowly by a tired old horse. In the wagon's bed, splayed over a stack of cut logs, lay the body of a long-legged, hooved animal. The man jumped down, revealing overly patched pants held up with suspenders, old leather boots that were on their last days, and a billowy cotton shirt, sheer from use.

He handed William the reins without taking his eyes off the three strangers. A fine dusting of dirt clung to his sweaty face, solidly caked in the creases around his eyes and mouth. Mae wondered if one of them should speak first or let this intimidating hunter-lumberjack make the first move. The man locked eyes on Toke, him being the largest, then slowly took the gun from the woman while she sunk back behind him.

Forcing a neighborly smile, Toke held out his open palms. "Hey dude, man, we just need to call someone. I swear, no need for guns."

The man's eyes narrowed and chewed them over for a good while. His expression slowly changed from fear and suspicion to flat-out curiosity of these peculiar-looking people and his finger loosened on the trigger.

"We're trying to make a call to our parents and need to find a phone or even a computer," Mae begged, using a flurry of unnecessary hand movements. "It's probably considered a local call, depending on your provider, but if not, we'll pay you back triple every cent."

Taking a step closer, Dexter added, "Or if you can possibly give us a ride, we'll give you gas money and payment for your time, just to drive us."

"And a huge tip." Mae tugged at her blanket, making sure she was covered where it mattered. She didn't want him to get the wrong idea.

The gruff man backed up warily and motioned for his family to do the same. "Stay here." The resonance in his voice was so deep, he appeared much bigger than he was. With the gun still aimed at them, he backed up and joined his family. William began explaining to his parents what had happened, and every so often the man or woman glanced over at them with a look of suspicion or disapproval.

"We don't have lice and aren't sick," Mae called out after them. "A few Band-Aids might help, though."

Chapter Twenty-Three

With no place to sit, they just stood there and perused their surroundings. About fifty yards back sat an old-fashioned log cabin dutifully puffing smoke from its stone chimney. Mae felt its shoddy DIY design worked well with the unpainted barn, its constantly creaking door, and the small stable that butted up to the side of the barn. Occupying the back of the stable were a dozen or so chattering chickens busily running in and out of their wooden eyesore of a hen house—and everywhere else for that matter. On the sunny side of the cabin struggled a pitiful garden that grew a disarray of scraggly plants. Wrapping around it stood a useless stick fence to keep the two goats out, but evidence proved they had been quite successful at poking their heads through whenever they wanted a munch. And, everywhere else grew apple trees—lots of them. No way this place was just some primitive vacation cabin in the woods. These people actually *lived* there.

After ten minutes, the family seemed to come to an agreement. The woman left, disappearing into the cabin, and the other two walked back to face the three of them. Clearing his throat, the man spoke sternly in a pronounced Scandinavian accent, "My Villie tells os dat you are from de Sacramento River."

"Well, we don't live *in* the river, but near it. We go to the city college and—" Dexter slapped his hand on his chest. "I'm sorry. My name's Dexter, and this is Mae and Toke." With a gun still pointed at them, no one held a hand out for shaking.

"This is my Pa, Jack. Jack Fox," Willie said.

"Can you tell us where we are?" Dexter glanced around briefly.

"Dis here is de Fox's land. My land. My house."

"Dude, can you at least stop pointing that gun at us? We're unarmed, see?" Toke held up his hands and spun around revealing his bare butt where the vest didn't reach. Jack grunted disapprovingly but did lower his gun.

The wife came back over carrying a small pile of clothing. "And, this is my Ma, Mrs. Fox." She nodded her head in greeting. With a nervous smile, she handed Toke the pile of clothes and quickly stepped back next to her husband.

Turning away from Jack's hard stare, Dexter asked Mrs. Fox, "We're hoping you can tell us if you've seen our friend that we've lost. His name's Greg."

Jack moved protectively in front of his wife. "No travelers here. Wat dose he wear?"

Toke took over. "He's in a shredded white t-shirt. Well, it used to be white. But not him. He's black, average height, big fro."

"Black as in negro?" Jack scratched his chin. "Dere's no negroes in dese parts. Is he a free man?"

Mae smiled politely. "Not a Freeman. He's a Stalls. Greg Stalls."

"Maybe an escaped slave den?" Jack asked, concerned.

Mae blinked in disbelief at his absurd question. Toke snorted and said under his breath, "What an ass." Then turned their attention on the clothes while running a constant commentary as he held up each piece.

Mae reached for the pair of threadbare, patched, drawstring pants and her face lit up. "These are so cool. Real vintage, not acid or stone wash."

Finally catching Mae's attention, Mrs. Fox motioned for her to follow. Mae handed Dexter the pants making a face and pleading "help" with her eyes.

She walked up the steps of the covered wooden porch, past three roughly made log chairs, and entered the front door of the cabin. A dark interior greeted them, with the only light coming from two small glassless windows draped by sheer curtains. Instead of flicking on a light, Mrs. Fox lit a candle and took it with her, leading Mae to the back of the room and behind a partition, curtained off from the main room.

While Mrs. Fox busied herself sorting through clothing, Mae took in her surroundings. The tiny room was stark and simple. In the center stood a narrow bed and judging by the two pillows, was meant for two very narrow people who had to sleep as straight as sticks. Next to the bed sat a chair and a shelf with a small collection of folded clothes—a crudely made, slender pine table butted against the back wall, holding an antique style pitcher of water and a large ceramic bowl. Under her feet was dirt. In fact, the floor of the entire house was dirt. Packed down so hard it was almost shiny. No wonder they didn't offer them their phone, they couldn't afford to own one. She took a silent step back and peeked back out through the curtain to the main part of the house. She saw no lamps or lighting fixtures anywhere, just a scattering of candles and a couple of old oil lamps, but continued hunting for the clue that would be the tattletale of this fake rustic living. A plastic container, a roll of paper towels, a clipped coupon, the "ah ha"—but found nothing.

"Here we are now," Mrs. Fox said, revealing a trace of a southern accent. "I'm hopeful something here will fit you."

"Thank you. You've no idea how much we all appreciate this."

"You speak English quite well." Mrs. Fox proceeded to lay a few pieces of well-worn clothing on the patchwork quilt covering the bed. "What tribe do you come from?"

"Tribe?" Mae wanted to laugh having been asked this for the second time. "I'm from Sacto. Well, just outside."

"Sacktowe," she repeated, with no recognition.

"I hope you don't mind if I ask, but are you like Amish or Quaker or something?"

Mrs. Fox arched her eyebrows, looking amused. "No, we're Lutheran."

Not knowing what to say after their awkward conversation, Mae started shuffling through the clothes on the bed. When she looked up, Mrs. Fox was staring at her hairless head. Mae half-smiled, embarrassed. "I know. Freaky, huh?"

Pulling down a green linen cloth from a hook on the wall, she held it out for Mae. "You might wish to tie this around your head…to stay warm." Then she filled the large bowl with water from the pitcher and lay a small folded cloth next to it. "Let me know if there's anything else you need. I'll be right out here." Stepping out of the room she pulled the curtain closed behind her.

Splashing the cool water on her face, Mae found, to her horror, chunks of dried fish still on her cheeks and chin and hastily scrubbed them off. Secretly, she'd miss being able to let loose and live like a cave troll where being gross was completely acceptable. She closed her eyes and draped the wet cloth over her entire face. Her tortured skin rejoiced under the soft weave of the fabric while drinking in the moisture it so desperately needed.

A small broken piece of mirror hung on the wall above the bowl of water and Mae glimpsed her image. Catching her breath in a startled gasp, she quickly turned away. Small tears pooled in her eyes while she slowly reached up, touching her face, then her scalp. She had gotten used to seeing Toke and Dex like this, but not herself. Not even one stray hair anywhere. Her skin was smooth and polished, but with her bloodshot eyes, she looked like she was strung out on something.

Seeing the skin of her face with its nice, even color, not like Dexter and Toke with their pink blotches of sunburn, Mae felt grateful that her darker Mexican genes were much more dominant than her light Spanish ones. No wonder these people couldn't relax around them, they really were a disturbing sight. She took the green cloth, wrapped it snuggly around her head like a turban, and finished it off with a bow for a dab of femininity.

After scrubbing the rest of her body clean with the cloth, she searched for panties and perhaps some kind of bra, but found nothing. Just some giant floppy capris. Was she supposed to wear them under the dress or instead of the dress? She started to put the pants on, but her foot went right through a giant opening between the two legs. She couldn't tell if it was a rip or a convenience hole.

The drab colored dress was hand-stitched and very soft from many years of washing. It proudly wore its faded stains like an intentional design, and its edges were badly frayed. To make this dress work like it was supposed to, Mae needed to put on another curious thing that tied around her chest tightly stuffing her bosom in like a sausage. Her sensitive fingers painfully buttoned up the front of the small dress, then she patted down the ridiculously cumbersome skirt.

Holding out the mirror, she took a look at the whole ensemble, and her mouth dropped open. This was the first time she *saw* what two weeks in the tunnels had taken from her body. She lost so much of her always-inconvenient giant boobs and flabby upper arms. Her pillowy belly was flat for the first time in her life—though Greg would not like this, he loved her squishy tummy.

She stood silent for a moment, feeling humanity slowly return to her being. Then, before she forgot, and long overdue, she took out her diaphragm, cleaned it, then wrapped it in a small rag.

Chapter Twenty-Four

Mae emerged through the bedroom curtain and paused to breathe in the intoxicating aroma of food. Salivating excessively, she spotted Dexter and Toke sitting at the table with Jack and Willie across from them. Empty wooden bowls licked clean must have contributed to their thoroughly satiated faces. Without time to wonder where her bowl was, Mrs. Fox appeared. "There, now. You are comely once again."

"Comely," Mae repeated quietly. *What kind of word was comely?*

After collecting the empty bowls from the table, Mrs. Fox crooked her finger to follow her into the kitchen. Mae walked the four steps it took to be on the other side of the room where a long wooden counter stood to separate the kitchen from the dining room.

The kitchen, if one could really call it that, puzzled Mae. It held no appliances large *or* small and she could not find a single electrical outlet anywhere, but still, there was no mistaking what purpose this room had. In fact, each room in this house held names far more grandiose than their reality. Actually, the word "house" should be changed to "cabin." Compact and crowded without much wiggle room. Like having to wear your little sister's shoes. *Dis here is Fox land. And dis is Jack's wee cabin.* Mae giggled as she neutered Jack's boastful claim.

Shown to a seat on the far side of the counter, Mrs. Fox set in front of Mae a large wooden spoon with a polished bone handle and a steaming bowl of stew. Without waiting a beat, Mae loaded the spoon with the chunky root vegetables and potatoes smothered in the thick aromatic stew. She closed her eyes and leisurely swallowed. It warmed her throat all the way down, and she never wanted this wonderfulness to end.

Mrs. Fox brushed off her apron, and began loading a tray with four metal cups, one half full of water, a pitcher of hard apple cider, and a wedge of white cheese. "Please excuse me, Mae." She delivered the tray to the table and returned with a steaming kettle from the fire.

After filling the teapot with the hot water, Mrs. Fox noticed the meat piling up on one side of Mae's bowl. "Is there something wrong with the meat?"

"Oh, no, no. So sorry. I'm a vegetarian, and there's plenty of other things to eat in the stew." Mrs. Fox gave her a blank stare, so Mae felt compelled to explain, "I don't eat animals. Animals are my friends, and I don't eat my friends." She quickly glanced over at Toke, who would use this opportunity for a crude joke, but he was too engaged in the cider to have heard.

Sitting down on one of the stools, Mrs. Fox poured them each tea. "Well, then, here we are."

"Would you happen to have any vanilla soymilk? I usually put it in my tea."

"I'm sorry, but we don't have milk from that animal. We only have our goats."

This woman was so ridiculous, Mae turned her head away, afraid she'd start laughing.

"We don't often get visitors up here, so we just have what we get in trade or when Jack gets down to the ships."

Mae could hear Toke and Dexter laughing, and she wanted to be out there too. "Do you mind if I grab some of that cheese?" She inclined her head toward the table.

"That wouldn't be good. The men are talking."

Whatever that meant. Mae rolled her eyes. Mrs. Fox's easiness with being so submissive to her husband was nauseating. And so was this bitter tea. "How about if I pour a mug of cider?" Again, she referred to the table.

She could tell Mrs. Fox was holding back her annoyance with Mae's apparent hearing problem. "It is best to let the men talk."

"How about if we drink cider, eat cheese, and talk with them, too?" That should have solved everything.

Mrs. Fox regarded Mae curiously. "Jack prefers a man's company when he drinks his cider."

Not knowing how to respond politely to this, Mae just drank her tea. This "men only club" seemed to match the rest of their antiquated lifestyle. Did Willie stand in for "men" when they had no outside company? In fact, Mrs. Fox didn't even seem old enough to have a twelve-year-old son. She was maybe in her late twenties.

"So, Mae," Toke said loud enough so she could hear. "Jack here was telling us not only do they not have phones, they don't know what they are." Sounding a bit sloshed on the hard cider, he confined his laugh to a series of snorts. "Guess what else? He's never heard of a city named Sacramento! Just the river."

Dexter added with the same intoxicated slur, "However," and held up an index finger to make a point, "he does *know* they live in California."

"No car, TV, or radio neither. Don't even ask about a computer." Toke found this so ridiculous, he turned his head away to hide his giggling.

Deciding she'd had enough of this chauvinism, Mae thanked Mrs. Fox, pushed her stool back and marched right into the "men's" room. Then, before she lost her backbone, she blurted, "Can we just get a ride into town or the next city? Even on your horse or something? We are desperate to get home and will happily send you money for this incredible meal and transportation."

So disturbed by her intrusion, Jack did not look up at her, just clenched his teeth around his pipe like he wanted it to break. With a slight edge in his voice, that had to skirt around his pipe, he finally said, "As I was saying to your friends, I might be heading dat way in a few veeks to do some trading in de valley. Come back den, an I'll load you in de vagon."

"You don't understand. We have to get back home to our families," Mae pleaded. "We've been gone a very long time, and our families will be sick with worry."

Jack drew on his pipe steadily for what seemed like forever, squinting at Mae through the smoke. "All right. Dis is wat I can offer. I vill take you wit me to de Indian willage down de road."

Mae scowled, not liking the politically incorrect term, "Indian" but as she had learned before, she needed to keep her mouth shut and just be grateful.

"Sounds great!" Toke stood up, wiping his mouth with his arm.

Mrs. Fox took a seat next to Jack at the table, quietly telling him something, then nodded her head in Mae's direction. Jack's brows lifted, stupefied. Then belted out a raucous laugh. "You don't eat meat? Sounds like your head isn't hammered on straight."

What a little tattletale, that Mrs. Fox. Why were they even having this conversation when there were far more important things to worry about? Mae stepped closer to the table. "It's not like I'm saying I enjoy trucks running over my face, I just prefer other forms of protein. I do dairy and eggs. I love tofu, seitan, and all those meatless proteins. Well, I'm not all that fond of tempeh." Jack studied her disapprovingly as if she should be committed to a mental hospital.

"Mae, give it up." Toke crossed his arms over his chest. "Look around. Do they look like they read Vegetarian Times?"

He was right. Everything was made of either animal fur, bones, dried guts, or skins with a little wood and cotton thrown in—just one big happy slaughterhouse. Dexter pulled the conversation back on track. "How soon can we leave then?"

"Not till de morn. Ol' Gruff is as tired as a sock. It was a big haul we had."

"Morning? But it's still light out." Mae attempted to sound patient, but her frustration was squeezing out of her pores. She sat down instead and put her head in her hands.

They all sat in silence for a few minutes.

Extending open palms across the table to the Foxes, Dexter asked, "Would it be possible, by chance, for us to stay here just this one night? We have no place else to go, and our blistered feet won't let us walk very far."

Jack and his wife looked at each other as if they were asked to house three rabid skunks. Toke quickly added, "We can work for the room and board. We'll do anything."

Getting up from the table, Jack stretched and belched loudly. Willie tried to do the same but sounded like a kitten next to a lion. "Lizzie, I'm tinking dey can chop a little vood for de fire, and I shore could use some help unloading de vagon."

Not able to hide her hesitation in exposing her family's vulnerable situation by sharing their own home with strangers that were truly strange, Elizabeth looked utterly unnerved. Allowing guests in their home for merely a snack was one thing. But, the order was given and with no time wasted, Jack hustled Dexter and Toke out the door and put them to work immediately.

As if she were frozen on the spot, Mrs. Fox held the same worried expression with her hands folded in her lap and shoulders hunched in protectively. "Mrs. Fox, we're good people," Mae assured her. "We're not sick and would never hurt you. We're just asking for your help for one single night."

This seemed to help, and her posture relaxed some. She gave Mae a courteous smile, then pulled herself up from the table. "Well then," Mrs. Fox breathed, and brushed off the front of her apron, a nervous habit she'd done frequently since they'd arrived. "Let us start in the kitchen." And that was fine with Mae, anywhere she didn't have to look at a poor murdered animal.

Chapter Twenty-Five

With the wood unloaded, they carried the sizable dead animal onto a massive flat rock about table height. Willie handed Dexter and Toke each a knife and expected them to help him start skinning the beast.

"What the hell is this thing?" Toke cocked his head hoping for some sort of recognition.

Willie gave a short laugh, then realized Toke was serious. "Elk. Have you never shot an elk?"

"Uh, *no*." Toke raised a brow, looking amused.

"Okay, just hold her here, and I'm going to..." They watched his skillful twelve-year-old fingers cut around the animal's anus, tie it shut, then slice into the stomach and arrange the insides like a surgeon. Eventually, Willie handed Dexter the knife and directed him on where to cut.

"So, I'm guessing your mom is also your dad's sister. Am I right?" Toke said, amusing himself. Willie looked at him puzzled, unsure what to say. "Okay, come on. You've got to admit your family's not just a little *weird*."

Willie stopped what he was doing and stood, scanning his eyes over Toke from head to foot as if putting him in his place. Then he turned and continued with what he was doing. One bucket full of bloody guts later, he called out, "Pa, come get her!"

Immediately, Jack appeared, made a few swift cuts in the animal's legs, slid a sturdy stick through the new holes and hoisted the heavy thing onto his back as if it were only a rabbit. Willie followed him to the house with the pail of guts.

A scream flew out the windows of the house and soon a very distraught Mae stumbled out onto the porch. She held fast to the railing, trying to rid her brain of the scene she just saw. A disemboweled animal hung in the kitchen dripping blood into a pan. She ran down to where the two stood, whose hands were still drenched in blood. "You both act like this wacko house is normal."

Toke leaned into her and said through unmoving lips, "Just go with it."

"But these oddball cave people living in a pitifully sad little log cabin out in the middle of nowhere are just plain weird."

"Yes, these people are a bit unusual, but we need them." Dexter seemed to be happy just having food in his stomach. "My best advice is to just blend in, like Toke said. It's only one day, and we'll all be home tomorrow."

The thought of home and her soft pillow-top bed, the full refrigerator, her laptop, favorite TV shows, her friends, and maybe even Greg having made it home by now, gave her some focus and a little more strength.

Coming back with a sloshing bucket of water, Willie cleaned up the bloody dregs from the rock, then washed it all down with water. Toke snagged Willie's rag and attempted to wipe the drying blood from his hands. "Hey man, can I use your can?"

"Can? For what do you need a can?"

"Bathroom—john—latrine—restroom—commode—shit-hole—what the fuck ever." Toke spoke with uncomfortable urgency. Willie understood now and pointed to a small log shed behind their house.

Toke scrutinized the structure of vertically aligned sticks bound together with twine that could topple over in a heavy wind. "Ohhh…Dude. An outhouse? You use an outhouse?" With a broken spirit and head hung low, he walked toward it, muttering, "Damn, after all we've been through, I was really looking forward to a smooth porcelain toilet seat and a stack of magazines."

With their brains and bodies dueling over being exhausted from their journey and excited to be back on the surface, Mae and Dexter made their way to the porch and sat on the steps.

Twenty minutes later Toke plopped down next to them. "Mae, you are definitely *not* going to like it in there. There's no toilet paper." Then, looking at his hands, he wiped them on his pants. "And no sink." Mae grimaced, and he continued, "But don't despair. You'll have your choice of leaf from an entire basket of leaves and, if you're lucky, a scratchy corn husk. But nothing remotely close to toilet paper." Mae felt that surely Mrs. Fox would let her use her private bathroom. They must have something for guests.

Jack came out and waved Willie in, then turned to the three of them. "Vell, it's getting dark, let os be in bed now." Their bodies felt immediate relief, having expected still hours of chores.

Standing in the doorway, Mrs. Fox wiped her bloodied hands on a towel. "Well, seeing how it's such a warm night out, you boys might want to sleep on the back porch instead of in the barn." Her voice was as sweet as butterscotch—but artificially sweetened, like with one of those pink packets. "Willie, would you mind showing them where to get some sacks and straw?"

"Hey." Toke shrugged. "Anywhere is fine as long as there's a bathroom, or rather, outhouse. Speaking of which, that one out there is out of toilet paper." He looked at her expectantly.

"I promise there is plenty in there to clean up," Mrs. Fox assured, looking a little embarrassed to be speaking to strangers of this private matter.

"Mrs. Fox?" Mae mustered up her own version of butterscotch. "Like your family, I am very much into the eco-environmental-sustainability-conservation of water and all, but would it be possible to get a hot shower before bed?"

Mrs. Fox smiled with that familiar expression of patronizing pity, like the ones your friends give you when you think the most popular guy in school has a crush on you. "I'll bring out a bowl of water and rags so y'all can clean up on the back porch."

Oh, eww. Were they all really expected to share the same small bowl of water?

With hands clasped together in a fisted prayer, Toke said, "Mrs. Fox, we thank you very much for your kind hospitality, as well as Jack's. We appreciate everything you've given us and owe you big time."

Feeling a little stunned, Mae had never seen this sincere side of Toke and hadn't thought he was capable of it. She and Dexter nodded in agreement.

"Mae, I plan to set you up by the hearth. I would not make you sleep next to the men. I'm sure you would agree."

"Definitely. I am way too much of a lady." Mae ignored Toke's protesting cough and followed Mrs. Fox back into the house. Her first impulse on walking into the darkened house was to feel for a light switch, but Mrs. Fox handed her one of the lit candles and showed her the bench where she would sleep.

Mrs. Fox shook out an old blanket and then plumped up a grain sack stuffed with wood shavings for her pillow. She then instructed Mae how to latch and bar the door from the inside. "Since you will be out here, I'll leave the fire to you. Being summer, you won't need to get up too often to keep it lit."

Mae nodded, preoccupied with the strangeness of it all and her separation from Toke and Dexter for the first time since they fell down the well. She thanked the woman and settled down on the hard bench while Mrs. Fox disappeared behind the curtain to her own room with her husband.

It comforted her to know that, just outside the back door, Toke and Dexter lay in their beds, not far from sleep. She hunted around for a faucet to clean her teeth and was not surprised that they didn't have one. She filled her cup with water from the kettle and dipped the hem of her dress in and rubbed her teeth as clean as a wet dress could get them.

After unbarring and unlatching the heavy door, she stepped onto the creaky back porch to begin her long trek to the outhouse. She couldn't believe the guys were already sound asleep and felt a sense of unease. Too alone.

Nervously stepping off the porch, she let the candle lead her way. In the distance lonely, hungry animals howled back and forth to each other and seemed to be getting closer. It was sort of a blessing when her heart began thumping so loudly, and she could no longer hear them. Distorted shapes flickered ominously all around her, intensifying with each step. By now Mae decided the outhouse at the end of the path was clearly haunted, so with a quick decision to turn around, she sprinted back to the snoring boys.

She found the long dress *did* have its advantage and soon understood the purpose for the convenience hole in the capris. She could just stand there, fully dressed, and no one would know she was watering the earth. Genius.

Once safely back inside the house, with the door barred and latched, she lay her tired and sore body on the ruthlessly hard bench and prayed her intestines would hold out till morning.

Firelight frolicked her sleepy eyes, and she let herself pretend Greg had squeezed in next to her on the narrow bench. They huddled together under the scratchy goat hair blanket and giggled about this bizarre family hiding away in the mountains. Mae took a deep, dreamy breath, smiling at the picture of Greg she held in her head and floated away into the welcoming darkness.

Chapter Twenty-Six

The next thing Mae knew she was surrounded by heavy footsteps, banging kettles and loud voices, using no effort to be silent. Jack threw open the front door greeting the overly brisk dawn with a yawn that used all his vocal cords, then stomped down the porch steps, leaving the door wide open. The chilling morning breeze rushed in, singing proudly the pungent scents of waking animals. Mae shivered, unappreciative of this gift from nature, and snuggled deeper under the blanket's warmth.

"Mae," a soft voice called down to her. "Don't you think it's about time you wake? You can help me make the biscuits. It's near light outside."

Mae yawned dreamily, rubbing her eyes and scratching her head—though finding her head completely hairless startled her back into her dismal reality. She blinked a few times, trying to shoo away her need for more sleep and focused on the log ceiling above. Her eyes went from one corner to the other of the small rectangular house, noticing for the first time the true size of the tiny dwelling. The day before, she remembered the illusion it gave of having separate rooms, probably because they were assigned official names, like "kitchen" and "bedroom." But in reality, they had simply partitioned off the areas using either a wall of sticks, a piece of furniture, or a hanging curtain.

"I went ahead and let you sleep a piece longer. It looked like y'all really needed it," Mrs. Fox said in her soft voice.

"I still do," Mae groaned.

"Since the fire went out last night, I was unable to bake the bread this morning. Thank heaven we were able to rekindle the flame early enough for biscuits." Mrs. Fox's humble face showed no sign of passive aggression, even though she was quite aware that Mae had let the fire go out. She was just laying out the facts.

To avoid looking guilty, Mae quickly ducked out for her first visit to the outhouse, and it was an event indeed. She remembered her promise to stop making judgments and just go with it. Sure, she could appreciate this family's sacrifice for rustic simplicity and even understood the whole outhouse thing. But who doesn't bend their own rules just a little—like springing for toilet paper? And what modern family cooks *all* their food in their living room fireplace? They've made their lives so unnecessarily inconvenient. Aren't they over it all by now?

When she stepped back into the house, Mrs. Fox had an apron tied around her waist in seconds. Why did this family have such a hard time grasping the fact that it was only *one* day ago that they emerged after being trapped underground without food, terribly dehydrated and weak from malnutrition for two weeks? The Foxes put them to work as if it were a typical day and they were just casual visitors at the Inn.

The sleeping boys weren't going to get off any easier. Jack stomped back up the porch steps, tramped through the kitchen and flung open the back door. "I shore shouldn't have anyting against some help out dere wit de vagon."

"Sure," Dexter said, stifling a yawn.

Toke rose, grumbling, and stumbled inside looking thoroughly distressed. "Mrs. Fox, could I trouble you for some coffee?" he said yawning through it all.

"No coffee op here," Jack huffed. "I hear some sheeps from Paris bring it in. Bot, I would be a rich man if I could get my hands on some of dat. Like I said, in a few veeks I'll be making a tour. Come back den an make your order."

Perplexed by their out-of-place decadence, Mae questioned, "You get your coffee from Paris?"

"Delivered by a flock of Parisian sheep wearing tilted felt berets, bright red lipstick, and all named Fifi," Toke added, mockingly.

Mrs. Fox scooted past setting three metal cups on the table. "I've made some delicious tea. It should be ready by now."

"Sweet." Toke plopped himself down. "Hope it's strong. I need something to prop my eyes open today."

Mrs. Fox filled his cup with the steaming hot tea, and one for Dexter. "Not strong at all." She smiled. "It will *soothe* you."

Toke regarded Mrs. Fox with an amused expression. "So, how do you all get up at dark-thirty, drink *soothing* tea, work your butts off, and still stay awake the entire day?" He was simply baffled.

"Well, occasionally, if we have a good crop of apples, Jack will make some trades for a small amount of coffee. But in truth, I would rather he bring home a couple of sheep, glass for the windows, imported cloth, or even a new stew pot."

"Have you recently been to a Peet's or Starbucks?" Toke said with a pained smirk. "You can't possibly trade a bag of coffee beans for an entire sheep."

After finishing their tea, Mae followed her friends outside. The first few times through the short doorway, Toke remembered to duck. But now he stood on the porch spewing an unintelligible string of profanity, rubbing the large lump on his forehead. "What elf built this house?"

"Toke! Are you okay?" Mae poured over him.

"Just a simple contusion," Dexter said, rubbing his own bump from the day before. For once, Mae felt grateful for her short height.

They were still for a moment as they stood looking out, surveying the land in the new morning light. Around the perimeter of the property, the Foxes had built a good-sized sturdy stick fence with gates on three sides. The majority of their apple trees grew beyond the fence, while their house, barn, garden, henhouse, and stable remained fairly secure inside. A tall, thick forest of pines, alders, and willows surrounded the entire area like a protective wall. To the east, a steep mountain incline rose one hundred yards behind a narrow row of trees, sheltering the homestead from harsh winters and cold winds.

"I remember watching a show once." Toke checked out the bottom of his blistered feet and winced before starting down the steps. "There was this family who lived such a secluded life, they had no idea what was happening in the modern world. But in the filming of the documentary, once they got a taste of the real world outside their isolated nucleus, they just couldn't go back to their old life. Or they all got sick and died. Something like that."

"No immunity," Dexter said, half-listening, and followed him down the steps.

After a few tries at mixing the dough, Mae finally gave up. "I…my fingernails are missing, and it's torture to touch anything." She was actually surprised Mrs. Fox even let her touch the dough with the grisly hands of hers.

"They do look like they hurt. Did you do that to yourselves? Pull your nails off?"

"No. Oh my God—*no.* It just happened when we touched the nasty hungry water that ate all our hair and anything it wanted to."

"Hungry water?" The look on Mrs. Fox's face was pity. Not for Mae's painful fingers, but pity for her lack of sanity. "Okay, dear, don't you worry. Just find Willie out there with the chickens, and you can bring on in the eggs."

Opening the stable gate, she found Willie at the far back next to the chicken coop. Weathered and creaky, it looked like he had built it all by himself and before he turned five. "So, Willie, can you tell me where I find the eggs?" He stopped shoveling chicken poop and regarded her, not sure how to answer such a stupid question. She admitted, "Yeah, you guessed it. I'm a city girl. Never even seen an egg that didn't come from a carton. But only cage-free, organic, free-roaming, of course. They've gotta be happy, you know," she added, fishing for a kindred spirit.

Taking a firm hold of the wooden door, Willie shoved it to the side. "I usually have to whack the side wall to scare them off their eggs. But since there's two of us here, I'll just lift the chicken, and you gather." He scooped up the first hen, but instead of snatching its eggs, Mae begged to hold the chicken. With a shrug, he handed it over.

She petted its orange dappled feathers adoringly while it struggled for freedom. "Aww. What's her name?"

Willie studied her face seriously for a moment. "You don't name your chickens. That'll make it harder to enjoy the taste of them."

"Oh." She turned her head away from the unsuspecting chicken, sadly handing it back to him.

After returning to the house, Mae proudly handed the full basket over to Mrs. Fox who nodded and motioned for her to have a seat. The woman wavered between a timid fear of the strangers and doting on them with nurturing kindness. This time it was the latter, and she had strips of rags waiting for her to treat Mae's nailbeds. First, she applied a pungent, sticky salve to each cloth and then tediously wrapped it around each of Mae's fingers. Mae noticed Mrs. Fox didn't seem to mind that she was actually touching her skin.

"Ohhhh…" Mae moaned as the ointment calmed her fingers' sensitive nerve endings. "You will have slaves for life if you did this to the guys, too."

"I'm not in favor of slavery. My father had them for a spell, but—"

"Your father had slaves?" But Mrs. Fox had left before she could get an answer. Mae really had to hear this one.

Chapter Twenty-Seven

When they finished loading the wagon and the last clean dish had been put away, Mae whipped off her apron for the last time. Before she walked outside to join the others, Mrs. Fox handed her a pile of old rags to wrap around their feet for protection. In the careful way Mrs. Fox folded the rags, Mae could tell that even ratty old cloth held high value to this impoverished family.

Then, whether it was an act of pure kindness or a, *farewell, please never come back gift*, Mrs. Fox walked to the wagon and placed a small bundle inside. "I've gathered some things to take on your way so y'all have food to eat until you find your fu…fi…"

"Phone?" Mae offered.

"Yes. Your fone."

Once they were all seated in the wagon, Mae distributed the rags for their feet along with some leather remnants Jack had given them for the bottom. They took their time, carefully wrapping each foot up securely, confident these temporary shoes would hold up for the short trip home.

Jack announced they were ready to get going and climbed onto the driver's bench. Mrs. Fox waved goodbye from the porch. Her relief to finally be rid of them was so transparent, Mae felt like laughing.

Dexter called back to Mrs. Fox, "Thank you very much for your food, beds, incredible hospitality, and healing!"

What he said was true. For Mae, herself, she would never let any freaky-looking drifters into her home, with or without hair and nails. She waved, adding, "Yes! Thank you so much, Mrs. Fox! I promise we will send all these clothes back to you. Cleaned and pressed."

Mrs. Fox nodded, adding, "The Ma'camo are good people. No need to fear them. We hope they have what y'all need."

Fear them? Why did she say that? Were the Ma'camo a gang or something? The name sounded like the place where Milok was from, and the kid seemed nice enough, although a bit odd.

Willie quietly slipped Toke a sheathed knife, not wanting his father to see, with the warning that a pack of large wolves was spotted recently. Had Willie maybe meant to say a large pack of wolves rather than a pack of large wolves? But, it really didn't matter, they were both just as terrifying. Mae cringed, remembering the howling from the night before. Who decided to release wolves back into the wild anyway?

The old horse had never pulled a load this heavy before, and even with Willie's horse sharing the load, his old body labored down the bumpy path. "Can you believe this ride?" Toke smirked. "I thought they'd at least pull out some rusty old truck hidden in the barn."

"If you're thinking they're Amish, I was assured they are not." Mae had to yell to be heard over the wagon's clattering. "I'm not sure if you noticed, but there's no fridge, no stove, not even a toaster. No electricity—just a fireplace! And do you know how she sets a timer for the biscuits? She makes a tick mark on the candle, and when it melts to that point, they're done."

"Extreme." Toke rested his arm on the side of the wagon while he scanned the surrounding mountains. "I mean, if I had a choice of any past era to build my life around, I'd choose the late sixties. VW campervans, plentiful free love before the fear of AIDS. *Real* hallucinogens, not mindful ginger chai ginseng drinks. Hell, people could smoke anywhere they wanted—even on crowded airplanes next to babies."

A squirrel seemed to be following them, jumping from pine tree to pine tree until it landed in an oak, scurried down, grabbed up an acorn, then disappeared behind a large rock. Mae smiled and gazed up at the bright morning sky and started to feel hopeful again as they inched toward home—maybe just a couple of hours away.

The last three days Mae had protected her heart, not considering any other possibilities than of Greg being alive. But somehow, the negativity climbed over her iron wall, torturing her with its dark thoughts. *What if Greg was badly injured and needed help? Or trapped? Or even worse, what if he was—stop it!* She knuckled away a tear, reminding herself that he *would* get out of the tunnels if he hadn't already. He *would* find the Foxes' house, and they'd tell him where his friends went. Maybe even give him a ride to catch up to them.

So wrapped up in her own pain, she realized she really never thought about what Dexter was going through. His lifelong friend was suddenly *gone*. She gazed over at him leaning against the side of the wagon with his eyes closed. Dexter was nearly impossible to read on the outside. For as long as she'd known him, he kept his inner feelings buried deep inside, completely hidden from anyone.

Ten more minutes went by and the ground began to flatten out. Jack turned them off the path to the left and continued forward as if randomly crossing a field. Dexter's ears perked up. "Music. I hear drumming." They all missed music, and soon they were bobbing their heads and tapping their feet to the repetitive beat. They rode through a small forest of trees and into another clearing where Jack slowed the wagon and jumped off.

Not sure why they had stopped in the middle of nowhere, they remained seated in the wagon. Toke's eyes foraged the scene, then abruptly stopped on something. "Check it out," gesturing his head toward the trees.

Mae squealed, "People!"

Nearly blending into the forest, people in costumes similar to Milok's slowly emerged from the trees, gathering where Jack stood. Toke snorted. "What the hell *is* this party?"

"From here"—Dexter's brows furrowed as he examined the crowd—"they look like an authentic tribe of Native Americans, straight out of a painting."

A nearly naked man stood in front of the others, and Jack handed him a jar of Mrs. Fox's preserves wrapped in a cloth and tied at the top. The man let out a grateful laugh as he opened the package, and showed the others standing next to him. The two men carried on a conversation involving many hand gestures, a few laughs, and large arm movements. A couple of times Jack pointed over to the wagon and both times the people looked over with blank expressions, showing no signs of welcome. Mae waved to Milok, but he didn't seem to see them or purposely ignored her.

"Jack looks like he's just trying to dump us on these people. How about we help him to speed things up?" Mae stood up, looking around for the best way down.

"I think we should wait for Jack," Dexter cautioned, remaining seated.

"Hell, we know Milok. That's got to count for something, right?" Toke slid down the side and brushed off his pants. Mae followed, struggling to climb out of the wagon, in her unwieldy long dress. Toke watched Mae's descent in wonderment, poking at the short white pants now hanging below her dress. "What the hell is *this* thing?"

Slapping his hand away, she answered in an inflated southern-belle drawl, much unlike Mrs. Fox's very *slight* southern accent, "Them thars my *drah-wuhs*." She proceeded to smooth down her dress, so it completely covered the showy parade of her unspeakable undergarments.

"Jack's one lucky man. Mrs. Fox sure knows how to do sexy." Toke coughed in his hand.

Dexter relented and climbed out of the wagon to join Mae and Toke walking toward the group. Toke held out his hand for a quick introduction. "Name's Toke." But, instead, the people nervously backed away ignoring his extended hand like he had leprosy. "What's up with that?" Toke said, annoyed, evidently forgetting his face was blotched like a confused rash, his head a pink, blistered mess, and each fingertip tied in a piece of cloth.

"Yeah..." Dexter murmured, straightening his clothes, attempting to look more presentable. "We need to think about how we look to them. I'd not want to touch us either."

Humbled, the three of them stood aside, as Jack unloaded his wagon of apples, ale, loaves of bread, a quilt, and other things. Then he reloaded it with a large bushel of dried beans, filled baskets of roots and herbs, dried fish, an adobe pot, and many sacks of unknown things. Both men seemed happy with the trade and Jack jumped into the wagon preparing to leave.

"Hey, wait—" Mae called, running over to Jack. "What's going to happen to us?"

"I'm very sorree bot I need to get back. Waho, de man wearing de cap, vill help you." Jack snapped the reins. "I vill pray you find your fone an' your toefew. Gud day."

The wagon flew out of there, leaving a scattering of dirt clouds in his wake. "Geez." Toke rubbed the back of his neck, looking more amused than frustrated. "Dude just couldn't get out of here fast enough."

Chapter Twenty-Eight

Mae stared after the wagon until the last of it disappeared behind the next hill. The loss of the familiar, however strange it was, and being dumped into the unfamiliar, had her feeling a little abandoned. She hated having to rely on the mercy of strangers. It made her feel so vulnerable.

Without waiting for Jack's dust to settle, they walked over to the man named Waho to plead their case. Though just five feet tall, he appeared much larger in stature. Sturdy, confident shoulders framed his broad, muscular chest, commanding an air of authority. The rest of the people stood behind and beyond him, treating his proximity like a human shield.

"Seems they're quite diligent in embracing their Native American roots," Dexter said quietly.

Waho wore an odd little cap with plain stiff sides and a flat top. The hat didn't look very functional for keeping him warm or blocking the sun, but it would have made a lovely Easter basket. A narrow stripe ran from his forehead to the tip of his nose, which Mae swore was a real tattoo.

Stepping closer to Waho, Dexter went through the whole, can-we-use-your-phone and we-need-a-ride thing, which landed on a face so expressionless, it seemed to be made of wax.

Finally, there was some movement and Waho turned and called out to Milok. He and another boy came rushing to his side. "Hi, Milok." Mae raised her hand and smiled warmly. Milok acted as though he was seeing them for the first time. Waho spoke to him sternly, and it sounded as though Milok fessed up to knowing them.

The three of them stood quietly and observed their surroundings while Milok and Waho spoke together in a language they didn't understand. By now, more Native Americans had come out of the trees and were studying them suspiciously.

Mae elbowed Toke hard. "Stop it. That is *so* rude." She felt embarrassed that Toke was so obviously staring directly at a woman's bare chest, wearing an adolescent grin.

"I can't help it. The fine handicraft of the beads and shells in their necklaces is utterly mesmerizing." Toke's eyes went from one necklace to another. Dexter too caught himself staring, but quickly averted his eyes out of courtesy.

They stood there waiting, though far from bored, entertained by the costumes and the dedication to the craft. One woman, with six or seven vertical lines on her chin, looked like she had grown a girl goatee. Only a couple of them wore moccasins, so most of their feet were severely calloused from years of going barefoot.

An older man, more ornately dressed than Waho, emerged through the trees, with a few others trailing closely behind. Judging by how the others reacted, he seemed to be highly respected. Waho attempted to catch the man up on the situation, but after listening for less than a minute, the man raised his hand, which brought immediate silence.

Barely glancing at the three of them, the older man abruptly turned and departed in the same direction in which he came. Waho and the group of people similarly retreated, following him out as if he were the Pied Piper.

"Wait, what?" Toke stepped forward a few paces, his thumbs clenched inside his fists. "They can't just leave."

"Are…are we supposed to follow them?" Mae asked with sinking hope.

"What about him?" Dexter motioned his head toward a single person still remaining, standing off to the side. The boy seemed to be about their age, or maybe younger, like seventeen or eighteen, with a slight body frame. The only clothing he wore was a small breechcloth, which left his hips fully exposed, appearing almost naked. His shiny black hair was cut bluntly at his chin, but roughly, as if he had used a plastic knife. He stood quietly, observing them for a moment before walking forward. Reaching out, he opened his hand to reveal some type of food he wanted them to take.

Toke eyed it suspiciously. "I'm not touching that." He pointed back to the guy. "How about you eat it first?"

So, the guy did, never taking his eyes off Mae. Without feeling the least bit uncomfortable, she simply stared back at him, curiously. Not wanting to hurt his feelings, she took the food, smelled it, and ate a tiny bite. The texture was a little gross, but it was made from some sort of flavorless fruit. "Yum." She smiled. "Thank you."

He seemed overjoyed and smiled broadly at her happiness. Dexter tried another round of questions about phones and cars while Toke backed him up with engine noises and did the international thumb-pinky phone sign. The guy just shook his head.

"Does that mean you don't understand us, or just don't have a car or phone? Then how about a computer?" Getting no response, Toke could not refrain from smiling and giggling a little. "Who *is* this guy?"

The boy pulled off one of his necklaces and reached out to put it on Mae. "For me?" She bent her head and let him slip it around her neck. She cradled it in her hand and admired the intricate detail. "This is lovely. Thank you so much!"

"I don't think we're getting anywhere with this dude." Toke turned and looked through the trees and across the open grassy area to the neighboring mountains. "How about we just get back on the main path Jack pulled us off of, then keep walking until we find something?"

"Seems that's our only choice at this point," Dexter agreed.

"If our feet will hold out." Mae glanced down at the rags she wore as shoes and winced. "Well, at least they're a *little* protected. Besides, we're bound to run into someone at some point."

"We can just follow the sun. It will take us west, toward home." Dexter squinted, trying to see into the distance. "Undeveloped land can't go on too far without a road or freeway."

They said goodbye to Mae's admirer, and she thanked him again for the necklace and food. He stared into her eyes as if he was searching for something until Mae broke contact when she turned to leave.

Crossing the grass was torture, and when Mae turned back, the boy was still standing there. And he remained there until they had completely limped out of sight. "He's adorable," Mae said between "ows," when stray stickers penetrated through the leather in her feet wrappings.

"Fellow must be starving for a woman. Damn, if you can catch him looking as lovely as you do now with your freaky potato head, he's definitely a lifer."

Mae narrowed her eyes at Toke. "Have you not heard of inner beauty? Besides, I'm Greg's." With that, Dexter looked down, and Toke turned away, as they had started to accept the probability that Greg didn't make it.

Chapter Twenty-Nine

Their steps were slow and deliberate, but they were able to pick up speed once they hit the main path and got accustomed to the unevenness of the rough ground. Toke stopped for a minute to give his feet a break. "Any guesses where we could be?"

"Well," Dexter said, picking up a rock. "This granite is a clear giveaway for the Sierras. And with all the mountains surrounding us, we're definitely in a much higher altitude than Sacramento."

Mae gathered a few dried leaves from the ground, broke a bay leaf in half and smelled it. "And this mix of trees reminds me of the Sierra foothills."

"We'll find out soon enough. We are bound to hit a road anytime." With confidence, Toke walked on, keeping an eye out for any sign of anything.

The unrelenting heat of the sun baked the sweet-smelling wild sage into the mountain air. Toke stopped and picked up a large pinecone, not to admire it but to throw it as far as he could, along with his usual stream of four-letter words.

"Toke, your head." Mae tugged his arm to slow down. "The blisters need to be covered, they're oozing and getting bloody. You know your coloring makes you a choice target for skin cancer. In fact, you both need head wraps like I have."

Ducking into the cool shade of a buckeye tree that was still hustling bees with its aromatic summer blooms, Mae tore pieces from the bottom of her long drawers. "Just hold still, and you'll be stylin' in no time."

With a big smirk, Toke mimicked Mae's voice. "And we'll return them pressed and cleaned. But someone forgot to say: and *ripped to shreds*."

Mae bit back a smile. "Oh, shut up." She began the careful process of wrapping the strips of fabric around each of their heads. "There we are," she added cheerfully.

Dexter reached up and felt his new hat. "Now we look like we're in some sort of cult."

"Dex, do you realize we have our heads wrapped in Mae's panties?" Looking guilty, Dexter immediately stopped touching his head.

A short while later, they stopped to rest in the shade and drink from the icy stream. Toke cupped some water in his hand and inspected it. "Hey, shouldn't we be worried about getting the shits drinking out of these creeks?"

"I know, dysentery. I was thinking the same thing." Dexter shrugged. "But, what other choice do we have unless we find a spring?"

Mae opened the satchel with the wrapped package that Mrs. Fox sent along. Inside were three beautiful baked brioches stuffed with fresh butter and berry jam, and covered in an egg wash glaze. Underneath lay a piece of dried meat and some nearly ripe apples.

"Man…" Toke chewed with his eyes shut. "I so miss Mrs. Fox already."

Mae looked back and groaned at the short distance they covered in the time they had been walking. The path was barely visible through the low grasses taking them through the trees. She worried they might be heading away from civilization.

The thickly forested mountain opened up to a grassy clearing, and they were startled to see the boy they had just left a couple of hours earlier sitting under a large oak. He was busily working on something with his hands but jumped up when he saw them. He wasn't barefoot anymore, but wore handmade moccasins cut from a single piece of leather, seamed up the front, and tied around his ankle.

"Hi again." Mae held up her hand in a half wave. He simply stood there, not saying anything, just looking at her.

"Uh, is he creeping you out?" Toke nudged Mae. "Maybe just a little?"

Intrigued by the small bone pierced through his nose, she stepped closer for a better look at the tiny feathers intricately knotted into each of its ends. "That's just beautiful. Where did you get that?" He seemed a little confused but patted his chest. "You made it yourself? Incredible." She smiled admiringly. "So, what is your language?" Then tapped her fingers on her mouth, but this only prompted him to reach into his satchel and present her with some dried red manzanita berries.

"Hmm. He understands *some* words, just not sure which." Mae decided to try it in Spanish since, by the looks of him, he could easily be Mexican. "Entonces, ¿qué idioma hablas?"

He straightened up. "Nisenan, Ma'camo." His voice was gentle, matching his delicate facial features and slender build.

"Okay, this makes it easier, but I'm not sure how much he knows in Spanish either." Mae pointed to herself. "Mae," then, "Toke," and finishing with, "Dexter."

On cue, he pointed to himself. "Yu'mi."

"Like, you me?" she asked.

His head made a swift nod down. "Dah."

Toke looked amused. "Did he just say duh?"

Mae sighed, exasperated. "It was daw. And it obviously means yes."

Toke crossed his arms over his chest. "So, what's your real name? You know like Wild River, Running Bear, Little Wiener? You know, like real Indian names."

Mae scowled, "Toke, can you at least *try* to say Native American?"

Yu'mi turned to Toke. "Not Indian. Ma'camo." Then he turned to Mae. "Not American. Nisenan." He didn't seem to be upset, just factual.

"Not so woke, eh, Mae?" Toke smirked.

"Sorry, yes, Ma'camo. Got it." Mae reddened, feeling humiliated to be politically corrected herself.

Dexter shaded his eyes from the sun and gazed down the path they were to follow. "Well, it was wonderful to meet you, Yu'mi, but we must get moving. We've been gone far too long."

Mae repeated, "Ha sido un verdadero placer conocerte, pero debemos volver a nuestro camino. Hemos sido idos demasiado tiempo." She hoped he'd be able to pick out some of the words in either language.

When they turned to leave, Toke had a thought and turned back to Yu'mi. "Sacramento?"

"Si. Sacramento Reeber," Yu'mi said confidently. All three of their faces lit up, and they scrambled back around him like he was the latest celebrity.

"How about Sacramento *Valley*?" Dexter attempted to shape a valley with his hands.

Yu'mi's ears perked up "Val-lee. Dah." Then pointed in the direction they were already heading. Relief brightened their faces, and Mae pulled him into an enthusiastic hug, forcing him to bounce up and down with joy along with her. He offered to escort them as far as he could, but first, he had to take care of something and promised to meet up with them a little later.

Dust stuck to salty sweat, and their feet screamed murder, mile after mile. Toke slapped mercilessly at the flies tasting his body, leaving pink hand-sized welts wherever he could reach.

True to his word, Yu'mi caught back up with them a couple of hours later. This time, following behind his own horse, there trotted a beautiful young filly. Her dark chocolate mane and tail were striking against her bright golden coat. An unusual marking lit up her forehead as if she'd been adorned with a large white pearl.

Yu'mi made it clear the horse was only for Mae and motioned for her to climb up. She glanced guiltily at Toke and Dexter but gladly accepted.

Though very familiar with horses from years of summer camp as a girl, Mae had never ridden one without a saddle. And never on a wild horse. She had never even *seen* a wild horse.

After a series of failed mounts, sliding completely over the horse's back and landing in the dirt on its other side, she finally did it. With her legs straddled firmly over the horse's back, she desperately hung on as the little horse rebelled. Yu'mi seemed to know this particular horse already, and it responded when he reached out to steady it and used his voice.

While Mae got a short demonstration on how to squeeze her legs together in order not to fall off, Toke and Dexter rested in the shade, taking the weight off their blistering feet. After knotting strips of leather into a harness, Yu'mi re-attached the rope leader from his horse to hers. This left Mae to just concentrate on staying on top since her little filly would naturally follow Yu'mi's horse.

Chapter Thirty

"I can't feel my feet anymore," Toke seethed through his teeth. "But somehow they hurt like hell."

"My entire body will be completely drained of blood if I keep walking." Dexter ambled over to the closest tree, collapsing against its trunk with Toke right behind him.

When Mae and Yu'mi got tired of waiting at the top of the next mountain, they rode back, startling Toke and Dexter out of their nap. Mae offered to let them ride on her horse, though only one at a time since it was such a small horse. But, Yu'mi quickly intervened, "Nuk. Mae horse."

"Well, I don't think they can go any farther on their feet today. How about we stop for the day and start fresh in the morning?" Mae suggested, and Yu'mi seemed to understand enough.

Yu'mi found a place near a creek with shade and a clearing in the middle. Too exhausted and sore to help, the three of them sat on the surrounding rocks watching Yu'mi make a fire.

Staring at the distressing sight of his bloody feet, Toke whined, "Is it time?"

"As good as any." Pain and apprehension distorted Dexter's beautiful face as he pried the blood and dirt-matted rags from his blistered feet.

Next, the pain belonged to Mae and Toke as they slowly unwrapped their feet and joined the chorus of "Ughs" and "groans"...followed by "ow ow ow" and sharp intakes of breath, until at last, the torture was over. Toke watched tiny flies suck at the bloody feast of discarded rags. "I am *so* done with these feet."

“Let’s get these into the stream. That is, if we can make it there.” Dexter raised himself to a crawling position, not daring to touch his raw feet on the ground.

The icy water of the stream revived their spirits and numbed the screams from their tortured feet. If the water wasn’t so agonizingly cold, they would have let their feet soak all night. They washed their bloody shoe rags, letting the slew of insects that had been breeding on them float away downstream. Then, they scrubbed down their bodies and draped the pieces of cloth to dry on the nearby bushes.

“I want a big, soft, fluffy towel hot from the dryer,” Mae said, sighing, then let them share her dress to dry their feet.

Dexter dabbed at his feet thoughtfully. “Yu’mi gives me a little hope. They let his tribe hold onto their language and culture for all this time and were not forced into the American school system and the American mainstream.”

“But, don’t all kids have to go to school by law?” Toke prodded the blisters on the bottom of his feet with gritted teeth.

“Yeah, I thought they pulled all Native American children out of the tribes and made them go to English-speaking boarding schools and live in foster families.” Mae glanced around, making sure Yu’mi wasn’t anywhere near. “But don’t these Ma’camos seem a bit over-the-top? Like, did you notice not one was even wearing a stitch of non-native clothing? Nowadays, indigenous people don’t really dress much in their traditional native clothing.”

“You know, I *really* don’t care. Let’s just get home already.” Toke, feeling hungry and impatient, stood up and hobbled back over to the campsite. Dexter and Mae gathered all their wet rags and moved them by the fire to dry.

In the short time they were gone, Yu’mi had made a steaming basket of stew, and dinner was nearly ready. “Holy crap. How’d you do this, man?” Toke slapped Yu’mi on the back. Yu’mi turned around with rage in his eyes, which changed to confusion after seeing Toke’s happy face.

Scents of cinnamon and wild sage caused Mae's stomach to growl like a hungry lion. And just a short time later, Yu'mi brought the steaming basket over to where she was stretched out and offered it to her first. By the time the basket came around to Yu'mi again, and he poked around at what was left, he made a sour face at Toke and Dexter. Mae went over and peeked inside the basket and scowled. "You guys just ate an entire rabbit yourselves and left none for Yu'mi?"

"I couldn't tell how much there was," Toke pleaded, defensively. "I was trying to save the vegetables for you."

"Same here," Dexter added, embarrassed. He tried to apologize to Yu'mi but got no response.

Instead, Yu'mi got up and went to work scraping the inside of the rabbit fur and then hung it over the fire to dry overnight. But he didn't stop there. He next collected eight long sticks and stacked them in a box shape. Two in one direction and two perpendicular on top of those, until it was five or six inches high. He gathered armfuls of dried pine needles and filled the center area, then covered those with larger leaves, topping it off with his saddle blanket.

Toke raised a hairless brow at the curious object that Yu'mi had built and looked at Mae and Dexter, who only shrugged back. But it was soon revealed when Yu'mi escorted Mae over and gestured for her to lie down, which she graciously did. He then proceeded to pack her bedding around her body, adding more pine needles under the leaves as needed.

"Damn, Mae." Toke smirked. "In what kingdom do you rule?"

Once assured Mae was comfortable, Yu'mi simply laid down on the plain dirt a few yards away and shut his eyes.

"So, just like that? Right on the dirt?" Toke muttered, looking around for a better option.

Dexter shrugged with indifference. "Well, it's just one night, and tomorrow we'll be in our own soft beds." Using the side of his hand, he brushed the ground smooth before lowering the rest of himself down. "Think of it this way," he grunted, turning onto his other side. "It's a lot smoother than the uneven, rocky floor of the tunnel."

After adjusting herself for comfort, Mae yawned luxuriously, washing away all traces of guilt. Behind her closed eyes, she pictured Greg's smiling face, missing him so badly. She wanted more than anything just to hold him tight and never let him go again. Then with a silent vow to Greg, she made a promise to find him, no matter *what* it took.

They all lay silently under the stars until Dexter whispered to anyone still awake, "I can't shake this weird feeling I keep getting. It's like…like there's something's off…like out of place."

Toke gave a short laugh and responded thoughtlessly at full volume. "Yeah, like watch there be a motel just over that hill, and here we are lying in the dirt."

"No, I mean something else," Dexter whispered. "It's weird, I can't really explain it. Something just doesn't feel right."

"Give it a rest, man. We're almost home."

"Shhh. Toke, you're not even trying to whisper." Mae scowled. "You'll wake up Yu'mi."

"Shhhh," Toke retorted, insisting on having the last word. "We're trying to sleep."

"Shhhhh."

"Shhhhh, shhhh."

"Shhhhh, shhh, shhhhhhhh."

"Just stop." Dexter got the last word.

Chapter Thirty-One

"That was surprisingly a very nice sleep," Toke said, rising and stretching his back. "My back is killing me, and I'm coated in dirt, but it wasn't that bad."

"I agree." Dexter laboriously pulled himself to his feet and brushed the dirt from his clothes.

Growling noises once again roared from Mae's stomach, so she searched around for something to eat. Snatching one of Yu'mi's acorns, she cracked it open, then bit off a small piece, "Ack!"—and immediately spat it out. Toke, too curious, reached over and picked up the remaining piece. "Seriously, I wouldn't," she warned.

Toke screwed up his face and spat out way too much for such a tiny nibble. "What the hell? Is he trying to poison us? I'm not eating any of that psycho acorn shit."

Frowning at Toke, Mae put her finger to her mouth to shush him. Then, in her cheeriest voice, to make up for Toke's insults, she chirped, "Yu'mi, can I help you with something?" She gestured to the small piles of seeds, hazelnuts, and berries that he'd collected while they had been asleep.

"Dah." Yu'mi nodded once then handed Mae two rocks and pointed to the hard-shelled nuts and seeds. She tapped the stones together, wondering what she should be doing with them until Yu'mi made a motion with his hands and she finally got it. "Oh, grind. I'm to *grind*."

"Grind," Yu'mi repeated, absorbing the word.

In finding her job quite easy, Mae suggested to Toke and Dexter that they might want to offer to help too.

"Nah, he's doing good." Toke put his hands behind his head and leaned comfortably against a rock.

Holding out his hands to Yu'mi, Dexter asked, "Help?"

Yu'mi answered with a sharp nod and glanced into the trees. "Dah." He gathered up his quiver of arrows and bow, then handed them to Dexter, motioning him toward the thicket of trees.

With his inexperienced fingers, Dexter examined the bow and tested the points of the arrows. He flung the quiver over his back with awkward uncertainty, straightened his shoulders, and walked into the forest with forced determination.

"That's what you get for being nice!" Toke called after him, uselessly poking at the fire with a stick.

"I'm going down to wash up, nobody follow me." Mae gathered the saddle blanket and picked her way downstream where Yu'mi had bathed earlier. *Oh, what she wouldn't give for a toothbrush.*

"Hey, I'm dirty too," Toke called after her. "Let's save water."

"Oh, ha ha," came floating back from the trees.

Twenty minutes later, Mae returned, clean and refreshed, but wearing the same dirty dress. Toke looked utterly amused. "Sort of like putting a used diaper back on the baby, eh?"

He definitely nailed it, but she shook her head, not wanting to give him any pleasure. In her short absence, Yu'mi had produced, yet again, their entire meal, which sat steaming in the basket.

A moment later, an empty-handed Dexter sulked in, looking thoroughly beaten. He dropped the quiver with only two arrows at Yu'mi's feet, shamefaced. Yu'mi just motioned for him to sit with Mae and Toke by the fire while he passed around the gourd of dandelion tea.

After portioning out some chewy acorn mush called *ooti*, he topped it off with a sprinkle of nuts and berries. Yu'mi showed them how to use their middle finger to scoop up the mush and just suck it off. The feeling was strange at first, but soon became the norm. They all ate every single morsel of the ooti and found it surprisingly filling.

When it was time to leave, Yu'mi insisted they shuffle around the dirt, leaving no sign of fire or any human interaction.

With Dexter and Toke walking at a snail's pace in the hot sun, tiptoeing around the aggressive rocks and thorny weeds, they were all spent by the time they reached the top of the mountain. But soon it would all be over. Each looked expectantly down the other side for telephone poles, electric wires, scattered mountain houses, roads, ugly intrusive cell towers. Instead, they were met with a nightmare.

Toke threw his head back in tortured anguish and yelled into the open sky, "Fuuuuck!"

Sprawled in front of them was not a city, nor a freeway, not even a road, but another nearly identical, never-ending mountain range. It stood proud, throwing the twisted challenge in their faces like a mocking dare. What little energy Mae had left rapidly drained from her muscles and she slumped her head in defeat.

For the next few hours, they climbed mountain after mountain, listless, and feeling hopeless. But once Dexter pointed out that each new peak was bringing them lower in altitude, a little vitality returned. They were actually getting somewhere.

Occasionally they stopped to drink and eat pieces of the smoked rabbit from the day before. Yu'mi kept pushing the strips of rabbit to Mae, but she only held up her hand saying, "No," hoping something else would magically appear in their path.

"Vegetarian." Mae slowly pointed to her mouth, then stomach.

"Ve-ge-tar-i-an."

"Eat," Yu'mi still insisted.

"No meat."

"Meat. Eat," he ordered, pushing it closer toward her mouth.

"Nuk meat." She shook her head.

"Mae, you're going to need to eat something," Dexter coaxed.

"Geez." Toke smirked. "She hasn't even burned any calories sitting high on her royal horse. She's fine."

Gnawing on a woody root Yu'mi had given her, Mae said, "Don't worry. I'll find something. Or maybe I'm saving myself for our big homecoming feast."

"Suit yourself." Toke smiled smugly. "More for me."

Yu'mi's ears pricked up and, suddenly, he was on his feet, bow in hand, and slipping away like a cat, into the bushes. Within minutes he emerged with two rabbits flung over his back, necks broken, tied by their feet. Rabbits were the perfect size for traveling. They had scant leftovers and offered a soft pelt for something useful.

Dexter stood up, ready to start moving again. "We're probably almost home. Could even be over the next hill."

"Hot showers, fast food, and my PlayStation." Toke sighed longingly, gazing into the distance.

"That's what you look forward to the most? Not your parents and friends?" Mae studied his face empathetically like his hamster just died. "Well, *I* miss my mom and my friends more than anything."

"Yeah, well, you don't know my dad now, do you?" Toke swatted impatiently at a hovering fly.

"He seemed very nice." Mae smiled, remembering the cheerful man waving from Toke's front porch.

Toke groaned loudly. "He annoys the *hell* out of me. And out of everyone who knows him."

Chapter Thirty-Two

Once they settled on their camp for the night, Mae grabbed a basket and searched the nearby woods for a possible edible anything, while Dexter filled the larger basket with water.

Toke looked around until he found a large flat rock that would've made a nice table but plopped himself down on it instead. His body deflated, melting across the surface like butter on a hot pancake.

Moments later, Mae returned with a bountiful assortment of plants spilling from her basket, hoping something in there would be digestible. Yu'mi sorted through her collection, laughing at some of it, but still found plenty he could use.

Not appreciating Toke's self-entitled laziness, Yu'mi pushed him awake and emptied the basket of Mae's greens on the flat stone next to Toke.

Grudgingly pushing himself up, Toke poked suspiciously at the pile. "What *is* this crap? He's just feeding us weeds."

Mae shot him an exasperated look. "What are you complaining about? The fact that he's feeding us at all is a *huge* favor that we should be very grateful for."

"Yeah, whatever."

"You know, you could be a little nicer. I mean, just look at us." She wore an expression of "duh" on her face while circling her head and face with her nailless finger. "And Yu'mi's not questioning any of it. He's just helping us out, without asking for anything in return."

"Or so you *think*, Princess Mae." Toke winked.

With a startling thwack, Yu'mi flung a skinny brown rabbit onto the rock and pulled its entire skin off in one sharp yank. Mae's throat tightened a bit, and she quickly turned away. In just seconds, he had it gutted, skewered, and roasting over the fire. After shuffling the rocks that nestled cozily in the red coals, Yu'mi was ready for the greens and looked over at Toke.

And there they were, in the same untouched pile next to Toke, who sat playing an invisible drum to an imperceptible, indistinguishable beatbox, "Bf bs bsh bf chsh psh pf tcsh…"

Yu'mi's dark brown eyes narrowed slightly.

"What?" Toke shrugged, dismissively. "I don't know what to do with them."

"Geez, use your head." Mae sat down next to Toke and picked through the greens holding back yelps of pain every time a leaf cut across her raw nail bed—a horrific sensation like no other. She pulled off the woody stems, plucked out the bugs and larvae, then handed the dirty roots to Toke. "You can start by washing these."

After taking an unnecessarily long time scrubbing off the dirt in the stream, Toke began slicing the snake-like roots with the sharp obsidian rock. Soon he had a large pile, which Yu'mi gathered up and sprinkled into the steaming water, along with the collection of bugs and larvae from the greens. Mae had missed that part.

Dexter walked over to the fire and picked up the bent branch propped next to it. Yu'mi made this look easy, but it took Dexter a few failed attempts before he could finally secure it around a hot rock buried deep in red coals and successfully lift it out. When he dropped it in the steaming basket, the water rejoiced by exploding in a roar of bubbles and boiling instantly.

Very impressed, Yu'mi smiled big. Showing his confidence in Dexter, he now motioned for him to take over the roasting of the rabbit.

"What a kiss-ass," Toke muttered until he picked up the scent of the roasting rabbit and his mood shifted. "Oh—ho—man. Smells freakin' killer."

When Yu'mi began looking on the ground under the tree, Toke quickly joined in the search just to prove he was being helpful. Mae rolled her eyes. "You don't even know what he's searching for. That doesn't count as helping."

"And this?" Toke smiled smugly as he took over the stirring of the stew.

Instead, Mae's face paled to a greenish hue as she watched what Yu'mi was doing. "…oh…nooo…" She continued to mourn quietly as he added not just the chunks of rabbit meat to the stew, but also its slimy unidentifiable guts, brain, miscellaneous face parts, and *all* the hare's drained blood.

How was she going to do this? Picking around chunks of meat was one thing, but the thought of eating any of this stew was so repulsive she actually felt sick. Why did she have to see that?

As the day turned to night, and all things done, they gathered around the campfire and stared at the dancing flames. When Yu'mi began to pluck out his few short facial hairs, the flames became less interesting, and *he* became that night's entertainment. It was to Mae's relief that he turned away to pluck out the ones under his breechcloth. "Heh," Toke mused. "So that's the trick. Get each hair out by the root as soon as it comes in." He stroked his chin, considering this approach.

Toke and Dexter succeeded in making themselves softer beds, and aside from the scratchiness, they were successful. Waiting until Yu'mi fell asleep, Mae said quietly, "We need to reward Yu'mi with something good when we get back. He's done so much for us."

"I'm down," Toke whispered back.

"I'm sure our parents will be very generous. They'll be so happy to have us safe and home."

"Not mine," Dexter exhaled, desolately. "He'll just be missing the money from my job to pay rent." Dexter rarely revealed details of his unhappy home life. He was still haunted by his tragic past, which took his mother away from him much too soon. She was the only person Dexter really loved with all his heart. He was only eleven when his drunk father drifted off the road and hit a tree, killing his mother instantly. His father spent three years in prison, but Dexter got very lucky and was assigned to a loving and kind foster family. He would have given anything to stay with them forever, but when his dad got out of prison, he forced Dexter to move back in with him to gain access to *all* of his mother's insurance money.

Fortunate for being given so much love from his mother and kindness from his foster family, Dexter didn't turn out anything like his father. He never really got over losing his mother and was at the perfect age for her death to burn a huge hole in his heart while his self-esteem plummeted. He withdrew socially, focusing everything on his studies, and then later, his Chevy. Dexter decided to never put himself in a place where he could feel vulnerable again, so he kept his emotions and inner feelings well-guarded. This made it hard for people to get to know him too well, so he didn't have many close friends. Except for Greg.

"We got you covered, bro. Your dad sucks. A complete douchebag."

Mae's heart went out to Dexter, remembering the things Greg had told her. She felt unexpectedly emotional and shut her eyes. This sweet, trusting boy, raised by his hateful, violent father, had to go to school unfed and full of bruises. She wanted to hug him, but he was too far away. Plus, he might feel betrayed that Greg confided so much to her about his best friend's private life, so she'd have to wait until he opened up about it.

The change of subject onto Dexter helped Mae put the anxiety of getting home aside. She let the peaceful night work its seduction, serenading her with the now-familiar chorus of wild nature…

Until something large and unseen rumbled a dark and hungry growl just a few yards from where they lay. Yu'mi bolted up, alert, and jumped to his feet in a defensive strike position. His eyes searched the darkness until they fixed on a direction.

Mae lay frozen, eyes wide and unblinking like a deer in headlights. The horses whinnied nervously and began stomping their feet and tugging at their ropes. It was their instinct to flee and quickly escape their predators, but now they were easy prey, being tied to a tree. Yu'mi swiftly seized his bow and quiver of arrows and sliced through the dark toward the horses.

Mae squealed, "It must be after the horses!"

Toke shot to his feet and picked up the nearest stick. "Who the fuck cares about the horses? What about us?"

The brush rustled in the direction that Yu'mi had disappeared. Suddenly an upheaval of snapping branches and crunching leaves exploded about twenty yards away, and the color drained from Toke's face. Mae's heart pounded, and her entire body trembled. *Did Yu'mi need their help? Or should they run and hide?* Dexter grabbed Yu'mi's obsidian blade and stood next to Toke, both conflicted on what to do next.

Then it came—the blood-curdling shriek of a creature's painful death and the savage tearing of flesh.

Chapter Thirty-Three

Mae felt like crying. It was their fault the innocent horses were tied up and couldn't run away. And what if it got Yu'mi too?

Then they all heard it—something big was heading through the dark, pushing through the thick bushes and low tree branches, right toward the center of their camp.

"It must be attracted to the fire!" Mae gasped and jumped to her feet. And, without any other words needed, the three of them sprinted in the opposite direction of the noise, into the blackness.

A six-foot-high boulder stood in their path. Toke boosted Dex and Mae to the top, and they helped pull him up. They crouched down defensively and just listened. Mae couldn't hear anything through her heavy breathing and pounding heart, but Toke could see the camp from where he was.

Suddenly Toke stiffened like he could see something. Mae gasped, "What? What is it?"

Toke's shoulders relaxed, and he released his breath. "It was just Yu'mi. And he's fine." Mae's hand flew to her heart in relief, waiting for the rest of Toke's report. "And he's got a horse."

"Just…one?" Mae squeaked, barely above a whisper. She already knew what the answer would be, so she crawled next to Toke to see for herself. She was just in time to watch her own little horse emerge from the trees, and her hand flew to her heart in relief.

"Let's get back," she said, hurriedly sliding down the side of the boulder. Dexter and Toke were right behind her. Sharp thorny oak leaves mercilessly punctured their feet, a sensation they hadn't noticed on their desperate escape the first time.

Mae limped into the clearing. "Yu'mi! Are you okay? What happened?" She rushed over to him, relieved at only finding a few bloody scratches.

He nodded with a "dah," and proceeded to tend the fire like this sort of thing happened daily.

After tethering the two horses within view this time, Yu'mi took off his quiver and sat down. Without all the gory details, he explained as best he could that they didn't need to worry anymore tonight. The panther had plenty of food for himself and others. *Panther?* Ice shivered down Mae's spine.

It took a while to relax their terrified minds enough to sleep, so they just lay there in silence. Mae gazed up at the stars as they screamed for attention against the velvety black sky, playfully nipping at the trees on the horizon. She refused to admit to herself or anyone that, as each day went on, the less confident she felt of ever seeing Greg again. Her prayers became more insistent, almost bossy, and this night, like each night before and each night to come, she fell asleep with wet eyes and an aching heart, craving his body next to hers.

Mae slowly woke to the soft hissing of the crackling fire and opened her eyes to a fresh morning sky. She stretched out her arms and yawned, gazing up at the cluster of chittering birds in the laurel tree who were far into their day already.

A few yards away, Yu'mi crouched with his hands together under his head, and slowly raised himself to a sitting position. He spoke softly into his hands, cradling a few seeds and acorns. He gazed into the sky and closed his eyes, quietly chanting, fully at peace. His prayer to his gods was sweet and personal, not the big showy stuff they reenact on TV with an enormous headdress and dancing around with jangling moccasins.

Awaiting the late sleepers sat a hot steaming basket filled with morning porridge. *How did Yu'mi do this all so silently?* Mae couldn't help but show her gratitude and sprung on him with a smothering hug. "I just love you!" He had no idea how to respond to these physical expressions of hers, so just remained still until she was done.

"So, Mae," Toke launched his back into a deep stretch. "You do realize what all your touchy lovin' means to him, right? In his eyes, you're as good as married now. Just helping you out here. In fact, I'm going to encourage this kinky adoration he has for you. It's getting us regular hot meals." Mae rolled her eyes as usual to his unappreciated comments and dug into her cereal.

After putting out the fire, Yu'mi handed Dexter and Toke each a basket of greens and motioned to the horses. "Caballo hungry."

"Oh, c'mon. You don't allow the Princess to feed her own horse?" Toke grumbled. "Whatever." And followed Dexter to the creek where the horses were filling up.

Not needing any further resentment, Mae chased after them, insisting she could feed her own horse. There stood Dexter and Toke, staring wide-eyed at two new horses standing with the others.

"I take it all back, Mae. Your guy's a saint," Toke said while cautiously inching his way over to the larger of the two. The horse was thin but strong, with a chestnut brown coat and a black mane, and the other could almost pass for a twin except with a smaller build. He reached out to pet the horse but jumped back when it snorted angrily and stomped its foot several times on the ground.

When Dexter held out his hand to make friends with the other one, it nipped back. "These don't appear very tame. Where'd he get them?"

"They must be wild." But the logic in Mae struggled. "This is just too weird. How can there still be *all* these wild horses running around free in the Sierras? How come I've never seen any here before?"

Luckily, the basket of special greens worked its magic, and the horses became a bit more amiable, and the angry jerking back and forth of their tails stopped. The only problem was, the horses wanted more of that delicious green candy and got a little aggressive with their insistent nudging.

"Okay." Toke covered his face with his hands, caging his frustration and exhaled. "I don't want to look a 'gift horse' in the mouth but"—he dragged his hands down and distorted his face like it was made of rubber putty—"why did he wait so long? Why didn't he give us these sooner instead of watching us stagger along in mother-fucking-bloody-blister-hell?"

"Actually, why *would* he help us?" Dexter reasoned. "I don't think he liked us very much. He probably saw us as wimpy and lazy, just sitting around for hours nursing our wounds. Also might assume that we, being male, would want to fend for ourselves out of pride."

While lovingly caressing her horse's coat, Mae added, "Well, I think he's rewarding you for helping out so much last night."

"So, that's all it took?" Toke threw up his arms as if blaming the sky for not telling him earlier. "He'll probably find us a car once I put on my Mr. Helpful apron."

After a brief and extremely embarrassing horse-riding lesson from Yu'mi, he tethered one horse to the other, letting each follow behind him in a line, and they were off.

Sort of.

Chapter Thirty-Four

The tunnel's underground river grabbed hold of Greg and tore him down the right side of its fork, far away from Mae and his friends. It all happened so fast, he didn't even get the chance to panic. But his right leg felt like it was on fire, and he was in such agony all he could do right now was keep his head above the water's surface.

Greg wasn't prepared for the river's sudden change in temper when it went from a fiercely accelerating raging bull into a terror-driven cheetah. Sharp, jagged rocks scraped his skin raw as it shot him through the narrowing limestone tube like a spiraling missile. He began to feel the euphoria like on one of those spinning rides at the fair. The kind that always ended in vomiting.

Just ahead of him, something exploded in a deafening rush of water, and suddenly, as if dynamited out of a water cannon, he was shot out of the dark underground tunnel and into intense brightness.

For a moment, he floated in air, until gravity took over, and he fell—*fast*. His body slammed down onto hard wet dirt, landing in six inches of water, which did nothing to cushion his fall. Then water began to move in a circular current with strength enough to pull Greg along. His fingers found a small rock protruding out of the ground and clung to it tight—and just in time.

Two seconds later, like the powerful flushing of a pressurized toilet, the tunnel greedily sucked all the water back down into the earth. With a force so mighty, the four-foot boulder vacated its new perch and rolled back into the indentation where it normally sat.

To a passerby, it was just an old rock. No one would suspect the terrifying secret it hid beneath the earth.

Still shell-shocked from the last five minutes of hell, Greg lay quietly, covering his eyes from blinding light, and waited for the motion sickness to subside.

One thing he knew, he was breathing fresh air, tree-spiced air. He could hear insects and birds, felt a breeze on his skin, and the heat baking his face was definitely *real.* He slowly opened his eyes to a squint, then a little more…and cried out lustily, expressing the crazy high of freedom coursing through his being.

His clothes were in tatters from nearly being skinned alive, but mostly still attached. As much as he tried, he couldn't ignore the intensifying pain in his leg, so he propped himself up on his elbows to take a look. He could see it swelling right before his eyes through the fabric of his jeans, and it appeared that his bone might be broken.

Pulling himself up a little further, he scoped his surroundings. No one was anywhere, so he yelled for them. Anyone. "Help!" Then listened. Shouting louder this time, "Call 911!" Then switched to calling his friends' names, just by the off chance they'd been shot out of the ground too. The only response he got was some chattering from a couple of bothered chipmunks. He exhaled and flopped his head back down in the dirt.

Nearby, above his head, something slapped the mud a few times then stopped. Then the sounds repeated. "Hey—is someone there?" Biting back the pain, he sat up again and turned toward the noise.

Gasping, on its last minutes of life, flopped the ugliest fish he had ever seen in his life. Greg's only thought was to get as far away from it as possible. So, he gritted his teeth, and dragged himself on his butt across the mud and out of the hot sun, under a shady tree. He leaned against its trunk and tried calling out for help a few more times, and even shouted, "Fresh Fish!" But still, no one responded.

Accepting the dismal reality that he was on his own, he needed to figure out where he was and which way to go for help. After a quick glance around at the manzanitas and madrones, the familiar color of the large gray boulders, and just a small scattering of pines and granite, he could tell he was in the mountains, and thankfully, not that high up. But where were his friends? Were they still in the tunnel? What if Mae was hurt? He needed to figure out a way to get to her, even with his injured leg.

The shadows were lengthening, and at this point, the way things were going, there was a good chance he might be staying out here all night. And if his leg *was* broken, he didn't want the bone to set in the wrong position just to have it re-broken once he got to the hospital.

Three fingers gripped each side of the hole in his jeans. He licked his determined lips, mustering up the courage—and tore the fabric open.

Others might react to a broken leg in anger, cursing the world at why this had to happen to them, and what did they do to deserve this? But in seeing his broken bone, Greg was actually happy. What luck he had that the bone hadn't cut through the skin! Having a glass that was naturally half-full, no matter how hard the world tried to pour it out, served him well when he needed it most.

In a few short minutes, he had gathered five sturdy sticks to use as splints and tore strips off his already-shredded pants for ties, then got to work. It took using every cuss word known to the human race to straighten out his broken bone and line it up with exact precision. But once the splints were tied in place, and his leg was immobile, the pain became much more tolerable.

Now it was his stomach that hurt him, growling loud enough that he might be mistaken for a bear. Just a few feet away, the now-dead fish's wide eyes stared up, blankly. "Ugh. I guess you're it, creepy-ass." Luckily, a long, thin tree branch lay within reach, enabling him to spear the fish and bring it back.

He held the fish and stared into its wrinkled eyes, which looked eerily human and made Greg's skin prickle. "What the hell kind of fish is this?" Too hungry to think any more about it, he reached into his pocket and pulled out his keys. Using the jagged side of his house key, he hacked away at the fish's leathery skin with the tiny dull serrated edge until he worked free a small piece of its pale pink insides. With hesitation, he brought the flesh to his lips but had to wait until he could get his mouth to open for it. "It's just sushi, man." He then shut his eyes and shoved it into his mouth. He scrunched his nose at the dirt-like taste, but kept going, eating away at it like corn on the cob until he was almost sick.

A welcoming, cool mountain breeze refreshed the fishy air, bringing along with it the dusky grays, to stage the last hour of daylight. Greg knew he needed to find shelter since his cropped t-shirt and tattered jeans wouldn't be enough to keep him warm through the night.

Bracing himself against the tree, he pulled himself to standing using the fishing spear as a crutch. Not too far off, he found two large boulders that would give him refuge in the tight space between them, and he was more than ready to sleep away the pounding pain in his leg.

It took a while as his body searched for a comfortable position to lie in, but he couldn't seem to move away from this one lump under his side. When he finally realized it wasn't something on the ground but in his pocket. He reached in and pulled out Mae's crushed water bottle. "I'll find you, Mae. I won't stop until I do."

Morning light reflected brightly off the bleached rock and woke Greg from his restless night. With his body so stiff and sore, he baffled over why anyone would *choose* to sleep outdoors on purpose? He could maybe do car-camping, but this extreme camping was *nothing* like that. Plus, the nighttime sounds of the forest were utterly unnerving. Twice he woke to a raccoon or something walking over him, and too often he felt creepy things crawling inside his clothes.

After a loud and lengthy yawn, it was time to sit up to see how his leg was doing. He winced at the sight of the giant purple plum that rose from under his skin above the break in his bone. But surprisingly, his pain was minimal and having a full stomach gave him strength he hadn't felt for nearly two weeks.

With the support of the rock, he raised himself to his feet. So far so good. Next, he needed to find water, so he picked up Mae's bottle and shoved it back in his pocket. "Thank you, Bae," he said with a loving pat. Then he traded in his stick crutch for a good sturdy branch and set off.

He limped a fair distance before finding a creek. Far past thirsty, he drank as much of the water that he could from the leaky bottle, and then dipped his t-shirt in the water and dabbed at his bloody wounds.

Before heading off again, he stuffed himself with wild blackberries that grew along the creek and patched the holes in Mae's bottle with pitch oozing from the bark of a nearby pine.

His leg wasn't happy with all this walking and began to throb, but Greg ignored it and kept going. When the pain got too brutal and relentless, he was forced to give it a rest in a large flat clearing.

After propping his swollen leg up on a decaying log, he leaned back on his arms with a defeated sigh. How was he ever going to find Mae and his friends being *this* crippled? He had to find a higher place where he could see far in all directions, and so, when he yelled, his voice would carry even more. Since climbing a tree was out of the question, his eyes scoped his surroundings for maybe a small isolated mountain, or even a giant rock, like…like—"Holy shit!" He sat straight up. "Is that Sailor Rock?"

Most teenagers and anyone under twenty-one knew Sailor Rock all too well as the best place to hang out and party. It was hard to get to and hard to get caught.

With the relief of at least knowing where he was, he felt a surge of energy. "I'm coming, guys! I'll get help at Sailor Rock," he said, speaking his thoughts out loud as usual. "Or maybe you're already back home by now. And if not, I'll get choppers after you."

Giddy and motivated, he wanted to get going but knew he had to wait until the swelling in his leg went down a little. He hadn't been to Sailor Rock since high school, and from what he could see from where he sat, someone must have *really* cleaned it up since then.

Chapter Thirty-Five

The morning's excruciatingly slow ride had a number of unpleasant and painful mishaps, but Dexter and Toke eventually made it over an entire mountain.

Riding without a saddle, blanket, and bridle was an even bigger challenge than their horses' temperaments. Each step the horses took, their bodies slid to that side until it took the next step, then they slid to the other. Their thighs cramped fiercely in the constant battle to keep a hold over the insanely uneven rocky terrain. Watching them, Mae was reminded of baby monkeys desperately clinging to their mother's back as she swung from tree to tree.

Her thoughts went to summer camp and the time the horse trainer took in a new filly that needed to be saddle broken, and when they arrived back the next summer, he was still working on her. She decided to ask Yu'mi not only where he found all these horses, but how he could possibly tame a wild one so quickly.

It took a while for him to get his explanation across, but she finally got the gist of it. Many herds of wild horses inhabited these mountains, and the people who lived here caught the horses easily, and quite often. They would ride them for a while, and, when they finished with what they needed them for, they'd be released back to the wild. Mae raised a skeptical brow and planned to Google it when she got home. Yu'mi then added that he captured these particular horses because they showed to be accustomed to an occasional rider—although, to Toke and Dexter, this wasn't evident in the least.

They rode for hours up and down the endless mountains, filling up at a small fresh spring along the way.

These long boring rides gave Mae way too much time to worry about Greg. What if something really horrible happened to him? What if he's still in the cave, hurt and unable to walk, calling for her and she just abandoned him? What if…? She could feel tears building and blinked them away, but they kept refilling. She wished she could tell him that they didn't abandon him. It's just that the quicker they got back home, the sooner they could send professional, fully equipped search and rescue teams. She'd send helicopters filled with Navy SEALs, Green Berets, and the entire Delta Force to go back into the cave and get him out.

They were nearing the top of the next tall mountain when the narrow trail abruptly ended. Yu'mi got down and tethered his horse to a tree. "See vallee." He pointed farther up the mountain where they needed to go.

Too excited, Mae squeaked the question, "Sacramento Valley?"

"Oh, man, yes, please." Toke scrambled off his horse and stretched his legs. Yu'mi insisted on helping Mae off her horse, then motioned for everyone to follow him on foot.

They entered a dense, bushy area, climbing rocks and boulders, places no horse could travel. Snagging skin on sharp branches, scraping knees in tumbles, and resting only when they had to. Continuing up and up, drinking from Yu'mi's water bladder until, red, sweaty and sunburnt, they pulled themselves up the last part of the enormous rock top. This was it. They had actually made it and scanned their eyes over and down into the expansive valley far below the mountain.

"Vallee!" Yu'mi beamed, proud to have finally gotten them here.

"Dude. That's not the Sacramento Valley." Toke eyed Yu'mi like he had brain damage. "Check it out. There's no Folsom Lake, no buildings, not even a freeway. Wrong valley, dude."

Yu'mi pointed to a river far in the distance, "Sacramento Reeber. In vallee."

Slowly shaking her head, Mae felt depressed, knowing they still had a long ride ahead of them before they found a ride home.

"All this way for nothing? This is shit. The whole time, we've been heading to some bum-fuck place, way the hell away from anybody." Toke trudged over to the far side of the rock and kicked a small bush struggling to grow out of a crack. "There's no roads, no cities, no houses, no nothing, anywhere. So then, where the hell *are* we?" he demanded, peeing over the backside of the rock.

"Actually," Dexter pursed his lips as he reeled in a faraway thought. "Yu'mi's not saying what we see out there is the Sacramento Valley. He's simply showing us the Sacramento River in a valley. This could be any part of the Central Valley that the Sacramento River travels through."

"That means we could be hundreds of miles from home." Mae let out an exasperated groan and rubbed her forehead that was beginning to throb. "We couldn't have traveled *that* far or we'd be dead."

"Let me see if I can give us a rough idea of where we are." Dexter patiently scanned over every inch of the immense valley that lay in front of them. Having exhausted all her remaining optimism, Mae had to admire his tenacity and threw her head back to gaze into the sky.

A mere moment later, Dexter's head jutted forward. "Is that…? No…" He squinted, trying to focus on something in the distance, then took a step forward. "Is it?"

Only a little curious, Mae stepped up next to him, angling her neck and trying to see what had caught his attention.

Toke looked over with half-lidded eyes. "What, dude?" His doubting tone lacking any enthusiasm.

"There." Dexter pointed to a far-off rock formation propped atop a forested mountain. He leaned into Mae so she could follow his finger. "Even without my glasses, there's just no mistaking Sailor Rock."

Chapter Thirty-Six

Though close in distance, Sailor Rock was much harder for Greg to get to from its north side, rather than from the dirt road he'd always taken from the west. He limped the entire way on one good leg, maneuvered over rocky and uneven ground, and had to elevate his leg every two hours, so it took him two full days to finally reach the level ground below Sailor Rock.

After searching for far too long, he was unable to locate the wide well-worn trail that opened up to the clearing at the base of Sailor Rock. All he found was an unaccommodating narrow trail that lead him through the thick carpet of prickly bushes and a scattering of small trees to the clearing that wasn't much of a clearing anymore. Even the official trailhead entrance that was usually marked by a parade of bras and prayer flags tied to branches had been taken down and was so overgrown with vines that he almost didn't recognize it. In the center, instead of the five old logs that had been pushed together in a circle, a young sapling now grew. "Hello! Anyone here?" It was way too quiet and annoyingly clean. Where were the scattered piles of beer cans and tequila bottles? Not even *one* cigarette butt. Must've been one of those damn anti-drinking parent groups who came out here, cleaned the place up and gated off the road again. But, for some reason, this time their plan actually worked, and everyone stopped coming. Greg frowned and shook his head. "What a waste of an awesome place."

Heading across the ground toward the entrance, something caught his foot, and he lunged forward, nearly falling. He looked down to see tangled with his foot in a homemade net, a wild hare. It was nearly dead and exhausted from trying to escape. His first instinct was to rescue it, but, having only eaten a few wild plums and berries in the last two days, he was starving and needed the protein to help his bone heal. "Mae, I'm so sorry, but I really need this." Then, without untangling the fear-paralyzed rabbit, he snapped its neck in one quick move and pulled it from the net.

With vigilant caution, he made his way halfway up Sailor Rock where the easy part ended, and the steep part began. Gazing up, he scanned the side of the rock formation and tried to pick out the best way to the top.

Dragging a stiff, heavy leg behind him like a bag of bowling balls made this steep part something he never wanted to climb again. He'd never seen this place so empty and he sort of felt abandoned, but once he began to recognize the old familiar turns, grab hold of the same old cracks, and rest on the same old ledges in the stone, he didn't feel so alone. And when he reached the small "cave of firsts" where he and Dexter had smoked their first joint, where he first felt under a girl's shirt, and where he first did most everything, it meant he'd made it to the top.

"Holy shit." Greg dropped the rabbit. "What the hell did they do?" He shuffled from end to end in disbelief. Those overzealous assholes didn't just clean up the trash, they eradicated all the years of art it proudly displayed. It wasn't just graffiti, but actual history. Sons found their father's 'Fuck you' and added to it twenty-five years later. "It was beautiful." He sniffed, leaning his hand on the sailor's stone ear.

Being this close-up, nothing of it looked like a sailor, just a rocky mountain. But Greg knew his way around and stepped across the flat part of his beard to the far edge where he could see for miles and miles and far up into the Sierra Mountains.

After ten minutes of scrutinizing each and every mountain, he found the trees just too dense to see much of anything. He started waving his arms around manically and shouted Mae's name as loud as he could, then the same for Dexter's and Toke's. When his voice became too hoarse, he took off his shirt and tied it to a long stick and waved it around like a flag. When he got bored with the waving, he made up fancy flag routines until he could no longer move his arms. Hopefully, they caught some part of his flag show and were already on their way over. And if they didn't come by tomorrow, he would head off to find the road home and send help to rescue them.

As a precautionary measure, even though it had been out of water for days, he set his phone out on the ledge along with the meager contents of his wallet to let the sun dry them further. With his dying battery, he might only have one chance to make an emergency call and wanted to make it count.

The noon sun was getting too intense, and he needed to find shade. He remembered Sailor Rock as always having shade, part of why it was so popular. That's when he looked up and groaned. "Bastards even cut down the oak tree that grew out of his hat. What a bunch of effin' A-holes."

Then, thinking for a moment, he eyed the barren rock, finding the perfect platform to lay out the letters 'SOS' on the very top of the sailor's hat. The dark sticks would contrast nicely against the sun-bleached rock and would be hard to miss from the air. But, peering down at his broken leg, he knew it would be some time before he could do that last part of the climb. Only rarely did anyone go all the way to the very top of the sailor's head; too many had fallen to their deaths. Though being intoxicated contributed to their brave stupidity.

By now, hunger was angrily clawing at the insides of Greg's stomach, and he needed food. After thoroughly assessing his useless surroundings, he pulled out his keys and got to work on skinning the rabbit with his house key "knife."

Looking down at the raw, unappetizing muscles of the animal, he struggled over how he was actually going to eat it. Why couldn't his family have watched useful shows like Survivor or MacGyver instead of how the Beaver learns a new lesson on how to be even more of a geek? Then the idea came to him. Grabbing a rock, he smashed open the miniature flashlight that hung dead on his keyring and pulled out the tiny glass lens. Stacking a few sticks in layers to make a square, he filled the center with dried leaves and anything that could easily burn. Next, he concentrated the sun's rays through the tiny lens and into a pinpoint dot, much like he did as a kid to melt his plastic Army men. And later, his sister's Barbies.

It took some time, but, finally, a small black dot formed on one of the dried leaves and started to smoke. Carefully blowing on it, he got the little red embers to grow larger and larger until they ignited into a delicate flame. He placed smaller twigs on top of the flame, then larger ones until it became a full fire. He felt quite proud of his accomplishment and wished someone was there to hear him brag. "I'm smarter than the av-er-age bear."

He separated and skewered each appendage of the rabbit, then roasted them over the small fire, turning each slowly on the toy-sized rotisserie. Too hungry to wait, he pulled small pieces of charred meat clean from the bone with barely anything left to cook.

Not sure what to do with the rabbit's skin, head, and guts, he ended up tossing them over the edge. His rationale was that any wild animal catching his human scent would be satiated with this easy meal and not bother with the climb up the Sailor to kill and eat him.

Before extinguishing the fire, he silently collected the remaining rabbit and then ducked into the cave of firsts, barricading the entrance for the night with as many branches as he could find against the hungry howling and growling of the unseen animals.

Waking refreshed, Greg stood at the far tip of the Sailor's beard and gazed out over the mountains. He breathed in the fresh mountain air and noisily beat his bare chest like Tarzan. "Today is the day. I just know it!" With his t-shirt tied to the stick, he was ready for a full day of flag-waving and this time he'd make a fire so they'd spot the smoke if they were far.

Suddenly there came a noise from far below, and he froze. There it was again.

Hoof-beats!

Giddy excitement tore through Greg's body when the horses come to a stop at the backside of the rock. Laughing silently with relief, he quickly hobbled his way to the other side, ready to climb the path down. He stopped mid-stride, and his jaw went slack. *Where'd they go?* His head darted around like a bird, searching the surrounding trees and bushes. Shouting after them proved useless since his voice was still hoarse from the day before, and barely made a croak.

No way in hell was he missing his only chance. He started climbing down as fast as he could, scrambling over, ducking under, and scraping past every obstacle in his way. Loose pebbles skittered past him as he half slid, half hopped on his one good leg, and down the final stretch. Then, with an unexpected jerk, the foot of his uninjured leg caught in a crevice, but his momentum kept going, flipping him over his foot and tumbling him to the bottom. With a sickening thud, his head hit the dirt, detonating a deafening clang that reverberated in his skull. His eyes fluttered twice, fingers twitched, then everything in his world went dark.

Chapter Thirty-Seven

"No way. That can't be right..." Mae frowned skeptically, searching for more proof.

"We're just seeing Sailor Rock from a different perspective. We're used to his side-view from Highway 50. But, look closer." Dexter sidled next to Toke, pointing. "See his hat with the notch in the brim? And the rock pipe sticking out above his beard? His two-hump nose...his lopsided ear?"

"Nah, looks just like it, but not the same." Toke shook his head, his voice firm. "Notice. No graffiti. The *real* Sailor Rock has decades of shit scrawled all over it."

"It's just too uncanny," was all Dexter could say.

"And, most importantly, there's no oak tree growing out of his hat." Toke crossed his arms, satisfied.

"You're probably right, Toke." Mae could feel her logic unbraiding. "But, then, how could there be this identical face of a sailor with the same white granite rock embedded in the same place of his gray rock beard?" She had to smile a minute, reflecting. "We always called it a piece of cheese from his last meal."

"Nah, it's always been a chunk of vomit."

"How about a regurgitated piece of cheese. Truce?" Mae said with a small laugh. Then something caught her attention. "Wait a second...I can barely see it, but it's definitely there." She squinted even harder. "The crack on his knobby nose. It's in the exact same place as it's always been."

Toke shifted uncomfortably, considering this. "Shit—I know that crack well. I tagged 'Fuck the whole fucking world' myself senior year along the south side. This side." He formed his hands around his eyes like binoculars and took two dangerous steps forward. A minute later, he announced, "Okay. Same crack, but no Toke wisdom. Not the same rock. Hell, it's even missing the massive collection of gum snot some other fucks added under his nose." Though confident in tone, Toke still eyed it suspiciously.

Drawing his hairless brows together in a crease, Dexter said with a gravely sobering voice, "Something's *definitely* not right about this."

Mae took a moment to digest what Dexter had said. "Yeah…" Her voice wavered with uncertainty. "It's sort of like…like as if…like we're definitely seeing Sailor Rock…but a much younger version." Then she wiped her eyes with the palms of her hands for clarity. "Like we're looking back…back in time."

Mae, Dexter, and Toke stood on top of the highest rock on the tallest mountain for a full hour, staring out as far as they could, haunted by the vacant valley that stretched out in front of them. How could there possibly be this familiar undeveloped valley where the overcrowded, freeway-tangled city of Sacramento should be? With a feeble, half-hearted laugh hiding his sinking heart, Toke pointed out three well-known mountain peaks.

Feeling her eyes growing wet, Mae said weakly, "Please stop."

"And over there, at the base of that mountain," Toke stretched out his arm haltingly, pointing slightly left, "there should be that massive cluster of identical houses wolfing up the hillside. And, to the right of those, that mammoth outdoor mall…" Toke's voice trailed off as the gravity of their plight had begun to sink in.

"The highway should be coming in between those two mountains." Dexter pointed listlessly. "And down through this valley." He let his arm fall limply to his side. "Right here." His voice, so pained, was almost a whisper.

Trying to cope with facts too bizarre to accept, tears pooled in each of their eyes. Bit by bit, their reluctance surrendered, and they began to see everything for what it was. Toke and Dexter sat slumped over, legs hanging flaccidly over the rock's edge as their reality painfully peeled away, exposing the raw truth. Mae stood behind them, swaying somberly, anguish distorting her joyless face.

It was Dexter who first spoke. "Why didn't we see it before? It was all in plain sight."

"Why *would* we see it?" Toke said slowly, sounding defeated and lost. "This just doesn't *happen* to people."

Counting on her fingers, Mae began, "The Fox family in the woods and their simple lifestyle. The natives in their ancient costumes, fluent in a lost language…"

"Not one power line," Dexter added to her list. "We've heard nothing remotely mechanical. Not even a chainsaw." He pulled up his legs and crossed them in front of him.

"Hell, not even a passing airplane." Toke picked up a pebble and threw it into the air. "Since when has the sky only flown birds and butterflies?"

"There's no trash, no gum wrappers, no cigarette butts, not even a beer can, no nothing." Mae tightened her lips as her chin began to tremble.

No one noticed when Yu'mi had left nor when he happily scrambled back up with two lifeless rabbits hanging down his back. But his smile fell the instant he took in their tortured faces and the heaviness in the air. He stayed silent, crouched a few yards away, not knowing what to say or do.

Mae let out a small agonized laugh. "I want to find the hidden camera. I want someone to jump out and say, 'Punked!'"

Raising his chin, Toke said with a little hopefulness, "Maybe we should go farther down there, just to make sure."

Annoyed, Mae turned her exhausted reddened eyes to him, but, in seeing his shaken face, she softened, realizing he was just being hopeful. "Yeah, maybe there's someone down there. We might be able to get some real answers."

"We're too physically and mentally vulnerable right now." Dexter's voice of reason stopped that line of thinking. "We might actually get ourselves killed. We don't know what's *really* down there, but we *do* know what's not."

The afternoon sun was getting low, so Yu'mi decided it was time to speak up. "We go."

Chapter Thirty-Eight

Vacant of mind, as if on autopilot, the three of them mounted their horses in silence. The intimidating quietness left Yu'mi unsure of what to do next. So, he just turned them all downhill to take them back the way they came.

They stared straight ahead, depressed and confused, grieving the loss of their families and friends, their hopes and dreams and their life as they knew it. They didn't care where Yu'mi took them, as long as they didn't have to make any decisions.

"So...where do we go from here?" Mae's words trickled out so tiny and sad, she could barely be heard.

Lost in a faraway daze, devoid of his ingrained logic, Dexter slowly shook his head. Toke, slumped completely forward with his face planted in his horse's mane, answered with a grunt, his brain seemingly immobilized.

With an aching heart, Mae thought of her life back home. Her disappearance would *destroy* her mother.

Would she never see her friends again? She didn't have any siblings, so her friends *were* her sisters. Marissa would just call her to talk about every minute of her day. Mae would put her on speaker, and they'd laugh for hours while she cleaned her room or did homework. Her other BFF, Jessica, lived down the street, and they were friends since the first grade. She could tell her anything, all her secrets, and knew she would never repeat them to anyone.

When Yu'mi glanced back and saw the tears running down Mae's cheeks, his face fell. He decided they would make camp right where they were. This time, so numbed of mind, no one complained that it was still light out and simply got off their horses. Like zombies, they gathered at the base of a large rock and just peered into the darkening sky, for a long while.

A big vocal yawn from Toke broke the silence as he noisily adjusted himself against the rock, showing his frustration. “So how is this all even possible? *No one* can time travel. It’s total bull, just sci-fi…made-up stories…not real. It simply can’t happen.”

“Yeah, I’m right there with you.” Dexter thumped his head a few times as if trying to declutter the mess inside. “My brain can’t make sense of this aberration.”

Before long, Mae decided to ask the question they’d all been wondering. “Yu’mi, what year is it?” He looked up at her and cocked his head, unsure if he understood her question.

“Maybe give him examples like 1930 or 1890,” Dexter offered. “Something he might be able to relate to.” But Yu’mi still had no answer for them. With brains so overloaded with questions, their thoughts continued to swirl around and around like in a toilet that just wouldn’t flush.

Mae wrapped her arms around her knees, hugging them tightly to her chest. “I keep asking myself, why us?”

“Yeah, same here,” Toke said, shifting to a different sore spot on his butt from the day’s ride. “Maybe it’s cosmic, like one of those wrinkles in time.”

“That was no wrinkle. We almost died like nine hundred times,” Mae said bitterly, beginning to rock.

Through the next hour, they shared thoughts and theories of their predicament, which helped their moods lighten a bit. Dexter added to the list, “Or what if we’re in an alternate universe or our subconscious and we’re still back home living our lives as usual?”

“Oh shit. My stash. My effin’ dad’s going to find my stash.” Toke sat up. “I’ll never see my custom bong again. Or my buddy’s weed garden.”

“Toke, don’t you think we have more important things to worry about?” Mae shook her head in disbelief. “Like, how are we going to survive, for one? What about our families and friends, will we ever see them again?"

"They haven't even been born yet." Toke yanked off the hot and annoying wrap from his head. "I can't miss someone who doesn't exist."

This got Mae thinking. Since Greg wasn't there with them, maybe he wasn't in the past. Would that mean he wasn't born yet?

"I say we go back to the Foxes, who actually don't seem all that weird anymore," Toke said with a pained half-smile. "They're sure to know something about when and where the hell we are."

"Yes, that seems like the best course of action." Dexter nodded. "We'll have a place to stay while we work out a strategy to get back home."

"I can't do that tunnel again. I just can't," Mae said shrilly, tightening her shoulders.

"But"—Dexter held up his finger to calm her—"we'll need to take the time to plan it out carefully and find the right equipment, so we make it back *alive*. For now, it's important to get our health back before we can do anything."

"And sanity," Mae added.

"Agreed. And I think sitting here mourning and focusing on regret is not going to help with anything. Probably the best way to deal with this inconceivable situation is to keep ourselves busy." Dexter stood, taking his own advice.

Yu'mi had no idea what had happened to them, but knew they were hurting, so he remained silent. He carefully laid the two dead rabbits on the rock, preparing to skin them. Dexter walked over to the rabbits and held his hand out to Yu'mi for the blade. In two swift moves, Dexter skinned them both like he'd been doing it for years. Seeing this, Toke sprung to his feet, grabbed a basket, and left to get water.

Mae just watched them, utterly bewildered. How on earth could they get it together so fast? It must be a guy thing. Her brain still felt numb, and she was hurting throughout her entire being. Besides losing Greg, she had to accept the most unbelievable, inconceivable, bizarre transformation to her life she could ever imagine. Wanting for this day to be over as soon as possible, they went to bed right after dinner. Bonding together in misery, they forcibly squeezed their eyes shut, begging for instant sleep. Dexter whispered, "Tomorrow will be better."

"It has to." Mae's tears blurred all the stars in the night sky into ghostly blobs. "It can't get any worse."

Chapter Thirty-Nine

Foggy-headed and emotionally hungover, Mae woke to a steaming gourd of tea and Yu'mi delicately tucking fresh flowers into her hair wrap. She smiled sweetly and sat up slowly, feeling frail. "Oh, Yu'mi, thank you." Closing her eyes, she breathed in the Christmassy incense of the pine-scented tea and took a luxurious sip. "Ack! This is awful!" And spat it out. When Yu'mi laughed, she joked back, accusingly, "You *knew* it was awful."

"Drink." He crossed his arms.

"No, absolutely not."

"Give it here." Toke made a come-hither motion with his hand. "If it tastes that bad, probably has some awesome swarmy psycho effects, which is what I need real bad right now." His first sip was slow, but he eventually drank the entire thing, only gagging at the end. "I feel nothing. What is that shit?"

"Meddy-cine."

"Medicine for what?" Mae wiped her mouth on her arm, still trying to rid her mouth of the taste.

Yu'mi pulled up the skin of her arm between his two fingers, showing how dehydrated she was. Then pointed to their ashen faces. "Sick."

"We're not sick. We're just depressed," Mae said, pouting.

Shading his eyes from the bright morning sun, Dexter scanned Mae's face, then Toke's. "Actually, for all the sun we've been getting, you both look strangely pale. Sallow. And I assume I must too." He lifted his arm and examined both sides.

The next cup of the bitter pine needle tea went to Dexter, which he obligingly forced down, having to stop quite a few times before finishing.

“Okay, Princess, your turn.” Toke took the refilled cup from Yu’mi and handed it to Mae. “You don’t want to make him lose interest and start making *me* the platform bed each night, do you?”

She took the cup and sipped, keeping a running commentary about its awful taste. Yu’mi patted her free hand the entire lengthy process. And when finally finished, she let out a climactic wail, which Toke honored with a high-five.

Yu’mi picked up the small basket of scented flowers and herbs he picked for Mae that morning and finished weaving them into her hair wrap. All his attention and care flattered Mae and never seemed the least bit sexual. He treated her more like a baby doll or pampered poodle than someone he lusted over. And, as far as she knew, she *still* had a boyfriend… somewhere, and she would wait for him as long as it took.

The mountains rose quickly in altitude as they began their long ride back to the Foxes, easily tiring the horses with the steep inclines. They made a point of stopping often for water or for Yu’mi to run into the forest and come back with a handful of something or other. He was constantly thinking of the next meal.

After lunch, Mae lay in the shade on a narrow strip of soft grass at the water’s edge. She stared up at the treetops, envisioning positive scenarios for Greg’s whereabouts. When he finished a long drink from the stream, Dexter sat back, following the flight of an orange dragonfly as it darted in and out of the spidery reeds lining the bank.

Toke found a shaded rock and dangled his legs in the cold creek water, watching Yu’mi repair one of his arrows. This got him to thinking. “Hey, maybe we can get Yu’mi to teach us how to use his weapons. As we found out a couple of days ago, we really don’t know *what’s* creeping around in the dark. Next time could be a grizzly. Or a family of them. Hell, just because they're extinct back home, they're still pissing all over the place here." The thought made them *all* bristle. "I agree." Mae turned on her side to face him. "We really need to be able to defend ourselves against dangerous animals."

"And hunt for our own food." Dexter walked over to Yu'mi and sat. He picked up one of his arrows to use as a prop to help explain what they wanted.

Yu'mi understood immediately and was quite pleased they wanted to learn his ways. With no hurry to be anywhere, they took their time with their blow dart and bow and arrow lessons. Their moods brightened, and it was even sort of fun. It felt good to laugh again.

Like the night before, sleep didn't come easily. They lay awake listening to Yu'mi's even breathing, gazing up at the explosion of stars that sparkled like tiny diamonds in the tuxedo black sky. "I wonder if Greg's staring up right now at this same exact sky," Mae said, thoughtfully, suppressing the desperate ache that constantly pained her stomach.

"Let's hope," Dexter said, concentrating on the sky. She knew how depressed he was about losing Greg, but he kept his emotions together far better than she ever could. Suddenly his arm shot up. "There's one." He pointed at a shooting star, following its path. "Make your wish."

Mae squeezed her eyes shut and mumbled a wish. But, she thought of another so she had to wish for that one too. Then, another popped into her head that should have been her first wish and she had to rearrange the order of her wishes. Then, she added another few wishes. This went on for a while.

Eventually, Toke interrupted with, "Dexter used the single word *wish*. Not wish *list*."

"Did you know we can tell what month it is by the stars?" Dexter shifted slightly, noisily crunching the pile of dried leaves beneath him. "For instance, right now, it's late July."

Toke smirked. "Cheater. We all know it's July."

Dexter ignored Toke's negativity. "We can tell by the constellation that's in the sky at the time." He pointed to a grouping of stars. "See Leo?"

"Ah…" Mae said, scouting for more. "Try it, Toke. You have to use a lot of imagination."

"I never see shit in the stars. They all just look like a bunch of glowing dots. No bear, no warrior, not even the virgin, and you know how much I'd like to see her."

"You won't see her until next May," Dexter corrected, pointing out two more constellations.

"Okay, then. I'm good for the Big Dipper. That's mine. Don't say it." Toke plumped up the pile of moss under his head.

"Great Bear." Yu'mi had woken and was watching the night sky with them.

"And the Big Dipper makes up part of the Great Bear," Dexter explained. "Toke, find your Big Dipper again, and now follow the handle. That's the tail of the bear. Do you see it now?"

"They shouldn't call it a bear. Bears don't have long stupid tails like that. It looks more like a cat." Toke turned on his side, then added, "Hell, find me some weed, and I'll see your bear, your unicorn, and anything else you'd like."

Chapter Forty

Yu'mi worked hard to keep them fed each day, and, the more new skills he taught them, the more they lightened his load.

Mae wanted to know his trick for making acorns taste good, so Yu'mi gave her a lesson. First, he had her dig a small sandpit near the creek and add a layer of fern leaves. On top of those, she was to place a pile of shelled and ground acorns, then cover everything with a branch from a cedar tree. Next, he showed her how to pour warm water over the top, so the bitter-tasting stuff in the acorns leached out and into the sand. That had to be done a few times before the soggy pieces of acorns were ready to be smashed and lastly cooked into mush.

When the lesson was over, Mae proudly announced her new skill to Toke and Dexter. "I can now make my own ooti and could live off of it if I have to," she said, though she was already getting a little tired of it. "Also, I made us all toothbrushes. Well, not really toothbrushes, but, it's what Yu'mi uses and look at his white teeth." She handed Dexter and Toke the sticks she had hammered and frayed on one end and sharpened to a point on the other.

"Thanks. I so need this," Toke said and began using it immediately. "I need floss next. Go get on that now." He brushed the air with his fingers to get her to move.

"Toke, it's time you learn to skin a rabbit," Dexter said, holding out a sharp piece of obsidian for him and pointing to the dead rabbit on the rock.

Picking up the dead rabbit by its ears, Toke held it out in front of him. "This one looks nothing like the bunny I used to have at home. Look at those ridiculous donkey-sized ears on his tiny head and those long gangly legs. Not the cuddly type you'd find in your Easter basket with a bow."

Once the skinning lesson was over, the butchering class began, and Dexter taught Toke what he had learned so far. "So now, hold it like this and cut across here. You want to separate out the tendons. This white stuff here is called *sinew*. It's incredibly strong and shrinks when it dries, so it's perfect for tying things together, like an arrowhead to its shaft."

Toke was especially intrigued by the sinew. He asked if humans had sinew. And what if they happened upon a dead body, would it be okay if he cut out that person's sinew? Mae thought his question was so absurd she answered it herself. "Yes."

When Yu'mi showed up with a four-foot rattlesnake for dinner, Mae thought she was going to have a heart attack. But, she fought through her fear and stood strong instead of bolting like she really felt like doing.

With his fingers clamped tightly behind its head, unable to bite, it twisted and writhed hopelessly. Then, without a moment of pause, Yu'mi slapped the snake down on the large rock by the fire and held its body captive with his knee. Toke and Dexter leaned in, wide-eyed and curious, never really seeing this deadly creature so close before.

After extracting the venom by squeezing it repeatedly behind the snake's jaw, Yu'mi filled a small shell with the vile yellow fluid, which, to Mae, looked more like it came from someone's runny nose. This he'd use later to dip his arrows in for a faster kill.

Once beheaded, the snake's body continued to flail around as if possessed. Mae's upper lip curled in revulsion, but she found she couldn't take her eyes off the headless body with a life of its own. Toke held down one squirming end of the snake and Dexter held the other while Yu'mi sliced through the entire length of its underside. Yu'mi gripped the top edge of its skin and slowly peeled it off as if he were removing a tight sock.

Mae hoped that was the end of the gruesome demonstration but was sadly disappointed. Yu'mi reached his hand inside the snake and carefully drew out a long transparent sack that looked like a soggy overused condom. After he stuffed the entirety of the snake's guts inside of it, he put it to the side. What Yu'mi intended to do with it, she didn't want to know, but was wise to the fact that he never wasted anything. The remaining body of the snake was skewered and slowly smoked over the fire. How could anyone possibly have an appetite for it after all that? But she was wrong.

They started to notice that every time they spoke, Yu'mi quietly repeated each word to himself. After a little while, he began to get louder, realizing no one was listening, nor cared, and he didn't seem to be bothering anyone, so he just kept on. Soon, he was repeating whole sentences pretty clearly, punctuated by the same sigh, snort, grunts, or laugh that the bearer of the original words had added.

At first, they thought it was funny and even cute, but having to listen to him all day long quickly got on their nerves.

"Okay." Toke gestured his chin toward Yu'mi riding ahead of them. "He's been pretty much silent the first few days, speaking only when spoken to or out of necessity. He kept busy hunting, cooking, crafting frequent unnecessary gifts for Mae, then more gifts for Mae and basically helping us stay alive in the wild. But this new thing he's doing? Is it me or is he bugging the shit out of you, too?"

Mae looked back at him. "We owe him our patience. He's not hurting anyone."

"And…" Dexter paused a second to wipe the sweat off his face with his sleeve. "He only wants one thing from us. Just a little help."

"Don't forget. He also wants Mae." Toke gave a lopsided grin. "But, well, he has her already."

"No, he does *not*. I'm still with Greg if you haven't forgotten already."

"Geez, lighten up little princess, just sayin'. As anyone would. He's got something big for you—and I mean *big*."

Mae narrowed her eyes. "Oh, ha-ha. Just stop."

"Ho, ha-ha. Just sthop," Yu'mi repeated.

Toke glowered. "Can I punch him?"

"Kanneye ponch heem."

"Freakin' stop that."

"Freekeen stopbat."

Toke groaned and buried his face into the horse's mane.

For the last couple of hours that she'd been riding, Mae felt a little light-headed, but ignored it, hoping it would go away on its own. When it finally got so bad that she felt nauseated, she decided to say something. "I'm…I'm not feeling all that good."

"Duh," Toke said matter-of-factly. "You're eating like a rabbit. A *sick* rabbit."

Dexter pulled his horse next to Mae's. "Mae, you need to remember you had barely eaten anything for weeks in the tunnel and you're still in recovery. You should be nourishing your body, not starving it because of your humane concerns."

"Be careful." Toke held up his hands to cover his head in fake defense. "Don't go there dude, I'm warning you."

"I'm not feeling…" Mae's weakened body fell sideways off her horse, landing painfully in the stickery weeds and dirt.

"Oh shit!" Toke grabbed his water sack and jumped off his horse. Yu'mi was at her side before anyone else, holding her face and looking into her eyes, then feeling her skin. He put her head in Dexter's lap, then rushed over to his horse, poking around in one of his satchels. Toke got her drinking water, talking to her calmly, which was totally out of character from the Toke they all knew.

Yu'mi piled a small handful of unknown substances on a nearby rock and pulverized them to a powder with another stone, releasing intense aromatics. He stuffed the small pile into Mae's mouth followed by water, forcing her to swallow.

"Yuck." Mae wanted to scrape her tongue. It was awful and tasted like snails. "What *was* that?" she asked groggily.

No one answered, so she just lay there quietly for a few minutes. "I'm feeling a little better. Just dizzy and a little sick to my stomach."

"You need to eat some meat, Mae. That's your best form of protein at the moment." Dexter held her chin, turning her face to his, and looked sternly into her eyes. "This is getting out of control. You need to put your ethics aside. Just until you're healthier."

"What about eggs?" Mae said, hoping that was the answer.

"Nuk. Nuk eggs."

"Why not?"

Yu'mi made a flying movement, and they realized he was saying the eggs have hatched and the birds have flown. She *knew* she had to eat better to survive here, but her strong determination to make her ethics work was making her sick. "I've been doing this vegetarian thing most of my life." She weakly thumped her hand over her heart. "It's part of who I am." Slowly, she raised herself, propped up by her elbows. "When I was little, I asked my dad where the meat in my hamburger came from. When he told me, I got so upset, I never ate meat of any kind ever again."

Toke cleared his throat and raised his brows.

"That was different. Eating the tunnel fish meant life or death."

"And life or death is what our situation here might become," Dexter reminded her.

Mae closed her eyes for a moment and took a deep contemplating breath before answering. "But what he cooks scares me. Skunks, snakes, gophers, and all sorts of little bony birds."

"Squirrels, bunnies, and ducks aren't scary, and they're hella tasty," Toke said, rubbing his stomach.

"Those are too cute to eat," she whined. "It's not like you're asking me to eat a hamburger. In my head, it feels like you're asking me to eat a little kitten."

Yu'mi walked back and announced firmly, "We stay." Then he left to begin setting up camp.

Dexter fed Mae some jerky, which she grudgingly chewed and swallowed. "Just don't tell me what it is. Please?" She turned to Toke with pleading eyes. "Okay?"

"Damn, what fun is that?"

In no time, Yu'mi had a fire going and hot food ready. Toke and Dexter helped Mae to camp and propped her against a rock. Yu'mi settled down next to her and with such gentle tenderness, hand-fed her the meaty stew. She enjoyed being the coddled baby and reminded them once again not to divulge what they were feeding her.

But, as expected, Toke couldn't contain himself and insisted on giving her little hints. With her first bite, he trumpeted like a baby elephant, and on her next spoonful, a chattering dolphin. He followed these with a sprinkling of exotic creatures, finishing with a tiny kitten. This was the most fun they had had in weeks. Sick, but funny.

Mae lay curled up in her bed, feeling better for the first time in days. She insisted it was the awful pine needle tea Yu'mi kept making them drink, rather than adding meat into her diet.

The fire crackled warmly as her brain puzzled over the grisly ways of nature that just didn't make sense. Why would animals be given so many emotions and be able to feel such incredible amounts of physical pain, only to suffer and die painfully in the jaws of another? The world was such a brutal and savage place, it seemed unfinished. It had to still be in God's *alpha* phase. This couldn't possibly be beta.

PART THREE

Chapter Forty-One

With the air growing cooler and the firs and pines beginning to replace the oak and manzanita trees, Mae knew they didn't have long to go. Having mixed feelings about getting back to the Foxes, at least they could stop and rest, sit in real chairs, and get the answers they so desperately needed.

Yu'mi slowed his horse and looked into the trees for some kind of mark. He made a few realistic-sounding bird calls, then turned his horse, which turned them all. Dismounting his horse, he walked back behind them, the way they had just come, and brushed over the trail they had just made with their horses.

"Aren't you being excessively tidy?" Toke raised his brow. "Deer don't even cover their trails."

"I think it's for safety," Dexter observed. "They seem to be fairly vulnerable up here. Did you see a gun or other destructive weapon besides knives and arrows in his tribe? They seem peaceful. But in order to stay alive, they probably need to conceal their location."

"Actually, I think you're right. I remember something about this in one of my history classes," Mae said, thinking back, ignoring the loud bored sigh from Toke. "The Incas were conquered because they built these awesome roads all up and down their country so they could quickly communicate with the other tribes. People living in the mountains didn't have any finely made roads leading directly to them, so they remained hidden and survived." Mae was one of the few kids in her class that actually loved history. She wasn't good at remembering dates and names, but she definitely remembered the stories.

They followed Yu'mi as he picked his way through the trees, bushes, and rocks until they came to a small clearing. He untied Toke and Dexter's horses from Mae's and handed them each their own horse's rope, then motioned them to keep going in the same direction.

"We'll just follow Jack's wagon tracks. He's not the least bit stealthy." Toke attempted to steer his unwilling horse, but it wouldn't move.

Yu'mi continued on, leading his horse with Mae in tow through the narrow passages in the trees toward his village. "Wait. Yu'mi, I'm not staying here with you. I'm going with Toke and Dexter. No me voy contigo. Estoy ir con Toke y Dexter."

After stopping, Yu'mi turned around, his face cheerless, but he still made no move to untie the rope. Mae slid down off her horse then walked over to Yu'mi. "We'll come back and visit you soon."

After thinking about this for a moment, he took Mae's hand and with the saddest posture in the world, put it to his chest and then his cheek. Mae moved his hand to her lips and kissed it. "I promise." With that, she pulled away and turned toward her horse. She looked into her big brown eyes and stroked the side of her firm golden jaw. Ending with a kiss to the furry white pearl on her forehead, Mae walked back to Dexter and Toke.

"Mr. Yu'mi, we absolutely owe you our lives." Toke saluted a goodbye. "We'll make it up to you. Promise, dude."

"Thank you, Yu'mi," Dexter added, warmly. "We couldn't have done *anything* like that without your help. You kept us fed and taught us how to survive on our own. I owe you, man."

He reached down and pulled Mae up onto his horse. After adjusting the skirt of her dress, so it bunched to the side, it left more room for her. How was she going to face giving Mrs. Fox's torn and shredded clothes back to her? "Um, do you think the Foxes really *expected* to get their clothes back? I mean, we're total strangers and all and they just handed them to us, right?"

"Nah, I wouldn't worry about it. I think us *returning* will be disturbing enough for them." Toke snorted and started them on their way.

"Speaking of which..." Dexter's horse lurched to follow, and Mae quickly wrapped her arms tightly around him. He continued, "What's the best way to do this?"

"Let's just lay it all out." Toke sliced his arm through the air. "Tell them the truth up front. It's not like they're going to do anything besides kick us out, holding a gun to our heads, right?"

"You know, I agree with Toke." Mae patted one of her hands on Dexter's chest. "We have nothing to lose."

"Although..." Toke winced. "I have to admit, when Jack belts out his commands in his unnecessarily loud voice in that deep Scandinavian accent. Brrrrr. What—is he deaf? Or just wants to make sure the grizzlies know who's boss?"

Dexter gave a friendly rub on his horse's neck, trying to win it over. "The problem is, these might be the times when anyone who acts a little odd is labeled a witch. And who knows? The Foxes might be the type of people that would hang a witch for their own family's safety."

"So, what if we come up with a more sensible, believable story? Like how we lost our way and a bunch of crap like that."

"Hmm, maybe. If only we had a little beard growth to help us appear more human. More like them." Dexter squinted, calculating a convoluted fabrication versus the truth. Mae could feel his muscles tense as he worked hard to control the uncooperative horse. She'd never been this close to him before. He felt good and solid in her arms, and she felt a little safer. He finally announced, "Okay, I agree. Let's just lay it all out. The truth."

Familiar scents of burning wood, tree ripening apples, and baking bread wafted through the air, and they knew they were on Fox land. Mae's breathing accelerated. "I'm nervous."

As they approached, Toke slid off his horse to unlatch the gate, but first,

"Okay, here's where we do a special 'Team Future' handshake and flash into our future costumes." He held out his superhero fist to Mae and Dexter and was happily surprised when they bumped it back with theirs.

After walking their horses through the gate, Willie came running over from across the orchard. Through panting breaths, he asked, "They gave you horses? What'd you do for those?" He rubbed the horses' hides while talking to them, which the animals didn't seem to like too much.

Toke jumped in first. "Mae became Yu'mi's girlfriend, and he bought Dexter and me off with horses." Mae wanted to protest, but it was kind of close to the truth. In Yu'mi's eyes, that is.

Crossing his arms over his chest, Willie eyed the horses warily. "These are wild mustangs. And untamed. They won't do well being kept." He took Toke's rope, then Dexter's. "You're lucky, these two seem pretty calm. Must be used to being ridden." He turned and shouted at the house. "Ma! Pa! Those people are back!"

Emerging too quickly onto the porch, giving away the fact they had been spying from the window, Jack and Mrs. Fox reluctantly walked over. Jack covered his nervousness with, "Looks like you didn't find your fones. Wat can we do for you?" He placed one hand on his hip, the other casually touching his rifle, while Mrs. Fox nervously brushed off the front of her apron.

"We would like to have a word with you and your family." Dexter smiled, staying back where he was.

"Vell." Jack looked around at the sky. "Ja, dat vood be fine. Wat is it you vood like to say?"

"We mean," Toke explained. "We need to sit down with you and discuss something." Then he looked at Mae and Dexter for back-up. "At length."

Jack cocked one of his eyebrows and tugged at his bushy beard. He gave a slight nod to his wife that it was okay with him and now was up to her to decide. As if in answer, Mrs. Fox boldly took a few steps forward and handed Mae something wrapped in a handkerchief. Mae guessed she was trying to buy them off with a gift, but soon enough felt the familiar rim of her diaphragm inside. Mae hid her smile, knowing Mrs. Fox had never seen anything so strange in her life and would never have touched it if she knew where it had been.

Seeming to relax a little, Mrs. Fox almost smiled. "Would y'all like to come in? I've a berry pie fresh from the hearth."

"Pie?" Toke nearly collapsed at the beautiful word. Mae wiped her chin, finding she was, in fact, drooling. They didn't need to answer.

At the base of the porch steps, Dexter pulled Mae and Toke aside. "We need to be sensitive to these people's feelings and watch what we say. We really need this family right now."

Impatiently waiting for them at the doorway, Jack thumped the butt of his rifle on the porch.

Once they were seated around the table, Toke looked around for Mrs. Fox, then finally asked, "So, there's pie you say?" For the first time, Mae felt grateful for his audacity.

As promised, Mrs. Fox emerged from the kitchen with the promised pie and a pot of tea, and then slid next to her husband at the table and began serving.

"Okay." Dexter drummed his hands on his thighs and looked at Mae and Toke. "So, where do we start?"

"What year is it?" Mae started.

Jack looked distrustful. "Forty."

Toke's face lit up in surprise. "That's around the beginning of WW2. Holy crap!"

"Toke," Mae huffed. "Do you seriously think this looks like the twentieth century?"

"Okay, um…what century *is* it then?" Toke shrugged at Mae for her "approval."

Jack cocked his head, considering Toke for a moment. "Are you dimvitted, son?"

Standing up straight, Willie clicked his heels and reported proudly, "It is Thursday, July the twentieth, in the year of the Lord, 1840." Then he looked to his mother for approval, for which she gave him a nod.

A stunned silence followed.

"1840..." Mae breathed in shallow rapid breaths, a crease formed between her eyes.

"That's like twenty-five years before the freaking Civil War." Toke knew his combat fighting more than anything else, any history that involved guns. "This is even before the Mexican-American War. Man, we are *way* the hell back." Toke rubbed his head, trying to unbraid the giant tangle in his brain. The Foxes looked at Toke, waiting for a translation that never came.

After Mae's head cleared some, she got back to their immediate problem. "We are in a pretty desperate situation and need your help."

"We wouldn't involve you if we knew another way." Dexter smiled weakly.

"An' you remember, we don't hef any of dose fones and cars and all dose oter tings you want," Jack said, now more curious than skeptical.

"One thing, though, you'll need to keep an open mind." Toke shoveled a heaping forkful of pie into his mouth.

With a concerned glance at Jack, Mrs. Fox said, "We can try to help you, but is it something we should send our Willie away for, so as not to hear?"

Toke looked at Willie with a cocked eyebrow. "Nah, he'll be fine."

"I think it's best if we start at the beginning." Dexter shifted to a more comfortable position on the hard bench. "And everyone needs to stay and listen to the complete story."

"The very, *very* beginning," Toke added.

"And, remember what Toke said about keeping an open mind," Mae reminded them, smiling painfully.

To show his sincerity, Dexter caught Jack's eyes and held them. "We're probably going to use some words and terms you've never heard before." He moved onto Mrs. Fox's blue eyes. "You can just let those pass by, and we'll answer all your questions at the end." Lastly, he looked at Willie's pure and open innocence, completely unaware they were about to muddy it all up. "We'll sound crazy at first, but please hang in there."

After each Fox gave their hesitant nod, Dexter cleared his throat and began. "There were four of us…"

Chapter Forty-Two

Their story went on for a good hour. Every once in a while, Mrs. Fox and Jack would look at each other or squeeze Willie's hand a little tighter. Dexter finished at the part when they met Willie and Milok for the first time and the room was silent. Not even Jack knew what to say.

Mrs. Fox thoughtfully rubbed her lips together until she formed her question. "I'd like to know if you found out what happened to your friend Greg?"

"Interesting." Toke raised an eyebrow. "So, of *all* the questions to ask of our ridiculous sounding time travel story, your big concern is the whereabouts of Greg?"

After reliving the events of Greg's departure, Mae couldn't shake her wistful look. It was probably best not to admit to the Foxes of her relationship with him. At least until she knew how they'd handle this controversial interracial—and most likely illegal—relationship.

Repositioning himself noisily on the bench, Jack attempted to hide the condescension in his voice. "Vell, I don't know wat I shall say. Most of de tings you talk about are strange indeed."

"Yeah, we thought you might have some trouble with the truth," Toke said with a half-laugh.

Still looking sad for the loss of their friend, Mrs. Fox said, "I must admit, your story sounds fascinating. I want to believe it. And you. But it's a little unreasonable to think we would accept something so…so…"

"Insane?" Mae firmly planted the flat of her hands on the table in exasperation and leaned toward them a little. "Do you think *you're* the only ones having trouble believing this?"

"This is all new to us, too," Dexter explained, calmly. "We're working on accepting it ourselves."

Jack let out a short burst of a laugh and snapped his suspenders. "How can someone *really* come from de futore?"

"We just told you how." Toke ran his hands over his head in frustration, forgetting there wasn't any hair to grab onto. "Or look at it this way. You are in the past, and we are from the present."

Mae finally blurted out what they came to ask. "We would like to offer our help around your house and yard in exchange for room and board."

When her charitable heart and sympathetic soul dominated over her fear, Mrs. Fox turned to her husband. "Just looking at their tortured bodies and hearing their stories that don't make any sense, it's obvious these people have been through some kind of ordeal. The Christian thing to do would be to take them in. Now, wouldn't you agree?"

Snatching up his pipe, Jack removed himself from the table and walked to the fire. He pulled out a glowing ember and drew on his pipe until it lit, and then began a deliberate pace around the table. "I am sorree dat I cannot find mysef wit belief in your tale." He stopped and planted his hands on the table. "Bot, your circumstance did come trough. You hef no place else to go." Jack parked himself back on the bench next to his wife. "We hef already lived wit you for one whole day an' night, an' you came to os wit no veapons an' appear to be non-violent."

Expecting him to say more, he didn't. Should they thank him, or did he even *give* them an answer? The silence was too loud, even Toke was quiet, afraid to mess this up. Mae shifted on the hard bench and let out a small cough to avoid the uncomfortable silence.

"So." Dexter politely cleared his throat. "If you don't mind me asking, where does that put us now?"

Jack teetered back, the whole bench leaning with him, and sucked on his pipe. "Vell, you can see we do not hef much to offer 'cept for our animals, which are few, an' de apples. How can we feed all of you?"

Mae perked up. "That is where we can help. We can clear some land, plant crops, chop wood, and help this land become more productive." She held up her bicep to show off her shrinking unused muscle.

With a hearty roar of a laugh that coordinated well with his large dark beard, Jack nearly toppled the bench over, taking his wife and Willie down with him.

Quite humored, Toke added, "Mae, I don't think he approves of women working outside of the home, if you don't remember."

"He just doesn't know what I can do. I am not a baby and bread-making machine." Mae shut up when Dexter gave her a stern look with a slight head shake.

Jack thought for a moment, then stood. "We would require some tings."

"Lay them on us." Toke smiled at their future brightening.

"Dis is a God-fearing home. If you do not trust in de Lord, you may not sleep under dis roof."

Toke nodded. "Sure, no problem." Though he wasn't sure what he believed.

"I'm Catholic. I hope that's okay?" Mae grinned with pride, hoping to score some Christian points.

Jack and his wife looked at each other. "As long as you don't try to convince os of dose strange ways of de Katoliks."

"They aren't strange ways." Mae glared defensively. "Plus, I'm one of those Catholics that *do* believe in birth control."

After giving Mae another head shake, Dexter added confidently, "We were all raised with God as part of our daily lives. We are good people, and we would never do anything against God's wishes."

Jack put his hands on the table and leaned forward, taking turns looking each one of them in the eye. "You vill do your deal of vork, if not, you vill be denied food an' shelter. De vork is not easy, an' I vill put you in de yob dat best fits your strengts." After a short drag of his pipe, he used it to point to Mae. "Mrs. Fox could use your help in de kitchen."

Torn between feeling grateful for a place to live, but outraged at the workplace gender discrimination, Mae forced a clenched smile.

"So, is that the end of it, Jack? You're not even going to *try* to believe our story?" Toke felt a little cocky now that the decision had been made.

"Let os leave it at dat. An at some point, you vill take os to dat hole you came out of so we can look at it for oursefs." Jack noisily tapped the burnt remains from his pipe and began to repack it.

"We rise at dawn and head to our rooms soon after dark," Mrs. Fox explained. "Sleep is extremely valuable for a fully functioning farm." Mae toiled with her use of the word 'farm' but, okay, with some imagination, she could make that work.

"Ja." Jack's thick fingers drummed on the table. "See, our Villie's not quite old enough, an' his muscles hef not developed to be much help wit de heavy vork. My wife's fingers are practically worn to de bone." They all looked at her once delicate little hands, where a lifetime of cleaning and scrubbing had written its story. She hastily tucked them inside the pockets of her apron.

"Thank you. We really appreciate you taking us in," Mae praised, even if they didn't find Catholics charming.

Jack stood for another round of pacing. "De forst ting we need to vork on is de sleeping arrangements. Villie is behind dat curtain dere." This time he addressed Toke and Dexter with his pipe. "You can build a cople beds tomorrow to put underneat Villie's loft for yoursefs. Mae can sleep over dere by de fire an' dis time make shore de fire stays lit."

Oh, not that again. She had failed so miserably the last time. "How often does it need to be, uh, tended?" Mae blinked, trying to look earnest.

"Well, for summer, just a couple times in the wee hours," Mrs. Fox said.

'But if y'all are still here in the winter, you'll be up every two hours. Don't worry. Your body will wake you up from the cold as the fire is dying." Then she disappeared into the kitchen.

They found themselves alone at the table and listened to Willie outside as he freed their horses, then shooed them away. Mae wanted to run out and stop him, but understood why they needed to be free. Besides, wild mustangs seemed easy to come by up here, so they'd have to work on taming their own somehow.

Leaning into Dexter, Toke said under his breath, "They're counting on us being here a long time, building new beds and shit. Do you think they're desperate for help and just playing it cool?" Before Dexter could answer, Jack came back in the room and pulled out a long list of chores that needed doing. Many jobs on the list were unfamiliar but seemed acceptable.

Eventually, to their relief, his never-ending list finally went dry and Toke's question had been answered. They most definitely needed their help.

Chapter Forty-Three

Satisfied with the new situation, Jack whispered something to Willie, which made him smile and disappear through the back door.

A minute later, Willie returned with a jug in hand. "This is from Pa's harvest from last year. We call it the Golden Year Cider." He set it down with a thump in front of his father.

Raising the jug, Jack beamed with pride. "We chose de finest of de gold apples an' kept a good eye on dem until dey were at dere peak. Dose pesky vorms put op a good fight bot we got most of dem an' de rest vill add some spice." Relishing in this new captive audience, Jack continued to expand the lengthy introduction of his glorious achievement. "In de forst days of fermentation, I decided to take a chance on de…" That is, until Mae noisily plopped herself down at the table. The disdain on Jack's face for her rude interruption was almost humorous. For punishment, he ceased his boastful speech to deny her the enjoyment of his brilliance.

With a swift whack, Jack broke the wax seal and yanked the cork out with a ceremonious pop. Whether to speed things up or to straighten out future problems, Toke petitioned, "Jack, with all due respect, in our time, the women drink with the men. Hell, Mae can outdrink even you." After hearing this, Jack's expression shifted. But Mae couldn't tell if he felt challenged or just more condemnation, so she shot out her arm with her empty mug.

"Okay, Princess, I think you're on," Toke said with a wink and filled her up.

Ignoring Jack's disapproving glare, Mae raised her glass. "To our new communal living situation! Skål!"

Completely stunned how this woman would know such a Norwegian term, Jack's judgmental look thawed, and he raised his glass in return. "Skål!"

Mae tossed it back eagerly. "Oh, dear," was all she could manage while trying to look gracious. The cider had sounded so delicious, but it wasn't even close to being palatable. The putrid aroma of rotting cabbage clung to her nostrils and the taste of goat pee tortured her tongue.

Toke and Dexter quickly swallowed the cider just to get it out of their mouths. In no time, Toke had his glass raised for another toast. "To a full night's sleep off the hard dirt and without being stalked by mountain lions and wolves." They all took another painful swig.

Despite its ghastly taste and revolting smell, their cups quickly emptied, and they wanted more. The high alcohol content worked its magic and numbed their taste buds as well as their brains.

With a little straightening in his seat, Willie instantly appeared taller. Then taking out a temporary loan from his future puberty, he deepened his voice and presented his father with the ultimate question, "May I have a full-strength glass tonight, Father?"

Jack leaned away from the table and canvassed Willie from head to foot. "Son, you are half de size of me an' a tird de age. If you drink it full strengt, you vill be on de floor in minutes."

"Well, how about I drink half of what you drink since I am half your size?" Willie proposed.

"Nice." Toke nodded, impressed with Willie's bargaining.

Comparing his son's proposition to the enormous size of his empty mug, Jack crossed his arms. "Vell son, you make a good argument. Eider I drink less, or you fall flat on your face. Let me tink about dis some more." He immediately hammered down the rest of his mug and slammed it on the table with a throaty laugh.

Looking his dad square in the eye, Willie poured himself half a glass. "A deal's a deal."

Jack groaned, not happy with this situation.

Noticing that Mrs. Fox didn't drink any of the cider, Mae realized that if she were going to fit in and make this all work, she would have to put aside the hard-earned progress of the women's movement. All those years of women's suffering as they fought for equality, independence and women's rights. She had to step back into this stone age and try hard to be content being a Mrs. Fox clone. She would take one for the team. In fact, she would try to do an excellent job just to show them she *could.*

Mrs. Fox leaned into Mae a little. "You can call me Elizabeth."

Meanwhile, Toke felt quite jolly. "Ahh…Elizabeth…a beautiful name."

"Thank you." She blushed. "Jack calls me Lizzie as we call him Jack, though his proper name is Johan." She rested her clasped hands on the table. "Since we will be living under the same roof, I see it as acceptable not to use my formal name."

"Why wouldn't it be okay?" Mae shrugged disapprovingly. "Who says it's better to call you 'Mrs.' anyway?"

"Oh, I don't know. Townsfolk I suppose. But since there really aren't any…"

"Then who cares? Elizabeth it is!" Toke toasted to informality.

Uncomfortable with so much attention directed at her, Elizabeth fell into her usual meek posture. With a quick untie of her apron, she announced softly, "Best we all get to bed now."

Like Jack and Elizabeth's room, Willie's was partitioned off from the main room by two log walls and a curtain flap. The walls inside held wood pegs for clothing, a shelf, a basin, and his loft for sleeping.

"Vell." Planting his hands firmly on his hips, Jack studied the room then turned to consider Toke and Dexter. "You are quite tall for men, but I tink dese vill be good." He indicated the large lumpy grain bags hastily filled with some unknown substance deposited on each side of the room.

Plucky from the cider, Toke countered, "Maybe you're just short."

Since Jack didn't react right away, Mae cringed, glancing nervously at Dexter, and then back to Jack. Finally, he belted out a hearty dismissive laugh to everyone's relief.

"We're all taller in the future," Dexter explained. "Year after year, humans have been increasing in size. Bigger bones and bigger heads even. It's due to the massive amount of protein and food we have available in the future."

Jack lolled his head with an exasperated expression that read, "Gud God, not all dat futore stuff again…"

The curtain parted, and Elizabeth entered Willie's cramped room. She doled out fur skins to Toke and Dexter and a familiar scratchy blanket to Mae. "I apologize that everything is so humble. We try to make the most of what we have."

They were instructed to relieve themselves in the chamber pot under their bed at night and then to empty it in the outhouse in the morning. Elizabeth bade them goodnight and ducked behind the curtain into her and Jack's room, a few feet away.

Willie climbed the ladder to his bed, swaying clumsily from his adult portion of cider. The loft creaked and bent under his weight until he was settled. Then, with perfect aim to the shelf below, he spit the candle out.

Mae had to paw her way through the bedroom curtain in the dark but was greeted affectionately by the firelight on the other side. She wrapped the blanket around her body like a burrito, then laid down on the wide bench next to the fire. *And where was her chamber pot?*

Far from sleep, Toke stared up at the firelight cavorting on the log ceiling. "Mae, I just want to make sure you heard breakfast is at five a.m. I guess that means four a.m. for you since you have to make it." He seemed satisfied with her groan.

It began as a low rumble, like never-ending flatulence, then it grew in intensity until it reverberated through the walls and floor and beat itself into everyone's ears. That's when they knew Elizabeth had traded her husband in for a bear. And not just any bear. A big burly one with a severe head cold, chasing a honking goose using a gas-powered lawnmower.

Toke smashed his pillow over his ears, but it didn't help in the least. "Dude, this place needs doors. You're probably stuck listening to your parents always going at it too."

"Going at what?"

"You know, fornicating, screwing, fucking, making little critters like you."

"I'm not sure…" But now Willie was curious. "How does—"

Toke quickly changed the subject to avoid explaining the birds and the bees. His version would scar the child for life. "So, who's president now?"

"In the United States or Mexico?" Willie steepled his fingers across his stomach. "In the U.S., that would be President Van Buren. Don't ask me about Mexico. They keep changing them, and no one can keep any of them straight."

Amused at the little show-off, Toke asked, "Why would I care who the president of Mexico is?"

Willie paused a moment before answering. "You *do know* we live in Mexico, right? I thought you said you were from around here."

"How can we be in Mexico? This is California, dude." Turning on his side, Toke wrestled the assortment of furs covering him back into place. "Little man, I think the cider's got a hold of your brain."

"Right here, the land where my family lives, is Alta California, which is part of Mexico. And the governor of Alta California, *here in Mexico*, is Juan Bautista Alvarado." The fact that Willie knew more than Toke, who was much older than him, gave him a charge. "Alta California is *huge* and goes on and on. Over lots of mountains to the east, and even touches parts of the United States, then it goes all the way to the ocean, that way." His grandiose arm movements went unappreciated in the dark room. "Dex, did you hear that? We're in frickin' Mexico, man."

"Oh yeah." Dexter yawned. "I forgot about that part. I can't remember exactly *when* the Mexican-American War was, but the U.S. will eventually take all of California for themselves. But..." He yawned again. "I think we have a few years."

"What war?" Willie rolled onto his side, trying to see their faces in the dark.

"There will be a lot of wars," Dexter continued, sleepily. "But the one I'm thinking about, the Mexican-American War, is when the U.S. snatches all this land you call Alta California. They end up *paying* Mexico for it, but not that much. It's a huge piece of land, so the United States divides it up and only calls a small piece of it California. The other parts they named Nevada, Arizona, New Mexico, and...some other state." Then he yawned himself out of the conversation.

"What will happen to us then?" Willie's voice pitched higher with worry.

"First, they'll kill all the Indians, and then lie about it," Toke said. "But since you're not an Indian, they probably won't kill you."

"Will they kill Mae?" Willie asked, showing genuine concern.

"Hmm, that's actually a very good question," Toke puzzled thoughtfully. "Dexter, do you know?"

Half asleep, Dexter still answered, "Her heritage is Mexican, not Indian." But, a moment later, he startled himself awake in realizing what he just said. "Actually, in these times, your time, 1840, most of the *Mexicans* are considered white since they're predominantly from Spain. It's only over time, after mixing with the natives on the land, the skin of the European Mexicans will become all shades of white, brown, and everything in between. Mexico didn't kill their Indians like the United States did so Alta California still has large populations of Indians and people with dark skin like Mae." He considered this for a moment, and when he spoke, he sounded worried himself. "So, yeah, I guess she *would* be considered Indian *here*."

"Yep. Not a good time for Miss Mae. Sorry dude." There was no answer from the troubled Willie, so Toke just yawned. "Good night."

"Okay, um, good night." Not knowing what to say or think, Willie's brain swam with too many unfamiliar thoughts and scary images, so he pulled his quilt up over his head and forced his eyes closed.

Chapter Forty-Four

Dawn slowly painted the sky while a half-asleep Mae diligently cracked eggs. Next, she carried water in from the large covered barrel outside, kneaded dough, ground spices, and brewed tea. All this under the light of two candles.

"We set the fire up according to what food we'll be making that day. If you will notice, I've already set up the flame for the baking of the wheat bread." Elizabeth decided to explain even the most basic things, seeing Mae's ineptness at everything. She gave her a quick lesson on getting the toasting and roasting flame on the left side of the fire while the other was a smaller flame for boiling or stewing. "We use the bellows to fan the fire, and once the coals are red, we shovel them onto the oven."

Relief flooded over Mae. "Oven? You have an oven? Where is it?"

"This large iron pot here is the oven." Then seeing Mae's expression, she added, "Well, a Dutch oven as some call it. We set the red coals underneath and on top, so the contents cook evenly." She unhooked a smaller iron pot that hung to the side of the hearth. "We use this one when we want to cook from the bottom." Above the flames, a metal bar with several hooks stretched from one side of the hearth to the other and attached to two crudely made iron stands. "Jack built this so I can hang it from the handle over the flame and it will not burn." Mae could see the respect and admiration Elizabeth had for her husband, the same that Jack showed for his wife.

Mae was assigned to make the bread dough and searched the pantry for flour. It took all her strength to lift the three-foot barrel's heavy wooden lid. A spray of insects flew into her face, so she slammed the lid back down. Every barrel she opened held only whole grains of one kind or another, but no flour. Elizabeth came to her rescue, swatting away the insects and showed her to the flour she'd already ground that morning.

By now, the sun was starting to show itself and Willie came in with a bucket of goat milk. Mae poured the spice-scented tea into the cups sitting on the table. "So, you drink tea with all your meals?" Mae longed for a cold glass of chocolate almond milk.

"If we had a cow, milk would be delicious to drink. We make butter, cheese, and curds from most of our goat milk, and the leftover milk, the buttermilk, no one likes the taste of it here." Elizabeth made a sour face. "I use it for the baking."

Elizabeth walked over and rang a bell that meant "time to eat." She removed two place settings and cups of tea Mae had laid out and placed them on the kitchen counter. "We don't have the leisure of sitting down for breakfast. Even with your help, there is just too much we need to get done."

Well, this wasn't all that different from her life back home. She spent half her life eating in her car, rushing, always late for something, downing her latte as she ran up the street. While the men ate their breakfast in leisure, the women grabbed bites of their own between chores, eating most of it cold.

"Next, we will plan out the meals for the day, gather and prepare what we can, wash clothes, iron, sweep, fill water pitchers, knead dough, grind grains, and build up our regular supplies." Seeing the look of dread on Mae's face, Elizabeth smiled kindly. "Don't worry, we leave the sewing for our leisure time, at night by the fire."

Was she for real? So, in her time off, she was still working? Mae sighed, knowing she had to accept it all with no complaints. The three of them needed this gig. At least right now.

Mae amused herself by listening to Jack's grunts and Scandinavian ramblings as he fitted Toke and Dexter for hide gloves on the back porch. She poked her head out the back window in time to see Willie push through the men to empty another bucket of river water into the large barrel that stood behind the kitchen. Then, without a pause, he scrambled off to get more. Mae was out of breath just watching him.

Toke worked his fingers in his new gloves. "That kid works hard as hell. No way any twelve-year-old kid's doing that where we're from."

"Vell, he knows wat's good for him." Jack tied off the last stitch and started on Dexter's.

By mid-afternoon, they finished their two new beds and they were nothing like they'd ever built at home. Instead of nails or screws, they held the wooden frame together by embedding wooden pegs. Strips of hide were stretched across the frame and securely tightened. And now it was time to test the new beds out with a nap.

But Jack cracked the whip, once again. "We hef got to get some old trees felled an' de land cleared for more apple trees. Straight ones put aside an' de oters we cut for vood. Needer of you vill use my ax and hammer." He pointed to the word Fox possessively carved in their handles. "You hear dis?"

With an obedient nod, Toke and Dexter walked to the edge of the orchard, exhausted before they had even started.

The sun ducked behind the trees, but it would still remain light for a couple more hours. Dexter and Toke walked into the house with freshly washed faces. They found Mae comfortably slumped over in a chair, her face smashed against its side post, one arm limply holding on to a long wooden spoon supposedly stirring a pot. Not one spark of energy remained in her body.

Willie and Jack funneled through the door, plopped down on the bench and began taking off their boots. Toke groaned and rubbed his arms. "My muscles, they're completely dead. Hey, I could use some aspirin or Advil if you have it."

"Ass per wat?" Jack picked up his boots and dropped them by the door.

"Never mind," Toke said under his breath. He sat down and untied the old boots that Jack repaired for him, making them somewhat wearable. "And what did *you* do all day Princess? Stir?" His mouth curved up in a half smile and proudly added, "*We* only built two finely-crafted wooden beds, chopped down large trees with teeny tiny axes, and cleared land."

Mae felt her face boil to a dark crimson. If only her eyes could shoot bullets.

"Nah, you know I'm messing with ya." Toke glanced over at the table. "I see you made some tea, too."

"I guess you don't realize who will be washing and sewing your clothes and cooking your food." Mae wrapped her hands in a cloth, then lugged the steaming pot to the kitchen. "Let's just see what happens with comments like that." Jack nodded in the background, knowing first-hand.

Elizabeth placed the elk stew on the table followed by Mae with freshly churned butter and the biscuits she'd made earlier. Without a thought, Toke and Dexter plopped themselves down at the table and began loading their plates. They dove into their meal as if they had been starving for months.

Jack and Willie sat speechless, staring at their ill-mannered guests. Lacking any more patience, Jack forcibly cleared his throat. Dexter glanced up and then lowered his fork. "Sorry, man."

"Oh, yeah, sorry," Toke mangled through a mouth full of food, then wiping his hands on the borrowed pants.

After punishing them with a long icy stare, Jack bowed his head and led a lengthy Lutheran grace.

Jack eyed the biscuits on his plate suspiciously before taking one. He turned it over, revealing its tragically burnt underside and frowned. Mae quickly looked away as if she found something vitally important on the empty wall.

With supper done and the day's chores complete, they gathered with the family around the fire. Though exhausted and wanting sleep, Mae was handed one of Jack's shirts for that night's mending. She attempted to sew the coarse cotton fabric as best as she could, pulling skills from her *one* day in Girl Scouts at the age of eight when she sewed a cat-head pajama bag. When she looked up, Toke and Dexter were gone, crashed out on their new beds. Without a word, Mae put down her sewing, and sprawled her depleted body across the bench and was sound asleep in seconds.

Chapter Forty-Five

The next few days seemed like grueling carbon copies of the first, but they made it through each having a little more energy each day.

Mae didn't get how the Foxes kept up this unrelenting amount of work, day in and day out without any complaints. They just went about everything at their own comfortable pace using what they had, knowing it would eventually all get done. They weren't living competitive stressed-out lives like most everyone else with all the modern conveniences to make life "easier." Technology actually seemed to make life harder and just easier for people to get ulcers.

Elizabeth drew the curtains closed against the evening chill and wrapped herself in a knitted shawl. Willie sat at the table cracking walnuts, which he accompanied with his own version of a folk song. "Willie cracked nuts, and no one cares…" Occasionally he tossed one to Dexter who waited patiently with an open mouth. Elizabeth picked up Mae's earlier knitting mess and attempted to untangle it while Mae kept to her sewing.

With a grunt, Toke rammed a rod down the barrel of the musket he was cleaning. "Have you thought about how this place is so remote, hidden away in the mountains, the Foxes probably have no clue on what's going on in the rest of the world?"

"Ha. I do." Jack stomped through the front door, dropping his heavy boots to the side. "But I admit, I came almost directly from Norvay." He heaved his spent body into his chair by the fire and propped his feet up. "Watever I hear is from my tours to de port towns, but de rest is from my Lizzie." He smiled at his wife. "Lizzie was still in school op to de time we met."

Chilled by the cool air Jack brought in with him, Mae tucked her feet under the blanket draped over her lap. "So, how did you two meet, anyway? Especially since you're from Norway and Elizabeth's a Southern gal, and you ended up all the way over on this side of the continent."

"Yeah." Toke laughed. "Could you not find a farther, more isolated place to end up?"

"Vell," Jack began, packing and lighting his pipe, filling the room with the sweet-smelling tobacco. "If you've got some time." Mae screwed up her face and batted the air with the shirt she was sewing.

"Hold on, let me check my email first." Toke smirked and kicked his boots off as well.

Purely out of habit, Dexter flicked his head to get his hair out of his eyes, which wasn't even remotely long enough to be anywhere near his eyes. "I'd be interested in hearing this too."

"Vell, Lizzie, wat do you tink? Are you ready to relive dis again? Been a long time."

Elizabeth lowered her head, then nodded. "Yes, it's been a long time. I can talk about it now."

After a vocal stretch of his arms and a crack of his back, Jack began their story. "I grew op in de soutern part of Norvay. My fader was a German soldier on holiday who found his way to a small willage one drunken night. My moder was a Norvegian farmer's datter whose tick, sturdy legs, and wide hips brought fifteen children into deir family. After a hard winter of nearly starving, dey tought it would be good for deir eldest son to get a yob on a British sheep to America, as many oter young men were doing. Maybe buy some land in de United States an' start a family wit de vages I'd earn."

Jack looked around and nodded at this good idea, and they nodded back. "Bot, I picked de worst sheep possible. De English crew on dis boat were scoundrels an' went by deir own rules. As we got closer to America, instead of paying me my vages, dey accused me of stealing anoder man's valuables an' said de crime for teft was hanging. Dey decided to wait ontil we got to land, so I could be legally tried, den hung. A body washing op on de shore might make trouble for someone.

"It turns out, I may have done exactly what dey wanted, for as dey neared shore, I jumped sheep an' swam for my life. I ran penniless trough de streets of de port town, an' tanks be to God, I was able to find vork on a sheep leaving right den, bound for somewhere an' I didn't care where." He picked up his pipe and gave a soft nod for Elizabeth to continue.

Her cavorting knitting needles ceased their frisky dance, and she set down the beginnings of Willie's new sock in her lap. She closed her eyes and dug around in her head for the old box of memories she'd buried deep inside so many years before. First, she blew off the thick layer of dust, then mustered enough emotional strength to pry off the lid.

In the beginning, her words trickled out cautiously as if testing the ice on a frozen lake. Vulnerable emotions paled her haunted face as she bravely liberated more and more of her broken memories and the words began to flow.

"Childbirth stole my mother from us, leaving my grief-stricken father alone with three young children and an infant. I watched him become so depressed, he could hardly do his work. And, without my mother around to ease the hot tempers of her overbearing father, my grandfather began to take his anger and frustrations out on my father. Life on her family's plantation became unbearable.

"The day finally came when Daddy had enough, and we left my mother's family and everything behind, to begin a new life on a small settlement in North Carolina. It was just my father taking care of us now, until I got old enough to help out.

"This particular day was wash day, so I was down at the river. I was the last one left and just finishing up when I heard screams coming from the village. I dropped the laundry and ran toward home, toward the smoke, taking a shortcut through the trees. I stopped short when I saw Indians in our village that I did not recognize. They were everywhere. Looting the neighbors' houses, then lighting them on fire. A couple of the warriors swung their weapons at anything that moved, even hacking people down as they ran out of their burning homes. I wanted to run out from my cover and scream for them to stop, but I had no weapon. What good could *I* do? So, I stayed where I was, petrified and shaking, having to watch people I knew my entire life getting their throats slit, and scalps ripped from their still-living bodies, then set on fire." Her southern accent that was usually so light grew with intensity.

"I was desperate to find my family, praying to God they were still safe. I kept myself hidden, sliding silently behind the trees until I could see my family's house."

Elizabeth had to stop for a minute, putting her hand over her mouth to hold back sobs. Jack put his hand over hers, and she continued, "I…I saw my father fighting an Indian man who had a painted face and made yipping sounds like an animal. He held a tomahawk, and I saw him whip his arm back, then swing it forward and wedge the blade deep into my daddy's head." Elizabeth was visibly shaking, with tears streaking down her face. Mae took her blanket and wrapped it around Elizabeth in a hug.

"My father fell to the ground with the tomahawk still sticking out of his head. Then the Indian put his foot on my father's face and yanked his hatchet out of my daddy's skull just to use it again on someone else. I had to clamp my hand hard over my mouth to muffle my screams.

"But now I knew, my little brothers and sister were unprotected and free to be killed. Suddenly, the Indian who killed my father turned and looked in my direction. He must have heard me and was heading my way. I ran with everything I had back to the river and without looking back swam to the other side.

"The air was thick with smoke and the sickly smell of burning human flesh. But all I could do was hide behind a large rock, and listen to men, women, and children screaming. Somehow I knew, without having to see it for myself, that they had massacred the rest of my family.

"I'd nothing left. I tormented myself that I was a coward and could have saved my family. I too wanted to die. But instead, once it was dark, I ran, and kept running. After two days without food and only small amounts of water, I finally came to a house with people who gave me a hot meal, a safe place to sleep, and a ride into the next town over. I needed to get as far away from this place that killed everything I loved." She took a sip of her tea and set her cup down so softly it made no noise.

"I wandered around the town, until I came across a man at the dock, loading a ship. I begged him for passage in exchange for work, but he informed me they could not employ women on the ships. I was at my end and collapsed in sobs. Seeing my desperation, he said he'd speak to the captain since they were quite short-handed."

"Oh, Elizabeth, I'm so sorry you went through this." Mae reached out and held Elizabeth's hand tightly, increasing the tears in both their eyes. Everyone, even Jack and Willie, who had heard the story before, were stunned to silence.

Filled with empathy, Dexter looked deep into Elizabeth's eyes. "Do you know if any of your family or village survived?"

"How could they? They burned everything." Elizabeth buried her eyes in her handkerchief.

"Your family is wit God now, Lizzie." Jack gave her arm another few rubs.

"I had always thought the old stories about the hostile Indians scalping people was totally exaggerated to justify the horrible things Americans did to them," Mae said.

After dabbing her eyes, Elizabeth continued, "The tribes around where I'd lived were very angry at all white people and, in my opinion, had good reason to be. I saw so many try to conform to our ways so they could remain on their land and live a peaceful life. My father told us stories about colonists picking fights with the Indians so they would have an excuse to kill them in defense. Or, since Indians had no legal rights, colonists could just use the law against them. They'd accuse the Indian of being violent and then he'd be forced off his land *legally*.

"The colonists didn't understand or even care that this land was the Indians' *home*. A place their family had lived for not only hundreds, but *thousands* of years." Elizabeth paused and folded her hands in her lap.

"Even in my own family, we didn't know, nor care, that we were building a house and planting crops on top of their dead relatives and ripping apart their sacred sites."

"So, was that why they annihilated your village? Just to get their land back?" Mae asked.

"It was more than that. I remember hearing two American soldiers brag about scalping three young Indian warriors for petty crimes. White men do as much scalping as Indians around those parts. But our town should have taken heed of this particular group of Indians that these young warriors belonged to. They had a reputation for unspeakable violence. No one expected them to get their revenge by murdering our entire village instead of just the two soldiers who did the scalping.

"But when I look back at it all, this was exactly what the colonists were doing to the *Indians*. They'd punish the actions of one tribe, by killing people in an entirely different tribe that had no relationship at all to the other. Thinking all Indians were the same. Both sides are guilty of blaming the races as a *whole* and too many innocent people are being killed for the despicable behavior of others." Elizabeth wrung her hands together as if they were wrestling.

This was the most wound-up Mae had ever seen Elizabeth. The room remained silent while they digested her heart-wrenching story. With deflated shoulders, Elizabeth bowed her head. "I'm sorry to admit that I was not innocent of those feelings either. After having my family savagely murdered in front of me, I, too, had a deep hatred and fear of all Indians at the time."

It now became clear to Mae why Elizabeth was so content leading such a non-eventful life, tucked away in these secluded mountains. It was self-contained, nearly self-sufficient, and fairly safe from people with hateful hearts.

Chapter Forty-Six

Toke stood to stretch his legs and placed another log on the fire. The wood blazed in rebellion, hurling wild shadows around the cozy room and a tantrum of snapping sap.

Studying Jack, Dexter sipped his cold tea. "What I'm curious about is how you ended *all* the way up here in the California foothills of the Sierra Mountains?"

"Yeah, it's a little extreme, don't you think?" Toke plopped back into his chair.

Jack smiled warmly at Elizabeth and leaned into her lovingly. This was the most physical affection they had ever seen between them. "Vell, as luck would hef it, we were on de same sheep. I changed my name from de Norvegian Johan Fuchs to de way of de United States. Dat day, I became John Fox. Bot since dere was already a John on board, my sheepmates called me Jack.

"I spoke no words of English and Lizzie spoke needer Norvegian nor German. I was quite sorprised for a sheep to employ a woman on board, bot soon learnt it was hard to find a full crew for *any* sheep going around Cape Horn. Dat's around de entire Sout America, de bottom of de world. Dey called it a sailor's graveyard, wit de treacherous waters an' large floating ice mountains. But dat's de only way to get to de ports in California an' Oregon, so it was to be done. Dey put Lizzie to vork helping de cook, an' she cleaned de sheep as vell as any sheepmate could."

So impressed that this delicate woman lived the rough life of a sailor, Mae nodded approvingly to Elizabeth, which caused her to blush.

"Bot, true as was said, de voyage was unnerving. It was very long, wit too many dangerous trading stops along de way. By de time we got to port in California, Lizzie an' I were already married by de sheep's Captain. Elizabeth was wit child and not able to hold any food down wit de constant rocking of de sheep. We chose to take our chances and collected our vages, then got off at de forst promising port town.

"We had enough silver to buy a horse, vagon, an' some basics. By now, Lizzie was terrible wit sickness an' began to bleed—" Jack cleared his throat instead of giving details. "So, I confined her to lie in de back of de vagon ontil I found a safe place to set op camp.

"Knowing her history wit Indians, I kept hidden how many tribes an' willages we had passed an' traded wit. I had never met Indians before bot found de tribes here quite peaceful, not like de ones dat haunted Lizzie's memories. No one I met seemed to care where we were headed, so we jost kept going. Away from everyone, far from people, where we could feel safe.

"De land jost kept getting better an' better. Hunting was easy an' de wetter must be kind for we found much food growing on dis land. It almost felt too good an' we knew dat oters would soon settle here too, so we kept moving forward trough fields and forests following no trail at all. It would soon be too steep to pull de vagon wit only one horse, so I scouted around for a place to call home. An' dat is where we are sitting right now. One ting about a Nordman, we know everyting about farming, especially in de cold lands. We always do vell where an Englishman would perish.

"It had been only eight monts, bot baby Villie wanted out right den an' dere, causing his moder to scream like noting I had ever heard before. Remember, in my family, I am de oldest of the fifteen, so a woman giving birt, I'm no stranger to. Bot, I could tell someting was terribly wrong, an' I knew Lizzie's own moder died giving birt." Jack reached over and ruffled Willie's hair. "I didn't know wat to do. I was crying like a wee babe, so afraid I'd lose her.

"Over de past few monts, I had been trading for sopplies wit a gentle Indian tribe not far away. Gruff was young den, and he took me as fast as I'd seen any horse go, straight to deir willage. God was wit me dat day an' I was able to bring back one of deir women to help deliver Villie into dis world. She gave Lizzie some birth root, which took much of her pain away. Little Villie wanted to come out bum first, so she had to turn him around while still inside of Lizzie.

"I could not watch an' turnt away. Next I knew, de woman was holding my son who was screaming like a stabbed pig, an' my sweet wife was alive. Bot dere was no mistaking de fear in Lizzie's eyes as she watched de Indian woman clean her an' de infant. De woman had a kind smile an' stayed to teach Lizzie how to get her milk to come out an' feed our new babe.

"Fear soon left Lizzie an' got replaced wit gratitude. De woman covered dem bot in a soft woven blanket, singing softly till my Lizzie an' baby Villie were bot asleep."

"That's Yu'mi's Aunt Jalulu," Willie said with pride. "Milok's mother."

"I felt I owed her my life, bot she wouldn't take anyting in return for her services." Elizabeth's face brightened with memories of Willie's birth. "She returned the next day with her own tiny baby Milok, strapped to her back. She brought a soft skin blanket to wrap around Willie, and a basket with special things for me to eat for good milk. She even taught me how to make diapers by mixing moss with algae."

"Ouch." Toke patted Willie on the back.

Jack went on, "She knew so many ways dis vild land could provide for a new babe an' she took de time to teach os. A friendsheep grew dat didn't require a common language. Our boys grew op as tight as broders, an' Milok speaks English as vell as Villie. The Ma'camo, dey're good people. Dey seem to hef a medicine for everyting. Bot most important," Jack said, trying to contain himself. "We still—we still hef our scalps!" Then he threw his head back and roared in laughter, so scary loud, it made Mae shudder.

Dexter and Toke gave polite laughs, but Mae just rolled her eyes. She couldn't laugh at something that was not only offensive, but also not even funny.

"Oh, c'mon Mae," Toke said, showing his irritation with Mae's constant braying of political correctness.

"Many of the Ma'camo still keep a fair distance, mostly due to the difference in our cultures. But we trust each other, for the most part, and rely on each other for trade and protection." Elizabeth put down her knitting, rose and collected the empty cups.

Emotionally taxed as if they'd just sat through a three-hour movie, they were *all* looking forward to bed.

Mae knew her mind wouldn't let her sleep until it exhausted itself replaying vivid pictures of their horrific story over and over. But one thing was for sure, she felt a new bond with this family and a little more a part of them now.

Chapter Forty-Seven

The following night, Mae waited for Elizabeth to hang up her apron, pick up her knitting, and join the rest of them at the fire. With everyone together, she felt it was finally time to broach the subject to the Foxes. "So, I was thinking…since tomorrow's Sunday, our day of rest, I thought we could show you the cave. You know, the one we came from. Maybe pack a picnic lunch."

Jack looked up from sharpening his ax, handling it carefully like it was a newborn baby. "Ja, I soppose we can do dat. Den you vill stop all dis nonsense of de futore?" He ran his finger across the newly sharpened blade. "Lizzie, you vill come?"

Elizabeth paused her knitting. "Well, if you want, I will go. I can't help but be curious about this story they told us."

"Sounds good to me." Dexter leaned back in his chair.

"Let's do it." Toke held out his fist for anyone to bump it.

Mae's mood lifted. "Then it's a plan."

Toke patiently waited while his fist hung suspended in the air. "It's going to just stay like this until it gets the love."

"Willie, you're up," Mae said.

Mae woke in the morning, knowing the sun would be shining extra bright today. Even the birds were singing her favorite songs. She popped her head into the boys' room with a huge smile on her face. "Ready?"

"Aren't you a little early?" Dexter groaned, stretching his back.

"It's Sunday, the day of rest for God's sake." Toke slapped his bed a few times for the snooze button.

"Omelets today, get a move on." Mae danced her way out of the room.

"You know, with all this perkiness of yours, I don't miss coffee anymore." Toke slowly pulled himself out of bed and leaned to the side to crack his lower back.

Dex tied a knot in the rope that held his pants up. "I'm a little afraid of finding out what's *actually* in the cave. All the other stuff we didn't see."

"I hadn't thought of that. Could be anything. Maybe the animal bones weren't animals at all." Toke gave an over-dramatized shudder.

An hour later, Willie pulled up with Milok's horse on loan and tethered Petey and Ol' Gruff along with it to the wagon. Once the lunches were packed and the cart loaded, they were on their way.

A delicate breeze cooled the air and waved through colorful late summer wildflowers dotting the hills. Mae held in her anxiety about facing the tunnel that stole Greg from her. She worried she would burst into a sobbing mess at the sight of the cave, confusing the Foxes with her love of their missing friend. Especially a *black* man.

Peering over the side, Toke studied the large wooden wheels that labored them along. "Cool thing about wagons is we can go anywhere. There's no rubber tire to get a flat."

Willie squinted at Toke and cocked his head. "Rubber tire? What's that?"

"One more thing apparently not invented yet." Toke winked.

On cue, Dexter took his usual role. "Tires are wheel coverings made of vulcanized rubber and filled with air. The rubber is so hard that the tires can reach an extreme temperature and not melt."

Toke made the Vulcan sign to Dexter and added, "In other words, air-filled bouncy wheels." Willie looked down at the large wooden wheels rimmed by a thin piece of metal. Then he looked back at Toke and smiled, wondering what other interesting things were in Toke's head.

When the ground became too rough to continue in the wagon, Willie dropped the log, which dragged behind them until the wagon came to a stop. After tethering the horses to a spot in the shade, Mae and Elizabeth served up the picnic lunch before heading the rest of the way on foot.

Entering the section of woods that was thick with thorny bushes, low hanging trees, and spiny grasses, Mae cringed with the memory and was grateful their nails had grown a thin protective layer. But they still had to be careful.

Surprisingly, the steep climb down the side of the cliff to the tunnel opening was a breeze for this tough Fox family. Elizabeth was an expert at moving her long skirt out of the way while still remaining dignified and not showing anything but boot. Mae, on the other hand, caught the skirt of her dress on all the branches, and eventually giving up, she just pulled her dress between her legs like pants. Thankfully Jack and Elizabeth were focused on their own climb, or she would surely have gotten an earful.

One by one, they climbed through the opening the three of them had emerged from only two and a half weeks earlier. The cave echoed hauntingly with their voices. Once they lit the tallow candles and lanterns, their shadows jumped around on the walls, highlighting the plentiful spider webs, making it even eerier. Below them, on the far side of the cave, the water revealed itself, reflecting back the light. They climbed down the large boulders and followed the narrow path leading to the water.

Kicking the small bones aside that covered the ground, Toke muttered, "So far, none look human."

Standing at the water's edge, Jack peered down into the liquid. "So, you come from dis little pond of water den?" He was not hiding his patronizing tone.

"Looks innocent, doesn't it?" Mae stared into the water, trying to deflect the incoming memories.

Toke picked up a small bone, showed it to them, then tossed it in. The water instantly erupted in an iridescent blue causing gasps and wide-eyed disbelief and Jack's, "Gud God!" Elizabeth stepped back and pulled Willie with her.

"It appears to eat anything that isn't alive," Dexter explained.

After repositioning the lanterns, the water lost its surface reflection, and they could now see a few feet down. Willie cleared away bones so he could kneel comfortably at the edge of the water. "Yuck," he said, once he got a whiff of the surface. "These animals must've been pretty thirsty to drink this stuff."

Dexter squatted to examine the stiff, dried carcass of a skunk. "Even though they were alive at the time, possibly the water poisoned them or found something internally to destroy."

Mae bristled, remembering how she almost drank the water too, before Toke stopped her. "Poor little things must have come in for a drink and stayed forever. Let's make sure to seal the opening back up this time so the animals can't get in."

"Or get back out," Toke meanly teased. A tortured expression flashed across her face, to Toke's delight.

Chapter Forty-Eight

Willie held his walking stick over the water and then slowly lowered it in. Mae instructed, "Okay, Willie, now pull it out." All he could do was stare in utter fascination at the end of his stick that was no longer there.

"Careful, son, don't touch it." Jack's eyes darted from the water to the stick and back to the water. "Wat the devil is in dere?"

"We don't know." Mae locked eyes with Jack so he could read her sincerity. "But we *do* know that we swam through this liquid just hours before we met you for the first time."

"What this water did to Willie's stick"—Toke held up the remaining piece—"is what it did to us."

The cave lay dormant, asphyxiated in silence as Jack and Elizabeth looked each of them over, unbolting their closed minds to revisit their impossible story, and searched for answers.

Elizabeth slowly raised her lantern to Dexter's face and studied it closely. Next, she moved on to Toke. For the first time, she noticed the growth of fine baby hair fuzz all over their heads, the tiny strands that sprouted from their brows and dotted their lash lines and the barely visible patches of emerging beards. She motioned for Jack and Willie to come close to see what she was seeing as she moved onto Mae.

Tears welled up in Elizabeth's eyes, and her cheeks began to flush. Her hand flew to her mouth, then lowered it gently to her heart. "I'm…" She swallowed and started again. "I am so very sorry about the way we treated you. We couldn't imagine the things you told us nor understand."

Something caught Jack's eye, and his arm shot out, pointing at the water. "Joess! Look dere. I see someting."

Everyone rushed to the very edge and scanned the dark water with their lanterns. An object rested on the ledge a few feet out, throwing back the lantern's light. Toke tossed in another bone, and the water blazed its brilliant blue, casting its light on everything around them.

"My lenses!" Dexter trumpeted, so elated, he looked like he was going to jump in after them. But, instead, he ran the other way, returning five minutes later with a long thin green tree branch. "This tree branch is alive, so the water will leave it alone." He tied a loop at the soft end of the branch and knelt at the water's edge, working the lenses closer. Then with Toke joining in with another branch, they balanced each lens between them and carried them out.

"So, why didn't the water eat your spectacle lenses?" Willie asked, completely puzzled. "They're not alive."

Dexter admired the surprisingly pristine condition of his lenses. "Perhaps because glass is made from sand, and sand is rock, and rock is what holds all this water in here." He wiped the water from his lenses on his shirt, creating a hole, then held them up to his eyes. Laughing with relief, his face glowed as bright as the water. "I was starting to get headaches having to squint at everything just to focus."

Mae strained her eyes farther out into the blue liquid. "There's some rivets and a belt buckle, nothing we desperately need, except—" She picked up Dexter's branch and extended it as far as she could, working at something, and drawing it closer.

"Wat is it?" Jack leaned closer.

"You'll see," she grunted, while the others looked on anxiously. "Got it!" Not waiting for it to dry, she picked up the small round object up and dropped it into her palm, letting the water turn her skin pink.

Staring back at them, was a bright copper United States Indian head penny from the year 1877.

"1877—what the hell?" A crease formed between where Toke's brows would be, his brain consumed with questions. Just like the others.

Mae held the coin up to the light. "I've never even seen one of these. I thought Lincoln was always on the front. Maybe it's fake."

Taking the coin in his hand, Dexter inspected it thoroughly, and concluded, "Definitely real. We're obviously not the only ones who've found this tunnel."

"Let me see dis." Jack plucked up the coin. "Dis says it came from de United States of America. Look Lizzie, it has an Indian's head on de front for land-sakes!" He exploded in a thunderous laugh, for which the echo boomed back even louder torturing their ears for far too long.

"It is too small for a one-cent coin." Elizabeth frowned. "The United States one-cent coin is much larger and has a woman on it, not an Indian."

"Ja, dis is clearly a coin for de Indian tribes." Jack scoffed, "De United States would sooner kill an Indian dan put one on deir coin."

Willie took the coin and turned it over and over, examining it closely. "This is the first one-cent coin I've ever seen. Can we buy a lot with it?"

Toke listened in disbelief, then wiped his face in exasperation. "You're missing the freaking point. *The date!* Look at the *date*!" He tapped the coin a few times in Willie's hand. "This year hasn't even happened yet."

Jack's brows creased as he studied the coin, then turned to Elizabeth for her impression, but she shrugged, lost.

"We're not even close to the United States." Willie was still not getting the reality of the situation, but it was clear he paid attention in his lessons. "So, someone put that little coin on a ship on the East Coast of the United States, then sailed it all the way down the Atlantic Ocean, then around Cape Horn, and up the Pacific Ocean, to Alta California. Then they put it on a horse and rode it all the way up here to these mountains, climbed down the side of this cliff just to drop it into this small pond of water in a hidden cave that no one knows about?" His face contorted with skepticism and he gave the coin back to Jack.

Jack rubbed his forehead as if getting a headache. "Son, dis coin is from 1877. De year dat we live in, right here, right now, is 1840." He paused for a moment, seizing Willie's eyes. "Remember," he said, motioning to Dexter, Mae, and Toke. "Dese folks were telling os dat in de futore, de United States owns dis land we live on. De land we have our house on, an' de land we are standing on right now will be part of de United States. Den how on God's Eart is it possible dat we find a coin from de United States dat was minted in de futore year of 1877? Right here in dis cave, unless dey might be telling os de trut, as crazy as it may sound?" Elizabeth nodded along, agreeing with his reasoning.

Taking a moment to put everything together, Willie finally understood. But since he had believed their story from the start, he didn't seem too impressed. Jack took the coin from him and flipped it over to study the other side again. "Mind if I hold onto dis?"

Toke shrugged. "Sure, it's not ours."

Stepping closer to the water, Dexter held his lenses up to his eyes. "I want to show you something. But you can't really see it from here because it's below the ledge." He stretched his arm out, pointing to the far end of the water. "If you follow the back wall down a ways, you'll find an underwater hole. On the other side, it connects to the tunnel and what we swam through to get out here."

"No one would ever know an opening under there existed unless they originally came from the other side," Mae explained. "Speaking of which…"

The three of them each took a section of the cave and combed every inch of the walls, searching for any sort of way to bypass the hungry pond for their much-anticipated trip back home. To their own time.

Discouraged, without finding anything remotely close to an alternate escape, Toke decided to explore the sea of boulders behind them instead. He bulldozed through the grisly bone orchard and desiccated carcasses, keeping his lantern low to illuminate the shadows. As he rounded the next large rock, his light picked up something unusual, tucked away at the rock's base.

First, he kicked at it like he expected it to move out of the way. Then, pulling out his knife, he lifted it cautiously with the tip of the blade, keeping it at arm's length as if it were a venomous snake. "What the *hell*?" echoed through the cave. This caught the others' attention and they quickly scrambled over.

Dangling from his knife hung a man's stiff, crusty old moccasin, decrepit with age. "Dude's probably long dead."

Picking up the other moccasin, Dexter held it up to the light and examined every inch of it for clues. Mae studied the tattered remnants of past ornamentation meticulously sewn into the top. Drawn on the back of the heel, once in a brighter red, were four faded diagonal stripes with a line connecting them at the bottom.

"Let's think about this for a minute." Mae paused to corral her galloping thoughts. "Since the shoes are on *this* side of the water, the owner probably left them for when they return. So maybe this person plans to come back. And maybe he can help us get home." It was a long shot, but she needed the hope.

"Still say he's dead. These pieces of crap are *older* than ancient." Toke dropped the moccasin and kicked it back into the shadows.

Were these somehow connected to the bones of the child they'd found back in the tunnel? Just thinking of the haunting memory sent shivers down Mae's spine, and she hugged her arms to her chest.

A new sense of foreboding crept in and hovered around them like a chilly fog. The once-soft echoing of their voices now sounded eerie, and their own shadows, menacing. Elizabeth shivered and pulled Willie close to her. "I would rather we leave now." And not one person objected.

When the last exited the cave, they neatly stacked the stones across the opening, sealing it closed, and climbed back up the side of the cliff. Before leaving the site, Jack and Willie helped them study the ground above and beyond the cave to confirm what they didn't want to know. They found no way to access the tunnel from the top either. The ground was mostly solid rock and twisted tree roots for about one hundred yards down.

The ride back was nearly silent with everyone lost in their own thoughts. Jack and Elizabeth looked pained, trying to wrap their heads around this new reality they had no choice but to believe, and Willie seemed only to be affected by the intense mood, so he remained quiet.

Mae gazed out at the passing landscape, ruminating over the coin and moccasins and the storm of new and troubling thoughts they brought with them. Had earlier travelers come through this tunnel and already changed the past? Maybe the life she knew back home had already been altered by someone else…

Chapter Forty-Nine

Upon returning home, they all jumped back into their routines, almost as if nothing had happened. The Foxes would need some time to digest the events of this strange day and modify their rational thinking.

By dinner time, the tone had lightened, and conversations about the coming weather, their animals, and the garden returned to an unexciting normal. When Elizabeth and Mae had finished cleaning up the meal, Jack called for everyone to sit around the table for a talk.

Once everyone was seated with a steaming cup of spiced tea nestled in their hands, Jack opened with, "Vell, I tink it would be best if you explained as best you can of your life from de futore. We need to understand your situation better an', to be honest, I *am* a little curious." Jack picked up his pipe and packed it with tobacco.

Dexter looked to Mae and Toke, not knowing where to start. Mae blurted out, "There are fifty states now in the U.S., *including* California." Not looking the least bit surprised, Jack took a short draw on his pipe.

"We have a thing called electricity," Dexter continued. "It flows through a wire covered in rubber and comes right into your house and powers everything. It powers light bulbs that you can flick on with a switch, illuminating the room better than a candle ever could." This got Mae thinking about how archaic it was to have dangerous wires of electricity running through a home with all the other advancements in the wireless world.

Jack's mind steeped on this for a moment. "So, wat are you saying? Like dere's a little sun in your house?"

"Well, sort of," Dexter said, realizing this was going to be harder than they thought.

"We have a box that washes our dishes for us," Mae remembered fondly. "A box that washes our laundry and a box that dries our laundry." Elizabeth stared off, trying to picture a simple box doing these things.

"We have a thing called a car, or automobile," Dexter explained, using his hands. "It's much like your wagon. It can carry us all over the place, and all we have to do is push our foot on the pedal, sit back, and steer. It runs on liquid fuel, sort of like the oil you use in your lanterns."

Jack raised a curious brow. "So, if we feed Ol' Gruff de lamp oil, he vill run again? Joess, dat would shore be someting to see."

No one bothered explaining, so Mae continued, "We tap a screen, and we can see someone who's clear across the ocean, and we can talk to each other as if we're in the same room."

"So den, can anyone fly in de air like a bird?" Jack leaned back, crossing his arms, knowing he *really* stumped them now.

"Hell yeah, and hella fast." Toke's enthusiasm lit up in a subject he knew. "We climb in this thing called an airplane that flies us through the sky. Some even carry guns and bombs and can wipe out entire cities."

"Is it a giant bird with wings?" Willie cocked his head, fascinated, trying to picture this enormous bird clenching guns in its feet and people on its back.

Dexter squinted an eye, trying to explain it better. "Well, it was originally designed like a bird, but it doesn't flap its wings."

"It can fly us from a freezing stormy winter to a hot, sunny summer day in a few hours," Mae added.

"And, we have toilets *in* the house instead of outhouses," Toke bragged. "When we push a button or pull a lever, the crap's gone, out of sight—whoosh!" Toke's arm flew too close to their faces making them jump.

"We can write a letter and have it delivered to the person in just seconds." Mae wasn't getting the astonished reaction she wanted so she smacked her hand loudly on the table for emphasis. "Seconds!" Instead, they just looked at her hand that had made the loud noise.

"Yeah, and if your heart dies, doctors just cut it out and slap in a new one." Toke nodded, agreeing with himself.

"Ha! I can do dat too!" Jack stabbed his knife into the table.

Frustrated, feeling like Jack wasn't even trying to understand, Mae spoke more to Elizabeth now. "If we want to see a performance, all we do is click a button, and right in front of our eyes, the actors instantly appear inside a little frame. And, these actors could be long dead, but we can *still* see them as if they're alive, still acting out the play."

"Same goes for music." Toke nodded, confidently. "Just push a button, and you can hear something cool, even if the musician's rotting in their grave."

Hoping for some kind of reaction from Elizabeth, Mae spoke with enthusiasm. "Machines freeze food without ice, blend anything to liquid, and cook dinner in three minutes. There's even a machine that will suck up dirt on the floor into a bag." This only got Elizabeth to look down at her dirt floor, unsure why she would want that. "In fact, there is so much done *for* us, we just sit on our butts all day and have to *plan* exercise just to get movement in our bodies."

"Can you shoot muskets over and over without reloading?" Willie acted it out with gunpowder blasting sound effects.

"Unfortunately, they've done that a little too well." Dexter shook his head disapprovingly.

"Yeah, and it's awesome!" Toke's face lit up. "In fact, there's things we call video games where you can shoot and kill as many people and aliens as you want, blood everywhere, and not even get thrown in jail."

Shaking Toke's comment away with his head, Dexter continued, "If you're cold, you just push some buttons, your house is heated. Or if you're too hot, you push other buttons, and your house gets cold again." Elizabeth fingered the buttons on her dress, looking puzzled.

"You can talk to a person across the world from a small watch, or rather, a clock tied to your wrist." Mae pretended to speak to someone from her wrist. But instead of Jack being amazed about talking to someone from this tiny device, he was more enamored with the idea of a little clock attached to his wrist instead of from a chain in his pocket.

"If you're depressed, they give you pills that make you happier." Toke pushed the corners of his mouth into a dopey smile. "If you're a man and want to be a woman, they will cut off your dick—" He heard Dexter clear his throat. "I mean, doctors will do surgery and make you into a woman. If you're a woman and want to be a man, they will make you your very own man-part and stitch it on." Toke seemed to enjoy the terror on their faces, so he continued. "Men can marry men and women can marry women."

"Son, I would radder you not speak of dese offensive acts in front of my family. We are a respectful home of God."

"God loves everyone, don't you believe that?" Mae couldn't help herself. "If you're going strictly by the Bible, you do realize the other things it condemns, right? I see quite a few you already practice..."

"Oh, haha, Mae." Toke kicked her under the table. "You behave you silly ol' Catholic girl."

"Why should I? You're not." Mae kicked him back like a squabbling sibling.

Dexter jumped in. "They can fix your bad eyesight with a tiny red light, and then you can see perfectly." He looked away, wistful, obviously wishing he had done this before they left their own century.

"We have shopping bags we use once and throw them away." Mae was unaware that her hand made a tight fist on the table. "We ship mountains of garbage across the ocean so another country can dispose of it."

Afraid Mae was starting one of her eco-rants, Toke barged in again. "If you don't like the size of your tits, you can get them made bigger." He quickly turned to Elizabeth. "Sorry, I mean boobs. No, breasts—mammaries. Not tits." He smiled at Jack for approval. Jack scowled and puffed on his pipe so ferociously Mae had to manically wave a towel around just to breathe. But Jack's point was made.

"Bosom is the word you're looking for," Dexter said. Elizabeth subconsciously looked down at her compacted chest straining against the buttons of her dress with a look of "Why would anyone *want* that?"

This went on for another hour and, every once in a while, Jack would put his head in his hands like he was sleeping. They shared topics covering high-rise skyscrapers, world wars, antibiotics, cash machines, the moon landing, presidents, fast food, computers, internet purchases, drones, telephones—

"Tell a fone, is that like your sale fone?" Willie perked up finally hearing something familiar.

"You're getting it, dude." Toke held his fist out for a bump from Willie. "And you don't even need a phone, really. You can lie in bed and talk into the air, requesting a pizza. In half an hour it's outside your door." Willie scrunched up his face, unsure of this, mouthing the new word "peetsuh."

"You know, we do have it pretty easy." Mae smiled and shrugged. "But most of us are always stressed and unsatisfied and have to have the newest thing. Then when we get it, we just want more and better."

By now, Jack and Elizabeth were staring straight ahead. Lost. Completely drained. Finally, Jack spoke up, "I don't know wat to say."

Elizabeth rubbed her temples for a miserable moment. "Maybe just tell us what has *not* changed."

"Well." Mae closed her eyes to think. "People still get old, get sick, and die. People still kill each other, even children, just for religious reasons. People are still dying of starvation while others throw food away. People are still homeless while others have five homes. Mothers with young children have to work outside the home and leave their children with other people—"

Toke groaned in agony. "Mae, you're depressing everyone."

"Fine," Mae said smugly, feeling slighted.

"We still have to go to school to learn things. We still need to work to earn money to buy stuff." Toke shook his head in disgust.

Dexter held up his finger to make a new point. "Almost anyone can become president. A stage actor, a black person, a peanut farmer—"

"A moron." Toke hijacked the topic. "Hell, even a woman can become president." He rolled his eyes in mock disapproval for Mae's sake.

She refused to satisfy the pleasure he got out of pushing her buttons. "In fact, people can marry anyone, no matter their race. Women go to college alongside of men, and black people can go to school alongside white people, share the same toilets and don't have to call anyone master or ma'am. Women become scientists, doctors, astronauts, lawyers—anything we want! We can own businesses and a house with the deed in our *own* name and not our husband's. That is, if we even *want* to have a husband at all."

Elizabeth sighed. "I do not want to be rude, but these stories are overwhelming. I do not know how to handle them in my head. I do not have a place to put them and it is exhausting me." Jack pushed himself up from the table, helped his wife up, and announced they were going to go to sleep.

As Mae prepared the smaller fire for the night, Willie continued to ask question after question, too excited to be sleepy. Toke and Dexter were enjoying themselves, tossing a dried bunny tail between them with no sign of weariness, much unlike herself. When she couldn't keep her eyes open one more second, she curled up in the chair and eventually fell asleep against Dexter, who wrapped his arm around her.

Chapter Fifty

A small breeze blew in from the south, flapping the clean shirts on the clothesline, whipping up the music of the wooden chimes and bringing the savory aroma of roasted duck to the entire farm. The hungry men stomped up the porch steps, but were immediately stopped by Elizabeth. "You men will eat out here. You can't bring that dirt into the house."

Willie smiled at the word "men."

"But the damn floor *is* dirt," Toke muttered as Elizabeth walked away.

"I'll not have you making disrespectful comments to de women. An' you must be watchful of your curses. Lizzie is not accustomed to dat sort of language. It must be understood, dis." Mae could hear Jack's scolding through the open door and smiled to herself.

"Yeah, okay." Toke looked embarrassed, being held accountable for one of his many snarky acts of sarcasm and unconscious use of profanity. Mae emerged from the house with a tray of hot biscuits and drinks and passed them around. Toke squinted up at her, adding, "Does that include Mae, too?" She squinted back at him mockingly, and "accidentally" spilled some of his drink into his lap before heading back into the house.

"You're a fellow full of spice an' goat dung," Jack said, laughing heartily. His humor was so self-entertaining that laughing *at* him was far more fun than laughing *with* him.

The second Jack inhaled his last bite, he slapped the table and stood. "Now, we get back to vork." He grabbed up his hat and fitted it back over his greasy head then lumbered down the porch steps. Dexter followed close behind with his mouth still full of food, while Willie shoveled the last of his lunch in his mouth, pocketed the remaining biscuit, and raced down the steps.

Toke caught Willie before he got too far. "Hey, bud," he coaxed, draping a heavy arm over Willie's shoulders, slowing him into a leisurely walk. "Mind showing me how to make a pipe like your dad's?"

Juggling an armful of dirty dishes on the porch, Mae called after him, "Remember Toke, you've been clean from nicotine for over a month, why not stop while it's easier…?" Unfortunately, her words didn't find a welcoming ear and just floated up into the trees. Shaking her head in disappointment, she exhaled.

Elizabeth looked up from wiping down the table and gave her a sympathetic smile. Her protective wall seemed to be melting away as her feelings toward the three of them warmed, and she relaxed.

And then there was Jack. No one could miss how happy he was to have their extra help now that he'd opened up to the truth. Even though his disappointment in their lack of experience at *everything* was very apparent, Toke and Dexter skated through chores in hours, that in the past, had taken Jack and Willie *days* to complete. And all those years of hard labor were etched on Jack's weathered face. Who would guess he was only thirty-seven?

After shaving a few flakes of soap into the scalding hot dishwater, Mae dumped in the greasy plates, suffering a painful splash. Alongside her, Elizabeth got busy carving up the small skinned body of an animal that might have been a squirrel. Glancing back over her shoulder to make sure they were alone, Mae felt this was a good time to ask Elizabeth some of the more private questions she'd been worrying about.

Since she was feeling healthy again, her menstrual cycle would be starting back any day, and she wanted to be ready for it. How did women handle it with no supplies? She saw nothing in the outhouse to indicate women even lived here.

Elizabeth surprised her and wasn't embarrassed by her candid questions, but rather factual. She made sure to wear dark colors on those particular days and just bleed into her clothes. Also, she applied a scented oil to her skin to mask any odor it might bring. Maybe women in the nineteenth century didn't bleed like women in the twenty-first. There was absolutely no way some dark clothing would hide the massive quantities of blood that poured out of her own body for five entire days.

Seeing Mae's horrified expression, Elizabeth explained further while finely mincing the squirrel's tiny organs. "But, now, with more people living in the house, I attach a small pouch that I've filled with rags onto a string belt that I wear around my waist. I'd be happy to make you one of your own." Then, as if she timed her next move, Elizabeth drained the dark red pool of the creature's blood into a bowl. "When the time is over, I slip away and wash my soiled rags in private." Mae nodded, understanding all too much, vowing to herself she'd invent the first disposable tampon.

Far above them, a scattering of songbirds clutched the high branches and boasted their cheery carols to those who would listen. This daily concert had become Mae's unappreciated substitute for her beloved Spotify.

But today it unpleasantly mutated into a loud brawl of unmerciful squawking and Mae couldn't change the channel.

"What do you suppose is happening out there?" Elizabeth said, without looking up.

Mae strode to the window, and her ears routed her eyes to the twitching bushes just beyond the gate. "Those sure are some pretty large birds!" she called outside.

A minute later, Yu'mi and Milok walked through the wooden gate with their horses close behind.

Mae smiled and waved from the doorway—just in time to see a third horse trot through the gate. She gasped and yanked off her apron so fast it almost tore, then flew down the steps.

There the little horse stood, sun-kissed in golden honey with a perfectly round white spot on her forehead. Joy welled up in Mae's heart just seeing her again. But when Yu'mi handed her the rope, her eyes teared up, overcome with happiness.

"She better horse now." Yu'mi smiled proudly.

The rope Mae held in her hand felt so unreal. *Was this little horse really her very own?* No matter how much she begged her mother when she was young, they never had the money to own a horse.

"Yu'mi has been working on this horse since you left her with him. And…" Milok reached up and smacked the sturdy leather seat of her horse's saddle a couple of times. "One of my brothers gave you his old saddle."

With a squeal, Mae wrapped her arms around the little horse, then around Yu'mi. Milok backed up, afraid he was next. Yu'mi was getting used to this body touching open affection so he didn't flinch this time. "You give horse name."

Mae peered into the mustang's big brown eyes as if searching for a secret. A moment later, she announced, "Trixie. Her name is Trixie."

"What the hell kind of name is Trixie?" Toke scoffed, walking up with the others. "She sounds like a little horse prostitute."

"It's in honor of Greg who was forced to watch Speed Racer anime reruns his entire childhood because his sister had a secret crush on Speed Racer." Mae ran her fingers over its shiny sun warmed coat. "Trixie was Speed Racer's girlfriend."

"Excellent idea." Dexter nodded.

Yu'mi tried out the new word, "Trisskee."

"Trixie."

"Tricksty."

"Almost. Trixie. Trick see."

"Treeksy."

Mae affectionately ran her fingers through her mane where Yu'mi had braided in seeds and feathers. Trixie was truly beautiful, and Mae was completely in love.

CHAPTER FIFTY-ONE

Over the past three weeks, Mae's vegetarian brain had been adjusting to her new life. It wasn't easy, but she was determined to adapt—she *had* to if she wanted to survive. Now, she could pluck the feathers from a warm chicken that was alive just minutes before without shedding tears or feeling queasy. It also helped to know the bird's feathers would be put to good use. The bulk of them would be stuffed into the mattresses, reserving the soft wispy down feathers for the layer next to the skin. And, when a new container was needed to store something, she'd simply hollow out an antler or a sizable hoof. She could finally think of these as by-products of the animal's death like she'd done so far with leather and fur. Using each part of their body gave the creature's sacrifice so much more meaning than just becoming food.

Elizabeth pointed out that the goats were due for a good combing, and Mae volunteered just to get out of the house. Goat hair was rough and coarse, but Elizabeth knew how to blend it with other softer animal fibers before spinning it into yarn. It was still too miserably itchy no matter what she mixed it with.

She sat in the shade in the orchard beyond the fence, letting one goat graze while she worked on the other one. The breeze carried over entertainment in bits and pieces of Toke's one-sided conversation with Dexter while they repaired yet another new hole in the fence. When the last goat was finished, she stuffed the hair into a sack and rambled over to where they were working.

Toke's ax came down hard, splintering off a long sharp piece of wood for a "poke." Dexter stuck the poke through to the other side of the fence, wedged it securely in place, and tied it down. These pointed sticks faced out to help keep the hungry would-be intruders from breaking through and making its next meal goat and chicken. Toke continued, "Did Jack steal this idea from *The Walking Dead*? Never mind, you're probably a documentary sort of guy." Arching his brows expectantly to Mae, she just shrugged, having never seen the show. With another heave of the ax, Toke buried the blade at the perfect angle and neatly trimmed off another poke. "So those guys would just leave the bodies there skewered on the pokes, which is not such a bad idea really." He kicked the new poke over to Dexter and dropped the ax. "It'd be like serving fresh meat-on-a-stick. This way, the hungry invader gets fed and leaves our animals, on this side of the fence, alone." He wiped his forehead with his sleeve and finished with, "I'll sketch it up for Jack and sign your name, Dex."

Squinting against the sun, Mae peered down the length of the fence. "So, do we know what keeps trying to plow through this?"

"Jack's pretty sure it's a wild boar," Dexter answered, finally joining the conversation. "And unless we do something about it, it'll keep making a lot of work for us."

Mae reached over and tested the sharp tip of the poke with her finger, mouthing a silent *ow*. "Will these keep a grizzly bear out?"

"A grizzly? Hell no," Toke scoffed. "Those suckers are mammoth—tall as a house. To one of them, this fence is made of toothpicks. And Ol' Gruff? He'd just be an appetizer. Jack says they're around, but we just haven't seen any yet." Mae had an image of the huge bear, like a visiting T-Rex, squeezing through the trees, snapping them off at their stumps, and simply stepping over to their doll-sized fence. Toke went on, "I hope these pokes also keep out the little asshole black bears that climb over and nab the gut ties I'm drying."

"Jack seems to take care of the real nuisances," Mae said with conflicted emotions.

"What the hell does bear taste like anyway?" Toke made a face like he didn't want to find out.

"Well, if you liked last night's stew, you like bear."

After the last dinner dish had been washed and put away, Mae wiped her red, chapped hands on the towel and flung it over her shoulder. She lugged the leftover dishwater from the kitchen to a worn spot on the floor in front of the bookshelf and poured it out. The grease and grime from the dirty water would help the muddy mess dry into a hard, protective seal.

"I must say, you're just turning into the perfect little housewife, Mae." Toke smiled at Jack for approval of his respectful comment, but Jack was lost in thought, and smoke.

Without a minute of rest, Mae picked up her sewing and sank into a chair. Over these weeks with the Foxes, she found her body adjusting to the second-hand smoke, and not getting the headaches like before. After all, she couldn't ask a man in his *own home*, especially in 1840, to step outside to smoke. Besides, they hopefully wouldn't be living with them for that much longer, so it shouldn't do too much harm. Anyway, tonight, she had a different battle to fight.

Every day of trying to convince Elizabeth only resulted in protests, but if Dexter stepped in, he being the voice of reason, she might actually listen. "Dexter, would you like to tell the Fox family why it's important to boil water when it comes from the creek?"

But, before Dexter could answer, Toke blurted out, "I can tell you." Mae rolled her eyes, wishing he would shut up. His role was just to agree.

With a skeptical smile, Dexter crossed his arms and sat back. "Okay, let's hear it."

Toke stood and paced a few steps, tapping his fingers together with the confident air of a professor in front of his classroom. "You might think the act of washing your hands with water is good enough, especially when your hands look clean, right?" He singled out Willie, who nodded, then continued. "But, did you know that bacteria don't die in cold water? In fact, they live happy lives, fornicating like crazy, raising large families of even more bacteria who move on, go to college, and have families of their own. Soon, there's whole cities of bacteria, then suburbs of cities connecting all the cities. Now, there's just a swarming mass of bacteria wanting more fast food and Super Walmarts killing everything that gets in their way."

Exhaling impatiently, Mae said, "Stay on topic please."

Continuing, Toke held up his hands. "Just think, your freshly washed hands could be harboring some of the most vicious killers out there."

Jack crossed his arms across his chest. "So, wat's dis, bac trerea an' wat makes it so bad den?"

Toke looked cross-eyed at Jack. "Geez. Has *no one* discovered bacteria yet?"

Jack shook his head with a shrug. "Nei, not dat I know of or at least it hasn't reached dese mountains. Not a lot makes it dis far op."

"Excuse me for a sec." Toke ducked out the back door and filled a clear jar from the water barrel, then placed it on the table in front of everyone. "There's evil stuff in this water that you can't see. It can make you sick and maybe even kill you. If something bad gets in that barrel, it will never leave. Your barrel stays full and never runs dry, thanks to your diligent water boy." Willie's face beamed with pride.

Elizabeth lifted the jar and peered through the water, looking unconvinced. "But it's clear as crystal."

"Bacteria are so freakin' small, they're pretty much invisible." Toke put his finger inside the jar and stirred it around. "Let me put it this way. Have you ever known anyone to die from cholera or yellow fever?"

"Too many," Jack said, with Elizabeth nodding.

"And there you go. It was bacteria that killed them. Just because they call it a name like cholera or yellow fever, it's all from *bacteria*." Toke leaned on the table, taking a teacherly pose. "The cup of water you drank this afternoon might have held an entire empire of bacteria."

Jack looked at the jar of water distrustfully then back at Toke. "So den, how dose dat backtrea get dere in de forst place?"

"The suckers get into the streams from things like shi—I mean, *poop* from animals and even poop from people." Toke began to pace again. "There's tons of crap that comes from living bodies." Dexter opened his mouth to add to the conversation, but Toke held up his hand for silence and turned back to his pupils.

Willie crinkled his face in a question. "So, should I stop emptying the chamber pots in the creek?" Mae cringed. *Blech. How had she missed him doing that?*

Toke groaned, but went on, "The insides of your bodies are probably already running rampant with parasites and crap, but you're so used to feeling the way you do that you don't notice how bad you really feel. You'll probably also expect to die pretty young because that's just what happens to people, right?" He slapped his hands down on the table and leaned over them. "But it doesn't have to be this way, people. You can kill the bacteria yourselves. One. Use soap when you wash your hands. It's their mortal enemy. Two. *Boil your freaking water.* You've been lucky so far because you drink so much of that flippin' tea. You've been killing it without even trying." Toke wiped his brow proudly and sat back down. "Dexter, I think it's your turn."

With a curt nod, Dexter cleared his throat. "There was this man called Louis Pasteur—"

"Boil or not?" Mae was losing her patience just to get a simple point across and raised her hand in a vote.

Toke raised two hands. "Boil. Duh."

"Yes, boil." Dexter raised his hand. "Except if it comes from a fresh spring, then you can use that directly. Or if you had a well, which you don't."

"We do have a spring, but it's a good long walk." Elizabeth made a gesture with her hand, which suggested miles rather than yards.

Willie's eyes widened in a flash of fear. Keeping the water barrel full was one of his primary chores and both his arms shot up. "Boil. Duh," he said, sounding like a mini-Toke.

Chapter Fifty-Two

Sunday couldn't come fast enough for Mae this week. The habit of their early routines left them not able to sleep in until noon like they wanted.

Breakfast and its lazy aftermath rolled the morning into the afternoon. The sun threw sparkles over the farm, scenting the air with baking pine needles. Mae took a deep cleansing breath and leaned back in her chair. "It always feels weird just sitting here. The only work I'm doing is to lift this teacup to my lips. I'm feeling useless and rubbery. So relaxing…but weird."

"Yeah." Dexter lifted his head up from a project of leather, twine, and sticks he was working on and rubbed his eyes. "I used to feel like I would give *anything* just to have one hour to work on my car. But now, I'm so preoccupied with working on things we need to *survive*. I don't miss her like I used to when we first got here."

"Same here. Now, I only think about my PlayStation half the day instead of twenty-four-seven." Toke kicked his feet up on the porch railing and reclined in his chair. "So, with all we've been through, what do you miss the most right now? In order of priority and not including people."

"If you asked me a month ago, when we first got here, I'd have easily said mascara, nail polish, my phone, a full-length mirror, and my fuchsia heels. But now, definitely a refrigerator."

"Flush toilets." Dexter meticulously sliced a thin strip off the scrap of leather. "And toilet paper."

"Drive-thru fast food and Cocoa Puffs." Toke slapped his armrest. "Wait, no—I miss my weed."

"My deodorant," Mae added. "In fact, I miss *all* our deodorants." She followed it with a gagging cough.

"Electricity. Or rather I'd love anything that actually *needs* electricity." Dexter diligently tied a series of knots and sliced off the excess.

Mae perked up. "Hey, isn't that something you can make *now*, with just a potato?"

"Hmm. I probably could." Dexter looked up. "But then, what would we use it on? So, I guess I should get to work on that part, too."

"What about inventing the telegraph, if they haven't already?" Mae's face brightened.

"Hell, why stop there? Go directly to the telephone. Then we could finally make our calls," Toke said, so seriously, Mae couldn't tell if he was joking.

From that point, their conversations went all over the place, entertaining themselves with their theories, complaints, memories, and similarities. "Okay," Toke said. "This isn't a bitch, but I don't feel like shit all the time like I did back home."

"It could be all the exercise we're getting in the fresh mountain air. I've never worked so hard in my life." Dexter had to stretch his back just thinking about it.

"Also, you're not eating enormous value meals, and the food is super organic. I mean, whole grain bread, tons of fiber, unrefined honey, no pesticides, no preservatives, no antibiotics and hormones in your meat, just good pure food," Mae said, looking over the farm, resting them on the humble garden. "Well, except, they do need to plant more greens and find a good source for vitamin C."

"The bread's a bit chewy, don't you think?" Toke wrinkled his nose.

"Chewy? You're complaining about the bread?" Mae sat up. "Do you realize we have to grind our flour every day? We don't have pre-sifted flour sitting around in bags. We make our own everything, from the source." She decided not to tell them how much time she spent sifting out the accidentally-ground bugs. "And when you men come in from the outside, you just see the finished food and us women simply lifting a little needle and thread."

"Sorry, not chewy. Fluffy bread made for angels." Toke smiled to fend off her steely look.

Mae sighed. "I would give anything to modernize this kitchen, but, each time I have a great idea, it requires something that we don't have or hasn't been invented yet, so I'm back to nothing again."

"Same here." Dexter rifled through the small pile of tools on the table until he found what he needed.

"Yeah." Toke let out a frustrated breath. "If we could only talk Jack into going down to the valley to pick up some things. Hell, it's just a week's ride, but he acts like it's a trip to Africa or something."

Mae added, imitating Jack's voice, "We need to vait to get more apples blah blah to trade wit blah blah to return wit enough guds to make de trip blah blah wortwhile." She rolled her eyes.

Toke joined in the rant. "Shit, if they *really* want to grow more apples, we'd have to clear more land, and it's not just the hacking down of the trees, it's removing the stumps that bites the most. And the tools we have suck a rat's ass. Even when Jack's not using his precious pickax and hammer that would do the work in half the time, we can't even look at them. Who chops down a tree with a tiny handheld ax? It's like using a feather to cut through one of Mae's burnt biscuits." She opened her mouth, wanting to protest his second jab at her cooking, but he was right. She had yet to master baking in a fireplace.

"It's bull." Toke stood and leaned on the porch railing, leering contemptuously at the orchard. "To make more money so we can buy better tools, we need to grow more apples. To grow more apples, we have to clear more land. And to clear more land, we need better tools. Shit keeps going."

"Maybe we can just leave." Mae stood, impatiently. "I feel so *stuck* here. I'm suffocating! I want to see what's out there." She swung her arms wide over the trees to the west. "We can take things to the next level now that we've got a horse. We can look for Greg further out, we've searched everywhere we can up here. Yu'mi and Milok persuaded everyone they knew to scour these mountains, and no one's turned up even the smallest clue." She shaded her eyes, trying to see past the milky haze of the distant mountains. "He'd most likely head down to the valley to find people, rather than further back in the mountains, like where we are."

"Let's be logical for a moment." Dexter stopped working for a moment. "We'll need money to start out with or something good to trade. We have neither. So then, we'll have to find jobs right away and what will we do when the bad weather hits? We'll end up spending all our earnings on food and shelter with nothing left to travel anywhere."

Mae slumped back down in her chair, losing all her momentum. "Okay, then. How about we make this our focus. Work hard, earn their trust, and maybe they'll give us a starter package to trade with."

"Yeah, because they're just swimming in surplus," Toke added sarcastically.

With a long, defeated sigh, Mae itched her sweating head under the green scarf. "Oh, I forgot," she said, shifting to a brighter mood. "Check this out." She began unwrapping her scarf to reveal small patches of hair about a quarter of an inch long. "It's *really* growing."

"You're doing better than us." Dexter rubbed the short fuzz his own head.

"Heh, so what about other places?" Toke was interested now.

"None of your business," she said, scowling and letting her fingers explore her scalp. "I always thought having hair grow in would feel scratchy. Like when I'd kiss Greg after he hadn't shaved for a couple days. But this is soft, like fine baby hair."

"Yeah, must be the difference between being chewed off by an invisible creature or being sliced off with a sharp razor." Toke itched the tiny hairs on his arm.

"Or dissolved." Dexter brushed off the table under him.

"So, what do you think that water is made of anyway?" Mae said, wrapping the scarf back around her head. "Is it organic like some sort of microscopic piranha? Or maybe a chemical, like acid?"

"I'm at a complete loss over that one—but!" Dexter raised a victorious arm. "They're finished!" Smiling proudly, he held up his new pair of handcrafted eyeglasses.

"Dude!" Toke walked over for a closer inspection. Dexter had framed his old glass lenses with thin strips of soft leather to hold the lenses securely in place. These he hinged to two carved and polished sticks with braided twine.

"Let's see them on!" Mae encouraged.

Dexter looped the sticks around his ears and adjusted a few times until they sat straight. He fidgeted uncomfortably under Mae's far too long of a stare. How could he still look so hot wearing a contraption like that? "You really rock those, Dex."

Toke's lips twitched as he stifled a giggle. "I'm changing your name to Poin-Dexter."

Mae broke into a laugh and slapped Toke a high-five for the retro-future-brilliance of his joke.

Chapter Fifty-Three

After two more nights of molestation, unable to flee its post, the ravaged fence trembled vulnerably under Jack's glare. "Enough of dis!" His words smacking away the peaceful calm of early dawn.

A moment later, Jack stomped out of the barn like Rambo, brandishing his loaded rifle, three hunting knives sheathed to his belt, and wearing a murderous smile.

Knowing what this meant, Willie let out a whoop and excitedly ping-ponged around the farm. "Get your weapons—we're bringing home the wild boar!"

Elizabeth peeked out the kitchen window at all the ruckus. "Goodness, we haven't had a boar for nearly a year. Maybe one day he'll catch one of those toefews you like so much, Mae."

Mae turned her head away to stifle a snort. "Aw, that's okay. I'm sure they're nowhere around here."

It didn't surprise Mae when Toke had the excuse that he wasn't feeling that well and should stay home. He always wore the tough guy shell, captivated by guns and violence, but, when it came down to the actual *killing*—to snuffing out a life with his own hands—he had no stomach. This farm life could be a bit brutal for a secret empathetic soul like his.

With the hunting party gone, they ate an early dinner and retired before dusk. Mae cozied up under her blanket in the chair and closed her eyes to the gentle hush that shrouded the farm. Elizabeth's fingers softly rustled through bags of goat hair as she sorted and combed and prepped it for spinning. And even more quiet, straddling across the bench, Toke practiced his important new skill of pumping out a string of smoke rings, then stabbing them through the center with a sharp spear of smoke.

So thoroughly relaxed, Mae's mind let its protective walls down, and she felt the pain of her heart wrenching for Greg. She craved to bury her head in his chest and feel the warmth from his strong arms as he wrapped them tightly around her. No one in the world could make her feel as happy as Greg could. She missed him so desperately, she felt crumbled inside, and her throat began to tighten. Wiping away her tears, and before she became a sobbing mess, Mae burrowed deep in her blanket and forced her mind shut.

As dusk's shift came to an end, it punched its timecard out and took what remained of afternoon's warmth away with it. Elizabeth wrapped her shawl around her shoulders, drew the curtains, and lit the evening lanterns. She carried one to the porch where she waited for the hunting party's return.

Startled out of her nap, Mae jumped to her feet. "They're back!" She grabbed a lantern and ran outside just as the noisy parade of pounding hooves and excited voices burst through the gate. In with them came the body of an enormous boar, dangling by its feet from a long wooden pole.

Toke raced over to help with the load while Willie brought in the horses. As soon as Mae caught sight of Trixie, she flew down the steps to check on her. But, when she got close to the dead animal, she couldn't take another step. As it passed her by, she stared into its lifeless eyes and felt consumed with profound shame. This beast, so magnificent and powerful once, now hung flaccid and vacant.

They carried it across to the table rock and hoisted its monstrous body up. With its front half now supported on the rock's edge, Jack adjusted the pole so they could roll the rest of the animal forward but, suddenly, with an earsplitting crack, the pole broke in half and the full weight of the boar slammed to the ground, thundering the earth up through the soles of their feet.

Elizabeth was startled and dropped her lantern, so Mae rushed over with hers. The light illuminated the creature's gray bark-like skin that sagged heavily from its immense corpse, splaying its suffocating mass on the ground like a beached jellyfish.

"Dexter!" Mae screamed when her light shined on Dexter, who was trapped underneath.

"Oh, shit—Dex!" Toke quickly seized the boar's neck to free Dexter's head. Each of them grabbed an appendage of the boar, and they heaved the dead weight off of him.

Mae rushed to his side. "Dex, say something. Please."

Pain overtook his beautiful face as he bit back his intense agony, squeezing his eyes shut. Through gritted teeth, he said, "I can't move…I can't move my back."

Jack sent Willie to get the wooden ladder, and Elizabeth covered it with a blanket. They carefully lifted Dexter onto it, wincing sympathetically as he howled in torturing spasms. When they got to his bed, each of them took a corner of the blanket and transferred him gently.

"I'll make him some tea." Elizabeth left to go to the kitchen.

"Tea? Really?" Toke smirked in utter bewilderment. "Dex might have broken his back, and she's making *tea*?" He grabbed the blanket from his own bed, shook it out, and laid it over Dexter.

Mae tucked it around Dexter, just like her mother did when she was sick. When she got to his feet, she untied and slid off his boots, then lightly pinched his toes. "Do you feel that?"

"Feel what?" Dexter groaned.

Mae and Toke met each other's pained eyes with shared understanding.

"Dude, you might want to check with Jack, I'm sure he's got workers' comp," Toke offered, awkwardly sidestepping the serious probability that Dexter could be paralyzed from the waist down.

Once the tea had cooled, Mae raised his head while Elizabeth spooned the barely tolerable bitter tea into his mouth, explaining its purpose. "This tea is steeped from a highly prized herb the Ma'camo trade for in the far South. We're quite lucky to have some."

The tea had surprising potency, and soon Dexter lost all lucidity. Without his high functioning brain working out the world's problems, he was set free and floated away into a tranquil sleep. Mae picked up his empty cup and sniffed it. "Geez. What's in this stuff?"

Chapter Fifty-Four

Dexter's pain had worsened by morning, and he still had no feeling below his hips. After propping him up, Mae helped him drink a mug of willow bark tea, which the Foxes used like aspirin, then fed him biscuits smothered in elk gravy. It occurred to her that he would need to go to the bathroom. "Um, I'm going to leave the chamber pot right next to you here and give you some privacy." Did she seriously expect him to aim it in the pot? He could barely move his arms. "Let me know if you need Toke to help you with anything bigger…" This last part was way too awkward, so she selfishly slipped out of the room.

When she informed Toke of his new nursing duty, all he said was, "Hellllll no." But he was also told he didn't have that choice to make and had better hurry up.

Between breakfast and the short time Mae had been away, the kitchen was transformed into butchering central, and she had no idea what was in store for her squeamish self. In the past, she'd been able to duck out of the slaughter at the goriest moments since Elizabeth and Willie could handle it fine. But, with the boar at least three times the size of anything before, Elizabeth needed everyone's help. In no time, and without vomiting or fainting, Mae earned an unwanted degree in advanced animal anatomy.

With the lack of refrigeration, the boar had to be preserved as quickly as possible in this heat, or it would decay and provide a delicious feast for hungry maggots. If it wasn't smoked, salted, or pickled, it would have to be dried or preserved in brine, and the whole family got involved.

Once skinned, Jack needed his ax to cut through the boar's dense bones and cut its body into manageable pieces. He and Toke hauled away the skin and left the rest for Elizabeth. She began by cutting away large hunks of meat and putting anything one wouldn't find in a typical grocery meat department to the side.

Mae laboriously sliced the raw meat into thin strips and brought each batch outside to Willie. He smoked the pork over three large fires using special wood they'd saved up for this occasion and basted it in the dripping fat. For hours, the farm marinated in smoke, intoxicated the senses to a carnivorous delirium, and caused constant pilfering from his dad and Toke.

The boar's two large back legs were laid on a bed of salt where Elizabeth packed more salt and spices into their every little crevice. Both of these hams were strung up in the pantry where they'd hang for about six months until they lost a third of their weight. For the belly piece, Elizabeth smothered it in salt with a little sugar which would cure into a slab of bacon in a much shorter time than the ham.

Mae was impressed. For people who had no knowledge of bacteria, at least they were aware of the need to dry the meat out to prevent bacteria from growing without a refrigerator. And just like with Yu'mi, the Foxes refused to waste any part of the animal. This is where Jack and Toke joined forces for creative "fun," visiting often to pull from Elizabeth's "miscellaneous" pile.

Out of the boar's stomach sac, Jack showed Toke how to make a water container that one of them could wear. Then with the tusks, they'd be making new handles for broken tools. And that was just the beginning…

Mae's hands ached from slicing, so periodically she'd check in on her sleeping patient to give her hands a few minutes rest. With each visit, she found herself lingering longer and longer after he fell asleep. She was captivated by the pure perfection of his peaceful face, so beautiful it was difficult to tear herself away. Eventually, Elizabeth had to pop her head through the curtain. "I'm sure he's fine now, he's quite asleep. I could use your help out here."

A few brutally long hours later, Mae sliced the last piece of meat and delivered it to Willie. She raised her face to the sun and laughed, spinning around, feeling such relief that the blood was finally done. What she really needed was a serious bath and began walking toward the creek.

But somehow, Elizabeth's voice found its way to her ears and floated in like toxic fumes. "Mae, dear, I need you." Mae's shoulders slumped with a deflated spirit, being robbed of her small bit of joy. She slowly turned around and trudged back to her prison.

This was when Mae learned the conventional part was over, but it wasn't even close to the end. The large mound of miscellaneous wasn't to go into the trash, compost, or animal feed because this was the arena where Elizabeth shined. And so, for the rest of the afternoon, Elizabeth proudly shared all her gourmet secrets, using every butcher knife and meat cleaver the Foxes owned.

First, she instructed Mae to dig the four feet out of the pile while she prepared the fermented cider to brine them into a revolting-looking treat. Then onto the marrow, which they scooped from the bones and ground up with the eyeballs, most of the boar's face, his genitals, and even the anus, turning them into a large bowl of unpleasantness. By now Mae's mind had numbed entirely, sparing her from vomiting.

Next on the list was the putrid job of cleaning out the intestines. Most of them they used for the sausages, stuffing them with grain, spices, blood, and the mystery ingredients. The remaining intestines that she handed over to Jack were indispensable as ropes for tying wooden parts together that tightened snug as they dried.

The bones had been boiling for hours, and the sludge they created was used for things she never thought of and wished to forget. If she weren't a vegetarian before, she would definitely be one now.

With a little light still left in the sky, they carried the wrapped and preserved meat to the outside cellar. This was not like any cellar Mae had known, but simply a narrow and deep cavern dug into the side of a well-shaded part of the hillside. All through the summer, the cellar stayed fairly cool from the ice that Jack and Willie cut in the winter from the frozen creeks high up in the snowy mountains. Insulation gathered from nature was tightly packed over the contents, and a thick log door covered the opening to shut out any foraging animals. Jack had his gun for the bears.

The next time Mae checked in on Dexter, he was wide awake and wanted to hear, in full disgusting detail, all they did with every part of the boar. She swallowed the bile rising in her throat as she relived the barbaric mutilation all over again.

This day of blood was the longest day yet. All that remained of the boar was an enormous pile of fat, more than any human could possibly use. But Elizabeth cleared that up by explaining they'd put every bit of it to good use in the morning.

The turbulent momentum of the day rudely followed Mae into bed, and she couldn't fall asleep. Her mind swam with disturbing images of lost piglets crying at the gate looking for their daddy. She helplessly stood by as Elizabeth swooped down and yanked their little eyeballs out of their heads and chopped off their tiny feet. Mae tossed in her sleep so much the bench made bruises where her bones repeatedly hit the hard wood.

She squeezed her eyes shut and forcibly scanned her brain for something happy—and there it was. Greg's smiling face. He wrapped himself around her like a hotdog bun and softly cooed their special song in her ear. She could almost feel his soft face next to hers, his lips so warm on her skin. She felt safe in his arms, protected. Finally, her mind felt at peace, and she gently drifted into a sleepy twilight. Greg lingered for a while in Mae's cloudy subconscious...before slowly morphing into Dexter. And now it was he who kept her safe and protected in her dreams. But Mae was sound asleep at this point and wouldn't remember any of it by morning.

Chapter Fifty-Five

Greg lay unconscious at the base of Sailor Rock for nearly four hours. He woke to a raging headache that pounded through his skull and a stabbing pain in his broken leg, so horrific, it had to be hell.

Gritting his teeth, he worked up the courage to look down at his leg—but now wished he hadn't. His shin was bent where it should be straight, jutting unnaturally to the side. This meant the one remaining unbroken bone, the fibula, was fractured too. What, was he made of glass?

To mentally prepare himself for what he needed to do, Greg closed his eyes and wished he was somewhere else. He knew the precise splinting of *this* break was now more crucial than ever so it would heal right and be weight-bearing. And, judging by the severity of the pain, he knew the sharp splintered bones must have sliced through some of his muscle.

Scattered around were the sticks and ties from his old splint, but he was able to reach them with little effort. Anticipating the inferno of pain that would soon engulf him whole, he found a soft branch for between his teeth. After a series of slow, deep breaths, he bit down on the wood and began the torturous straightening of his leg and the careful lining up the narrow bones. But it took only fifteen seconds before he had bitten through the branch and almost broken off a tooth.

Nausea whipped through him when the pain was at its worst, but he was forced to push through it until he tied the last splint in place. He wiped the dripping sweat from his eyes and face and finished by buckling his belt around the outside of the braces for added strength.

His leg throbbed from deep within, almost numbing itself out. But, he had to start back up Sailor Rock before dark, and before hungry animals smelled the fresh blood dripping from his cuts and wanted the human meat encased within. He adjusted the belt around the splints until he could read his favorite quote that Dexter had gotten engraved into the leather for his eighteenth birthday. "Screw it, let's do it!" he repeated, over and over, hoping for inspiration…any minute now.

Something to his side moved and caught his eye. Then branches rustled, and his body tensed, acutely aware of the vulnerable state he was in. Bracing himself against the rock behind him, he turned his head cautiously in the direction of the noise, then exhaled with a soft deprecating laugh. Caught in the same net as the rabbit before were two fat quail, struggling for their freedom.

Dragging himself over to the birds, he pulled the entire net from its ties, wrapping the live quail up inside. A couple of feet away he also spotted a patch of miner's lettuce and plucked out a leaf—*a little sour, but not too bad*—and stuffed a few bunches inside the net with the quail before tying the entire package to his belt loop. A sharp splinter of pain ran up his leg reminding him of the agonizing climb back up to the top of Sailor Rock he had in front of him.

Nearly the entire night he wrestled in his sleep, delirious with pain, but, thankfully, at some point, his mind shut off, and he was able to sleep for a few hours.

He dreamt of horses and the hoofbeats stopping at the base of Sailor Rock, just as the day before. He fought frantically to get to them, but being asleep, it was only in his head. That is, until a man's voice shouted in the distance and another shouted back.

Greg suddenly awoke and bolted upright, banging his head on the cave's low ceiling. The voices were real, the horses were real, but growing fainter. *They were leaving!*

Panicked and beyond desperate, Greg heaved himself out of the cave, shouting so loud, he was mostly screaming. With careless speed, and so focused on getting to the other side, he was able to block out the tortured wailing from his leg and drag himself across on his butt. He stopped dangerously close to the edge and looked down.

No, no, no...not again.

All that stared back was a vacant patch of sunlit dirt. Not even the sound of hoofbeats could be heard in the distance, but he knew he hadn't imagined it. *Thanks for the pile of horse shit!*

An assortment of birds happily chattered "good morning" from the large oak below, and Greg greeted them back with, "Shut the fuck up!" With the excitement gone, the pain in his leg rapidly took over, and he forced himself to finally look. His head jerked back in alarm, and he sucked in air with a shuddering gasp. Swollen to twice its size, his skin painfully bulged out between the splints like soft caramel. The pressure was excruciating, but if he loosened his brace too much, he'd risk the bones separating.

His hand left a wet patch on his pants but how did his hand get wet? Looking around, he zeroed in on a dark glistening area under the Sailor's only ear. As he got closer, he spotted a tiny trickle and stuck his mouth right up to the wet stone and sucked thirstily. How could there be water? Sailor Rock had always been bone dry. Without further questioning, he propped Mae's water bottle under the dripping and waited.

No faster than a slug on a sidewalk, and a full bottle of water in hand, he worked his way out to the front of the beard, found a semi-comfortable position to keep watch, shout for his friends, and prop his leg up to help it heal.

It was now the third day of leaving his phone to dry out in the sun. He prepared himself with a deep breath and a little prayer, then pressed the power button. It powered on. "Holy shit—holy shit—" Greg quickly typed in 911, then the screen went black. He whacked it several times in his palm and pressed the power button again. *C'mon, Fender baby. You beautiful... beautiful*—but it had nothing more to give. "Piece of Apple shit!" He yelled profanities into the sky then slumped back down, defeated.

Every so often, he'd search the sky and listen for a rescue helicopter, but there was never anything. All he ever heard were the same old tiresome sounds of rustling wind, buzzing insects, chattering animals, and singing birds. But the hardest part of convalescing was being bored out of his mind. *Where the hell are all the people? Since when do teenagers follow rules? Why haven't any jumped the fence or cut the lock on the road? What's wrong with the youth these days?*

He started rubbing his brow to beat off a stampeding headache and let his eyes crawl across the giant pristine face of the sailor man. A slow curl began tugging at the side of Greg's lips as an idea formed in his head. "To hell with the parents and their overzealous, anal-retentive, joy-crushing, Sailor Rock clean-up squad!" he shouted out to the trees. His eyes brightened and he felt rejuvenated with adrenaline. "From this day forward, a new generation of art will grace this old sailor! Make an arrest and rescue me in the process!" With renewed optimism and sporting a devilish grin, he knew exactly what he would draw and turned the Sailor's northern cheek, with the largest flat area, into his grateful canvas.

After he collected the sturdiest rocks he could find, he chose one for a hammer and started chiseling the outline of the first howling wolf of his and Dexter's symbol. He found the stone's surface hard and solid, and he could only dig down an eighth of an inch, but that was enough. *This will be massive! No one on the road to or from Sacramento could possibly miss it!*

Chapter Fifty-Six

Through the next two weeks of his broken bone's painful mending, Greg never failed to keep a lookout from the sailor's beard every morning. Still feeling optimistic that any day his friends would see his shirt-flag flying high or someone might send a rescue crew. And, when the heat of the noon sun bullied out the brisk morning air, he'd retreat back into the shade where he'd tie his long hair back into a neat puffy ponytail, smooth his scraggly beard, and resume the daily etching into the Sailor's cheek.

By now, Greg's flesh hung from his emaciated body, but his leg looked much better. The swelling and pain had lessened dramatically, and he could stand for long periods of time. So, he'd made the decision that in the morning he'd be leaving for home. Besides, it had been two days since he'd eaten the very last piece of smoked quail and the squirrel he'd caught himself. If he stayed on the rock any longer, he'd have to start a new diet of insects.

After scolding himself for sleeping in so late, Greg hastily prepared himself for his adventure ahead. It took an hour to descend Sailor Rock, but once at the bottom, he realized he left his phone and wallet on the small ledge in the cave but there was *no frickin' way* he'd be going all the way back up.

His crutch still lay at the base of the rock where he left it, and he easily picked up the trails that the previous visitors' horses left. Feeling confident now in his survival skills, he might just pitch a new survivalist reality show to the networks. *How to kill, cook, and eat, using a house key and a broken flashlight.*

He limped along for an hour, but still hadn't found the main path everyone took to get to Sailor Rock. This was the path that would take him to the long dirt road that would lead him to the highway where he could flag someone down. He was starving and running out of energy.

"Ohh maaan..." he moaned when the horses' trail split, and he had a choice to make. Down the trail to the left, he saw nothing, and down to the right he saw a couple of piles of somewhat fresh horse manure and felt hopeful that there must be a ranch or a house not too far off.

Hurrying down the right with a furious limp, he called out for help, not holding back the desperation in his voice. When he stopped to take a break by leaning against a tree, his fingers picked up on a piece of twine tied all the way around its trunk. He gave it a little tug, then followed it a way until he came to the end. A small exhausted rabbit, nearly a baby, was frantically trying to wiggle free of the snare that kept tightening it in a slow strangle.

Even though Greg was beyond famished, he didn't have the heart to kill a baby anything. He loosened the twine around the bunny's neck and it immediately darted away, disappearing into the low brush. "That was for you, my Mae."

Continuing down the path, he passed two more empty snares hanging like nooses, waiting to asphyxiate the next unsuspecting animal. But the third one he came to held a large rabbit that had fought so hard already, it had extinguished its own life. Greg had become so weak he could hardly keep walking, so he pierced a hole in the rabbit's neck and dripped the disturbingly warm blood into his mouth.

Fwap! Suddenly, an arrow pierced the tree next to Greg's head. *What the hell?* He quickly ducked, falling onto his butt, and looked around in fear as much as in disbelief. Dropping the rabbit, he raised his arms in surrender and attempted to stand, which was futile without his crutch. Then with one arm still up, he slowly lowered the other and was finally able to pull himself to standing. *Fwap!* All at once he had a painful, peculiar sensation like being punched and stung at the same time by a dog-sized bee. When he looked down, he found a thin arrow with short white feathers sticking a few inches out of his shoulder. Paralyzed with fear, he just stood there, watching the dark crimson spot on his shirt slowly expand.

Far too bizarre to comprehend at the moment, but either way, it was real. Someone was trying to kill him! *Whoosh!* Another arrow whizzed past his ear, startling him out of his stupor. Without looking back, he took off through the trees, dragging his leg behind.

He would keep going north, uphill, the opposite direction the horses had gone, putting as much distance as he could between them. If he didn't come to a road or a house, he would just keep going until he did. He could be safe in the mountains, with plenty of places to hide.

Chapter Fifty-Seven

Mae awoke on the hard dirt floor, tired and sore. She stared at the ceiling without moving, trying to psych her stomach up for another day of carnage. She scratched at the dried blood and crusty boar fluids spackled to her body, feeling like the wretched mess she looked.

Her first task was to chop the fat into smaller pieces and load them into the large iron kettle. This was then placed in the hearth over a low flame so it could slowly melt for half a day without burning. All too soon, the entire house was filled with the putrid odor of five soaking wet Labradors fresh from rolling in pig poop. The sickly stench found its way into every corner of the house and yard, and Mae needed to escape or she would vomit.

It was Elizabeth who suggested Mae take a break and give herself a good cleaning in the creek. Mae was on that in seconds, however, with something much better in mind.

She grabbed a small towel, saddled up Trixie, and the two of them took off through the gate, following the creek up the mountain. A short ride later, they emerged through the dense forest of trees and into a small humble clearing. In the center stood a large shady oak tree with massive roots, one which clamped over the narrow creek like a giant wooden claw. The delightful sound of the water slipping through its burly maze of crooked fingers gave off such a tranquil charm, Mae took no time to tether Trixie, kick off her shoes, and declare it her own private day spa.

Desperate to rid her body of all piggy bits, she completely submerged herself in the freezing water, clothes and all. She swished around like a washing machine, belting out a confusing mashup of tunes until she felt sufficiently laundered like a clean popsicle.

With her wet dress draped over a sunny bush, and her undergarments over another, she lay her bare body on the small towel. She closed her eyes as her mind immersed in the rich spectrum of nature's chorus.

She woke in a start to Trixie's whinny and an anxious stomp of her foot. She sat up and for a moment forgot where she was, feeling a little dazed from her nap. The shade had moved, and she must have been asleep in the direct sun for hours. Once she got her shoes on, she collected her chemise and underdrawers that were already thoroughly dry. How long had she been out?

The bush she remembered draping her dress over was now bare, even the ground beneath it. In fact, her dress wasn't on *any* of the bushes, nor branches, nor anywhere. She stopped a moment to gather her thoughts and retrace her steps in her head. Just then an eerie feeling came over her like someone was watching her. Mae's heartbeat quickened, and she edged toward Trixie. That's when she noticed Trixie's rope had been untied from the branch. Someone had been there while she slept. Her heart gave a lurch, and her stomach clamped, and she stood there frozen, not sure what to do next.

Then to her extreme relief, a shot rang out, and Willie called her name from further down the mountain. Suddenly, in the shadows just a few yards away—a lashing of branches followed by a flurry of snapping twigs and whoever had been in there—was gone.

Without another thought, Mae hurtled herself onto Trixie and raced from her former piece of paradise back down the mountain toward Willie.

When she found him, he looked down, embarrassed, seeing her only in her women's underclothes. "Willie!" Mae said breathlessly. "Someone's up there! They stole my dress—and almost Trixie."

"Stay here, I'll get it back," he insisted.

"No, it could be some sicko, let's just get out of here."

"Well, all right." He turned his horse around grudgingly. "But only because Ma needs you back."

Never feeling so happy to be back at the farm, Mae raced into the house, leaving Willie to put Trixie away. "Someone stole my dress!" she cried, pulling her only other spare clothes out of the dirty laundry.

Elizabeth didn't know what to make of her story since Mae's exposed darkened skin revealed she had clearly been without her dress for a long time in the sun. "If I could offer some advice, my dear, I wouldn't be telling Johan about this. He's got a good mind to go out there shooting at anything that moves. And, since no one got hurt, it's probably best to forget it happened." She dismissed the incident like that so they could get back to work.

When Mae tracked down Toke, he just laughed it off, wishing he'd been there to see it. Her face steamed and she let out a frustrated huff then stormed back to the house to find the one person who would understand the true seriousness of what just happened. And he didn't let her down. Dexter's voice was full of worry and concern, and he vowed when he got better, he'd be right out there with a gun, hunting the thief down.

By the time she walked back into the kitchen, her nerves had calmed some, so she pulled a stool up to the counter ready to at least watch. Elizabeth was finishing pouring the last of the melted fat through the cheesecloth—which, to Mae's relief, did an excellent job at straining out loads of creepy things. The transformation from the hideous massacre of fatty pink into this ketogenic liquid gold inspired her. "My first tallow," Mae said proudly. "It's beautiful."

"My dear," Elizabeth kindly corrected. "We can only make tallow from elk and deer, or even cattle and sheep if we can get them. The fat from them hardens quite firm, so theirs is best used for candle making and strong soaps for dishes and laundry." Mae took a pinch of the cooling fat and rubbed it between her fingers. Elizabeth continued, "Since the fat we have here *today* is from a pig, it is much too soft for tallow but will make excellent lard for cooking and soap that will be much gentler on our skin." Mae looked down at their rough, abused hands, cracked from the hours spent gripped around a hard bar of soap, scrubbing stains from clothes or in the dishwater where it brutally etched away at their skin like an acid bath.

"And now, I've something special for us," Elizabeth added with a confiding wink. Into a small black pot, she added three ladles of the semi-liquid lard. Then, from around the kitchen, she collected a special mix of dried and fragrant herbs which she crumbled into the pot. With a quick stir, she took it to the hearth and suspended the pan over a single flame. It took only minutes for the heat to kick awake the dormant herbs and perfume the room with its expressive sass, chasing away any lingering tallow funk.

Once off the heat, the liquid in the pot cooled to a creamy white. Elizabeth gave them each a generous scoop of the fragrant healing balm to rub into the chapped and thirsty skin of their overworked hands.

The very last remnants of boar had been put to good use, and hopefully, they'd never bring another animal of that size in this house again. Mae sat by the fire with the satisfied feeling of completion and began the first stitches into what would one day become her new dress. Tomorrow she'd find Yu'mi and Milok and tell them about the predator and her stolen dress and see if they knew anything. She didn't want to admit it, even to herself, but she actually looked forward to the morning and the return of her boring daily routine.

Chapter Fifty-Eight

Mae was only two hours into her morning chores when she noticed the three large baskets of apples sitting on the kitchen table. A feeling of dread clouded over her meager ray of sunshine. Willie came stomping up the porch steps carrying a bucket overflowing with even more apples. "Harvest time," he announced, and dumped them in with the others before heading back out again.

After setting down the large kettle she hauled in from the back porch, Elizabeth sat at the table. She handed Mae one of the paring knives and began to peel the first apple, looking expectantly at Mae to do the same.

Mae looked distrustfully at the small knife in the palm of her hand and then at the ease in which Elizabeth carved away each peel in a perfect, unbroken coil. She made it look effortless, so Mae scooted in across from her and started on her first apple.

Without the use of an apple peeler, Mae felt like a toddler giving a gentleman a close shave with a straight-edged razor. Though trying to be careful, she sliced off his chin, gouged out his cheek, lopped off his nose, and sheared his lips completely off before sending him on his way and starting on her next victim.

For every apple Mae peeled, Elizabeth finished six. She despairingly eyed the three baskets whose contents never went down with the constant replenishing from Willie. Stopping for a moment, she examined the beginning of a blister where the knife handle dug into her hand. "Don't they have machines that do this?"

"Perhaps. I just know that we don't have one."

Mae tried another tactic. "Did you know that the healthiest part of an apple is right under the skin? The skins that we're *peeling off*?"

"Don't you worry any. Johan uses the peels and even the cores in his hard cider. And we get our cider vinegar from his failed batches."

Studying the colorful mound of peels between them, Mae plucked up a spiral of red streaked with brilliant flames of yellow. Then she pulled out another of bright green that blended into a candy pink at its base, thinking they would make beautiful earrings.

Elizabeth picked up a coil of golden yellow and orange and looked at it admiringly. "As you can see, my Johan experiments quite a bit with his apples. There should be probably ten or twenty kinds by now." She smiled with fond recollection. "It all started when he met a man that sold him some apples quite different than he had ever seen. Johan asked the man to teach him how he could grow these unusual apples to take home to his farm. The man was eager to share his craft and demonstrated how to experiment by splicing together parts of one tree that could survive the freezing winters, disease, and rot, with another whose roots were too fragile to survive those conditions but bore delicious fruit." Mae picked up one of the apples, examined it, then picked up another. Elizabeth nodded toward the apple. "That one is best for cider and vinegar, and those over there, for pie." She handed Mae another she had just shined. "And this one is for eating," she said with a wink. Like Mae had any desire to eat an apple after she was mercilessly tortured by them all afternoon.

Just as with the exhausting days of boar, Mae had to use every excuse she could to give her hands a break and check on the convalescing Dexter. She found herself unusually drawn to these visits. Not just to relieve her painful blisters or take a break from the tedious monotony of peeling and slicing, but she simply liked being close to him and taking care of him, and she especially liked him needing her. Earlier she had brought him a basket of apples and a knife to relieve his boredom. This turned out to be a tremendous help in strengthening his hands and arms. Sometimes Mae felt jealous with the attention he gave each apple, and he was often completely unaware she was even there.

Quite unlike the giant boar, apples could sit around for weeks before getting soft. But, Elizabeth was a workhorse and constantly worried about preparations for the winter, so they peeled nearly non-stop for days, taking only short breaks to cook quick meals and do the most basic of chores.

A portion of the apple slices were strung and dried, while others were made into apple leather to eat like candy. Many were sliced into wedges, cooked with sugar and water, loaded into glass jars and small glazed pots then sealed over with melted wax. Mae thought about how glass was so precious here, and how hard it was to come by. Then she thought about her recycle bin back home, filled to the top with perfectly useful jars that Elizabeth would have cherished.

Mae watched in awe as the Energizer Bunny unloaded bucket after bucket of apples without taking a break. But this time, she caught him before he headed back outside. "Willie, don't you get sick of apples? I mean, they seem to be a part of *every single* meal in one form or another. I'm so sick of them already, I feel bile rise in my throat with just the smell of them."

He stopped at the door and looked thoughtful. "I guess so. But Ma mixes lots of things in with them so they taste different. And we trade for other food like dried fish, corn, and even medicine from the Ma'camo with them. Soon, Pa will take a few barrels down to the big valley and come home with sacks of grain, salt, sugar, and so much other stuff we need." He squinted and looked down at his feet. "I guess I'm afraid to say I'm tired of them because if God hears me, he might make them not grow one year to teach me a lesson."

"Don't worry, he won't hear you. I'm too busy monopolizing his ears with things that *I* want." Willie didn't quite know what to say to that, so he smiled politely and left.

After three long hours, the blessed time had finally arrived. Mae raised the last peeled apple over her head and cheered to the end of the dreaded apple days. She nearly cried she was so happy.

Elizabeth didn't join in her joy, but smiled empathetically. For some reason, she felt compelled to pop all Mae's party balloons and explain that the northern orchard, the apples best for making apple butter and apple jelly, would not ripen for a few more weeks. Mae buried her disheartened head in her folded arms and pounded her fist on the table. Please, *Dexter, please get better so we can get out of this nightmare.*

CHAPTER FIFTY-NINE

Sitting in her usual spot, doing her usual thing, Mae watched Dexter sleep. After two weeks of this routine, she knew each sprouted hair of his brows and lashes, the daily growth of facial hair that curled gently around his upper lip, and when his nose twitched in his sleep, she gushed with adoration. Sometimes, he'd have a troubling dream, and she'd hold his hand until he settled.

Now that he had full use of his arms, he didn't need to rely on her as much. He said his pain had lessened dramatically over the last week so the swelling in his vertebrae must have gone down. She worried if he never got the use of his legs again, not only how devastating that would be for him, but he also wouldn't be able to make their eventual trip back through the tunnel and hopefully back home. And they could never leave him here, so that meant all three of them would be stuck back in 1840.

With a sigh, she stood and walked to the foot of the bed, tucking the escaped blanket back under Dexter's feet. *Strange*. She had just tucked that blanket in when Toke returned him from his potty break and no one had been in the room since. "Hmm." Then she impulsively pinched his big toe.

Dexter groaned.

Mae's heart leaped. But it could just be a coincidence, so she pinched his toe again, much harder. "Ow," he bleated, batting her away with his foot.

Squealing, Mae shook him awake. "Dexter, you can move your legs!"

His eyes shot open with a mix of disbelief and wild elation, and he partially sat up. Using deliberate caution, Dexter slowly moved his big toe, darted a glance at Mae, then wiggled *all* his toes. He threw his head back in relief, drew a deep breath while kicking his feet, then let out a big laughing "Whoop!"

When he tried to stand, the muscles in his legs had atrophied so much from all his convalescence that his knees buckled, too weak to hold his weight. "I'll get working on these!"

"You do that." Needing a place to burn her excitement, Mae tore out of the room, slamming into Elizabeth, who was coming through the curtain. After a giddy, unintelligible apology, she flew down the porch steps and raced around the farm, spreading the good news.

When she found Toke, he was standing waist-high in the middle of a large hole he was digging for the new outhouse. He must have been at it for quite a while since his face, sweaty and red, looked like sizzling bacon. "Dexter can walk! He's not going to be paralyzed!"

He tossed a shovelful of dirt onto the growing pile a few feet away and gratefully took her cup, downing the entire thing without stopping. "Awesome news," he said breathlessly, then wiped his entire face with the bottom of his shirt. He repositioned the shovel, ready to thrust it in the dirt again until he noticed Mae was still standing there. "Uh…do you need something or are you just lusting after the gun show?" Toke lifted his arm and admired his bicep.

Disappointed by Toke's lack of enthusiasm, she rubbed the back of her neck. "Yeah…I mean no," she quickly corrected.

"Yo," Willie hailed, proudly using his new word, as he passed behind Mae on his way to the creek.

"Did you hear, Willie?" Mae spun around excitedly. "Dexter can walk!" Well, *he* gave her the response she wanted, cheering loudly and tossing his water bucket into the air.

Still smiling, Willie swung the pail dutifully over his shoulder before trampling through the tangled ferns and down the creek's steep bank. Mae followed him over. "Let me help you." She knelt at the top and Willie handed her the fresh icy water. She slowly straightened, but her eyes remained fixed on the creek. Willie held out his hand, but instead of handing Willie his bucket, she walked it over to Toke.

Placing it at the edge of his hole, she cleared her throat until he noticed her. Before she could say anything, he grabbed the bucket and poured it over his head and the rest down his throat. “Thanks. Brrr!” He bounced in place and shook off the water.

Willie groaned, disheartened, seizing back the bucket and slowly shuffling back to the creek.

“Do you know what will be in that clean, pure water you just drank if you keep digging the new outhouse here? It’s way too close to the river.” Mae felt horrible saying this seeing how deep he’d already gotten.

Toke gestured dismissively in the direction of the water. “I’m way the hell away from it.”

“I’m totally serious.” She straightened her shoulders and crossed her arms firmly. “The Sierra Club says a human cannot poo within two hundred feet of a water source.”

“Poo.” Toke tested the word.

“Okay, *crap*. Is that better?”

“I like shit.”

“You like shit?” Mae waited for a smile but didn’t get one. “Anyway, you *know* that’s where we get all our water. You’ll make us sick and die. Why didn’t you just dig it next to the old one?”

“*Hell* no. I can smell it in my sleep. Shit keeps me up all night.” This time he looked up at Mae for a smile.

“Mine was better.”

“Well, *poo* then. I wish you would have told me sooner.” Toke tossed the shovel out of the hole.

“But, seriously Toke, how do you not know this? Who was the person who gave us the lecture on bacteria?”

“I figured the dirt and rocks created a natural earth filter. Like how it works for a freshwater spring.”

"Maybe for small animals making tiny poos, but not the massive quantities that six people make."

"It's your fault with all those apple desserts and fresh baked bread you make us eat."

"Don't forget the elk and bear," Mae added.

Toke pulled himself out of the hole and began searching the ground, stopping ten yards away. "How about here then?"

"Still too close to the water."

Toke threw up his arms. "How the hell far is two hundred feet?"

"Just walk it off. Use your foot as a foot. It's close enough."

He winked, "You're right about that. You know what they say—"

"Remember, I've seen it."

Dismissing her comment, he planted his hands on his hips and chewed over the farm. "Thinking…maybe we should find out where the other outhouses were first, so we don't dig up some old poo-punch."

Mae wrinkled her nose, trying to keep the visual out of her head. "Just remember, two hundred feet, okay?"

Willie made a safe arc around them, passing with another full bucket.

Chapter Sixty

The gate jangled, and Milok and Yu'mi rode up to the house with Mae waving a cheerful greeting as they tethered their horses. After refreshing with a cup of tepid tea they didn't pretend to enjoy, Milok spoke first, addressing Mae. "We know your God has given you a day of rest tomorrow and Yu'mi would like to invite you over tonight to meet his father's people of the Ma'camo. We are celebrating and thanking the gods for the safe return of the chief's brother from the lower mountains." He motioned with his arm to the southeast. "He did much trading and returned with many needed things."

Mae looked at Willie, not sure what to say, and he nodded in approval. "I would love to!" she said, then added with a hopeful smile, "If Toke and Dexter can come too."

Judging from Yu'mi's disappointed expression, she knew Milok had been giving him English lessons. After all, Milok grew up with his best friend speaking English and soon became fluent, just like Willie did with Milok's language.

Discussing Mae's request, Yu'mi and Milok went back and forth until Milok finally answered, "Yes, they are most welcome as well." Yu'mi attempted to look stoic but was clearly not as happy as before.

Dexter declined Yu'mi's invitation, not anywhere near well enough to ride a horse. But Toke, all too anxious for something different to happen in his life, couldn't hide his eagerness, and quickly ducked behind the house to scrub up. Mae excused herself to change but ended up just removing her apron, smoothing out her only dress, and rewrapping her headscarf.

Yu'mi let Toke ride his own horse while he squeezed in with Milok.

Mae tightened the shawl around her shoulders as the sun, so indecisive of its departure, ducked in and out between the passing trees.

When they arrived at the Ma'camo camp, Milok ran off after tying up the horses. Mae lovingly ran her hand along Trixie's face and cooed a long goodbye, promising to be back soon.

Yu'mi stood unusually still, his body stiff like he was made of stone. Beads of sweat collected above his lip and his breathing was shallow and uneven. Mae leaned her head toward Toke. "Does Yu'mi seem a little nervous to you?" Toke just shrugged.

She was beginning to feel awkward amongst all these passing strangers with Yu'mi frozen in silence. Just how long were they going to stand there? Then, finally, he raised his head, and as if he were following a script, but looking like he had never done anything remotely close to this in his life, he moved to Mae's side and tenderly placed his hand on the small of Mae's back. This was the first time Yu'mi had ever made a move to touch her someplace other than her hands. Feeling a little surprised, she looked wide-eyed at Toke, whose eyes sparkled back in amusement. She didn't want to lead Yu'mi on but also didn't want to hurt his feelings for everything he had done for them. Besides, his advances felt innocent, and not in the least bit sexual.

Yu'mi held Mae tight to his side as they walked through the trees and on into the celebration. Toke found it amusing how Yu'mi had him walk behind them, rather than next to him or Mae. "Sorta thinking I'm just here to hold up the train of your wedding dress," he muttered from behind.

As they approached the man Mae and Toke remembered as Waho, Yu'mi puffed out his chest, and looked confident and proud in front of his father. Waho seemed far more receptive than the two weeks before, the day Jack traded them, or rather, dumped them, on the Ma'camos. Toke said under his breath, "Still got that attractive Easter hat."

Yu'mi placed Mae's hand on top of his and pushed their hands forward together, introducing her to his father. This gesture with their hands seemed quite formal, but then, she barely knew anything about this tribe. She would be sure to stop anything serious before it got too far.

A broad smile lit up Waho as he studied Mae's face—the shape of her eyes, her cheekbones, and angular features. She imagined he was searching for traits he did not desire in a person. Perhaps resembling certain neighboring tribes they were often fighting. But, he seemed to be especially looking for signs of their mortal enemies, the Yiptuati, with their distinct high noses, wide cheekbones, and small angular close-set eyes. Waho seemed to overlook any European traits that might have revealed themselves on her. He knew that, all too often, white trappers and Spaniards raped whoever they wanted and without permission. He felt no need to punish these victims twice.

Waho turned and motioned for them to follow him, without being introduced to Toke at all. "Now I feel like someone just brushed white-out over me," Toke called after Mae, while he hurried to catch up.

Mae corrected him, quietly, "I'm pretty sure it was the delete key."

They approached a festively dressed man whose white hair was trussed up under a headband made of quills and wrapped around his forehead. A large spray of white feathers garnished the top of his head with larger colorful feathers stabbing through the base and flaring out to the sides. Profound wrinkles consumed his dark face, distorting his once striking tattoos into something curious. Around his neck he layered what must be all the necklaces he had owned since birth. With heightened formal respect, Waho introduced Mae to the Huuk, Chief K'ut'im, by placing his hand on top of Mae's on top of Yu'mi's.

Mae whispered to Toke, "Huke? Like Luke?"

"That's what I heard." Toke lifted his shoulder in a half shrug.

The Huuk nodded in greeting as the large animal incisors making up his intimidating necklace clacked together musically. He covered Waho's hand with his darker wrinkled hand, topping off the stack.

Toke waved from behind. "Uh, should I be playing this, too?"

"Shhhh," was all Mae could say, thoroughly flattered by all the respectful formality.

By the next two introductions, it began to feel like Yu'mi had to prove his feelings for Mae to his father. She now started to realize he intended for her to be more than a close friend, which was odd because he hadn't displayed any physical attraction toward her. He never did ask if Mae had a boyfriend, or maybe he just observed the lack of a mate in her daily life and took it upon himself to claim her. But when Greg finally showed up, which he *would*, that would straighten it all out.

Toke muttered into Mae's ear, a little too loudly, "His dad's probably surprised, beyond belief, that his son's actually interested in a relationship with a female." Mae responded with a sharp elbow. Hearing this white man speak to Yu'mi's woman so casually, Waho and the Huuk both turned to look at him. As if noticing Toke for the first time, their eyes moved up to Toke's head, studying the spotty, uneven patches of hair and the scabby blistering sunburnt splotches in between them. But instead of looking horrified by some infectious, deadly white man disease, they seemed humored and moved on.

Waho then escorted them over to one side of the large circle of people standing around the fire. Toke looked around self-consciously, bending his knees a little. "Geez, I feel like a giant. In fact, your bitty five-foot-three is even tall here."

As dusk darkened their surroundings, the flames grew bolder, and the air became heavily scented with roasting meats and unfamiliar smells. Toke inhaled deeply, closing his eyes, savoring each exotic savory spice. "Oh, man. That's it. I'm staying right here." He took a seat on the nearest log, but Yu'mi motioned for him to stand back up. Mae explained by inclining her head toward Chief K'ut'im, who was still standing.

In front of them, a man, heavy with beads and feathers, danced around the inside of their circle, waving smoke from his burning smudge. The crowd hushed as a woman took the stage, dusting their ears with the musical patter from her elaborately ornamented dress of porcupine quills and seeded tassels. With graceful hands, she sprinkled a handful of powder into the fire. A beautiful coil of blue smoke rose, and she seduced it away with a dreamy dance of her hands, teasing it to follow. Her voice, so poetic, singing beautiful words, gently rose in timbre, sparking the smoke to life.

Her nurturing hands cradled it gently, then offered it up to the darkening sky where it would soon become one, forever watching over them from above, giving them life and protection as she had done for it. From the tip of her fingers, still reaching to the sky, her hands slowly began to coil, then her arms, followed by her body, twisting down, down until she seemed to disappear into the ground.

Mesmerized by this beautiful, spiritual show, Mae smiled sleepily while her body wavered slightly as if in a trance. Was she just starved for entertainment or was this woman really that amazing? She had no idea how she knew the meaning of the woman's moves, but she did. Mae slowly turned her head, her tranquil eyes catching Yu'mi's, and smiled. His radiated back the same peace. Then she turned to Toke, wanting to see him in the same enlightened state they were both in, but instead found him nearly finished carving his initials into the log he was sitting on behind them. Mae figured he must be in self-preservation mode because of all the topless women parading by.

Chief K'ut'im gave an order, breaking the spell, and everyone sat. He made a speech neither of them could understand, and the village reacted with jubilant noises using sticks and instruments. Mae felt relaxed. This night wasn't as awkward as she thought it would be. She and Toke were blending in.

But not for long.

Chapter Sixty-One

Chief K'ut'im drew his arm out, gesturing toward Mae and Yu'mi. All heads instantly turned to look at them, and the celebration of music and noises intensified.

"I feel weird. Who are they staring at?" Toke hunkered down, trying to disappear.

"Yeah, I'm feeling it too. Just look pleasant and humble." *Whatever that looked like.*

Food was being shared, and everyone used their fingers to scoop some out of the bowl, then passed it on. Mae tried not to think about all the germs being spread around. She dipped her fingers into the bowl while advising Toke, "Remember, they are still sizing you up. You had better let them know how much you love their food." She put the smallest portion she could in her mouth. It tasted like some sort of rodent with twigs for unpleasant crunchiness and found it extremely difficult to keep a polite face.

Toke put some in his mouth and nodded, expecting far worse. He leaned toward Mae, "Ask Yu'mi what's in this shit."

Mae turned to ask Yu'mi, and when she got the answer, she swallowed hard and turned back to Toke. She kept her eyes closed, concentrating hard on repeating his words without emotion. "Boiled skunk with ground trout bones, then drizzled with something's gland sap."

Toke blinked, trying to smile. "What's the word for delicious?"

Mae looked pale, trying not to think of the ingredients. "Let's just smile and rub our tummies. That's got to be universal."

While waiting in fear for the next course, they got a chance to look around. Mae said, "Just think what an opportunity this is to meet a real tribe, not dusty wax sculptures behind glass in a museum case." The colors the people wore were subtle and earth-toned, like they wanted to disappear into their surroundings. Many of the women wore aprons made of shredded bark with a smaller piece that they tucked between their legs when they sat. The men, as much as the women, added decorative trim of fringed or braided leather or animal fur along the edges of their clothing. Many had elaborate ornamentation strung with seed ornaments, tassels, and porcupine quills.

"What's with that ugly-ass nose tat?" Toke's head tilted toward Waho. "I mean, if you're going to ink your face—"

"Shh. You know some can speak English here." They sat quietly absorbing the strangeness of it all. Mae observed a group of girls, figuring out that the older ones wore their hair bound back while the younger ones cut their hair shorter and wore a headband which wrapped under their chin instead of behind her neck like headbands are usually worn.

Toke was passed a stick with something red and raw wound tightly around it. He pulled off a small piece then passed it on to Mae. This went on through the rest of the courses while they diligently smiled, looked pleased, and mimicked Yu'mi's actions.

"You're doing pretty good, princess." Toke gave an approving nod. "You're finding things to put in your mouth at least."

"I'm trying, or I make the most of the fine air I'm chewing."

Toke laughed. "Good girl."

Two women stopped in front of them carrying a ladle and a larger vessel of steaming liquid. They each had three or four vertical dotted lines tattooed on their chins. Mae couldn't stop staring at their faces. *Were these unappealing marks permanent?* The lines of the older of the two women continued unattractively upward, reaching the outsides of her eyes. Then, to top off her fierce look, she had small bird bones punched through the outer parts of her ear. Toke nudged Mae. "Those tats…he's going to want you to get those too, you know."

They were each handed their own bowl of a pungent hot liquid. Mae sipped hers and tried to give it back, but Yu'mi pulled it back in front of her. "Mae, drink." He extended his arm, motioning it toward the people, the fire, then the sky, wanting her to understand it was an important part of the ceremony. They were to sip the bittersweet tea after each person spoke.

After the fourth speaker, Toke screwed up his face. "Man, how much of this horrible stuff do we have to drink?" Toward the end of the bowl, Mae felt a little sick, like she was going to vomit. She leaned over to Toke to tell him she needed to leave to barf. Toke groaned, "I'm not feeling that great either. I'm going with you."

She patted Yu'mi on the hand and quickly slipped away, covering her mouth. They scurried through the outer bushes, past a dense patch of trees to an opening, far from the ceremony. Toke stopped and grabbed his stomach, but Mae insisted, "No, let's keep going, I don't want to embarrass Yu'mi." But as soon as she said it, her body convulsed, and she was on her knees retching. Just like Toke.

When Mae looked up, the most beautiful tree she had ever seen was standing right before her. Branches made of twisting rainbows wound around the tree's frosty blue trunk, sparkling like diamonds. Feeling euphoric with elation, she reached out to touch its soft fluffy tendrils that curled around her fingers and continued on, exploring the rest of her body. Toke had to see this amazing thing that was happening to her. "Look at this..."

But Toke was already on the ground, rolling and staring at his hands. "Mae...my fingers...they're little people with tiny hats, and they're talking. No—they're singing tiny songs!"

Mae screamed joyously then got distracted when she realized Toke's shirt was made of floppy pink taffy. She knelt beside him and tugged at it, and Toke laughed at the pain since she grabbed skin too, then they were both laughing as she started to try to eat it.

Yu'mi found them many hours later in the morning light, both naked, wrapped in each other's arms. He crept away silently, but the snapping branches woke them.

Mae's eyes shot open, and she looked around, horrified. She pushed Toke's arm off of her and untwisted her legs from his. Wanting to cry, she buried her face in her hands and squeezed her eyes shut, trying to erase everything. What had she done? Did she really have sex with Toke? She couldn't remember actually *doing* anything with him, but then, what she *did* remember was all swirled in her head, much like it had been the night before. How could she do this to Greg in just a month and a half? The thought sickened her. She calmed a little by not finding any physical signs of him on or *in* her body. Now she just had to slip away before he woke up and maybe she could pretend it never happened. As silently as she could, she pulled on her drawers and stood up, carefully stepping into her dress.

Toke groaned, wiped his eyes, and tried to sit up. "You look better without that." He reached out to stop Mae's hasty dressing, but his arm was too heavy and flopped back to the ground.

Sighing, she began buttoning her dress and nudged Toke with her foot. "C'mon. Let's get out of here before someone else finds us."

A few minutes later, they staggered out of the trees with raging headaches and found Yu'mi sitting on a rock, waiting for them. Neither knew what to say or how to act toward Yu'mi, even though he didn't look like he required any explanation, nor appeared jealous. He handed Mae a bag of water. "Drink."

Mae mumbled a mortified, "Thank you."

Yu'mi led them back to Trixie who was standing next to a couple other mustangs and Milok. He picked up one of the ropes that were attached to the larger of the two horses and held it out to Toke. "For you."

Toke was taken completely by surprise. "For real, dude?" He wasn't sure if he should shake his hand or give a buddy hug or what, so he just rubbed the horse's back. "Thanks, man. He's a beauty."

Milok handed him the other rope. "This one's for Dexter. We worked them both hard, and now they're ready."

Yu'mi tied down a horsehair blanket, so Toke had something to sit on. Once they were mounted and Dexter's horse secured behind, Yu'mi took Mae's hand in his and kissed her palm, then walked over to Toke and held up his hand as if to wave and nodded. He stood watching them leave and then disappeared back into the trees to his village.

Toke was doing much better on his new horse. He smirked, "Nothing like hustling off the shameful guests."

Mae felt so out-of-it still, but finally mustered, "I just feel so embarrassed. We were Yu'mi's guests, and we completely humiliated him. His father will think the worst of us, just as I thought he was beginning to accept us."

"They gave us horses so we couldn't have been *that* horrible," Toke said.

Mae nodded slightly with her eyes fixated ahead while she rode on silently, needing time to process the night before.

After a few minutes, Toke coughed. "Um, let's not let Dex find out about last night, K?"

"Definitely *not*." One thing she was finally able to appreciate here was her privacy. No one was going to snap her picture doing something ridiculous and post it somewhere. Nobody could record a private conversation and use it against her. No one was going to publicly immortalize her mistakes, like finding her and Toke naked in compromising positions. She finally felt free. Free to embrace her imperfections. Free to forgive the stupid things she did and the stupid things she hadn't done yet.

Chapter Sixty-Two

Willie's ears pricked up when he heard them coming down the path and he bolted across the yard to open the gate. Dexter hobbled across the porch using two sturdy canes as Mae and Toke rode up to the house.

Dexter's eyes glinted when they fell on the horse behind Toke. "Um..." with a quick glance to Mae, then Toke, and back to the horse. "For me?"

"Sure is," Mae said, jumping down to help him in his painful journey down the porch steps. He ran his hand softly over the sleek brown mustang's shiny coat, completely tongue-tied for words. "Yu'mi is a very generous person. Somehow he was able to convince his village to give us these mustangs they had been breaking in for others."

Dexter whistled. "We owe them big time."

"We're going to need to build a bigger barn," Willie said, examining the underside of Toke's horse. Mae glanced in Toke's direction, and they shared a knowing look like they were really planning on sticking around that long.

"And lucky for you, yours already has a name," Toke added, keeping a poker face. "Dexter, meet Queen Felicity."

With a slight wrinkling of his nose, Dexter nodded. "Okay, then. Queen Felicity it is." Mae couldn't tell if Dexter was playing Toke or was actually that gullible. Hobbling to the front of his mustang, Dexter pulled a small apple from his pocket he fed it to him. "So, Toke. What's the name of yours, if mine is so grand?"

Mae shot out—"Buckles."

"Touché, Mae." Toke dismounted. "Yes, my horse is named Buckles.

He is a strong, sturdy, virile male, so Yu'mi thought Buckles was a perfect fit." Then he lowered his voice. "He was first given the name Fuckles, for reasons I won't go into, but Mae made Yu'mi change it."

Testing out his strengthening legs, Dexter shuffled through the dust-filled afternoon air to investigate the small choking coughs originating from behind the hen house. He waved at the thick floating gray until he could finally make out the shape of a very sooty Mae. She held a shovel heaped with fireplace ashes and proceeded to dump them into a sizable funnel-shaped box filled with hay. This caused the calm to erupt once again into a dense dark cloud, blinding them both. "What a mess," he said, coughing.

Mae was startled, not expecting anyone to *choose* to breathe this murky mess and spun around. Squinting through the smoke as it settled, coiling and spiraling down like ghosts returning to their graves, she finally spotted him. Dexter took a couple of steps toward her, relying heavily on his cane. "What's all this?" said his muffled voice, filtering through his shirt.

Letting the shovel drop, Mae pulled the handkerchief off her mouth and wiped her face, which only smeared the soot around. "So, this filthy stuff is how we make soap. Ironic, huh?" She stooped to pick up a pail of water and poured it over the box of ashes and straw. "Voilà!" she announced, vigorously brushing her hands together. To her, this did not feel like "women's work," and she almost enjoyed it.

"So, now what happens?" Dexter moved next to her for a closer look, leaning on his cane.

"Watery stuff eventually leaches out from the bottom, and that's called lye. Isn't that cool? I'm making *lye*. I watched Elizabeth do this only once, so I hope I got it right."

"Well, I hear Elizabeth's very pleased with how hard you work. I'm sure you'll make some very fine lye." He put his arm around her shoulders like he often did, adding an assuring squeeze. When he smiled down at her, his white teeth flashed in that irresistible way she rarely saw anymore. Did he maybe see her as anything more than a sister figure? She looked up at his face, focusing on not looking too sisterly, but the stunning contrast of his vibrant turquoise eyes against his tanned face struck her like a bolt of electricity. Her lips parted unconsciously, and she couldn't stop staring at him. For a moment he remained still, returning her gaze with an expression she couldn't interpret. Then, with a small clearing of his throat, he straightened. The sudden movement woke Mae out of her drunken daze, and she self-consciously looked away as if searching for the shovel.

Dexter turned to leave, with a, "Well, it looks like you've got a lot of sooty fun ahead of you."

Mae responded with a half-smile, half-eye roll, stabbing the shovel into the pile of ashes, shrouding everything, once again, in gray. She waved her handkerchief around wildly, as much to clear the air as to clear the awkward and unwanted feelings that skittered through her heart.

Stopping for a minute, she rested her foot on the shovel's blade and watched Dexter on his laborious trip back to the house. An amused smile tugged at her lips as she thought about the transformation from his virile commanding presence a couple of minutes ago, into this hunched over frail man hobbling away on his cane. She yanked off the handkerchief that covered her mouth and blew in it hard, hoping to clear the heavy globs of soot squatting in her nostrils.

"Dude!" Toke praised Dexter's progress, crossing his path with Trixie in tow.

Mae looked up just in time, quickly stuffing the handkerchief back in her pocket. "Hey! Where are you taking her?"

"Ol' Gruff's been a little cranky these days. Just visiting her *neigh*-bor, giving him a little fun."

"Trixie's far too young." Throwing down the shovel, she marched over to Toke and blocked his way. "And that would make Old Gruff a pedophile."

"She's not that young, she's just small. In dog years, she'd be about fourteen. Hell, in these times, she's nearly a spinster."

"Give her back." Mae grabbed the rope and turned Trixie back toward her stall. "Try Queen Felicity. She's no innocent thing, as you know first-hand," she said, and then gave him a wink, quite proud of her joke.

Toke called back, "Are you calling Queen Felicity a whorse? How do you call a horse with no legs? It doesn't matter, it's not going to come. How do you know when a pony's sick? It's a little hoarse..."

Chapter Sixty-Three

Every couple of days, Yu'mi and Milok dropped by to check how the horses were doing. Willie always took off somewhere with Milok, doing things that twelve-year-olds do. And Yu'mi, so eager to learn English, followed Mae and Elizabeth around while they went about their chores, asking questions and absorbing as much of their language as he could.

Inspired by his dedication, Mae decided to help Yu'mi become fluent in English. First, she would find him a piece of slate rock to write on and insist he come every day to sit in on Willie's two-hour lessons. Maybe she could learn some of his language, too.

Elizabeth was an amazing teacher with the boys, so patient and understanding. At first, Yu'mi was confused why it was important to learn the alphabet to write words. His tribe didn't seem to have a written language, so they never needed to have an alphabet. In a moment of lucidity, Elizabeth admitted she couldn't recall ever seeing a Ma'camo word written on anything. "But how do y'all communicate or keep records?"

Yu'mi shrugged in a way that meant that they didn't need to do that. To explain further, he picked up the small basket of wild plums he had brought over with him and pointed to three small stripes stitched in dark twine near the top. "Aunt Jalulu make basket. Three lines mean Aunt Jalulu name."

Mae wrote his aunt's name in English on the slate, and Yu'mi just laughed at all the extra work it took with letters. Continuing on with *his* lesson to *them*, Yu'mi gestured to the intricately woven dark red grass throughout the coiled willow of the basket. He picked up the piece of chalk and drew a simple stick-figure bird with short legs and a little curl on the top of its head.

"Quail. That's most definitely a quail," Mae announced, not sure what it had to do with the basket, though.

"Kwayluh," Yu'mi repeated, setting it to memory. Then pointed to the design on the basket. "Kwayluh." Mae raised a skeptical eyebrow to Elizabeth. The design on the basket resembled more of an eight-legged invertebrate than any sort of bird.

He stood and went into the kitchen, coming back with two more baskets the Foxes had accumulated over the years. A repeating pattern of triangles decorated one, and diamond shapes running diagonally across was woven through the other. When Mae and Elizabeth gave up trying to guess, Yu'mi drew a picture of a flower for the first basket and a feather for the second. Mae mulled over each of them for a while, then smiled, nodding her head. She was humbled and embarrassed by her shallow thinking. They weren't simply random geometric shapes just to add color, the symbolism was conceptually brilliant.

Yu'mi started his lessons considerably behind Willie's level, but in no time, he soared far beyond Willie. Elizabeth told Mae that Yu'mi was unusually bright and that she'd never met anyone like him before. "He can recite a page from a book, word for word, like it was still in front of his eyes."

"Back home, we call that photographic memory. But that wouldn't make sense to you because photography probably hasn't been invented yet."

"I'm sure he would be declared a genius by physicians and the men of science. If they'd an open mind, that is," Elizabeth said, and Mae knew she meant because he was an Indian.

Elizabeth walked over to their library and ran her fingers across the books' spines with such pride. This "library" she was so proud of consisted of about ten or twelve books, three of them Bibles, one a doctor's book, and another a well-worn almanac. The rest were an odd assortment of novels and storybooks, all well read, way too many times. "Jack has been able to get some interesting books off the ships in the ports and was able to learn English that way."

Pulling one of Willie's storybooks from the shelf, Yu'mi began reading aloud. Mae walked over and gently took it from him. "You've pretty much got that one memorized. You need more of a challenge now, to see what you've really got." Mae scrutinized the meager assortment of books on the shelf. She finally narrowed it down to the Bibles and almanac and leafed through them. "So, even though the Bible is written in English and full of stories, it reads like a foreign language. That just leaves the Farmer's Almanac. Each day is exciting and different. Get ready for some real fun, Yu'mi." She felt bad when he didn't catch her sarcasm and looked excited. And who knew, maybe his knowledge of the almanac would come in handy one day.

With only a short time to spare each day, Yu'mi needed to leave and get back to his responsibilities in his village. This time he asked Mae to follow him to his horse so he could give her something. He drew from a satchel tied to his saddle, a tiny package wrapped in long green leaves and tied with brightly colored twine. "I make for you."

Seeing the pride in Yu'mi, she unwrapped it carefully and soon held in her fingers the most delicate needle she had ever seen. It was carved from bone and so sharp, the tip was translucent. This deserved Mae's biggest hug yet, which Yu'mi tolerated reasonably well.

On her way back to the house, she caught a glimpse of Dexter sitting on top of a large boulder out past the orchard. He had made it all the way to the other side of the surrounding fence entirely on his own just to watch the sunset. She hesitated for a second, not sure if he wanted time alone or if she could join him.

Hearing her footsteps, he turned around stiffly to avoid twisting his back and motioned her over. He sat cross-legged, gazing out at the changing sky, so she sidled in next to him and did the same. They sat in silence for a long while, listening to the earth as it peacefully made its transition into evening.

Dexter lowered his head and cradled the wooden carving in his lap. "I just really miss Greg," he said somberly. Mae nodded and leaned into him supportively. "He rescued me from my father so many times. He didn't make fun of me or judge how poor we were, he just made everything seem okay." Exposing to her his vulnerability and rarely seen emotions, Mae felt closer to him than ever before. He must have been feeling the same because he wrapped his arm around her shoulders, and it felt so natural.

His warmth radiated through her body, and she felt safe and protected under his muscular arm...but she was also starting to feel some other things, too. Little butterflies flittered around in her stomach and she felt her face get warm—No. She couldn't have those feelings. She jolted herself back to her senses. What was *wrong* with her? Dexter's in pain and mourning his best friend, Greg. The only person that meant anything to him in the world, and here she was, callously lusting after him.

Feeling ashamed by her inappropriate feelings, she tried desperately to push them out of her mind. She and Dexter were just good friends with a common best friend, and that's the way it had to stay. Keep it sisterly. Not incestuous. She tucked in her lips and bit down hard. Maybe her feelings for Dexter were just that she missed Greg so much? And maybe she was just drawn to that part of Dexter where she could feel closer to Greg. She wanted so much for that to be the reason. It was far more honorable than her confusing desires. Greg was, and always would be, the love of her life, and she would always be completely devoted to him.

With his free hand, Dexter held up his carving to show Mae. "Oh, Dex, that's beautiful!" He had immortalized his and Greg's boyhood symbol of the howling wolves in the flames by carving them in 3D on the piece of pine Willie had given him. "Greg would love this," she said, resting her head against him. They watched the sun peacefully slip away and graciously leave them a spectacular masterpiece to get lost in.

Suddenly something snapped in the thicket of trees just beyond where they sat. Their eyes darted to the trees and searched for the source. "Must be that pesky black bear again." Mae tried to sound calm but was not feeling it.

It snapped again. Like something heavy just took another step closer.

An unnerving chill gripped Mae, and she stiffened. “I should get going on dinner. Walk with me?”

With a deepening crease between his brows, Dexter scanned the dark trees once more. “Yeah.” He reached for his cane and Mae helped him get to his feet, not taking his eyes off the trees.

As they headed back to the house, each of them looked back a few times just to make sure nothing was following them.

Chapter Sixty-Four

Toke lumbered up the porch steps, so exhausted from three full days of digging, and plopped heavily in a chair. The wood protested for being treated this way and creaked back angrily. Jack's old boots fit him pretty good, but if his feet were a nine instead of an eleven, they would fit even better. Liberating his sweaty feet from the steamy leather, his smashed toes began to uncurl, and he groaned in relief. In a spontaneous decision, he unsheathed his knife and sawed the leather toes clear off the soles of both boots. "You are now free. These boots will bully you no more." He raised his toes in the air, wiggling them wildly as they celebrated their freedom.

"Ack! Get those disgusting things out of here." Mae swung the broom at him from across the room.

"Really? You get it from there? Guess I'd better then." He walked to the large barrel of water on the back porch and proceeded to ladle water over his feet.

Irked by the excessive splashing of water, Mae marched out, scolding, "No, you can't waste water like that! The amount you used took Willie one whole trip to bring up from the river. Just put a little bit in this bowl and wash your feet with a rag or your handkerchief."

Toke regarded her, his eyebrows scrunched in disapproving amusement. "Who is this person? Where's my Mae?" He took the bowl, filled it with water, and sat on the edge of the porch.

With a long, surrendering sigh, Mae's shoulders slumped, and she sunk down on the porch next to Toke. "I hate my life," she confessed.

"Yeah, I would too. But, it's just what it is right now."

"I just wish I could be out here with you guys, working my body in the outdoors, under the sun, fresh mountain air filling my lungs, feeling the energy of the green earth. I'm just not ready to be a housewife. I want a choice. I despise this caged domesticity."

"Nah, you'd be miserable out here. All day with the sun beating down on you, drenched in sweat, blisters all over your hands, dirt embedded in your new little bits of fingernails. And then you'd start whining about how you hate working outdoors."

"That's not true." She looked down at her clean hands. "It's just that all the jobs here have such stereotypical roles, and this family seems to like it that way. Neither Jack nor Elizabeth try to color outside the lines. Not even just a little."

Toke scrubbed at the dirt on his toes that seemed to be permanent. "Okay then, think about it. Would you like to be digging the new ten-foot-deep shit-house hole in this hard, rocky soil like *I* have to? Or, can you imagine Elizabeth out there chopping down trees and removing stumps with her pale, skinny little arms? Or, Jack's big rough hands and lack of patience, making tiny sewing stitches, stabbing himself with the needle constantly and cussing his head off?" Toke's toes were as red as cherry tomatoes now, but he got the dirt out and moved onto the other foot. "Shit, it's 1840, where men are in charge and women just obey and spit out kids. Life is strenuous, and they've learned to make it work by doing what they're best at. Just common sense, really." He wrung out the rag and looked at Mae. "Buck up girl, we'll figure something out." Mae was grateful Toke had a human side and wished he let it show more often. He held up his foot for her to smell. "Better?" When she didn't look, he stuck it closer to her face, but she still didn't move.

She slowly moved her finger to her lips for silence while keeping her eyes locked straight ahead. Toke followed her gaze, releasing his clean foot. "What is it?" he whispered.

"There's something out there. In the darkness of the trees, just outside the fence."

They remained still, soundlessly staring into the dark. Then finally

Toke heard it, too. A snapping of a large twig. Then another. "That wasn't the step of a four-legged animal. I think a person's out there," he whispered.

Mae shuddered. "Let's get back inside." She pulled herself to her feet and yanked on Toke to do the same.

"It's probably just Greg out there keeping an eye on you," Toke said, trying to lighten the intensity.

Nearly through the back door, Mae stopped in her tracks and turned around, bumping into Toke. "Toke…what if it *is* Greg? Maybe he's finally found us." She took a couple steps back onto the porch. Her thought process raced. "It's probably just too dark for him to see us. And maybe it was Greg who took my dress. He just didn't recognize me. I'm bald and at least fifty pounds lighter." Starting to believe her own irrational words, she took another step, hesitantly at first, then fully committed to her idea. "We need to let him know that it's us and he'll be safe here." She slipped off the porch and took one confident step forward. "I'll go open the gate."

"Whoa." Toke grabbed hold of her arm, stopping her in place. "I was just joking around. Geez. Your emotions have overruled your logic." She tried to yank free, but he held firm. "If it *was* Greg, he'd have already heard your voice and shown himself by now."

She stopped fighting back and looked broken. "Yeah, you're probably right." He watched her hopes crumble in a heap at her feet.

Toke finally coaxed her back onto the porch by saying, "Besides, it's probably just that creep bringing your dress back."

"What's going on out there?" Dexter called from inside.

"We're not really sure." Toke gathered up his boots. "We heard something out there. Not just a random animal noise, but deliberate, like a footstep." He glanced back once more before following Mae through the door.

"It was like two nights ago, Dex. It felt like someone was out there, watching us." Mae could feel that familiar anxiety snake its way through her body, and she shivered. "And when I was on the mountain and my dress was stolen. It's happened too often to be a coincidence."

Toke removed the smallest of his four sheathed knives attached to his belt and handed it to Mae. "Keep this on you at all times." After she searched her dress for a place to stash the knife, she gave up and stashed it inside the tight bosom of her dress. Toke snorted. "As good a place as any. Don't forget to always sheathe it first. Could be a little painful."

"I wonder if it has anything to do with the two missing chickens this morning," Dex suggested.

"Vell." Jack pulled himself up from his comfortable chair with a grunt and walked over to his gun on the wall. "Noting good can be creeping around at night. Or creeping around in de daytime needer. I'll just pull de trigger an' bring os dinner."

Mae's heart lurched. "Please, Jack—please not yet. It could be our friend Greg out there." She couldn't stop tears from pooling in her eyes.

"Does dis Greg taste good?" Jack laughed.

Mae's mouth dropped open, appalled at his insensitive joke, and stormed off to the kitchen. She pushed past Elizabeth as if she was to blame for her husband and pounded her fist into the rising dough.

Elizabeth stopped the grinding stone and turned to Mae. "Jack would never *purposely* shoot your friend, Mae," she assured with complete sincerity. She turned back to her grinding, then added, as much to herself as to Mae, "We can only hope he stays clear of the cider tonight."

What's wrong with these people? Mae shuddered and pushed the window curtain aside. The silhouettes of the orchard trees were unsettling, now seeming to resemble people just watching their house and waiting. Her fingers sought out the sheathed knife that pressed against her skin. This hard-edged little secret gave her comfort, and she felt braver—which wasn't always a good thing for someone who might run off into the woods at any moment to investigate a snapping twig she hoped was Greg.

Jack had warned them repeatedly of the woods at night and how their farm attracted an assortment of hungry and curious animals. Though he failed to mention people, his advice was sound, and it was best to stay inside the fence after dark.

Chapter Sixty-Five

Mae embraced the light of the morning and the feeling of safety it provided. However futile the idea that last night it was Greg out there in the dark, it renewed her belief that Greg was near and they'd soon find him.

She spun around with her straw broom, singing Greg's song. "Maaaae Baaaae. Before. Anyone. Else. Muh Mae baaaaaeee. Baaaby. Apple. Ears…" She was completely unaware that Toke had walked in moments before. He bit down hard on his lip and turned away to keep from laughing as she continued on, "… in your secret honey cave…"

He needed a moment to compose himself before being able to speak. "Hey, Cinderella." Startled out of her skin, Mae jumped and dropped the broom. He bowed and continued, "Your prince Yu'mi awaits you outside. He would like to escort you and your friends to the final match of their game."

Mae's face slowly brightened into an enthusiastic grin. "I am *so* all over that. Man, do I need to get away from this place, don't you?"

"Yeah. It sounds like a big-ass deal. The Ma'camo team and some other from the North are the only two left in the tournament."

"Should we dress up?" But then she looked down at her dress with a disapproving frown. Even the Ma'camo women's apron-like skirts of shredded bark were belted and fringed and looked fancy next to hers.

"One dapper gentleman, at your service. I'll just change to my other gray stained shirt and turn my only brown stained pants inside out. Piss a little on them to cover up the horse poop smell, and I'm ready."

This she related to all too well and threw her head back laughing.

Giddy with anticipation, Mae's face glowed. She just needed to spend a little time on her small amount of hair and make it actually look pretty. Then she'd grind things from nature of different colors to make eyeshadow and liner, maybe make some shiny red lip gloss by whipping beeswax and nut oils with berry skins.

The Ma'camo had it right. They dressed up for every occasion and celebrated often. It gave people something to look forward to and renewed the soul. Leaning the broom against the wall, she untied her apron and ran outside to find Yu'mi.

"So, what day's the big game?" Mae bounced with excitement.

"Now. We leave now."

"Wait—what? Now?"

"Dah."

Her heart wrenched. The one chance she had for glamming up was now a ten-second rush. With no time to waste, she raced back into the house and threw on her knitted shawl, fastening it closed to cover her stained bodice. She plucked a few wild daisies from the vase on the table and spruced up the drab hat she borrowed from Elizabeth. Then, fishing out a thin piece of charcoal from the fire, she carefully outlined her eyes and smudged them for a smoky look. Her eyebrows, though sparse, had grown enough to be passable, so she left them alone and finished up by dabbing crushed berries on her lips and lightly on her cheeks. That would have to do.

As she rushed past Jack sitting on the porch, he scowled and commented that the only women who painted their faces were prostitutes. She called back over her shoulder, "I'll be sure to let Ma'camo women know what you think of them."

She found Trixie already saddled up and waiting with the other horses, and when Toke and Dexter laid eyes on her, all they could do was stare. And she liked it.

Bursts of shouting, excited screams, and thunderous cheers reached their ears long before they arrived. Yu'mi explained the rules and stakes of the game with such passion they quickly caught his enthusiasm.

The ball was made of animal skin stuffed with deer hair, and it was kicked, thrown, and hit with sticks, not too unlike football and soccer with a little basketball thrown in—and sticks, of course.

This was the last day of the three-day game that went from dawn to dusk. The Ma'camo team competed against another village from the north and one from the west. Winning this game was highly significant for the Ma'camo. Not just for the ample amount of bead money that the winning village got, nor the notoriety and respect the village would have from this day forward, but the Ma'camo hadn't been in the final championship for twenty years.

Kin'ta, Yu'mi's cousin, was currently the Ma'camo champion, and if their team won today, he would be the champion for all the Southern Maidu tribes. This was one of the highest honors for anyone to receive. The youngest member of the team was Milok, and Willie was excited for his friend, if not a little jealous that he couldn't compete, too.

Throaty vocals and shrill calls, sounding bizarre to Mae, shouted encouragement. It was the loudest and most exciting game Mae had ever witnessed.

Suddenly, a heart-stopping burst of cheers erupted from the crowd, and Mae knew the Ma'camo team had won. The air grew thick with feverish drumming and a cacophony of sounds from various musical instruments that resonated through the cracks. Excitement buzzed through the crowd and they passed around food and drinks as they gathered around the fire to witness the winning team awarded their tattoos.

An elder tribesman holding a small shard of obsidian cut thin slices in the first man's arm, and, if that wasn't enough pain, he rubbed charred nutmeg into the open cut for color. It was an excruciating process for Mae to watch, but none of the men seemed to notice the smallest bit of pain, they only felt the jubilance of winning. In fact, with so much joyful celebration and happiness around them, this was the first time Mae didn't feel like any of them were under the tribespeople's scrutinizing eyes.

Willie pushed his way through the crowd and squeezed in next to Mae. "The Ma'camo people like your wide hips. They think you will make a good breeder for Yu'mi." Overhearing this, Toke snorted so loud people around them turned to look.

"I'm sure Yu'mi will tell them it's not like that." Mae shook her head dismissively. "He knows we're just friends." She smiled weakly. "Doesn't he?"

"You're on your own there." Toke gave Mae a twisted smile then turned to look elsewhere.

Watching Toke seek out the topless women and not even trying to hide his admiration, Mae let out a loud annoyed breath. "Aren't you over all the nudity by now? We've been here amongst the natives how many times? Four, five?"

"It's just the way I was put together. I can't help it." Toke's eyes got stuck on a woman dancing while shaking large beaded instruments.

"You mean how you were born attached to a penis? I don't see Dexter drooling all over the women, and I know he too has one of those."

"He just hides it better—there! Look at him now." Toke gestured to Dexter a few yards away, resting his back against a tree. Sure enough, Dexter's hand was to his face as his eyes slid slowly over a young woman standing near him who only wore two polished sticks through her ears and a tiny skirt made of feathers. "I could do that hand trick too." Toke covered his face and peeked through his fingers at Mae.

"Well, besides your ogling, being rude, and degrading to women, you also need to be careful. We don't know the Ma'camo rules for looking at another man's woman. They might think it's perfectly okay just to kill you for it, you know?"

With an involuntary sigh, Mae looked away. She didn't want to feel this way. Why would she be jealous that Dexter was looking at other women? She had no right to think this way. He wasn't hers and was free to do whatever he wanted. Plus, she had Greg. He was alive…somewhere…she hoped. No—she *knew*.

Disgusted with her own pathetic feelings, Mae sought out Yu'mi to let him know she was thinking about going home.

After twenty minutes of meeting more of Yu'mi's never-ending extended family and smiling so much her mouth hurt, she felt it would be rude to leave so early. However, the way they treated her and Yu'mi, as if they were a pair of lovers, was beginning to feel uncomfortable. How long should she let this charade go before saying something to him?

It was probably time to check on Dexter and Toke, so she excused herself to find them. Her over-imagination taunted her with the vision that she'd come back to Dexter leaning against a tree, talking flirtatiously with the girl in the feather skirt.

Instead, she came upon a group of young boys, including Willie and Milok, gathered around Toke. He seemed to hold their full attention as he demonstrated his "genius" on one of them. "You cover the cup with a cloth…" He paused for a moment while his eyes hunted around for a napkin or something in this fabric-less civilization. "Okay, here. Just use the bottom of Willie's shirt. Now suck the water up, but slowly, and keep sucking and swallowing all those fizzy air bubbles. Be sure not to stop, just keep sucking and swallowing…excellent." Once the cup was empty, the boy stood motionless, anticipating his next maddening string of hiccups. Which never came. The first stitch of a smile began on the boy's face and soon stretched across in a wide grin. "That worked, huh?" Toke smiled, nodding his head. "Next, you hold up your hand here, and slap mine." Not understanding a word Toke said, the kid ran off to tell someone that this white man got rid of his hiccups.

"You're a hero." Willie's face shone in admiration and he slapped Toke's hand still raised in the air for the other kid. "For them, it's quite shameful to have hiccups. It's a sign of eating more than your share of food too fast."

"Glad to help." Toke caught Mae's eye, giving her the okay to be impressed as well.

Chapter Sixty-Six

Much of the post-game celebration had moved into one of the hubos. A hubo was simply a circle of long bark pieces bound together at the top and dirt piled up around the outside which held the bark in place. The inside was surprisingly expansive, even with a fire occupying the middle. People sat around the perimeter on mats, and Yu'mi motioned for her to sit next to him. Dexter and Toke were told to sit behind the two of them next to Milok, Willie, and the younger children.

Because of the last time Mae and Toke indulged in drinks with them, she was hesitant about what was offered. She made Yu'mi promise to warn them about what they were drinking so they didn't end up like last time. Toke leaned forward, making it clear that he just wanted to be *warned*, not *kept* from it.

Milok tapped Mae's arm. "What does the word native mean? You call us this a lot."

"Well, it means that you were here first. You're the natives of the land. Where we come from, it's not polite to call you Indians. There's a country named India, and you are not from India."

"What do you call people from the country India then?" Milok asked, earnestly trying to understand.

Toke helped, "We call them Indians." He crossed his arms, looking amused, ready to enjoy Mae explain this one.

But all she said was, "I know, confusing, right?" She had hoped Dexter would jump in. Instead, he remained quiet, thoughtfully observing the surroundings and customs since he had not been around the Ma'camos as much as she and Toke had.

Deciding he would take this one on, Toke started, "Okay, it's like, you call me and Dex white men, right?" He held out his arms, exposing the pale undersides, and gave a "meh" shrug. "So, what would we call all of you then, so other people know who we're talking about?"

"But that is where the problem is," Milok explained. "All of us who you call Indians are not all the same. Our brown skin doesn't mean we are the same people. Us Ma'camo people are of the Nisenan tribe. If you don't know someone's village name, call them by their larger tribe name. The Ma'camo village is part of the Nisenan tribe, which is part of the larger Southern Maidu tribe. The small villages south of here are from the Miwok tribe. Northeast of here are the Washo, and then further north are the Northern Maidu. It's all quite easy. We look very different."

Toke wiped his face, expressing just how *not* easy it was. "Okay dude, the problem is, we have no idea how to tell one tribe from another like you so easily do. That's why we just group everyone together. Like, when you see a white person, and you don't know if they're from England, Spain, or the United States, you just call them white. Right?"

Yu'mi and Milok looked at each other for the answer that neither of them had. After speaking together for a moment, Milok affirmed, "Yes, we understand. If you cannot call us by our tribal name, then Indian or native is fine. Neither one is better than the other."

Mae turned fully around. "So, you don't get offended when we call you an Indian?"

"Why would we?" Milok shrugged. "It's not like you're saying it to be mean or to hurt us, so there's nothing *bad* about it. It's just something to refer to us as, yes?"

Yu'mi interrupted, "Not like name digger or savage." His face reddening with a brief flash of anger. "Those *said* mean."

Raising his chin and setting his jaw, Milok added firmly, "Just don't call us the wrong tribe name, that would be worse."

"Settled." Toke held up his hands in agreement. "Indian it is outside of the Ma'camo village, just to save us unnecessary blood loss."

Suddenly, everyone's attention diverted to a commotion right outside the opening of the hubo. At first, given the festive atmosphere all around the camp, no one took it very seriously. But then, a thump against the side of the hubo and another thud on the ground, accompanied by frightened chatter, pulled each of them outside.

A crowd had gathered around a man who was crouched on all fours, thrashing around like an angry wolf pierced in his neck by an arrow. With unexpected violence, he flipped himself over and slammed into the dirt, frantically arching his back as if he were trying to unglue himself from the ground underneath. One hand reached out, grabbing at nothing, and the other clutched his throat. Veins bulged from his forehead as his face grew dark pink, then crimson, and finally settled on purple.

When Toke reached the outer edge of the crowd, nothing blocked his view, so he easily saw over everyone. "Oh shit." Then he nudged Willie. "Watch and learn." Toke forced his way through the tight wall of people until he got to the man writhing on the ground. He immediately pulled him to his feet and spun the asphyxiated body around to face away from him. Arms reached out, trying to pull Toke away, unsure what this white man was doing to their tribesman.

Yu'mi yelled something to the crowd, which caused everyone to back off and let Toke continue. With his fist balled, he gave one quick thrust under the man's ribcage, after which a chunk of meat shot out of his mouth. Choking no more, the man launched into a frenzy of coughing while his family swarmed around in pained relief.

Toke had to crawl out of the mass of people to escape.

Once Toke emerged, Willie caught his arm, his eyes wide with admiration. "How did you do that?"

Toke straightened, tucking his loosened shirt back into his pants, and cleared his throat. "That, my friends, is called the Heimlich…I mean…the Toke maneuver."

It was time to leave, and they were saying their thank yous and goodbyes. The man whose life Toke had saved walked over with his eyes fixed on his boots and his toes sticking out of the tips. Untying the ankle strap of his thick fur-lined moccasins, the man held them out for Toke to take.

Milok gestured, opening the palm of his hand toward the man. "Red-Toothed Bear wants you to have his best moccasins for saving his life. He made them himself with skins from a great hunt."

"Aw shucks." He scraped his foot on the ground in mock humility but took the shoes gratefully.

"He thinks you have done something very brave, but extremely dangerous, working against the bad spirit who caused it to happen," Milok said, then knelt, showing Toke the correct way to tie them on. "The leather of these moccasins came from a courageous and fierce animal who fought strong."

The man's wife and children came forward, giving Toke offerings of nuts and berries and a gourd filled with drink. Toke downed the entire contents without any hesitation, just in case it contained some *special* ingredients, then handed it back with a "Thanks."

Mae added, "Toke would even drink rat pee if he thought it would get him high." The family smiled out of courtesy without understanding, then with a final nod to Toke, walked away.

Possibly taking advantage of his new hero status, Toke asked Yu'mi, "Hey, you have any more of that peyote drink we had last time? That shit was awesome." Mae cringed, remembering waking up naked in each other's arms.

Yu'mi always had a hard time with Toke's use of words. Especially when he compared human feces with everything. With Willie's help, Yu'mi explained that they only used peyote for their religious ceremonies so they could connect with the spirits. To them, it was not a drug to get high for a fun time, and they rarely had any since it didn't grow anywhere near their lands.

Toke held his head low until Willie asked Milok if he could make sure Toke sat at the ceremonial table next time so he could partake in the ceremonial pipe. This seemed to satisfy him for the time being.

They rode home, happy for the exciting night, and very grateful Willie was with them, along with his gun, to show them the impossible way back in the dark. Mae felt jumpy, on constant watch, listening for sounds in the darkness, and tried not to think about the possibility that someone or something could be watching them again.

Chapter Sixty-Seven

In the shade of Sunday's afternoon sun, Mae, Dexter, and Toke lay on their backs, sprawled across the table rock. Mae took a deep breath in and exhaled loudly. "I need more excitement in my life."

"Yeah, I'm right there with you. This is starting to get real old," Toke said, tossing around a small pinecone. "I watch Jack and Elizabeth day in and out, the same boring-as-shit routines. The only goal they have in life is just getting through the day."

"And the dreaded winter." Mae rolled her eyes. "Every conversation of theirs is about stocking up for the cold weather. Where are their hopes and dreams? Is this *it* for the rest of their lives?"

Tossing the pinecone away, Toke crossed his arms behind his head. "Maybe it's finally time to put our energy into ways of actually getting back home."

Dexter stretched, yawning through his words, "I'm open to that."

"We just…" Now Mae caught the yawn. "…need a way…to seal out the blue water so we can haul enough food and supplies through the tunnels to keep us alive the whole journey back." She cringed when she realized her totally rational plan sounded much the way her mother described childbirth. *A woman's brain is wired to forget the horrendous degree of pain we go through in passing a gigantic human head through our teeny tiny opening. If not, no woman would ever give birth again—wiping out the human race.*

"And then for *us*, what if we make, like, a glass globe helmet, and seal it with something to a body suit made from…" Toke thought hard for a moment, "… from something."

"Well, it's all those somethings that we need to figure out first." Dexter tapped his chin subconsciously. "I'd actually like to start testing other materials that the water won't eat, besides glass and certain metals."

Confining his laugh to a snort, Toke added, "Yeah, with all those other materials we have at our disposal."

"I keep thinking about all this knowledge we have of the future." Dexter folded his arms across his chest and exhaled. "There's got to be something we know that can make us money. Enough to buy the materials and equipment we need to get us through the water. I've even tried to work out a way to harness electricity and create a generator." He shook his head, defeated. "But the truth is, I just don't know enough about it."

"Well, how about we think of things *we* need that they don't know they need yet." Mae propped herself up on her elbows. "Like birth control, sunblock, clothes, and socks that stretch, hair dryers, ballpoint pens, light bulbs, cars—"

"Maybe something we actually know how to make," Dexter said with a laugh.

"Oh." That shut them up for a few minutes.

"I've got it." Toke rubbed his hands together. "We can grow a beautiful weed farm. Shit's not illegal anywhere yet, so I would just need to find some seeds. Hybrid strains."

"Let's try harder so Toke's idea doesn't sound like the best one." Mae bit the inside of her lip, searching her brain for ideas.

Every once in a while, someone would open their mouth to say something, then realize their idea would need something else that needed to be invented *first* and shut their mouth. Mae finally said, "Okay, so, what if we sought out inventors and helped them along with the missing piece to their puzzles and then share in the profits? Or, how about we pose as scientists and sell our secrets or equations to other scientists?"

"Like pi or something." Toke smiled, feeling brilliant.

Dexter crushed it with, "You mean E=mc2."

"And they can all be women scientists and inventors so women can rocket ahead of their time," Mae added enthusiastically.

"Good luck finding any," Toke said, sarcastically.

"Okay." Mae let out a loud, frustrated groan. "So, we've been here over a whole two months already and Dexter's feeling much better now." She slid off the rock and stood. "What are we waiting for?" she demanded with open hands, expecting an answer. But her impatience answered first. "Let's leave in a week. Dexter should be fully healed by then."

"Yeah!" Toke caught her buzz and sat up. "Damn time we get the hell out of these boring-ass mountains. Explore the real world. See what's out there, learn everything we can about this century and what they're missing. Make a shitload of dough, build a monstrous drill, and just dig our way past the hungry water."

Mae's tenacity crusaded on. "We're sure to find Greg down in the valley. It's a big place with very few people, so he'll definitely stand out. And, if we offer some kind of reward, then word about him will travel fast."

"Slow down." Dexter held up his hands. "We need to *seriously* think about this."

"You're hosing us down again. C'mon, let loose, bro."

"We could do some *real* harm messing around with the past like that. We might want to concentrate on other, more subtle ways to make money. If we change the past too much, it might have horrible and devastating repercussions."

Toke squinted, weighing it out in his head. "Yeah…I guess that's something to think about. We might not even be born. Or maybe we'd just disappear. Heh, like, what if Mae just vanished one day? Poof! That means she was never born, so she was never here. Would we even remember who Mae was to realize she disappeared if she never existed?"

Mae puzzled this over in her head, then nodded reluctantly. "Dex, you're right. Okay, let's stick with subtle. We can build our own shelter and eat off the land like Yu'mi taught us. Earn just enough money for the equipment we'll need, find Greg, and go back home to the future."

Toke stood up and planted his fists on his hips, determined. "So, when do we tell them?"

"Tomorrow," Dexter said with finality. "Once we have a chance to firm up a plan, we'll tell them after dinner tomorrow."

Chapter Sixty-Eight

The evening fire blazed, and their Sunday off was coming to an end. Toke creaked in his chair, bouncing his knee, working on trip plans in his head. Mae squinted in the dim light, sewing tiny dark stitches on dark cloth, stabbing herself with the needle every now and then.

"You know, we can hear you. You have one spicy potty mouth, princess," Toke said with a wink, and she scowled back, feeling in a bad mood because sewing wasn't considered "work" and still needed to be done even on their days off. "So, how come they don't even have a sewing machine with all the sewing you're both always doing? Hell, they don't even have a typewriter. These must really be the dark ages. We'll just add those to our list of inventions we can speed up."

Biting off the end of the thread, Mae held her sewing up to the candlelight to inspect. "Both of those could already exist, but maybe the Foxes just don't have the money to buy them." She wound up the thread and put away the sewing basket, lightening her mood. "Remember how Jack traded just his clock and got two goats, a wagon, *and* a horse?"

"Or it could be because we're way the hell over in California and they don't think anyone lives out here to buy their crap." Toke tapped out the black ashes of his new pipe.

Jack clamored through the door, hitching his battered hat on the wooden peg to his left. So used to taking charge, he spoke loudly, drowning out anyone else who might think they were talking. "So, I've been doing some tinking. De little farm has done vell wit dis extra help, an' now wit Dexter in good healt, I decided we vill build a room for Mae to sleep in."

Stunned, the three of them just looked at each other. No one knew what to say. They were all ready to spill their own plans. Jack plopped down heavily in his chair and began to pack his pipe. "An' if Lizzie gets wit child again, de baby can share de room wit Mae. It vill be big enough where Villie can move in dere as vell. He is nearly grown out of his bed." His good mood beckoned Elizabeth, so she picked up her knitting and joined them at the fire.

"Mae's quite comfortable out here, sleeping on the bench," Toke added. "And who would keep the fire lit?" Mae rolled her eyes but remained quiet.

Jack drew on his pipe, pulling the flame toward the tobacco until it lit. "It would not be easy adding on to dis old house. Makes sense to build a whole new house instead." Toke frowned at his empty pipe and showed it to Jack with pleading eyes until Jack tossed the bag of tobacco over. Mae automatically pulled the scarf from her head over her mouth. *Why did* both *of them have to smoke?*

"Den, in de few years time, Villie vill be wanting to start a family, an' he vill need his own place."

"A few years?" Toke raised his brow, looking amused. "Isn't he twelve?"

"Ja, you're right. Probably jost a cople years den. Bot we're hoping he vaits ontil he has fifteen years at de least." Jack rocked back in his chair as if daring the creaking legs to break. Elizabeth nodded along silently.

Toke scratched his scruffy chin. "So, we're basically building Willie's future fornication hut to procreate new Fox kits then?"

The rest of the evening felt as somber as a funeral while Jack worked out plans in his head and the three of them processed the new information. Finally, Jack stood, extending his hand to Elizabeth. "We vill start on de house in de morn. Got to get it done before de rains come. Gud natt." Then disappeared behind their curtain.

"What the hell?" Toke mouthed silently, then added in a low voice, "Let's just tell him."

Dexter took his glasses off and tightened one of the knots. "I'm thinking that perhaps we should just help him build it. Think about it. He's done us a huge favor by letting us stay here. The room is also for his future expanding family and not just Mae, so we won't have any guilt leaving right after it's finished."

"I guess that will work. It'll pay our debt and then some." Toke tapped out his pipe, stood, and yawned. "After that, I'll have no problems asking him for something good to take with us to trade."

Depressed and beyond frustrated, Mae threw her head back and let out such an anguished groan, she sounded like a stabbed bear. In her mind, the debt had already been paid, and she had the tortured body to prove it. "These are just more delays. Then there'll be more after this. We'll never get out of here."

"Mae, there are positives to this as well." Dexter swung his chair around to face hers. "Now, we'll have plenty of time to make a good solid plan for our trip. We'll have Jack's help in drawing a map, giving us tips, and hopefully something to trade with. This actually works out for our benefit too."

"And, I promise you, Mae"—Toke popped his head out through his bedroom curtain—"once we've got the new place done, we rest up for a few days, grab what we need, then we're out of here so fast Jack's head will spin completely off."

Chapter Sixty-Nine

Cradling a steaming mug of dandelion tea in her hands, Mae leaned back in her chair, propping her feet up on the porch railing. The tea's heat soothed her hands, sore from peeling a giant bucket of scrawny, twisted potatoes.

She closed her tired eyes to the peace of the morning—until Jack's voice barged in and boomeranged around the farm. He rattled off instructions to Dexter and Toke who followed at his feet like obedient dogs.

Now with Dexter's back stronger and nearly able to handle a full work-load, Jack made up for lost time. Stopping ten feet from Mae, Jack picked up a long stick and began to stake out his vision in the dirt. "From here to...here," he said, dropping rocks where needed. "Den over here, de door, vindow, beds, here an' dere." It looked like a modest-sized room to Mae's relief. That shouldn't take too long to build.

"See, we cut de logs to here, cut off all de notches, an' we strip de bark because it vill rot trough. We'll start by setting four good flat stones in de corners. Dese cornerstones vill serve as de foundation. We vill plan on de heart for de fire...here. De next few days we vill be cotting an hauling de logs an' large stones. It vill go op fast wit all os vorking. Bot de chimney an' firebox is someting else. If we vork sunop to sundown, we should have dis done in a fortnight."

Toke mouthed the words, "Fortnight?" to Dexter.

"Means two weeks," Dexter said in a low voice.

Toke groaned and looked over to Mae, but she had gone inside. "Who wants to give the good news to Mae?"

"We can put de girl in dere and divide it wit a dressing screen wit Villie on de oter half."

"Willie's going to like having a nice lady on the other side, don't you think?" Toke sported his mischievous crooked smile. "He won't be twelve all that much longer, if you don't mind me saying so."

Jack only grunted. "De door an' vindow vill be built to de sout for de sonlight…" Over the next few days, the sound of hammers and saws echoed through the trees, winning the duel over the chattering birds. Jack had four precious nails left to his name and those were going where they would do the most good.

Dexter put his hand on his back and stood, resting his sawing arm. "Toke, did you ever have Lincoln Logs?"

"Nah. I was less hands-on, more of a digital sort of kid. Why?"

"These logs we're cutting are just like them. Except the notches aren't precut." He picked the saw back up and started back in again.

"I guess you would be considered an architect at this point, having all that experience with Lincoln Logs." Toke put down his saw, taking this as an excuse to rest again. "We need to tell Jack so you get a promotion."

In the following week, they made a lot of progress, but it took its toll on their muscles, and their bodies ached all over. Once they had finished the stone chimney, fireplace, walls and door, they bore holes in the log walls and banged in wood pegs to hang clothes and other things up.

Stopping for a minute, Dexter pulled out his handkerchief and wiped the dripping sweat that stung his eyes. He gulped down a big cup of cold water and found himself studying the roof of the main house. Handing Toke a cup of water, he gestured to the roof with his chin. "Hand cut shingles. Do you think Jack split *each one*?"

Toke downed the cool drink before scowling at the roof. "Hell, yeah. You heard him. He made it all from scratch except for his four beloved nails. I guess now it will be *us* splitting that wood for each and every shingle on this roof." He glanced over at the house. "Maybe we can get Mae to do it since she wants to be working outside so bad."

When Yu'mi could spare the time away from his village, he was a great help with the outside finishes. He had much insight on how to finish a structure that could withstand the harsh elements. He advised them where to get the good mud, what grasses to collect, and which animal scat was best to firm up the clay mortar so it hardened in the sun. Jack said he wished he had known him when he was building his first house.

Anticipation grew each day as the cabin neared completion ahead of schedule. While Dexter filled the exterior wall holes with small pieces of wood, Toke and Willie packed them in with Yu'mi's special mud mortar. Jack built two crude shelves, then brought in the two new beds they had finished making that morning.

Once Jack inspected the outer walls, making sure not even the teeniest vermin-welcoming hole existed, he was finally pleased. Then he bragged how they never had rodent problems in the main house due to his diligence at patching and closing the window shutters each night. "If just one of dem demons gets in—" He slammed the blade of his ax into a stray log, splitting it in two. "Might as vell set de house on fire."

Toke raised his eyebrows mockingly. "Got some feelings about that, Jack?"

Next up were the dreaded shingles. Toke got the idea of hiring Yu'mi and his friends and paying them in food. They agreed, so the next day they went home with a loaf of bread and a dozen biscuits. The following day, a total of six joined him, so Mae and Elizabeth had to drop their other plans and bake like mad to fill the order.

With the shingles done, Yu'mi and his group of friends rested on the front porch, drinking fresh apple juice before going home. Mae wanted Yu'mi's friends to warm to her as they had with Dexter and Toke, so she was diligent in keeping their cups full and smiled a lot.

Suddenly Yu'mi straightened, splaying his hands out in front of him as if they were ears. A second later, they *all* froze, eyes wide and ears pricked on high alert. Without a sound, Yu'mi and his friends got to their feet, shouldered their quivers and bows, and soundlessly deserted the porch.

Yu'mi slipped through the wall of trees, and the others followed as if an invisible thread linked them together. They moved swiftly through the forest like light-footed gazelles, gone from sight and hearing in seconds.

Mae stood speechless, not sure what had just happened. Toke strained his eyes to see through the trees, but the woods were still, waiting for news too.

Dexter came around the house, noisily slapping the sawdust off his shirt with his gloves. Halfway up the steps, he stopped, noticing Mae and Toke's rigid stance with their eyes super-glued to the trees. "Oh man, is something out there again?" he asked, a little too loudly.

Mae put her finger to her lips with a partial shrug, keeping her eyes fixed ahead.

All of a sudden in the distance, the forest erupted in a blaring cacophony of calls and shrieks. Mae scrambled up a chair and craned her neck, but still, she saw nothing. None of them did. The commotion was moving away from them, growing fainter in the distance, until they could hear it no more.

Chapter Seventy

By now Jack and Elizabeth had joined them, and Willie perched himself on the porch railing, aiming his father's gun into the trees. "Should we go after them?" he said, sweeping the trees for a target.

"Y'all just stay put," Elizabeth said firmly, and no one argued.

It felt like forever before Toke announced movement, and soon after, Yu'mi and his friends emerged through the trees, shoulders drooped and heads downcast. Half of them left straightaway to report back to their village, but Yu'mi joined them back on the porch.

He explained to their worried faces what had just transpired, as best as he could, given his limited English vocabulary. There had been a Yiptuati warrior watching them from behind the trees. They chased after him and almost caught up, but once he reached his horse, he was too fast. But, before he got too far, they got two arrows in him. One in his shoulder and one in his leg.

Then, Yu'mi's tone turned bitter, telling them how the Yiptuati are known to steal people from one tribe and sell or trade them to another tribe. Or, sell them to the ranchos and missions to use as slaves. They came from far over the mountains on the other side of the Sierras, and the warriors were very dangerous. The entire area where they lived was considered Maidu land, but the Yiptuati made camp wherever they wanted.

A muscle twitched in Yu'mi's jaw as he tried to control his anger. He glanced over at his friends' grim faces and spoke for all of them. "They hunt our animals and steal our people. They not welcome in these mountains."

"How can you be certain he was a warrior and not just some Yip-twatty out for a peeping?" Toke asked.

"A Yiptuati warrior cut hair all off, like you, to show war scars. He have big scar." Then demonstrated with his finger a diagonal cut from his forehead to behind his ear. "And they mark horse with same scar in red."

His friends mounted their horses and stood by, waiting for Yu'mi to finish. He continued by telling them that many years ago the Ma'camo used to war with the Yiptuati often. Then, one of his uncles, named Bilba, who was just a young boy at the time, disappeared one night. The entire tribe looked for him a very long time, but he was gone. The Ma'camo learned that if they ever saw a Yiptuati around here, it couldn't be good. They only came to steal people.

"So, you're saying that guy was planning to take one of us?" Toke crossed his arms, contemplating their new danger.

"He have Mae's dress on horse. It cover over a big…" Yu'mi got stuck for a word so rounded his arms in explanation. "And tie with rope to back of horse."

Mae's hand flew to her mouth, realizing how close she came to being abducted that day. Her heart raced at Mach speed, and everyone looked completely unnerved. Yu'mi reassured them that the Yiptuati would not be coming around this area for quite a while since they knew the Ma'camo warriors would be on the lookout for them now.

How many times had Mae been alone and unsuspecting while washing clothes in the creek? Or, maybe it wasn't her they were targeting, but Willie who was young just like Yu'mi's uncle had been. Her vision blurred until she was full on sobbing, overcome with the horror that could have been and immense gratitude. Taking Yu'mi's hands in her own, she brought them to her cheek. "Thank you so, so much Yu'mi," she said, then turned to his remaining friends. "*All* of you!"

That night, they all took a while to relax and feel safe again. Mae felt a new trepidation about their upcoming trip. What if they came across people like the Yiptuati? And this time, they'd be on their own without Yu'mi's protection. Also, without a gun. How much could their little knives really protect them? She made up her mind to ask Yu'mi to give them a lesson on how to kill a living person with only a knife. She could do that far more easily than killing an animal.

Chilly early autumn winds swept through the farm, stealing leaves from unsuspecting trees, only to shamelessly toss them away a moment later. It was late September when Mae and Willie finally moved into their new room. Quilts that she and Elizabeth had sewn together from old clothes, more practical than pretty, covered their two sack mattresses. Large tule mats woven by the Ma'camo made up a dressing screen that divided the room between the two beds.

Trading the bone-bruising hard bench for her own soft bed had Mae a little less rushed to leave as she was before. But she struggled with the guilt that was eating her up inside. They had yet to tell the Foxes of their impending travel plans. The time just never seemed right to break such big news. And then, seeing the tremendous amount of work Jack, Elizabeth, and Willie had each put into the new house, made it all the more difficult to mention anything. But, now the time had come, and they couldn't put it off any longer…

PART FOUR

Chapter Seventy-One

A playful breeze whipped through the clothesline, filling the shirts, pants, and dresses with eerie human forms. Mae clipped the last wet shoulder of Jack's overly patched shirt to the line, cheerfully humming an old Katy Perry song.

Anticipation lightened her daily drudgery now that they'd decided to tell the family about their leaving that very night. Often through the day, she caught herself smiling, imagining the day she'd find Greg, her running to him, and them reeling around in a tearful passionate embrace.

"Incoming!" Toke's ear-splitting announcement obliterated any sense of tranquility Mae felt. Held in his fingers was the oblong ball he'd made from scraps of hide, stitched together with gut, and packed full of chicken feathers. He tucked it under his arm and sprinted to the goal line, pushing through the defense and trampling Willie to the ground. Toke pranced around in triumph, whooping boorishly.

Seeing Willie sprawled on his back in the dirt, Mae shouted, "Don't play so rough. Remember, you're twice his size." She groaned at all the dirt ground into Willie's pants, knowing she'd be the one scrubbing it out. Unless, of course, they were already gone by then…"Toke, don't you have real work to do?"

Toke grabbed Willie under the arms and pulled him to his feet. "Dude, you're supposed to try to tackle me. Not just stand there and let me hose you down."

After swatting hopelessly at the dirt on his shirt, Willie looked up at Toke questioningly, having to squint one eye closed from the sun. "I don't get why you call this game football. We use our hands and bodies more. It should be called handball or tackleball. Why can't we just play it like the Ma'camo do at their ball games?"

"Nah. Football's a *real* man's game."

Mae cleared her throat loudly.

"Hut, hut, hike!" Toke took a few steps back as he launched the ball. "Go long!" Catching it, Willie ran, holding his arm out in front of him like Toke had taught him, but was soon tackled flat to the ground once again.

"Duuuude." Toke shook his head with empathy, helping him up. "Okay. You know what we need? Team names!"

Willie jumped to face him, landing with bent knees and claws out, and ferociously growled. "I'm a mean grizzly bear."

"Okay, so we'll call your team the Grizzlies. I'll be the Niners." He clapped his hands together and started to move back for a throw.

"What's a Niners?" Willie asked, waving his arms around hesitantly, unsure if he should concentrate on catching the ball or protecting himself.

"The 49ers, you know, the football team. Or, rather, you wouldn't know."

"What a dumb name. Why not be called the 99ers or the 100s. That's far betterer."

"Nah, Niners is short for 49ers. It's when a shitload of pioneer dudes swarmed into California to seek their fortune—" Toke suddenly froze, and the ball fell from his open fingers to the ground. His eyes grew wide, and he breathed a deep and guttural, "Holy—beautiful—hell."

He took off running, barely stopping as he scooped Mae up in his arms and flew through the wet laundry toward the sound of chopping wood. Halting in front of Dexter, Mae flailed around, trying to get down. Toke just stood in front of him, catching his breath, and laughing like an unhinged whacko. Dexter smiled politely, shaking his head, before turning back to his chopping.

"Ow!" Toke laughed and finally released Mae.

"What's wrong with you?" She pushed him away indignantly. Toke could not wipe the enormous grin off his face and started to laugh again.

Dexter put his ax down and crossed his arms expectantly. "Okay, what's up?"

Mae started to walk away, and Toke reached out and grabbed her. "Wait. You need to listen." He paused for a moment to calm his excitement, then went on. "So, we know it's 1840, right?"

Mae rolled her eyes.

"And who's my favorite football team?"

She crossed her arms, impatiently. "The Giants."

"My other favorite."

"Niners," Dex said, getting a high-five from Toke.

"And…why were they called that?"

"Uh, they were founded in 1949?" She shifted her stance, still annoyed.

"Think about it." Toke laughed again, giddy with excitement. With a small jump, he skirted around them and ran off to find Jack, letting the two figure it out themselves.

A mere three seconds later, loud whoops and a happy scream trumpeted across the farm. Running footsteps caught up with Toke, and the three of them hugged and carried on loudly. The noise brought Jack out from the barn, and soon after, Elizabeth and Willie.

"Family meeting! Family meeting in the house!" Toke announced, so energized his feet barely touched the ground.

This new level of enthusiasm had everyone gathered around the table in under a minute. "Gud Lord." An impatient Jack rubbed his hands on his thighs, wanting to be elsewhere. "Tell os wat is so *terribly* important."

Toke's excitement was so out of character that he definitely had their attention. "Have you ever found a gold nugget or gold dust in any of the streams and rivers around here?" The Foxes shook their heads, perplexed by the odd question that had nothing to do with the productivity of the farm. Toke leaned in toward them as if revealing a huge secret. Which he sort of was. "There are massive amounts of gold, right *here*." He slapped the table hard. "On *this land*—all around you." He demonstrated by waving his arms in giant circles like an ambidextrous window washer.

"Gold?" Willie cocked his head. "I haven't seen any gold."

"So, where is all dis 'gold' you found?" Jack crossed his arms, with an air of condescension.

"We haven't found it yet, we just know where some *should* be, and we will have to look for the rest." Toke rocked back and forth, trying to contain his elation.

"We would like to take some tools and do an exploratory dig if that's okay with you." Dexter raised both his eyebrows, nodding encouragingly for a 'yes'.

"Me! Take me!" Willie bounced on the bench.

"Why are you just telling us now?" Elizabeth asked indifferently.

"Let me just say." Dexter held up his hand. "I am quite embarrassed for not remembering this weeks ago." He banged his forehead on the table a few times.

"Check your ego, Dex. Who the hell cares—it's G-O-L-D."

Dexter composed himself, recovering from his self-inflicted humiliation. "In answer to Elizabeth's question, I think that we were just used to the fact that gold had been discovered so very long ago. There was never a time in our lives that California wasn't known for its gold. People pretty much stopped looking for it since most of it was taken. We just didn't think of it anymore. Familiar habit, I suppose."

"Ja, so, den, where is it all?" Jack wore that familiar look of disbelief, not picking up their excitement in the least.

"Well..." Mae thought for a second. "There's a place called Coloma where they *first* found it. But Coloma might've had a different name back then. I mean, back now—in 1840."

"Still called Coloma," Jack grunted, impatiently.

"Coloma means beautiful happy valley," Willie announced. "I've met some people from there. They're part of the Nisenan like the Ma'camos. They call themselves Sickoma or something like that."

With bright eyes and eager faces, they stared at Jack, still waiting for his answer. He shifted his weight on the bench and leaned in on his arms. "Vell, I don't know. We're doing fine how we are." He squinted and looked out the window in thought. "Bot I soppose some gold could get os anoder pickax and maybe a pair of new boots for Villie."

"Uh, yeah," Toke said, amused at their humble requests, although boots were on the top of his list as well.

Mae turned to Jack. "About how far do you think we are from Coloma?"

"Soppose an hour or so by de horse." Jack pointed northeast.

"Seriously?" Toke beamed. "That's awesome."

"But, that's just where it was *discovered*. It's really all over the place up here." Dexter looked around hoping to find a map but gave up. "Here's what I remember, and some is just science. Gold was found all up and down where they built Highway 49. That was the biggest gold vein of all, and they called it the Motherlode."

"So, if we can figure out where they will put Highway 49, we'll know where most of the gold is." Mae's voice cracked with excitement. "The gold miners didn't even know exactly where the gold vein was until they dug everywhere it wasn't. So, we're *way* ahead."

Toke slapped his hand to his forehead. "Oh, ho man, now I see it. It was there all along." He smiled, tight-lipped, and shook his head at his own stupidity. "Mae, remember the scary demon with the gold eyes in the Ma'camo's wooden carving? And the evil snake embedded with gold on Chief K'ut'im's walking stick?" He let out a pained groan.

"Yeah, gold was all over the place back home, real and fake." Mae shrugged. "So, when we saw gold *here*, it didn't stand out as uncommon in our minds."

"The most important thing is to tell *no one*." Toke pointed his finger at each of them. "This place would get mowed down by hundreds of thousands of people in days."

"When California discovered gold, the world discovered California," Dexter added.

Jack rubbed his chin. "Ja, we vill go find a little, den buy a few tings an' be done."

"Nah. Then some other yahoo will come along and find it." Toke waved it away, dismissively. "For anyone from the east that wants to get to California, walking over these mountains is the fastest way to get here. And once the first person finds a nugget, it's all over."

"Den, we go find it *all* an' *den* be done." Jack made a decision, and it seemed to please them all. No one wanted to tell him just how *much* gold there actually was, so they left it at that. "We finished?" Jack scooted back the bench and slapped on his hat. "Now we get back to vork. It vill be dark in a few hours." Following Jack's lead, Willie and Elizabeth excused themselves to go back to their chores.

Faces still flush with adrenaline, the three of them remained seated, fantasizing about all the new possibilities open to them now. And none of their thoughts involved leaving the farm anytime soon.

Jack's impatient whistle from outside pierced the air and shook them back to the present. With reluctance, they stood, but looked forward to the time after dinner when they could talk in depth about how their lives were about to change.

From this day forward, life on the farm would never be the same.

Chapter Seventy-Two

Night had finally arrived, and Mae hurried through her chores to join them by the fire. Toke sat in his usual place and puffed on his pipe, looking ridiculous. "Yeah, I totally remember the field trips to Gold Country and Sutter's Mill. We had to go every couple of years with our class and sometimes an extra time when relatives came to visit. The panning for gold was pretty cool, even though it was all pre-planted."

"I know, we had to do that too. Let me think for a minute, and I'll try to remember some of the details." Mae cut a piece of coarse thread, waxed the end to a sharp point, and threaded it through her delicate bone needle. She stared, unfocused, at Jack's ripped trousers in her lap as her brain hunted through her childhood memories and history classes. "Okay, so, I think it went something like this. A man named Marshall left from Sutter's Fort to build a sawmill up in the mountains in a place the natives called Coloma. And something about Marshall having to dig a small channel to re-route part of the river so the water would flow through his sawmill." Mae picked up the pants and took the first stitch. "Or something like that."

"That sounds about right." Dexter leaned back and propped his feet up to be warmed by the fire. "The thing is, the rushing water in creeks and rivers slowly erodes their banks. It forcibly carves its way, creating new curves and bends for its water to flow, eventually moving the entire river hundreds of yards from where it used to be." Learning from his previous experiences, he looked around to make sure they were still listening. "We don't see this happening because it's super slow and takes hundreds of years."

Mae snipped off the thread with her teeth and folded the mended pants. "It turns out Marshall had dug the new water channel for his mill, right where the *old* river had been many years before and that's where he spotted his first piece of gold."

"So, it was just buried until he unburied it?" Willie blew two painfully shrill test notes from the flute he was whittling. Slumping into his chair, he frowned, discouraged, realizing it needed a lot more work.

"That's a helluva lot of digging we'd have to do." Toke lazily poked at the fire, not leaving his chair.

"Ja, we vill definitely need better picks an' shovels for dat part." Jack had the annoying habit of chomping repeatedly on his pipe between puffs. The clacking that Jack's teeth made against the bone tip of his pipe grated viciously on Mae's nerves.

Dexter continued, "So, since the gold's been in the water for hundreds of years, it isn't going to be still lying on top of the sand and rocks. It's the heaviest thing in the river, even heavier than the rocks, so it sinks. That's why you haven't easily come across it."

Willie blew into the soft part of his arm, making a series of farting noises. Then, Toke joined in, showing his real age. Mae rolled her eyes, poking Willie to get his attention. "So, where do you think most of it goes?"

"All the way at the bottom, and under that, even," Willie spouted triumphantly.

"You're getting this, little dude." Toke ruffled Willie's hair.

A thought occurred to Willie, and concern puckered his sun-bleached eyebrows. "But what if it kept sinking lower and lower and never stops—ever?"

"Nah, it will stop eventually," Toke assured him. "It might end up being like three feet down or so. But under all the sand, rocks, and other crap at the way bottom, it's solid rock. Bedrock, it's called."

"Most of the gold in these mountains is actually still inside the rocks. Veins of gold are usually found alongside veins of quartz that are within the rocks as well." Dexter glanced at Jack and Elizabeth, who remained silent, seemingly bored with the details. "We don't have the machinery to chisel any of it out, so we can just leave all that gold where it is. It's much easier to simply go after the gold that's already in the rivers."

"Works for me," Toke said. "There's got to be a truck load just hanging out, barely covered at the bottom or maybe a few inches down. We can leave the deep stuff, deep, safely hidden away."

"I say we start at Coloma, where we *know* it is." Mae put down her sewing.

Toke rubbed his hands together. "We could even go tomorrow."

"It vill still be dere. For devil's sake, wat's de hurry?" Jack held up his hands to slow things down. "You're going to want to get permission from de Indians to do someting like dis on deir land." Mae had a new respect for Jack for knowing the land belonged to the Indians.

"Like Jack said, we need to check with the Ma'camo first to see if it's okay." Dexter fidgeted with his short beard. "Then hopefully, they'll introduce us to the village in the Coloma Valley, before we just start pilfering from their land."

"I was just thinking." Toke paused to finish giggling. "If some people we never saw before just walked into the yard here and started digging, Jack would have a gun at their heads in seconds."

Mae laughed, agreeing with Toke. "Okay, so let's talk with Yu'mi first, and then his village. They might even know better places to start looking first."

Dexter slapped his hands on the armrests and gripped them tightly. "Sounds good, let's make a plan."

"Just be varned. Dey're not all as accepting of de white man as de Ma'camos have been. Not even to me."

"So, where does that leave me?" Mae raised her brow expectantly. "I'm not white, and I'm not a man."

Toke patted her on the back. "But you're Yu'mi's woman and that should get you somewhere." Mae batted his hand away like she would an annoying brother.

"We can start small." Dexter rocked back on the rickety legs of the pine chair. "Just find enough gold to buy a few crucial farming tools, proper equipment for mining, and some well-needed household things."

"And new boots for everyone!" Mae jubilantly shot her fist in the air.

"We'll throw in a big ol' ox to pull your stumps out, as easily as a weed." Toke plucked out an imaginary weed with two fingers and tossed it away like a feather. "Next time, we'll add a couple of sheep, and maybe get some glass on these windows."

"Imagine having a plow so you could grow your own grain." Mae hoped her enthusiasm would become infectious, but Jack just nodded as if she were telling him how many eggs Willie collected that morning.

Dexter persevered. "Soon you'll have a large, profitable orchard without having to worry about putting enough food on the table to feed your family."

"Let's not shoot sparrows with a cannon." Jack laughed. "We've got a good ting going now."

Mae squinted, trying to read Jack. "I don't think you're getting the whole picture. Gold also gives us the ability to get home. Back to our families. We'll be able to offer such a monstrous reward for our friend's return. We'll have all of California looking for him. Gold changes everything for us."

With a patronizing smile for something he let go a little too far, Jack stretched out his arms and yawned loudly, making his skepticism obvious.

"Dude! There's a ton of gold out there! No one's forcing you to have any of it. We just thought it would help you out. Make your family's life a little easier," Toke said, amused by Jack's ignorance but mostly annoyed with his smug pessimism. "Okay, Jack." He tapped the burnt contents out of his pipe loudly. "Tomorrow. I'll get you your proof."

Elizabeth got up and walked toward the kitchen. “I think we’ll need some warm milk in our tea tonight. Y’all seem a bit stirry for sleeping.”

And she was right. They tossed and turned through the night, brains alive with excitement. Except for Jack, who, as usual, was snoring like a rhino. Eventually, one by one, they fell asleep and the sounds of nocturnal wildlife took over.

Chapter Seventy-Three

The abrasive hacking of a pickax thundered through the sleeping farm, welcoming them all to the new day with the gentleness of a jackhammer. Out of pure curiosity, Mae followed the intrusion of noise and there stood Toke. He was barely visible, deep in the half-dug, rocky soil of the abandoned outhouse hole that had been too close to the river. She smiled to herself knowingly and walked back into the house with her fingers crossed.

When Toke didn't show up for breakfast, she brought it out to him, then slipped back into the house like a co-conspirator. At some point, Jack walked past the hole, and called down to Toke, "Maybe you can put your digging skills to better use and dig os a vell," then followed it with a patronizing laugh, as he walked away.

By their midday meal, Toke finally stopped and joined them. Breathless and drenched with sweat, he dropped a tied handkerchief in the center of the table. "There's your proof." And he took a seat.

Jack picked up the little package like it was a bag of dog poop and eyed it skeptically. With one last look around at their anxious faces, he untied the knot, letting the handkerchief fall open. Inside, shining up at him, were three small nuggets of brilliant gold. Mae and Dexter grinned, mouthing "thank you," to Toke.

Emptying the handkerchief into his hand, he brought the nuggets closer to the candle's light. The luxurious radiance of these valuable treasures looked entirely out of place in his leathery, calloused, dirt-embedded palm. It was like seeing diamond earrings on a bear.

Remaining silent, Jack took one of the nuggets outside and placed it on the table rock. The fact that it was still shiny and yellow in the shade where fool's gold wouldn't be, still wasn't enough for him. He picked up the hammer and flattened the piece of gold onto the rock's surface. The more he hammered it, the larger it grew.

"Lizzie, get me a cop of lye." She obeyed instantly. Peeling the paper-thin piece of gold off the rock, Jack examined it carefully.

"If you keep hammering that one nugget, it could seriously pave the entire floor of your house." Toke leaned an arm on the rock. "Not that you'd want to cover up that fine dirt or anything."

Elizabeth returned with the cup of lye, and he dropped the abused piece of gold into the liquid. "If it turns black, it is not gold," Jack announced a bit too smugly, as he stepped back, planting his hands on his hips.

They hovered anxiously. All eyes fixed on the gold, like cats watching a bird, waiting for the slightest fluctuation to pounce. Jack drew his brows together in a frown and leaned in closer. Finding a small twig, he poked at the piece of gold, then stirred it up a little.

Mae could feel her tense muscles melt and let out a huge breath she didn't know she'd been holding. The nugget's color remained its brilliant yellow, glittering brightly even in the shade. The hard line of Jack's mouth turned up at the ends, then grew broader until it was a full-on grin. "Ja, dat's gold all right." He pulled the gold piece out of the lye and dried it off. "Dis is nice. Real nice."

Meekly, unable to suppress her dire need, Elizabeth said, "A new kettle and some pots without holes patched over and over. They're so thin already, and the food burns too quickly. A bolt of cloth so I can stitch everyone new clothes. They're all so threadbare." Elizabeth fingered the many stains on her dress, then eyed her dilapidated shoes that looked a hundred years old, and her eyes began to glaze over. "Oh, how I miss my lovely dresses and tables overflowing with food—" She stopped mid-sentence and looked ashamed. "Please forgive my gluttony. We're quite fine with what we have." Jack gave her a nod for correcting her circumstances with the inadequacies he provided her.

The rest of the day and on into the night was far from silent. Filled with the chattering of plans, the exposing of dreams, and the unveiling of hopes until no one could keep their eyes open anymore and slowly surrendered to sleep.

Chapter Seventy-Four

They woke fresh and alive in this wonderful new land. Evidence of their original despair over these last ten weeks had vacated. It took most of the morning to gather the tools they'd need for their first gold mining trip. And what they didn't have, they cheerfully made, like elves in Santa's workshop. But, unlike the skilled work of two-hundred-year-old elves, their own finished tools resembled art projects crafted by kindergarteners.

Since Jack still had Willie's gun at home, he lent them his. Toke flung it over his back and mounted his horse, looking proud and confident with a cocky grin.

Mae glowered at his phony show of expertise. "Do you think we feel safe with your only shooting experience coming from video games and water guns?"

"There's not much difference, you'll see." Toke yawned, unconcerned.

"Um, except when it comes to actually shooting something *real*." Mae felt completely bewildered at Toke's perception of reality. "How many times have you even shot Jack's gun?"

Answering with a wink, Toke chose to torture her by not revealing his consistently expert score at the shooting range back home. He had sixteen years of shooting under his belt. Sure, it started when he was only three with empty paper towel tubes, which advanced to a broken chair leg, then a broom, and sometimes even just a stick would do. Anything over five inches qualified. He regularly gunned down his father, and when he was a little older, he mastered every gun in every video game he could get his hands on. Ron was firmly against violence, especially a ten-year old playing an M-rated game. But, using his self-taught psychology tools, he finally relented, figuring this might help his son release the bottled-up anger and frustration that constantly boiled inside him. If Toke were able to shoot all the fake people he wanted in a video game, then he might not feel the need to gun someone down in real life. He would soon become the loving son that Ron had always known was buried somewhere inside of him. At fourteen, Toke cleverly used his father's rationale to his advantage, explaining that there would be no need for him to join a street gang to get the physical shooting experience he hungered. So, perhaps if he just took him to a shooting range every week where he could shoot *real* guns at paper targets, it would satiate his hunger for violence. This worked, and Toke turned out to be a complete natural with incredibly precise aim.

The only real issue at this point was that he'd only fired Jack's gun a few times. Lacking the patience for reloading buckshot and gunpowder after a single shot, Toke didn't get the necessary experience to master the inconsistent fluctuations of this kind of antique ammunition. But Mae didn't need to know this.

Willie couldn't hide his disappointment when his dad insisted he stay home to help with the chores. But, once his tears dried, he pitched in to help.

The horses were loaded with a pick and shovels, blankets, pots and pans, tools, other essentials, and small buckskin bags to hold the hordes of gold they planned to find. And at the last minute, Elizabeth added a loaf of sweet apple bread and an assortment of bakery treats as goodwill gifts for the people of Coloma. She also snuck in a basket of apple hand-pies just for Yu'mi's family. The Indian culture wasn't much accustomed to wheat flour, so Elizabeth's baking was always well received, full of new tastes and unfamiliar textures.

Jack glared at Mae as she mounted her horse. "Dis vork is not for a woman. Your place is at home wit Lizzie." He held his hand out to help her down. Mae couldn't help but feel pity for the way Jack clung so fiercely to his throne of antiquated judgment. He needed to learn she was not chained to the house nor the kitchen, and his righteous authority was not always the final say.

"Yee-haw!" Toke shouted, and they began moving, but slowly due to their heavy load, unfitting to Toke's enthusiastic call. When Trixie passed in front of Jack, Mae held her chin up, keeping her eyes straight ahead, as if Jack had not spoken at all.

"Good luck!" Willie shouted, running after them.

Mae caught Toke's eye. "Thanks. Really. I was about to lose it." And she meant it.

"No problemo."

Ten minutes later, they came across a small group of Ma'camo children under a large oak tree. An older woman finished whacking the higher branches with a long stick, and the kids swooped in to gather the acorns and fill their baskets.

As they rode closer, the children froze with ears alert like startled deer. Mae waved, but no one responded. But, once the kids recognized Toke, they began jumping up and down calling, "Toca! Toca!" He answered with a wave of his hat like the celebrity he was.

Yu'mi had been alerted to their approach and emerged from the trees just as they rode up. His smile showed his pleasure in their visit, but he was not happy after they explained the reason. He just kept shaking his head. "Demons sent gold. My father say gold very evil. It kill people. Must keep buried."

"Can we at least ask?" Mae's eyes pleaded as much as her voice. "We feel very strongly about this."

Yu'mi reluctantly walked them over to his father who was sitting with Chief K'ut'im. When he explained what "Jack's people" wanted to do, the men's open expressions fell and turned grim. Waho answered first, speaking fast in harsh tones until the Huuk stomped his stick and stood. He spoke with sharp, biting words that continued to rise in volume. Swallowing anxiously, Yu'mi waved over for Milok to come and help. This didn't look good, and Mae glanced nervously at Dexter and Toke.

When Waho and Chief K'ut'im finally finished their rant, the Huuk impatiently gestured to Milok and thrust his cane toward Mae and the others.

Milok squinted, tightly rubbing his lips together until he found the right words. "There is no exact translation, but I will try. Gold is evil. It will take you over and make you sick with fever. People will lose focus on what is important and compete against each other for things that do not matter. Injure or kill over it. Tua has been put here as a test to us, to tempt us, and we do not want to fail the test from such an evil demon. We are happy now and want to stay that way."

The Chief rose and shuffled over to his hubo as if the conversation was over. Instead, he emerged carrying a small leather pouch and held it out until one of them took it.

With fading hopes but curious eyes, Mae and Toke looked on as Dexter emptied four bright gold nuggets into the palm of his hand. Mae sighed and said to Yu'mi, "Will you tell them that this is not what our plan is. We don't need *their* gold. We can find our own."

Yu'mi looked embarrassed at having to translate words he did not want to. He explained to Chief K'ut'im that they appreciated the gold but would not be taking it and were still planning on looking for their own. With that, Dexter handed the sack back to the Huuk, thanking him with a respectful bow.

Lacking his usual smile, Yu'mi turned to the three of them. "My father ask why you not happy with your life and why you need this gold."

Mae looked into Yu'mi's eyes. "We want to do good things with the gold. Jack needs to buy an ox and sharper tools to grow more apple trees. Elizabeth needs new pots and cloth, and we all need new boots." She failed to mention their primary reason for needing it. To find Greg and get back home. Plus, they'd want some to take back with them to live better lives. Who wouldn't?

Yu'mi was only halfway through explaining their reasons when the Huuk shut him down. Sitting with his cane firmly planted in front of him and his eyes fixed straight ahead at nothing, this was his way of saying the subject was over. Mae then turned pleadingly to Yu'mi's father, but his expression was just as hard and dismissive.

Disappointment slackened their faces as the three of them said their goodbyes and walked back to their horses, trying to figure out how to deal with this unexpected news.

Yu'mi caught up with them right before they took off. With a finger held to his lips for silence, he looked around cautiously to confirm they were alone. He said he'd be waiting for them further up the trail at the second red tree after the notched branch. Before they could ask him where any of these were, he disappeared back through the trees as if he were never there.

With hopes deflating like a leaking balloon, they ambled up the dusty path, weighing their other options. Toke punched the air angrily. "This sucks, big time. They gave us no help at all. Now we're just going blindly."

"And might die for it," Dexter added.

"Maybe Yu'mi's going to help us. Why else would he meet us so far up the trail?" Mae hoped more than anything this was true. They really needed his help to find the way.

True to his word, Yu'mi met them where he said he'd be. Though none of them saw his markers, they just figured he would appear by a red tree at some point. "I very sorry."

"Hey, no worries man," Toke mustered, sounding depressed.

"It's our fault." Mae lowered her head apologetically. "We shouldn't have put you in that awkward position. We should have asked Chief K'ut'im ourselves."

Looking directly into Yu'mi's kind brown eyes, Dexter stressed, "This is not your fault at all, Yu'mi. Please don't feel bad."

"I your friend. I want to help friends but not anger my village."

"Heh," Toke threw out. "Maybe we just say we're fishing…or hunting for beaver. Then—surprise! We find gold instead. Completely by accident."

Mae reached out and held Yu'mi's arm. "Can you help us find the big river and maybe introduce us to the tribe that lives in Coloma?"

Yu'mi squinted his eyes, sizing up the deceit in this proposition. He finally gave a sharp nod. "Dah." Then he added, "Very important. No talk of gold."

Mae felt suddenly lighter, like the elephant that was sitting on top of her got too drunk and toppled off. Smiles instantly returned to their faces and enthusiasm to their souls. She hurried the group to get moving before the elephant returned to claim back his seat.

One after the other, they headed northeast, winding their way through the narrow mountain trail. Dried leaves and pine needles crunched underfoot like people munching popcorn in a crowded movie theatre. The low hanging branches attacked them from all sides, trying to steal their supplies, but they fought them off bravely. Every once in a while, Mae looked back to make sure they weren't being followed. Toke told her not to act so guilty, or she'd give them away, and he was right.

They had a good plan that could actually work. Although very dishonest and deceptive.

But that part didn't bother them.

Chapter Seventy-Five

An hour later, the winding, narrow trail ended in a fork, with the left going north, the right south, and straight ahead of them, the river they sought.

Mae climbed down from Trixie and stood for a moment, just taking in its magnificent strength. Like a boasting dragon, its muscular current swept through the small valley with an intimidating roar. Where sunlight caught the shimmering waves, it turned them to dragon scales. No matter how many times she had seen this as a child, it felt different now. So young and unrestrained.

Toke finished off a piece of bear jerky and then cleared his throat, indicating it was time to go. Yu'mi turned them north for about a mile, taking them through sandy soil, large patches of grass, and a scattering of oaks. Darting across their path, a young deer and two fawns disappeared into the protective wall of cypress trees just as the Sekoma village emerged into view.

While Yu'mi assembled an impractical boxy hat on his head, Dexter and Toke tethered the horses. Mae gathered the gifts from the satchels and looked around nervously. They practiced their story until they heard soft footsteps a few yards away and tensed in silence.

A man attired in a deerskin breechcloth trimmed in spotted fur appeared and happily greeted Yu'mi but eyed the others suspiciously. Yu'mi asked in a formal way to speak to Mehaa, their village's Huuk. It was clear this man knew Yu'mi well and was probably related in some way, but there were always formalities upon entering another village. The man led them through the trees toward the village.

They walked past a large flat rock that was scattered with shallow holes like an industriously picked, pock-marked face. Happy chattering filled the air as women huddled around their own hole in the rock and ground away tirelessly.

"Look at the biceps on that broad," Toke said, getting Mae's "shoosh" back.

A nearly naked child ran up, refilling his mother's depleted basket before joining back up with the other laughing children cracking the shells off acorns. Mae had visited a place like this in her childhood. It might have been this exact place, in fact. She remembered how strange and abandoned it had felt and how inconceivable it was to understand how much life it had once held.

These people seemed very similar to the Ma'camos, which helped them relax a little. They had the same type of houses, and the giant raised baskets filled with acorns. They wore similar clothes, hairstyles, ornaments, and facial tattoos. Their language was even similar, making it easier for Mae to eavesdrop.

The group was led into a large roundhouse covered in dirt with grass growing on all sides. It reminded Mae of something that would be in *Winnie the Pooh*. The air inside was cool, almost like they had an air-conditioner running. They were not introduced to the chief as he stood before them, but instead, Yu'mi made a big show of the gifts these people had brought from the white Fox-man. For a fairly hairless culture, forests of bushy hair jutted from Chief Mehaa's nostrils, and Mae wondered, ashamedly, if he had trouble keeping small rodents from nesting inside.

Yu'mi started in with their planned story about their beaver hunting expedition. The chief only grunted. He was too busy scrutinizing these strange people.

Mae did not like the smirk on the taller man who stood across from her. She found herself staring at his gouged face, wondering if a bear had once snacked on it. He caught her gaze, and she quickly looked away. This seemed to provoke him, and he spoke up, asking Yu'mi why they were going beaver hunting when everyone knew all the beaver were hunted and gone. There weren't any left.

Yu'mi explained that he already told them this, but they still wanted to look just in case some were missed. The man with the chewed face took this as an insult to his hunting skills at catching the last beaver. He laughed, saying it would be funny to have them look for nothing.

Unmoved by Yu'mi's plea, Mehaa stood there, silent. His large, intimidating frame commanded authority while his intense black eyes bore into theirs as if trying to pull something out. He needed more explanation of these strangers and why they should allow them to hunt on their land.

Yu'mi looked frustrated, but not yet defeated. Impulsively, he reached over and pulled Mae in front of him, rubbing her tummy like she was carrying his child.

The chief looked quite surprised, yet oddly curious. He walked over to Mae and looked her straight in her face. Holding her chin in his massive hand, he turned her face one way then the other, studying every detail. She held her breath and tried hard not to tremble.

When he finally let go of Mae's face, his eyes remained on her while asking Yu'mi more questions, which he answered quickly and obediently.

The men in the room laughed and grunted something. This rudeness kept up for a while like they were there purely for the tribe's entertainment. But, in actuality, it was difficult for the three of them to take their eyes off the agonizing display of painful-looking nose piercings with bones, shells, and feathers.

After what felt like a week, the chief decided to smile, revealing beautiful, creamy white teeth. How did he do that without a toothbrush? Yu'mi motioned to her to stop staring into his mouth and look into his eyes instead. The chief spoke a few short words, then closed his eyes in approval. Yu'mi thanked him so profusely it was almost embarrassing.

When they turned to leave, the chief stopped Mae and faced her. He reached his arm out over her shoulder and clasped her back while looking into her eyes. Not knowing what to do, she just stared back. Without warning, his face moved in, and she flinched, but he merely touched his cheek to hers, and she answered with a warm smile. Yu'mi explained later that it was a way of saying "thank you".

The man who had shown them in and was now showing them back out told Yu'mi that the river ran fast but, they should look for the shallow crossing areas. He was glad they came at a good time and not in the winter or spring when the water was much higher. The river became a large writhing snake that ate many people who went into it. Lastly, he added, laughing, that they would need all the gods in their favor if they were going to find any beaver.

Once they were back on the trail again, heading south, Mae asked Yu'mi what the man meant by the beaver being gone. He explained that beaver skin was used as money to trade with the white man, so they were hunted everywhere and disappeared quickly. He hadn't seen any beaver since he was a young boy.

"Poor little things." Mae hung her head, feeling a heavy weight on her heart, knowing there was nothing she could do to help them.

Dexter met her eyes. "Remember, Mae. These are different times."

"Yeah. They didn't have faux-fur factories to make warm coats and shit," Toke added.

Dexter inclined his head toward Toke in agreement. "He's right. If it wasn't made from cotton or silk, it came from an animal."

Mae felt too sad to accept these new facts. "Did you know they sometimes use kitten fur in faux-fur from China?"

To avoid the heated animal anti-cruelty lecture that was coming, Toke abruptly called ahead to Yu'mi, "So dude, were you just telling them that you knocked up Mae?"

Dexter added, "Yu'mi, he's asking if you told them Mae was pregnant with your baby."

Yu'mi slowed his horse down to walk next to them. "Family very important to Nisenan."

“You little devil.” Toke winked admirably. “So, what was with the chief’s hands all over Mae’s face? Wasn’t she pretty enough for you?”

“Best to take wife from same tribe to keep family strong. He not think she look like one of ours, so I tell story.”

Mae’s mind stuck on the word “wife.” She needed to tell Yu’mi about Greg before their relationship got any further. This was getting too far, and she didn’t want to hurt him or anyone.

“Then I say to him that her tribe is lost. I found her face on ground, bloody cuts and bruises. Not yet dead. She had no…” He couldn’t think of the word so pointed to his head.

“Brains,” Toke helped.

Dexter tapped his head. “Memory? Like with amnesia?”

Yu’mi nodded and continued, “I tell them it not important because I put a Ma’camo in her belly.”

Mae hung her head and groaned.

“You see, there’s a pecking order, Mae,” Toke said, clearing it up. “The older tribesmen get first dibs on this season’s flowering virgins, so there’s nothing left for Yu’mi. He’s hopelessly smitten for you, and it’s not nice to disappoint him after all he’s doing for us.” Toke tried unsuccessfully to hide his smile.

“Stop enjoying this so much!” Mae scowled.

Chapter Seventy-Six

They rode downstream a few miles, back in the direction they came, passing the trail they had come in on. Toke glanced behind them. "Wait, we're getting too far from where the gold is."

"We don't have to find the exact place they discovered gold first. We just know it's all along this river." Mae looked once again at the fast-moving river, feeling small and helpless with their ambitious plans.

Dexter added, "But we do need to get far enough away, so they don't figure out we're not hunting beaver."

"I'm always hunting—" Toke started to say.

"Stop," Mae slammed.

The river split and Yu'mi took them to a spot where the water was shallow and far from any other people. With only about six hours of daylight left, they were anxious to get started. After tending to their horses, they grabbed their tools and supplies and hurried down to the river.

At the water's edge, Yu'mi protectively slapped mud clay all over Mae's face, which she wasn't happy about but figured Yu'mi knew best out here in the wilderness so she let him continue to cover her wherever she might burn. When finished, he washed his hands in the river and turned to leave.

"Uh"—Mae motioned her hand toward Dex and Toke—"can you dirty those white boys too?"

"I'm fine." Toke brushed him off, but Yu'mi ignored him and covered them both. Mae hid her smile as she watched their discomfort with Yu'mi's physical closeness. Guys were so funny with their built-in homophobia.

And in the end, they looked so ridiculous painted in mud she couldn't stop laughing.

Toke bugged his eyes at Mae. "Okay, you done?" Then he stepped into the icy water and plunged the kitchen pie pan a few inches deep into the sandy bottom, then pulled the filled pan out. He disappointedly poked around at the gray rocks and plain sand before emptying it back into the water. "So, how do we do this? Where can I get YouTube out here?"

"I think we swirl it so the heavy gold will sink to the bottom and the lighter stuff eventually floats out with the water." Mae wasn't sure, but it sounded logical.

They got to work trying different methods, trading tips back and forth. After half an hour, Toke took his hat off and wiped his sweating head. "I've still got nothing."

"Me neither," Mae whined.

"Nothing." Dexter dumped out his last pan.

"I'm going in deeper," Toke said, taking a few steps deeper toward the river's center, then stopped. "Holy shit—the water's frickin' freezing!"

Dexter followed Toke out, plucking his legs out as if doing some strange dance. "That's because it's run-off from the snow caps." Mae grimaced before tying up her long dress and following them in.

Though sacrificing their own comfort and enduring the excruciating pain of the cold water, no one had any luck finding gold. "So, how about we move upstream?" Toke shaded his eyes scouting for a new location. "It's shit pickins where we are."

Fighting defeat, they staggered over the uneven river bottom back to shore. Dexter dropped his pan and sat on a beached decaying log. "Okay, let's think about this." He smoothed the area of sand in front of him with his foot. "Since the water flows like this…" He used a stick to sketch out the winding river. "And gold is the heaviest thing in the water…it would make sense for it to collect in these bent parts. Here and here." He glanced up at them to make sure they understood so far. "This is where the water would be the slowest, right? It would have more time to drop out of the current and not be forced downstream, wouldn't it?"

"Hmm." Mae bent, looking over the drawing, then up the river. "Makes sense to me."

Toke studied the details of the design and nodded with renewed hope. "Yeah. That makes the most sense."

"Also, these places." Dexter continued with his stick. "Where the river turns, the bank probably ends up collecting tons of dirt and sand, a little bit at a time. Eventually, the sand builds up so much, that it makes a sandbar. See?"

"Okay. So, since the water can't go that way anymore, it moves over, like…" Toke smoothed out the old line with his hand and redrew the new river with his finger. "Here."

"Exactly," Dexter explained. "So, it would be *those* sandbars that we need to dig in and not just the river bottoms."

The three of them looked up and down the river, squinting in the sun, analyzing it with this new perspective. Toke mused, "Hey, look what's for dinner." He motioned downstream to Yu'mi, who was standing in the current with a twenty-inch salmon flapping on the end of his wooden spear.

Once a new spot, a little farther upstream, was decided on, they gathered up their tools and set off along the bank.

"Oh my God—oh my God—oh my God!" Mae squealed, staring into her pan. Toke and Dex crowded around. There, in the bottom of her pan, were three small yellow bits the size of couscous. Various shouts of "Woo hoo!" and "We did it!" erupted.

"Shhh." Mae giggled, covering her mouth, looking around guiltily. "Remember, there's no more beaver to find for us to be celebrating about."

With their new-found energy, Toke swiftly jammed his shovel into the bottom of the river and filled each of their pans, digging deeper and deeper, each time revealing larger nuggets. After a few more hushed triumphs, they grew tired of celebrating and just concentrated on their job, the satchels around their necks slowly getting filled.

By early evening, the savory scent of roasting salmon wafted upriver, driving the three exhausted miners back to camp.

"Holy shit. Yu'mi needs his own cooking show," Toke said, drooling over the skewered chunks of fresh salmon sizzling over the fire. But they were all even more impressed with the entire set-up Yu'mi built to cook the rest of the meal. He had dug a pit and lined it with stones, then made a fire inside, which heated the stones. When it was time to remove the fire, he added the washed plant bulbs he had dug up earlier that day, then covered it all up with dirt and leaves to let the hot stones bake the bulbs slowly.

To give the bulbs flavor, Yu'mi sprinkled on a spice, which he shaved from the bark of a nearby tree, that contributed a nutty cinnamon flavor. These he served on the side along with smashed roots and tangy wild plums mixed with greens. Mae had insisted on having greens with every dinner meal, and Yu'mi listened. Having no alternate source of protein, Mae grudgingly indulged in the fish as well. Dexter nodded in approval.

"Dude," Toke said through a mouth full of fish. "This is freaking amazing."

Mae noticed, since they didn't eat much salt anymore, she could taste every little tiny thing that would have been so painfully bland before.

When their evening meal was completely devoured and the mess cleaned up, it was time to check their day's work. They gathered around the large flat rock and emptied their satchels into a pile in the center. Dexter whistled, shaking his head in disbelief.

"Holy, holy mother of God." Toke grabbed the sides of his head as if to keep it attached. "We made a freakin' haul."

Mae couldn't take her eyes off the gleaming mound. "It looks too spectacularly unreal. What do you think this is all worth?"

Dexter picked at the loose sand under the nuggets. "If we can figure out how to get the gold dust out of all this, we'll have even more."

"So we got this all from just one river bend?" Mae's eyes danced in delight, and her feet wanted to dance even more. "Just think what we could do by the end of the week."

"But there's got to be an easier way to do this." Dexter rubbed his sore back. "We need to design smarter equipment."

"Yeah, like the ones the gold miners used made of wood and stuff," Toke added.

"Yes. I think they called it a sluice." Dexter tapped his lip as he ferreted through his brain. "Give me some time, and I'll figure out the details."

Mae began to scoop the mound of gold into the largest bag. "So I was thinking," she said, tying it off. "Now that we have something so valuable that a person would kill to get their hands on it, we seriously need to learn to defend our stash. And our lives, too. We won't always have access to a gun, but we're rarely without a knife on us somewhere, right?" Dexter and Toke nodded slowly, their minds playing out possible scenarios starring them as heroes.

Even though Yu'mi had never killed a living person, he had been trained for survival and agreed to pass his knowledge along. By the end of the lesson, they each knew exactly where to slice or stab for a swift kill or just to slow a person down. Mae never realized just how vulnerable their own bodies were to a knife-yielding assailant with any sense of human anatomy. At least now if she ran across the Yiptuati warrior, she wouldn't feel so defenseless.

Yu'mi wanted her to improve the power behind her thrust in case she hit bone, so after the lesson, she continued to practice by voraciously attacking a decaying log. Toke looked on, thoroughly amused by her contradictory enthusiasm for killing. So, for the rest of the night, he referred to her as the Wood Slayer, selfishly enjoying the double entendre each time he said it.

Sleep came easy that night for their tired bodies, but staying asleep was difficult. Mae woke often to her chattering teeth. It was colder up here than where they lived with the Fox family, and the frigid air went straight through their blankets. Yu'mi came prepared with layers of skins and a thick wolf fur, which, sometime in the night, he stretched over Mae's shivering body, shrouding her in a toasty nest.

Chapter Seventy-Seven

Yu'mi learned the easiest way to wake them early was with a hot drink he made from roasted bay nuts which had a stimulating effect like caffeine. He sweetened it with crushed dried manzanita berries that he always had handy and sucked on throughout the day. The drink was dark and smelled and tasted like fruity charcoal molasses. Almost instantly, their senses were alert and ready, and their stiff bodies forgotten. Forget coffee.

While Dexter scratched in the dirt, drawing up engineering plans for the new device, he started Mae on braiding twine into thin ropes. Toke got busy sharpening knives and tightening the shovel to its handle.

With plans finished, it was time to make the sluice a reality. Without flat boards, all the wood had to be chopped with an ax, split lengthwise and finished using their knives. Toke built the angled trellis and bound it together using the twine Mae had braided. Next, they lined the top with a couple dozen of the flat sticks, tilting each ninety degrees, creating a sort of stair-stepping effect, so when they poured a bucket of water over the top, the heavier gold would get caught while the lighter sand and other debris just floated over the top and back out into the river. It reminded Mae of one of those old-fashioned washboards, the kind she would give anything for now instead of using river rocks to pound the dirt out of the laundry.

They got the sluice as good as they were going to get it and felt ready to start their official second day of gold mining. Looking around, they finally found Yu'mi at the river's edge working on his third project of that morning. He was nearly finished knotting together a fishing net from twine he had braided before they even woke. He accompanied his work with a short repetitive song following each movement of his arm.

"Man." Toke sounded exhausted just watching him. "The guy's nonstop."

Dexter adjusted his grip on his end of the heavy sluice. "That's what they've always done to survive, constantly working for their daily food." They thanked Yu'mi profusely for all he was doing to help them and headed upstream to their next location.

To their surprise, the sluice actually worked better than they had hoped. The gold came in so fast and easy that it was hard to stop. Mae and Toke had to force Dexter to rest his back every half hour so that he wouldn't wrench it out again. That would be hard for everyone, not just Dexter.

Once again, Yu'mi's cooking permeated the late afternoon air, and they were too weak to resist. After washing off their sunblocking mud and pulling everything out of the water and up the bank, they were ready for tomorrow.

"So, this is what it was like for the very first gold miners. Gold was everywhere and easy to find once they knew where to look," Mae said excitedly. She helped Dexter cover the sluicing box with dead branches, eager with hunger to get back to camp.

Mae took a big whiff of the intoxicating air, letting her eyes close. "Ahh…incredible!"

Yu'mi turned to look at her. "In..cred..abow. Is this good?"

"Ohhhh, yessssss," she gushed.

Dexter explained, in his usual teacherly role, "There are a lot of words that you can use that mean the same as incredible. For instance: amazing, great, awesome…" Yu'mi ended up getting Dexter's English lesson well into the night.

Yu'mi seemed to never tire of learning English, and, in turn, gave them the opportunity to pick up some of his language as well. The problem was, they couldn't just swap out English words for Nisenan. Their Maidu language had single words for complicated emotions, wordy attitudes, and descriptive internal feelings that would take lengthy sentences in English to describe. Toke didn't seem to have much patience for it, and Dexter's mind too often drifted off on a particular word, getting lost deep in his own thoughts. It was solely up to Mae to take their language on.

Before settling down to sleep, Dexter and Toke added reinforcements to their sluice box and worked out any potential problems, while Mae smoothed some rough areas in the wood with a coarse stone.

"If this works as good tomorrow as today, we can even extend it out farther if we build a support." Toke put his hand where the piece should go, and Dexter and Mae yawned in agreement.

The next morning, they were knee-deep in the freezing water and in sync once again. With Toke's new improvements to the device, the gold was coming in even faster. They were grateful they brought larger satchels today and truly needed them.

At one point, Dexter straightened out his sore back, and his thoughts drifted to Yu'mi. "I'm still completely blown away by how fast Yu'mi picks things up."

Mae stopped working and stood up. "I've been telling you guys. He sits in on Willie's lessons, and I see it first-hand. He's truly a genius. Not just like smart, but the true scientific, clinical definition of genius. And not an annoying nerdy genius, but a pleasant well-adjusted guy."

"Dude believes in a lot of weird shit, though," Toke added, stuffing a handful of gold nuggets into one bag and gold dust into another.

Mae took a long drink from her water pouch and swallowed lustily before adding, "Yu'mi has lots of spiritual reasons for all sorts of things, if that's what you mean. And, yeah, some of it's weird and even ridiculous to us, but it helps him put reason to a lot of things he couldn't make sense of otherwise."

"Go on..." Toke said tonelessly, feigning interest as he sat to rest.

"For instance, they fear the spirits and gods, which are attached to almost everything. Like they feel animals, plants, trees, rivers, mountains, and even rocks have souls." Mae sifted through the gravel in the trough. "If you think about it, it sort of makes sense to have a separate god specializing in just one thing. Like the God of Rain, or God of Fertility, the Spirit of the Snake. Think how good the gods must be at their job, having just one specialty. Their gods don't have to spread themselves so thin, unlike our one God who has to be everywhere, twenty-four-seven, for everyone and doesn't always have time to answer our prayers and we have to make excuses for him to feel better. Sure, us Catholics have saints and all, but they have to funnel everything through the one and only God bottleneck too. Yu'mi's gods seem more of a direct route to the need, you know?" Mae stopped talking to pick out the gold nuggets and discard the rest. "Another thing, Yu'mi's way of religion seems to work a lot better than ours. I mean, they don't *kill* each other over different religious beliefs—"

"Okay, Mae," Toke interrupted. "Just because we're a captive audience, doesn't mean you can go all deep and political on us."

"Okay. I see you'd rather have me sing." Before he could answer, she punished him by bursting out a bastardized version of a favorite pop song. Toke and Dex, not successful in shutting her up, decided to join in, even though they had no idea what she was singing. It was a painful moment for the peaceful forest.

By noon, they were seeing less gold, and Dexter suggested they move everything up around the other side of the bend. The other two agreed, and they started to pack up. Dexter looked back toward their camp, "I think one of us should tell Yu'mi we're moving farther upstream and maybe grab a horse."

"I'll go." Mae needed the break. "You guys good to move everything yourselves?" No way would they ever admit needing her help, so she didn't bother waiting for an answer before heading back to camp.

As Mae approached their camp, she couldn't see Yu'mi anywhere. She sighed, trying to figure out how to leave him a note and headed to the horses.

Something she heard made her stop in her tracks, and she froze, listening. Loud scuffling noises were coming from behind the large boulder that sheltered their camp from the mountain winds. Mae walked toward the sound, hoping it was Yu'mi just wrestling with a big animal that didn't want to become their dinner. She couldn't help but think that something just didn't feel right.

Chapter Seventy-Eight

Feeling more curious than worried, Mae picked up the nearest stick for protection and walked around the large boulder toward the source of the ruckus.

Suddenly she froze in her tracks. Yu'mi lay a few yards away, face down in the dirt with a grisly man crouched over his struggling body. Rage tore through her, and she raced forward. "Get off of him!" Then using the full weight of her tiny frame, she rammed into him as hard as she could. The man remained firmly planted and just growled his annoyance. His nostrils twitched as he slowly lifted his head like a possessed sloth, revealing a wretched face consumed with pus-filled welts and oozing ulcers.

When her brain registered the horror of what she saw—the blood, the knife, Yu'mi's scalp clenched in the man's hand—she shrieked in murderous rage and slammed her foot into the attacker's side. He released his grip on Yu'mi's scalp, which was still attached to his head, and now turned his attention to Mae.

She dug frantically in her bosom for her knife, unsheathed it, but, in his sudden lunge for her, she stabbed it in the side of his cheek instead of his neck. He roared in pain and yanked the knife out, clenching it in his fist. His eyes bulged red with fury, and he bore his teeth in a deranged grin.

Her heart pounded fiercely against its cramped skeletal cage while she inched back slowly. A split second later, she was racing back to camp.

Her eyes darted around camp until she spotted the ax and bolted for it. All of a sudden, the man was right behind her and he tackled her to the ground. She fought desperately to get free, but, being without fingernails, her fight felt more like a declawed kitten defending herself against an angry bear.

The man flipped her onto her back, slamming her head into the hard dirt, then sat, straddling her between his thighs. Holding both her wrists with one large, paw-like hand, his other messed with his pants. Her mind filled a lifetime of terrors into a balloon that exploded into a scream so intense, it split the air like a razor, piercing the forest with manic desperation.

"Shut your damn hole, digger squaw," he spat. Then he released Mae's wrists to wrap both his hands around her neck. His hands tightened like a vise around her delicate throat. He was squeezing to kill. "You dirty digger whore. Red nigger squaw…" Mae pounded him desperately with her fists, catching his putrid drool with each vile word he squeezed through his rotting teeth. He dug his thumbs into the hollow of her throat, crushing her windpipe, and her face darkened to a deep shade of purple as her gaping mouth lusted for air. The pressure in her skull pounded savagely, and her eyes began to bulge…

Dexter's body suddenly slammed against the man, but only caused him to teeter slightly while remaining fixed to her neck. She could feel Dexter pulling hard at the attacker's hands to loosen them, to let her breathe, but the man's hands only squeezed tighter.

She couldn't get her arms to move—to fight back…her legs wouldn't kick anymore. Her aching head blended her thoughts into a raspberry smoothie, then they melted into a thick cheesy fondue…her brain dimmed…turning off…

An earsplitting bang ruptured the air. The attacker's head instantaneously exploded, spraying blood and a nauseating assortment of head guts in all directions. Dexter tore away the man's hands that still clutched Mae's throat, and she sucked in air so desperately, her entire body erupted in a violent cough.

The dead man's body, still sitting upright from muscle memory, finally toppled to the side, spilling the bowl of contents from the remaining half of the head onto the dirt. Dexter forcibly pushed the rest of him off Mae and began to wipe away the splatters of blood, bone, and clumps of gray brain matter off her face. Tears filled his eyes, and his lips began to tremble with intense relief.

Mae's head pounded, and her throat felt like she had swallowed a Brillo pad, but she was grateful to be alive. Toke put down the gun, visibly shaking, and walked to the dead man. He silently picked up the lifeless legs and dragged him out of sight, leaving a dark crimson trail.

When Mae's frantic breathing began to slow, and she was able to speak again, she wheezed, "Yu…mi…Yu…"

Toke looked up. "Oh shit—where's Yu'mi?" He immediately dropped the dead man and tore around their camp calling Yu'mi's name. Finding nothing nearby, he darted into the surrounding trees, scrambling over and around the adjacent boulders in his path.

Out of breath he stopped for a few seconds and looked around. And, there they were. Two familiar moccasined feet were sticking out from behind a large granite rock. "Oh, shit—*shit*!"

Yu'mi lay face down, his hair and neck drenched in dark blood which pooled in the dirt under his face. Toke swooped in and turned Yu'mi's face to the side in desperate hope. "He's still breathing!" He began dabbing at the blood which was flowing steadily from the back of his head.

With careful hands, he pushed Yu'mi's matted hair to the side to see the extent of the wound. "Holy mother…" Toke swallowed hard. Yu'mi's scalp had moved to the side along with the hair, exposing the raw pink of his skull. "The asshole tried to scalp him!"

In an instant, Dexter slid in next to him as Toke revealed a dirty, jagged six-inch cut across the base of Yu'mi's skull. Dexter drew in a sharp breath. "Oh man."

Mae struggled to crawl over to Yu'mi, crying, "No, no, no, no—" She could barely breathe, but finally managed to get to her feet and make her way to him.

"I just hope he passed out before he felt much." Toke moved aside to allow room for Mae.

Dexter had his hands clamped over Yu'mi's head, applying pressure to stop the bleeding. "He's pretty messed up, Mae. He's lost a lot of blood."

Buckling under heart-wrenching sobs, Mae forcibly composed herself enough to say, "It needs to be stitched." Her voice sounded hoarse and painfully weak. "I have a sewing kit in my saddlebag." She started coughing again and had to pull away from Yu'mi.

Toke jumped up. "I'm on it." He returned in less than a minute with her sewing kit and a pot of boiling water from the fire.

With delicate strokes, Mae washed the wound and Dexter passed her the threaded needle. She took a deep and painful breath, then set to work, thoughtfully stitching the scalp back in place while Yu'mi remained unconscious.

"Look at what the fucker used." Toke held up an old broken bladed knife with a crusty, ragged edge. "Yu'mi's lucky the blade was so dull, or his entire scalp would be a trophy on that asshole's belt right now."

"Actually," Dexter added. "Often, scalping doesn't stop at the head." Toke winced and covered his groin. Dexter stood. "We've got to get him home as soon as possible. Let's pack up what we can and get out of here."

Dexter and Toke stormed through camp, randomly stuffing their belongings into the satchels. It was a struggle to tie them to the horses who were still trembling from the gun blast. "Dude, let's just take him to the Sekoma, they'll know what the hell to do with him. They're just a mile upstream."

Considering this for a moment, Dexter finally said, "My only worry is they'll think you and I did this to him. I can't imagine they've had many good experiences with white men." He gathered the last of the scattered tools and baskets and tossed them to Toke. "If we ride fast, we can be with the Ma'camos in half an hour or forty-five minutes."

"Yeah, you're probably right. They know nothing about us other than we're stupid enough to hunt imaginary beaver." With the horses finally loaded up, Toke left to check in on Mae's progress just as she tied the final knot on Yu'mi. "Geez Mae, you need to lie down. You look like death and your entire body's shaking." He pushed in next to her. "I'll bandage him up." He began by ripping pieces from the bottom of Mae's dress.

Too weak to fight back, Mae let Toke take over, and she lay down next to Yu'mi. "Who can do this to another human being?" she cried softly. "The butcher didn't even know we had gold to steal."

With Toke at his head and Dexter at his feet, they lifted Yu'mi and shuffled him back to camp, with Mae holding his hand the whole way. The dead man's gruesome remains lay right in their path, forcing them to step around. Mae quickly turned her head but not soon enough. What she saw was by far the most repulsive thing she had ever laid eyes on, and she had the urge to vomit.

The man's face was completely missing from the nose up, and what little remained of his head was impacted with an excessive amount of buckshot. Dexter eyed the dead man as they stepped past. "Geez, what'd you put in that thing?" With that, Mae reflexively put her hand to her cheek, remembering the sharp stings of the deflecting buckshot.

"I was aiming for his arm just to stop him. I didn't mean to kill the bastard." Toke's voice shook, and his face looked pained. "I've never actually killed anything before."

When they got to the horses, they lowered Yu'mi down. "Hey, what's done is done," Dexter said. "If I thought of it, I would have shot him too." His words seemed to help, and Toke nodded.

It took a few minutes of gentle coaxing until the wild fear faded from the horses' eyes and it felt safe to lift Yu'mi onto Dexter's horse. He kept Yu'mi's head propped high until Toke had him securely bound to the saddle.

With a quick last check around the camp, they stashed away anything that would give them away as gold miners. Using broad, aggressive sweeps, Toke covered the dead man with a thick layer of pine needles and loose dirt. Then, picking up the dead man's pack, which was overflowing with rusty animal traps, he removed the string of freshly skinned animal pelts that hung from one side. "I'll take these, you dirty bastard, and you can keep your creepy sinew." He dropped the heavy pack on top of the grave and spat on it before walking back.

Mae buried her face in Trixie's mane, feeling calmed by her familiar scent. She turned her head to the side and mustered out in a hoarse whisper, "Promise me, if Yu'mi starts bleeding badly, we turn around and take him to the Sekoma."

"Just sit tight, you're barely alive yourself. You get to play princess once again." Toke gently patted her back with genuine concern before tying the bloody animal pelts to his horse.

In a sudden moment of clarity, nearly forgetting the whole reason they were up there in the first place, Dexter raced to where they buried the pouch of gold and dug it up with his hands. He distributed it among the three of them with only some going into their saddlebags, and the rest they stashed safely in and under their clothing. "Now, we're ready to leave."

"Wait…" Toke held up his hand for silence. "Do you hear that?"

"Hear what?" Mae moaned. "Let's go. Yu'mi needs to get home," she said, not raising her head, in a slurry of words.

By then, Toke was off his horse and forcing his way through spidery tree branches and bushes downstream, south of camp. And, in no time, Dexter was on his tail.

When the sound made its way to Mae, a sort of bleating, like a baby lamb, she sat up, fully alert. "What is it?" she called anxiously, but no one answered.

A few minutes later Dexter and Toke worked their way back out through the branches, and what Toke carried in his arms tore at Mae's heart.

Chapter Seventy-Nine

Bundled in her stolen dress and bound hand and foot, a terrified young native boy of about five or six stared back at Mae. Toke set him down in the clearing and cut through the ropes that had left bleeding welts on the child's wrists and ankles.

Mae didn't even notice when Dexter came through with a horse, only stared down in agony at the boy's bloody and beaten body. "Poor little thing," Mae cried, reaching for the child from her saddle. The boy's head lolled, and his eyes drooped like he was going to pass out.

Not forgetting the urgency to get Yu'mi back, Toke wrapped the child back up in the dress and slid him in front of Mae on the horse. She offered him water which he gulped down desperately as she took in the fresh burn marks on his legs. *What other unspeakable hell had that monster done to this innocent child?*

After a quick rummage through the objects hanging from the new horse's saddle, Dexter stopped on one in particular.

"Dex, you okay taking that horse?" Toke said, ready to get going.

"First, you need to see this." Dexter spread open a bloody cloth and its contents on top of the saddle. At first, Toke wasn't sure what he was looking at until Dexter flipped it over. Even after what they'd been through that day, it was still shocking to see any part of a person detached from their body.

Dexter traced a diagonal scar from one end of the shaved scalp to the other, and they both knew immediately whose it had to be. The horse then tugged angrily at the rope, and they took notice of the faded red stripe painted over the horse's head. "Holy shit. It's him." Toke smacked the scalp off the saddle. “Let’s just get the hell out of here.”

The small boy seemed more alert when they neared the Ma’camo grounds, but Yu’mi remained unconscious. The short ride loosened Mae’s throat, and she could speak without as much pain. “So, how do we explain all this without getting Yu’mi in big trouble?”

“I’m hoping they’ll be so relieved he’s alive that they’ll disregard all else.” Dexter turned his horse between the group of trees toward the Ma’camo camp, and they all followed in turn.

“Yeah, and it’s not like he just disobeyed his father.” Toke winced. “He disobeyed the *chief*.” He got down from his horse and walked to Mae’s. “And what about this kid?” he said, taking the child in his arms.

Mae slid off her horse and disappeared into the trees that hid the Ma’camo camp. Waving her arms, she tried to yell, as painful as it was, what she hoped was the right word. “Daka daka! Daka daka!” In seconds, she returned with a group of men and women in close pursuit wearing a mixture of confusion, anger, and fear on their faces.

The tribespeople carefully lifted Yu’mi off his horse, attempting to examine his bloody bandages while rushing him into one of the overcrowded hubos. When Milok set eyes on the three of them, he demanded, “Why is he bleeding? What happened?”

They hadn’t made time to get their story straight, so Mae decided to set it straight right now. But, before she could answer, a tiny woman with long brown hair, neatly woven into a bun, stumbled out of the hubo. Deerskin leggings cinched above her knees cushioned her kneecaps when she fell hard on them. She raised her arms to the sky, pleading and crying, letting her shawl fall to the ground.

In this woman’s extreme emotional state, it took a moment for Mae to recognize Yu’mi’s Aunt Jalulu. She rushed over to her, picked up the soft braided rabbit shawl and wrapped it back over her shoulders. Aunt

Jalulu turned her wet red eyes to Mae and began speaking so fast and full of emotion that no one could pick out a word. Toke held up his hands for quiet so Mae could explain what had happened as Milok helped his mother to her feet.

Mae turned to Milok and began her story. "We got permission from the Sekoma to hunt beaver downstream from their village. Yu'mi was back at camp cooking when some creepy trapper came out of nowhere and tried to scalp him." Mae started to cry. "We helped him as best we could and rushed him home as fast as possible." Since no one commented yet on the child in Toke's arms, they left that part out for the moment, for simplicity's sake.

Milok translated everything she said to his mother, and, as others gathered around, he had to keep repeating the story. As the facts of their story spread around the village, a group of men mounted their horses and took off in the direction of the big river.

Mae, Dexter, and Toke stood to the side, feeling helpless and guilty. Toke groaned quietly. "Shit, if they find out the truth, it'll just reinforce the evilness of gold."

"What's weird is the creep didn't even know we had any gold." Mae looked at the child and shook her head, trying to comprehend his barbaric cruelty. "He just seemed to hate all Indians."

"And the Yiptuati guy could have been an easy catch with arrows sticking out of him." Toke adjusted the dress around the boy. Mae shuddered at how easily Yu'mi and his friends could have hit the bundle on the Yiptuati's horse, not knowing it contained this boy.

Toke cleared his throat when he saw Yu'mi's father, Waho, walking in their direction. Waho motioned for Mae to come with him. After all, they saw her as Yu'mi's future bride. Toke and Dexter tried to follow, but the cousins held up a hand to stop them, meaning it was only family now. Mae certainly didn't have to fake her worry and concern, she truly cared about Yu'mi, and his father could see it even before she started crying again.

Once inside the hubo, they speedily escorted Mae to Yu'mi's side, opposite of the man known as Yo'muse, who was the tribe's medicine man. She took Yu'mi's hand and brought it to her cheek, wetting it with her heartfelt tears.

In an arc around Yu'mi's head, the Yo'muse shook a rattle made with dried cocoons that were filled with pebbles, singing a short phrase in a rhythmic chant that pulsed through Mae's body. Then, with sudden abruptness, he ceased his performance, and the room fell silent. Now it was down to business. The medicine man and his assistant assembled his instruments, herbs, and medicines around Yu'mi's slight frame.

Sensing she was getting in the way, Mae laid Yu'mi's hand over his chest with extreme delicacy and slipped away without a sound, joining Dexter and Toke outside. The three of them sat in silence, watching the entire tribe work seamlessly together, like an orchestrated dance, all for Yu'mi.

The younger ones collected a variety of wild grasses and flowering weeds. They passed these to the older ones, who ground or steamed them into preparations. With a flurry of urgency, the elders delivered the warm poultices and strong herbal concoctions directly to the Yo'muse, then silently retreated into the crowd for silent prayers.

An eruption of angry voices came from over where the horses were tied. Then, the commotion burst back into camp and an aggressive group of men stormed their way over to the three of them, demanding explanations. Thankfully, Milok rushed over to ease the communications. "They want to know why there is a Yiptuati warrior's horse with the others."

"First off, calm down. He's dead," Toke assured.

Mae took Milok's forearm. "Can you explain to them that the trapper who hurt Yu'mi, first killed the Yiptuati warrior? The warrior had this little boy tied to the back of his horse, wrapped in my dress."

This was the first time anyone took notice of the child in Toke's arms. One of the tribesmen examined the boy's face and then pulled away the dress. With a grunt, he gave a motion over the crowd and a woman came over and tenderly took the boy from Toke. Mae reached out anxiously after the child, having to release the protective bond she had developed. Milok explained that he was Miwok and the Ma'camo would get him back to his tribe. Toke offered Mae her despoiled dress back, which she took, walked over to the nearest fire, and dropped it in.

The intensity of the day took its toll, and the three of them needed to get back to the Foxes, back to normality, and crash. Mae thought about what the word "normal" meant to them now and hid her inappropriately timed smile. Yu'mi was in good hands now, and the boy was being cared for, so they felt it was time to take their leave. She peeked in, once more, on the sleeping Yu'mi and said a private prayer before leaving.

They arrived to a dark, sleeping house, so they unloaded their equipment and stabled the horses in silence, then tiptoed up the porch steps. The log door creaked noisily in greeting but was soon snuffed out, overtaken by the deafening snores of Jack.

It took a while to scrub the dried fragments of blood and debris from their tired bodies, if only they could do that to their minds. After dropping the pouches of gold on the kitchen table, Mae slipped into bed without the slightest stir from Willie. She looked forward to her dreams tonight, however awful they might be, because nothing could be worse than this horrifying day.

Chapter Eighty

Elizabeth tiptoed around, feeding Jack and Willie breakfast on the porch, thus allowing the three of them to sleep late. Mae was the first to wake and sat at the table, sipping hot tea and trying to wrap her head around the last three days, or actually, the last two *months*.

Relaxed and rested, Dexter shuffled in with a yawn which made Mae yawn too. A deep yearning ached from within her, and she had to stop herself from running over to him, wrapping her entire body around his and burying her face in his warmth and strength. She realized he was becoming her rock now and how much his presence made her feel safe and secure, just like Greg used to.

A loud belch preceded Toke emerging from his room. He plopped down on the bench across from Mae. "Where's my grub, toots?"

Mae frowned, being jerked unpleasantly out of her consuming thoughts. "Toots? It's Miss Sanchez to you, white boy."

As if the Foxes had been listening with their ears to the wood, Willie and Elizabeth burst through the front door. Jack sauntered in behind them, trying a little too hard to be casual and detached. "So…" he said, fingering the pouches of gold. "You going to tell os?"

Grabbing a pie plate from the kitchen, Toke proceeded to empty the sacks of gold into it. Mae nearly forgot the ones she had stashed in her clothes and dug them out immodestly. This reminded Toke and Dexter that the uncomfortable lumps they had slept on all night were worth thousands of dollars and added theirs to the plate.

Willie whistled. "Holy coyote! We can get an entire herd of oxen for that."

"And a small willage," Jack added with a loud, and, thankfully short, explosion of laughter.

"Yeah, we were surprised too at how much we were able to find in just two and a half days." Toke jiggled the plate like he was making popcorn, letting the bright yellow gold dazzle them with its flirty dance.

"But we need to tell you more." Mae's cheerless tone deflated the triumphant mood of the room, and she gestured for everyone to sit around the table. In the next twenty minutes, they summarized everything that had happened, causing Elizabeth to turn her face away often, as if that would help.

Jack looked repulsed, yet captivated. "So den, ven you got back to your camp, de intruder was in de process of cotting de scalp off Yu'mi's head?"

"More like sawing with a dull, rusty butter knife," Toke said, causing even Jack to wince.

"Yes. It was so awful." Mae's eyes reddened, remembering it all too clearly. "If Toke and Dexter hadn't come when they did, we'd both be dead." She pulled her collar to the side, showing them her bruised neck. Elizabeth gasped, and Willie tried to move in for a closer look. "We can only imagine what he did to that little boy and what he still planned to do to him if he hadn't come across Yu'mi."

Picking up on something they had said, Elizabeth searched each of their eyes. "I can't help but get the sense there is something more you want to tell us."

"Oh, there is so much more." Mae lowered her head solemnly, knowing the innocent joy they'd be taking out of this family's simple lives.

With a deep knowing sigh, Dexter took off his glasses and rubbed his eyes. "It's probably best if we give you the big picture. The things we *know* are bad that are going to affect everyone here."

"And, it's only a few years from now," Mae added.

"It's pretty brutal, though." Toke scrunched his face in warning. "You really gotta be ready."

"I'm ready!" Willie attentively scooted closer to the table.

"Wat can be worse dan wat you jost told os? Lizzie, would you like to hear wat dey hef to say?"

"Well…" Elizabeth swallowed, in preparation. "It is not something I would *like* to hear, but if it is something y'all think we should know, I suppose we must." She rose to pull the kettle from the fire and poured the boiling water into the teapot. It hissed in protest, resuscitating Elizabeth's latest tea creation, and permeated the room with its musty scents of sweaty compost.

"I only recall some of what's going to happen." Dexter gestured to his side. "But hopefully Mae and Toke can fill in the gaps."

With that, Mae went to the kitchen and brought over a small plate of biscuits and honey apple butter that were gobbled up before she even sat down.

Wiping his mouth with a napkin, Dexter cleared his throat and began to recall the history, or rather, the future story of California. "The eastern states have been growing fast, and the cities are way too overcrowded. You might not know this, living so far away from it all, but people have started to move farther west, where there's plenty of land to have a farm and to raise a family. But, in reality, although with good intentions for their family, they're moving onto the lands that Indians already live on and have been living on for *thousands* of years.

"These newcomers only used small pieces of their land and there were still plenty of food and animals to hunt. So the Indians, for the most part, but not always, rather than be hostile toward the small groups of intruders, found ways to live peacefully, so it benefitted both of them. They traded, shared knowledge, and enriched both of their lives, much like you and the Ma'camo do.

"But, soon enough, the United States acquired California after a long battle, and gold was discovered right here in these mountains. People swarmed to California like a storm of locusts. Some came from the East, over and around these mountains. Others arrived on ships that crowded the harbors, bringing thousands of people from all around the world to get rich from gold."

"All this rushing to California got a name, the Gold Rush," Mae added, sniffing her tea, and decided to let it cool for a few minutes. Or, forever. "The arrival of just a few gold miners wouldn't have made such a dramatic change, but try to envision thousands and thousands of men rushing into these mountains, like thick herds of buffalo, trampling everything in their path."

"Let me put this all in Fox perspective." Toke rose from the bench and walked to the end of the table. "So, picture this…" He held up his hands like a director framing the scene. "There's six of us sitting around this table, right?" They nodded. "Now, let's just imagine that for each one of you here, there are one hundred other people standing right outside that door." He pointed to the door, pausing for a moment for them to do the math. "Yes, that's six hundred sweating bodies crammed on your peaceful little farm." With that, Toke choked down his tea and slammed his empty cup on the table.

Dexter nodded and continued, "The Indians have always relied heavily on the rivers and always built their villages near them. Just like you did here. So, imagine what happened when the miners dammed up these rivers or re-routed them, simply to get a better source for gold. The villages were now cut off from their treasured water supply."

Toke tailored this to the Fox audience again. "Say, for instance, some miners are way the heck upstream from us, and they decide to dam up your very own Fox creek. This one right out there." He made a broad sweep with his arm parallel to the water. "So, without having a well, where would you get your water now? You'd not only have to pack up and move, but you'd have to build a whole new house, log by log, a new henhouse, and a new barn and stable, and if you have any energy left, surround it all with a new fence. But, worst of all, you'd have to chop down a gazillion trees and yank out their stumps before you can even begin to plant a new apple orchard. So, you think *you'd* be super pissed at these donkey-hole intruders?" Toke hammered his fist on the table. "You're darn-tootin' right!" He looked at Jack for admiration of his clean language, to which Jack nodded approvingly. "Oh, and the new river you just relocated to, like all the other rivers, happens to be downstream from a dozen miners' camps."

Biting his lip, Willie tilted his head in confusion. "But, isn't that good to be far from the mining camps?"

Toke answered Willie directly, "Without staying in one place for very long, there was no reason for miners to dig any kind of outhouse. To keep things clean, they just crapped in the creeks, and the water's current took it all away." Toke dusted his hands together, ridding himself of the matter. "And, guess who got it? The people downstream. That's right, the miner's poop was happily floating around in everyone's drinking water, including their own." He drove in his point by grabbing his mouth in a dry heave.

Willie added, proudly, "Backtrea," earning a high-five from Toke.

Chapter Eighty-One

Mae slid out from the table and returned with a bowl of rising dough that was ready for kneading. "And, don't forget about food. These massive herds of gold miners had to eat something. So, they hunted. Then, they hunted more, until they killed all the animals, leaving none for natives.

"Also, shelter was another thing the miners needed. They chopped down thousands of trees indiscriminately to build housing and have wood for their fires. These were the same trees where the natives got their fruits, nuts, and medicines to survive. There just wasn't enough for everybody, and the Indians began to starve."

Resting his arms on the table, Toke leaned in for his next translation. "So, it's morning, and you need to milk the goat and collect some eggs for breakfast. But, when you step outside, you can't believe what six hundred hungry people have done to your tidy, orderly farm. They've killed and eaten all your horses, goats, and chickens, which also means there's no more eggs, milk, cheese, butter, or wool. The outhouse is overflowing, so there's crap everywhere, and people are getting sick. Not only did they strip the apple trees of all their fruit, but they cut them down to make little houses. So now you have no sources of food and water, and nothing to trade with. And you're starting to get sick..."

"Great analogy, man." Dexter pointed a finger gun at Toke, then turned back to the Foxes. "As it turned out, some of the miners that weren't having much luck panning for gold found it much easier to steal gold from the luckier ones."

"And other miners found it more profitable to steal Indians instead." Mae's expression hardened. "The lucky ones were sold into slavery to help the wealthy women of the ranchos around the house. But, most of them were sold to mining camps, especially the women and children, where they were forced to do unspeakable things." She scowled, landing a few good punches into the helpless dough.

Toke opened his mouth to translate this part, but couldn't do it in front of young Willie.

"Crime became rampant, and they had no jails. Too many people, too soon." Dexter nudged his glasses back up his nose. "So, they just took the law into their own hands and hung any lawbreakers, miners, and Indians right there on the spot. No judge. No jury."

"So, by now, the Indians were super pissed and starting to fight back." Toke reached in for a pinch of raw dough and got slapped. "Everywhere became a bloodbath, with miners and Indians knocking each other off all over the place." Toke brandished an invisible rifle and preceded to have a shootout, with full-on sound effects, until a whistling arrow caught him in the heart.

With a grave expression and somber voice, Dexter added, "Outside of war there will never be as much murder than during the Gold Rush, at any other time or any other place in all of the United States history."

"And the Gold Rush is still killing. A century and a half later!" The volume of Mae's voice increased with each word. "A few years after the Gold Rush started, all the easy gold had been plucked from the water and was gone. So, the miners started with this thing called hydraulic mining—the *worst* idea *ever*." Disappointed, but undeterred by the Foxes' blank expressions, their eyes glazed over from their brains' over-limit, the environmentalist in her still forged on. "It used this stuff called mercury. And, guess what? The mercury is *still there* in our time! *Still* washing out of the mountains and into the rivers and streams in the twenty-first century. The twenty-first century!" Mae slammed the dough on the table. "It's causing cancer and deformities, killing people, animals, fish, birds, and so many other things we're not even aware of," she said, pounding the dough with each word.

Toke leaned heavily into Mae's side for a reality check. "Look how you've captivated your audience. They're stunned speechless. How about we move on?"

If Greg were here, he'd have her back. God, she missed him. Mae removed herself from the table, getting plenty of leverage from her bony elbows wedged into Toke's side. In the kitchen, she shaped the dough into a round loaf and dropped it into the greased Dutch oven. It took her every muscle to heft the iron pot to the hearth and skillfully placed the behemoth alongside the burning wood. Flames lashed out aggressively at the disturbance, then fought angrily against her shovel as she stole its precious embers to pack around the iron pot.

A noise outside caught their attention, and she put the shovel aside. A few seconds later, there it was again, a shrill whistle like from a small bird. "That's Milok's call." A chilling spark splintered through Mae's stomach, and she found herself racing out the front door toward Milok, who was barely through their gate. "How is he? Is Yu'mi okay?" she called to him, sweating with a confusion of hope and fear.

"He is doing well. They gave him medicines to make him sleep."

Mae's hand flew to her chest. "Oh, thank God." She walked alongside him toward the house, giving a thumbs up to Toke and Dexter, who stood on the porch.

Milok remained on his horse, planning for a short visit. "I came to tell you they found machi cree and brought him back to our village."

This only brought confused looks from everyone. "That's the evil dead man," Willie cleared up for them.

"Yuck." Mae grimaced. "Why would you want that horrible man's rotting corpse in your village?"

"Ma'camo have tribal ways to deal with the evil dead. We are just disappointed we could not punish him ourselves. I'll come back with more news." With that, he turned his horse around and nodded goodbye. Milok seemed so much older now, carrying around the gravity of this serious situation.

Toke shuddered. "What the hell are they planning to do with a dead guy?"

"Not sure if the Ma'camo practice this," Dexter considered out loud, "but some tribes like to keep their prisoners alive, burning them slowly, one piece at a time. They wake them up if they pass out so they don't miss out on any of the torture."

"Dude's real lucky he's already dead."

As they watched Milok disappear through the trees, Mae shared her chilling thought, "Do you think they have a similar punishment in store for what we did?"

Chapter Eighty-Two

Letting the desperate reality of the future sink in for a few hours, they all went about their daily chores until the bell announced lunch. As the men walked through the front door, the nurturing aroma of freshly baked bread greeted them with a tranquilizing embrace.

For most of the meal, the usual lunchtime banter remained absent, replaced by the internal conversations going on in each of their heads. Elizabeth laid her napkin on the table, folding it with the listlessness of a numbed mind and set it aside. "I feel so exhausted by all these emotional stories." She followed it with a discouraged sigh.

"Sorry to tell you, Mrs. F., but we just breezed over what they did to the Indians. That was just the Gold Rush." Toke took a second helping of sliced elk and drowned it in gravy. "Get ready for more."

"More? There's more?" Elizabeth's eyes pleaded with Toke, hoping he was making one of his jokes.

Jack put his arm around his wife, looking into her face. "Lizzie, would you radder excuse yourself? Villie an' I can summarize all dis for you if dat would suit you better." Looking thoughtfully at her husband, she shook her head and remained seated.

"You sure? It gets way worse," Toke said through a mouth full of food.

Elizabeth appealed to Mae, but she only gave her a tortured look back. Squeezing Jack's hand, Elizabeth nodded. "I'll be all right."

"Okay, then." Toke gave her the "I warned you" look and extended his palm for one of the others to start.

Knowing she was about to lose her appetite, Mae put down her fork, pushed her plate forward, and picked up where they left off. “Many people felt it was perfectly fine to kill a native since they were considered vermin. Hunting them became a sport. They'd often use these sensitive souls simply for target practice and snag the women for themselves as concubines. And rarely was one too young.”

“But, how could these murderers get away with this?” Elizabeth's face distorted with despair and the helplessness of injustice. “Surely there is some law against it.”

Dexter shook his head with a pained expression. “At this point, people realized they could rape, kill, or steal whatever they wanted from the Indians because Indians couldn't testify against a white person in court.”

“That means Mae could not testify,” Toke said to Willie. Mae shot Toke the stink-eye.

Dexter held up his index finger, ready to make a point. “Let me clarify that not all the people who moved to California were miners. Some were hard-working, honest people, like you, just trying to find a better life. Little did they know that they, too, killed the Indians, by unknowingly carrying diseases the Indians had no immunity for.”

“Yeah.” Toke tossed a sparkling nugget of gold from one hand to another. “But, there were also some depraved buttholes that brought diseases on purpose. Like infecting blankets with smallpox and then giving them like an act of kindness to the Indians as a faster way to knock them off.

“So, up to now, the way they got rid of Indians was by picking them off, one by one.” He slid a finger knife across his throat with sound effects. “California's first U.S. governor felt this was way too tedious and time-consuming. The fastest way to have them gone was to declare a war of extermination and wipe them all out.”

Willie cocked his head to the side. “What's wipethemallout?”

“It's also known as the Extinction of the Red Race,” Dexter said.

"Genocide of the Indigenous Peoples," Mae added.

Toke spread out his arms, sounding off an explosion like an atomic bomb. "Exterminating the Red Man."

"Eradicating the Natives."

"Indian Removal Act."

Mae slammed her hands on the table. "Ethnic cleansing."

Dexter crossed his arms. "The governor called in the military to slaughter whole villages. He paid money for each Indian scalp brought in."

Talking about the genocide triggered an unwanted slew of horrific images Mae had tried to forget. "They slaughtered them all. Even the little babies and toddlers!" The stories were still so vivid in her mind as if she was sitting in her history class right now.

As more details of the massacres were revealed, Elizabeth cringed miserably and shrunk low in her seat, wiping her hands on her apron repeatedly. It was hard to tell if Jack could actually hear what they were saying through his lusty bear-like eating. Or how he had an appetite in the first place with their ill-timed story.

Mae found Jack's eyes and locked on them. "Think of Milok, Yu'mi, and their entire Ma'camo tribe. These kind, non-violent human beings, who are just trying to live, will all be butchered, axed, and scalped alive, just to get them out of the way."

Mae glanced at Elizabeth, afraid the details might be getting too graphic, and she was right. Pale and clammy, Elizabeth gazed out the window as if a slideshow was playing before her in full, lifelike detail of her own family's slaughter. Jack tenderly covered her small, cold hand with his large warm paw. "Lizzie, now, are you shore you want to hear all dis?" She nodded limply, wiping her eyes, and forced her chin up, attentively.

"So now, at this point, it was all about efficiency and became a sort of white supremacy." Dexter took off his glasses and set them on the table, rubbing his eyes. "So, even though when the missions were under Mexican rule, and they used them to enslave the Indians, and the Mexican government treated them poorly, Mexico still acknowledged the Indians as human beings. Not something to exterminate like termites. But, now that California was under control of the United States, they brought their own rules."

"You won't know who Hitler is, but he is, by far, the most evil human being ever to live." Mae shuddered in disgust. "He modeled his own extermination of Jews on how the U.S. eradicated their Indians." She slid out from the table and began clearing the dirty dishes.

"God didn't even like Hitler." Toke felt the need to stress the point, tailored for this audience.

Jack squinted his eyes in doubt. "Nei, de ranchos need de Indians to farm deir crops an' tend to deir livestock. Dey vork hard for very little pay. A dead Indian would not be of any help to dem."

"People were too lazy and fired up with hate," Dexter said, shrugging. "The opportunity to kill freely was probably quite enticing to blood-thirsty vigilantes."

With a noisy swig of tea, Jack wiped his mouth on his sleeve and gestured to the three of them with his empty glass. "So den, how did you find out about all dis? Are you shore it's de trute? It sounds a bit exaggerated."

"Oh, the facts are true all right." Mae leaned back and crossed her arms. "Many people remembered it and wrote it down, documented it, lived it, and passed down the stories. It's even recorded in books and government documents. But, the whole gruesome truth you won't find in our school's history books. What you'll find are glossed-over stories, omitting facts that might upset people." She rolled her eyes.

"I got lucky for my U.S. history classes. Professor Callow was excellent." Dexter placed his hand in the middle of his back in an agonizing stretch. "Greg and I were in the same class, but the teacher still managed to keep our attention." Dexter let out a rare chuckle. "He was *that* good."

"Had him freshman year. Both times." Toke looked away, not wanting to explain. "A tough son-of-a-bitch. Dude told it straight. Held nothing back."

"I just finished his California history class in June," Mae remembered fondly. "He explained history like he was telling us a story. Not just cramming us full of facts and dates. I loved him. But then, history's my favorite subject."

In poised dignity, possessed with grief, Elizabeth floated to the kitchen in her new sad, sunless world. She returned with red eyes and a wet dishrag. "I'll never understand how anyone can kill children and innocent people."

Nobody said anything. Just a somber shaking of heads, shrugs, and downcast eyes.

"Hef you told Yu'mi an' Milok any of dis?"

"No, we didn't want to worry him until we needed to." Mae took the rag from Elizabeth and motioned for her to sit while she finished cleaning.

"We should probably leave them all in the dark for now." Dexter hesitated a moment and looked at his friends for support. "Plus, maybe there's a way we can stop most of it from happening."

"I think we're all on the same page, but let me just throw this out there." Toke held up his hands as if to block someone's punch. "There could be a big problem messing with the past too much." He shrugged, wincing. "I don't mean to sound selfish or anything, but we're not going to help anyone here if we wipe ourselves out before we're even born. We could use the gold to get back home and be wealthy beyond our wildest dreams."

Toke had an excellent point, and Mae couldn't help but feel a little conflicted. "Who knows how many people we love that might never be born, or be born to different parents, or however all that stuff works. But, back home, we could use our gold to help charities, feed and house the homeless, protect the wildlife and environment—"

"Support research to cure diseases," Dexter added.

"Yeah, all that too," Toke said.

After the retelling of the horrors that would happen to the people Mae personally knew, it completely changed everything. No longer were these just miserable historical incidents done to faceless people in the dusty past that seemed so unrelatable to her own modern life. "I don't know if I can simply stand by and do nothing for these living, breathing, human beings, knowing we could actually make a huge difference in their lives."

"Yes, this is no small decision that we need to make," Dexter said, crossing his arms over his chest.

"Then, I say we do both. Let's go for it all." Toke threw his hand up to vote. "If we're careful and keep reminding ourselves of the butterfly effect, maybe we can actually change the worst part of their crappy future. I mean, what the heck, right?"

This definitely gave them all something to think about.

Chapter Eighty-Three

It was good they had a full day to think through their new ambitious ideas. When they regrouped, they could speak less from emotions and more from rational thinking. Elizabeth had a fresh pot of tea waiting, thankfully a different blend than the day before, to accompany a freshly baked blackberry pie.

Though a little nervous about her grandiose plan, Mae decided to speak first. She fixed her eyes on each of their faces, one by one, especially Jack's, "Okay. So, the thing is, if we can somehow acquire *all* of this land and stop the gold from being discovered in the first place…there won't be a Gold Rush."

"So much for being subtle." Toke smirked.

Dexter stared hard at the table as if it would give him the answer. "So, if we all agree we want to do this, I guess the big question now is, where do we start?"

"Dey're called land grants. And de governor down in Monterey vill just give you one for de asking. You jost draw a little map of de land dat you want to settle an' hand it to him."

Mae asked, "Is that how you got yours?"

"Nei, we don't need dem op here." Jack dismissively waved the idea away with his hand.

"Wait. So you don't own this property that you've built two houses, an orchard, and a farm on and now just discovered gold right under your feet?" Toke flicked the side of his head. "Holy crap, man."

Mae blinked a few times, confused. “But, if a land grant’s free for the asking, why haven’t you just asked for it?”

“Not wort de troble. No one else wants to live op here. Dey all want land near de sheeping ports an’ we’re a four to five day’s ride.” Jack stroked his beard. “Anyway, I could not get it even if I wanted to. I would hef to be a Mexican citizen.”

Dexter leaned forward with intent. “Well, maybe there’s a way we can get it for you.”

“So, den, how are you going to do dat?” Jack said with a condescending smile. “To become a citizen of Mexico, you must hef lived here for a year, an’ hell if you’ve even been here six veeks.”

“And be baptized Roman Catholic,” Elizabeth added, disapprovingly.

Jack released a booming laugh that ricocheted unpleasantly off the walls. “Can you see me a Katolik, Lizzie?”

“Yes, but, certain details might get overlooked with a little gold.” Toke rubbed his thumb and fingers together with a devious smile.

Dexter nodded. “There’s a lot of lust and greed in desperate people. Especially out here in the Wild West.”

“So. Wat you’re saying is dat we take as much gold as we can out of dese creeks, streams, an’ rivers. Den we use dis new-found wealt to buy op land an’ bribe de officials to get de law changed in our favor?”

Dexter, Toke, and Mae looked at each other until Toke said, “Uh, yeah, basically.”

“Isn’t bribing illegal?” Willie asked innocently.

“Willie, dear,” Elizabeth said thoughtfully as she refilled the sacks with the gold. “There are times that one needs to break the rules when good people’s lives are in danger.” Not wanting to go into details about this sinful way of handling things, she got up and went into the kitchen.

“We’re going to have to get this all weighed somehow.” Toke lightly tossed one of the sacks in his hand. "See how much we've got to work with."

"Bot de bigger problem is, you hef to come op wit an amazing story if you plan to bargain wit raw gold nuggets. Dese aren't coins, remember, an' de spoken word travels fast."

"Good point, we'll have to work on that one." Dexter studiously chewed on his bottom lip.

Elizabeth returned with an old chipped clay jar from the kitchen and piled the small sacks of gold on top of Toke's first three nuggets. She placed the pot on the highest shelf in the kitchen, then wiped her hands together as if cleansing her soul.

"So, while we're down there getting our supplies and crap, we can pick the brains of the locals. Learn something about their government's"—Toke put air quotes around his next words—"less official ways."

Leaning forward, Dexter flattened his hands on the table. "We can start small, get your Fox property on paper, also add in the Ma'camos' land, and however far you think we can get. Especially if the government sees this land as undesirable as you say."

Jack went to the bookshelf and tore a blank page from an old storybook of Willie's. He placed it on the table and began to sketch a map of their farmstead.

"So." Dexter contemplated, drumming his fingers on the wood. "Once we've got this first part finished, we can start on Part Two. For that, we'll need to collect enough gold to buy as much of these mountains and foothills for the tribes as we possibly can."

"That's one heckova lot of gold we'll need to pull out of the water." Toke scratched his short, scruffy beard.

"Dey don't have a big problem giving Indians land. Bot, dey usually take it away ven they decide dey want it back."

"That's exactly it." Dexter took a bite of pie and mumbled a "delicious," hiding his berry-stained teeth. "For Part Three, the hardest of them all, we'll need to come up with a creatively brilliant plan to legally keep the land the natives live on permanently in their hands."

"Yeah." Mae twirled her fork as she searched her thoughts. "But nothing like a reservation. Even in our modern twenty-first century, the Indians don't even *own* their reservation land. They just *live* on it."

"Besides the gold, the other thing we've got going for us is we know what's coming in the future." Toke put his finger to his temple, with a cunning wink. "We just need to figure out how to use what we've got, then work it."

Mae stood and began to clear the plates away. "Our biggest problem will be when the U.S. declares war on Mexico and forces them to sell California to them."

"There's still a small chance the U.S. might still honor the Mexican land grants." Dexter downed the last of his tea. "But, then again, they might not honor any land grants given to Indians and just sell their land to the highest bidder."

"Which will be the people with tons of gold," Mae added, confidently. "As long as they figure the gold came from somewhere else entirely."

Nodding slowly, Elizabeth was beginning to understand the bigger picture. "Do y'all know how much time we have before the United States takes this land?"

No one said anything, so Dexter spoke up, "I don't really know. All I remember is they signed a treaty and took over California right before they discovered gold. I mean, like the exact same month or week, completely by coincidence. So that would be around 1848. That's all I know. I was never good at remembering dates."

"Geez." Toke looked guilty for the greediness of the United States. "That completely sucked for Mexico."

Returning from the kitchen, Mae wiped her hands on her apron. "It's kind of a long shot to think that not one person is going to find a nugget of gold in some random stream and start a gold rush."

"The way I see it," Dexter said thoughtfully. "We won't be able to stop *all* the brutality done to the natives, but we *do* have a chance to stop the killing and damage caused by the Gold Rush."

"And that means California won't be the popular new girl anymore." Toke shook his head in faux sympathy. "People will take their time checking her out. Then the government won't be in such a desperate fury to paint over every single Indian."

"That's right." Dexter crossed his arms over his chest and nodded. "Because of the push West, also called manifest destiny, people will still be coming to California, but at a much slower pace. Word will get out about the great California weather, the huge redwood trees to log, the rich fertile soil to plant their crops, and miles and miles of open land to graze their cattle."

"Dey're already doing dat. De entire valley has been ron over by dose large defecating beasts." Jack let out a sound somewhere between a belch and a cough.

"Stinks awful down there." Willie scrunched up his face.

"Well then, shit's begun already." Toke waited a second, holding out his fist, then nudged Willie. "Pound it, dude. I made an awesome use of word-play."

Willie's small fist bumped Toke's back, saying, "Dude, that was an awesome use of words playing."

"That means the valley natives are already taking a hit." Dexter rubbed his forehead. "The ranchers have already planted their new species of grasses so their livestock will have plenty to eat wherever they roam."

"So, wat's wrong wit a little color?" Jack leaned back, stretching his arms wide with a loud, infectious yawn.

Mae rolled her eyes and tried not to sound annoyed. "Those new grasses are tough and intrusive. Spreading way too quickly, in all directions, bullying out the unsuspecting native plants that the Indians have relied on for thousands of years." She covered the pie and began wiping down the table, working around the oblivious elbows.

“You know,” Toke said with an amused expression and a partial smile. “Here we are, making all these massive plans, but have we forgotten? We’ll still be mining in the native’s territories without their consent. I mean, who are we kidding? It’s not like they won’t catch us. Ever.”

Chapter Eighty-Four

With their minds completely engrossed in plans of their terrifying future, they were unnerved to hear the latch on the gate slide open. Mae let out a startled chirp. Willie tore away from the table, grabbed up his gun, and dashed to the window. Gun out first. With the stealthiness of a cat, he peeked out from the side, let out a short laugh, set down his gun, then ran out the front door. Seconds later, he was right back inside. "Milok says the Ma'camo want to see you," he panted. "All three of you. Right now."

Mae followed Toke and Dexter outside, a little embarrassed by the raggedy bottom of her dress. Maybe she could get the bandages back from the Ma'camo and merely sew them back on. That was if she could get the blood out. Milok dismounted and stood to face them. "They want to hear everything you know about what happened with the machi cree. They're not angry. They just want to talk." His little bit of reassurance only slowed her racing heart a tiny bit. The rest of her wanted to run.

Once the horses were saddled, they followed Milok to his village. Mae took a few deep breaths, but felt her anxiety return the closer they got. She looked at Dexter for support, and he gave her the reassuring nod she needed.

Once the horses were tethered, Milok walked them into the center area of their camp. So, just how "not angry" were the Ma'camo?

"Behind you, Mae," Toke said under his breath. "Aunt JuJu coming up fast."

"It's pronounced Aunt Ja*lulu*." But, as soon as she said it, the woman was already beside her, speaking rapidly, using hand movements and gestures to help carry her words. Mae, not wanting to be rude, just nodded along. When she caught Milok's eye, she motioned for him to hurry over.

"She forgets you don't speak our language like Willie can." Milok put his hand on his mother's shoulders. "She's trying to explain that he is doing much better thanks to you three. Yu'mi says you three saved his life even though he doesn't remember anything that happened. Waho and everyone are hoping you can fill them in on the rest of the details."

Milok walked them over to a sizable mud-covered structure and pulled them aside. "Inside will be many elders, and I need to teach you some things, so you do not make them angry." He looked into each of their faces, and they nodded. "Not all the old are considered elders. An elder is someone who has acquired large amounts of knowledge and wisdom over their lifetime, especially about our tribe's traditions and customs. An elder would rather you listen without asking why. To learn, it is best to sit mutely with patience, absorbing what the elder shares of their wisdom. Questions are considered rude." Milok put extra emphasis on the last one. "But, it's okay to get clarification or to comment."

"So, we treat elders with the utmost respect," Dexter said, confirming he understood.

"We listen and keep our traps shut," Toke added.

Milok nodded and handed them over to Yu'mi's cousin since he was too young to enter. They were taken to the center of the hut and were motioned to sit.

Seated opposite of them were three distinctive men: Yu'mi's father, Waho, a much older man who seemed important by his showy ornamentation, so they figured him to be an elder, and Chief K'ut'im. Tightly packed around the sides and back of the hut stood other male village members. Mae was not happy with the women to men ratio, but it was their tribe, their rules.

The elder began speaking directly to the three of them, but Mae could only pick out a scarce word or two. He spoke much faster than Yu'mi, who she now realized slowed his speech down for her. Seeing their bewilderment and lack of response, the elder turned to Waho, where they discussed something in low tones. Waho stood and gave a command, then two men moved forward from the back, stamped their heavy sticks into the ground, turned sharply and left through the doorway.

After a few minutes of sitting and looking blankly at the three men in front of them, it got too uncomfortable. Mae found reasons to look at her hands, admiring her tiny new fingernails while Toke found the beams in the mud ceiling fascinating and Dexter stared straight ahead, focusing on nothing in particular.

Mae could feel the eyes around the room watching them, studying their souls to pick up any trace of betrayal. Or, was it just her own feelings of guilt? It was unsettling no matter the reason.

A noisy rustling parted the group that crowded the entrance to make way for the two returning men. They carried in a woven tule chair which held a bandaged, ghostly pale Yu'mi. His Aunt Jalulu quietly slid in against the back wall.

Mae immediately rushed over to him, squatting by his side. "Oh my gosh, Yu'mi. I'm so glad you're okay! I've been so worried!" She put her head down on his arm and then lifted it to see into his face. She could not stop her tears. Seeing her friend like this tore her heart in pieces.

"I okay," Yu'mi said in English. "They want me to say what they talk and tell them what you talking."

"Dude, so glad you're here." Toke picked up Yu'mi's hand and swiped it across his own in greeting.

"Glad you're okay, man." Dexter gestured with his chin and smiled warmly.

Three loud raps from the chief's cane, and everybody fell silent. Chief K'ut'im spoke at length, and Yu'mi kept up, nodding the entire way.

Yu'mi turned to face them, already looking exhausted. He spoke slowly and carefully, translating everything he said. "Very important to thank you for coming. Tribe men found machi cree dead." Then he paused for a moment, trying to use the correct words but only came up with, "He very dead. They ride his evil body back to village. Huuk ask if you know dead machi cree."

They all three said, "No!" which was clearly understood by all.

The chief spoke some more. "People worry there more machi cree in mountains."

Mae wanted to ask a question, so Yu'mi introduced her by her full first name, her father's last name, and where she was from. Maegan Sanchez Sacramento. Next, he introduced the elder, Ono'ha, as the healer for the tribe's spiritual side. The elder nodded slowly, keeping his permanent frown. She nervously cleared her throat. "That dead man, he was a very bad man. But please don't assume that all white men are bad and are out to scalp all natives."

Yu'mi translated and returned with, "That please him. Huuk family and all village thank you all for saving me." Mae could see tears in Waho's reddened eyes that threatened to fall. Then Yu'mi spoke directly to Mae. "My father see marks the night you bring me home." He motioned to her neck. "He want to know if machi cree make those marks."

"Yes." She blinked a few times. "Would you like to hear *everything* we know about what happened that day?"

Mae could see that Yu'mi was quickly fading but still managed to explain that the elder Ono'ha would like to give her truth medicines. Dexter and Toke looked at her as uneasily as her stomach felt. Not knowing what to do, she merely shrugged and agreed.

With extreme physical effort, the elder healer stood. His flesh seemed to fall from his bones and linger behind in his chair. It took ten minutes, but the walking skeleton eventually relocated himself in front of Mae.

Performing for the entire crowd, he opened his palm, revealing a thick leaf. He snapped it in half with his knotted fingers and held it up for all to see. It oozed a clear gel, which he promptly wiped across Mae's forehead. He motioned for her to come forward and sit at his feet.

In his next act, he presented a large acorn cap he had filled with a ground substance. This he handed down for Mae to eat. Afraid she'd be able to identify its contents, she snapped her eyes shut and tipped the concoction into her mouth. She chewed the crunchy bits, not trying too hard to hide her misery. Toke had to turn his head to keep from laughing since he saw exactly what Mae was munching on.

Chapter Eighty-Five

Yu'mi spoke again, but much weaker this time. "They say…to please tell all. Everything." Then to just Mae, he assured her, "It okay."

Sitting cross-legged on the dirt facing the elder, she began to tell the whole story. She was able to avoid the reason they were there in the first place by starting from when she found the man on top of Yu'mi, cutting his head. She told of Dexter's role, and, when she was telling of Toke's, he added sound effects to his shooting, which made the elder jump.

When she finished, Toke raised his hand like a third grader. The chief nodded for him to speak. "I'd like to mention that Mae was barely alive herself, recovering from being strangled to death, but she still sewed Yu'mi's scalp back on—herself."

Dexter added for clarity, "This stopped his bleeding and kept the wound clean until the healer could stitch it back together properly." More eyes looked upon Mae.

The room was hushed as Ono'ha, Chief K'ut'im, Waho, and Yu'mi discussed among themselves for a few minutes. It was a pensive moment. Dexter reached out and squeezed Mae's shoulder while she hung her head, biting her lip.

When the discussion was over, the men retook their places. Yu'mi announced with as much gusto as he could manage, "The elders believe your story." Instant relief washed over Mae, and she smiled at Toke and Dexter. Yu'mi added, "They want to know what we doing hunting beaver and why I not advise you beaver gone. They want us be husband and wife because they hear from Sekoma you grow my baby, a Ma'camo child, inside you."

"Oh…shit," Toke breathed.

But, Mae, still loose tongued under the influence of the truth medicines, did not hesitate. "Yu'mi lied to the Sekoma about the baby so they would like us more because they would see me like family. We need to get better tools and an ox for the Fox family's farm. We went behind your back. We hope you can find a way to forgive us for deceiving you and lying to the Sekoma leaders."

Toke and Dexter wondered if Yu'mi was translating these same facts. Besides not knowing the entire English language, he was also not wearing the truth gel, nor did he take the truth medicine.

Yu'mi turned to Mae, "Huuk want to know if you hunt gold and not beaver." Now sweating heavily and looking sickly pale Yu'mi requested for Milok to take his place.

Once they retrieved Milok from the outside, he stood in front of Chief K'ut'im with a bowed head and repeated the oath of truth. Mae then answered the question, "Yes, we were digging for gold. We need gold to buy an ox and some better tools for the Fox family farm," Mae said like a repeating robot.

Milok spoke the chief's answer a little more theatrically than Yu'mi. "Why did you disobey the Huuk when he said you could not hunt for gold in these mountains? It is a sickness, and now you all have the sickness and infected Yu'mi. The machi cree came to punish you. It has already started!"

Why did the dirt have to be so hard under her butt? She shifted a little but felt no relief. "The machi cree didn't even know we had any gold. So, as much as you'd like to think, it was not the evilness of the gold that did this to Yu'mi." She looked at Milok, then back at the men and swallowed. "We have an excellent reason for hunting the gold and want to continue to hunt the gold. But, this is not a sickness. This is to save all of the Nisenan tribes and many, many others that will soon die at the hands of invaders." A murmur rolled through the people like surround sound.

Milok turned to Mae, but his voice spoke to everyone. "They want to know what you mean? More invaders like machi cree?"

"Oh, there's so much more…" For the next full hour, Mae filled them in on the entire future of their beloved homeland. Unable to hold anything back, all the heart-wrenching details of the bloody massacre of the innocents, the hellish slavery, the extermination—*everything* poured out. Even more than they had told the Fox family.

The entire time she spoke, her eyes fixed on the faces of the villagers that surrounded her. She watched their expressions change from disbelief to worry, then alarm, and lastly, to utter and complete horror. Many wiped away tears, but, as Mae feared, others looked angry at her for telling them these abominable fictitious stories. She hung her head, unaware of the tears running down her face, feeling sick to her stomach.

No one spoke. There was no noise at all—just absolute quiet.

Breaking the silence, the elder spoke. Milok nodded, then turned to Mae. "He would like to know how you know this will happen. You are not Ono'ha, and only Ono'ha can see into the future, and then only when the spirits wish him to. They have not shown him this. How could you see this?"

"I'm telling the truth. I've seen the future. There's no doubt this will happen unless we stop it," Mae summarized. "And, we know how to stop most of it. But, we'll need to acquire many government papers from two different countries, and that'll require an awful lot of gold."

The elder bent, with creaking bones, to examine Mae's face in detail. He straightened back up, turned to the people, and spoke. Sounds of alarm immediately followed, ricocheting through the people.

Milok explained, "He has announced that what you said was true as far as you believe it yourself."

Mae felt relieved but also a little skeptical. "But, how does the elder know it's the truth?"

"The elder put a truth sap on your forehead. He is able to see it turn a shade of green if you are lying by somehow outwitting the truth beetles."

Mae gagged, repeating weakly, "Beetles?"

When the crowd broke, everyone filed out of the mudhouse, forcibly avoiding eye contact with the three of them. "Geez, Mae." Toke looked around uncomfortably. "Do you think you could have held *some* of the baby gore back?"

"No," Dexter assured Mae. "They needed to hear it all."

Mae let out a tortured sigh and stood. She nearly fell over, finding her leg had fallen asleep. "Let's find Yu'mi," she said, miserably limping out of the hut.

Chapter Eighty-Six

They spotted Yu'mi, sitting outside in his tule chair, looking slightly better. Aunt Jalulu walked over with an adobe cup filled with a green-colored fluid and told him to drink. He cringed at the smell but did as he was told, nearly gagging.

From inside the mud hut came an uproar of voices with intense, mixed emotions. People of the village began to file back inside. Milok held up his hand for the three of them to stay put.

Toke strained to see inside. "What? What just happened?" Yu'mi shook his head, as confused as they were.

Ten minutes later, a middle-aged man wrapped in a deerskin vest fringed with feathers and tiny bones emerged and motioned for them to come back in.

"I don't like it in there," Mae complained. "It feels like a courtroom."

"I think it actually is one," Dexter said, stepping into the hut. They took their old seats across from the three men. Yu'mi still looked sickly, so Milok remained the translator.

The elder's decision was strangely brief, no lingering questions or long pauses. Milok stepped forward and delivered their decision with his usual full drama. "They have considered your lies and your stories and have come to a decision."

Lies? Gone was the sense of relief as Mae's stomach sank. Milok spoke with such confidence, not like the kid Mae remembered, jumping around with Willie, but a full-grown adult. He sort of reminded Mae of a TV lawyer on court day without the suit and tie. Plus, his English was far better than Yu'mi's, and even Willie's for that matter. Milok straightened his shoulders and continued, "You saved Yu'mi's life at the risk of losing your own. That, above anything else, grants you the elders' consent to continue to collect gold on these lands."

Mae was so stunned, she started to laugh. Then, she pulled Dexter and Toke in for an epic hug, her smile so broad it covered her entire face.

Clearing his throat, Milok continued, "Chief K'ut'im will speak to the Sekoma and the other Nisenan tribes nearby to ask them to let you have full permission to collect gold on their land as well. The Huuk will be meeting with the other headmen at the annual Bear Dance and will discuss this matter with the attending tribes.

"We will let it be known to the Miwok and Washoe of our recommendations. But lately, the Nisenan have been warring with the Miwok, and you may have to wait a great many moons to work on any of their lands." Milok smiled briefly. "But, once the Huuk lets it be known that it was you who saved the young boy, that may change. To those they speak with, they will not share the entire story, for the others may not find truth in it. But they will explain the circumstances in such a way that the other tribes will listen."

The three of them could not hide their relief and happiness. Not sure of the Ma'camo custom for thanking, they chose to bow and overly praise them with thank yous and more thank yous. The middle-aged man with the vest came forward and presented each of them with a soft leather lanyard, intricately woven with seed beads, polished wood, and tiny black feathers. These gifts represented the bond of their new agreement.

Mae beamed brightly and clutched her new necklace to her heart. Her mind and body radiated with such warmth, it made it all the way to her heart, awakening a part of her that had lain dormant for so long. She turned to Yu'mi and hugged him, being careful not to injure him more. Yu'mi's father quickly turned his head away from this shameful public affection, as did others.

Regrouping back outside, they watched the tribespeople go about their daily lives as if nothing huge and life-changing had just happened. Toke leaned into Mae. "Did you see that doll they're making?"

"Yeah, I think so why?"

"They were making it out of skin. *Human* skin."

Dexter joined the conversation. "Milok alluded to a ceremony. Since the man we killed was missing much of his head, thanks to Toke"—Toke took a mini-bow—"and they needed to burn the evil man's body in its full representation to rid this land from his evil so it can never come back in a different form, they probably had to recreate it."

"Voodoo, perhaps?" Toke flicked his eyes around in mock suspicion.

Mae caught sight of Milok, heading their way, and waved. They all got to congratulate him on a job well done. Milok looked prouder than they had ever seen him. Willie would surely notice the change in his best friend the next time he saw him. Yu'mi mentioned that Milok would probably get his tribe name earlier than the other boys his age.

After first speaking with Yu'mi for a few minutes, Milok turned back to the three of them and said in his new adult voice, "You understand that this is a great sacrifice for our village. It will be a difficult task to convince the other villages and tribes that the gold will be put to good use and not used to spread the sickness."

"We understand and are very grateful." Dexter thought for a second. "Do you think the elders really believed what we told them? That it's not simply a story, but the future? The actual future, unless we fix it?"

Looking shameful, Milok said, "Willie has spoken to me of your cave story, and I had spoken to Yu'mi and the elders. I am sorry, but I did not know it was private."

Mae nearly choked. "Wait, what? You *told* them where we came from?"

"Did they believe you?" Dexter stared as wide-eyed as Mae.

"Yes, they do believe you speak from what you know," Milok explained. "Through time, the Ma'camo ancestors have met a few visitors that came the same way. Ma'camo do not like the cave and do not want to talk about it or go there. They are worried that one day much evil will flow out of it and darken the world. Our ancestors kept the water happy by making sacrifices into it, but not anymore. They stopped about two hundred years ago. It was when they remembered seeing your missing fingernails, toenails, and hair that made them put it all together today."

"So, Yumes." Toke smiled sheepishly. "How long've you known about the cave?"

"I hear stories about cave from elders. Just stories we think." Yu'mi gestured to include Milok as the "we." "Elders tell many..."—Yu'mi tapped his head for the word—"dream stories. I think not true until Milok say you came from same water cave. Then I know too."

Milok nodded. "The truth that I told about your coming from the water cave helped the elders understand the urgency of your request. They are content with their decision. They are risking the gold sickness for peace."

Mae reached out for Milok's hand and held it. "Thank you, Milok. That was a very good choice."

Milok straightened up, looking even prouder. Mae had no doubt that Milok would grow up into a strong influential man. Possibly even their chief one day.

Chapter Eighty-Seven

For the first time since they arrived at the Fox farm, Mae sat with the men for breakfast. Their work for the day involved preparing for the trip, and they needed to include her in every detail. They had the blessing of the elders, so nothing could stop them now. Their plan had to be solid, or they might speed up something they were trying to eradicate.

Jack held the candle, Dexter the quill, and they started the beginning of a very long list.

"I think we should only take a few days to prepare," Dexter said, awkwardly dabbing the quill in the ink, trying not to make a huge mess with this new sort of writing tool. "It will be autumn soon, and we need to get back before the rivers get too cold for us to mine."

Smiling agreeably, Mae hid the inner celebration she was having at missing the second apple harvest. But then, with their new wealth, couldn't she just hire someone to help Elizabeth? With disheartening clarity, Mae realized that they couldn't if they wanted to keep the gold a secret. She and the Foxes were going to have a talk about priorities when they got back.

Dexter proceeded to scratch a list which was unreadable due to long stretches of missing ink and numerous ink globs. The tired old storybook on the shelf lost another page to Jack, this time for the travel map. Unlike Dexter's writing, Jack's quill sketched the paper's surface lustily, leaving thick, erratic black lines looking like confused snakes in a chaotic garden. But, once he labeled the coast, mountains, and rivers, it began to make sense. He added in the approximate location of the missions, large ranchos, best river crossings, Monterey, and various other landmarks. He consulted with Willie, who made a few changes and then turned the map around for them to see.

Mae pored over the barren map. The distance they needed to travel was barely tolerable in an air-conditioned car, but riding horses in the direct summer sun for a couple hundred miles would be torturous. "Is there a chance any of these lines here could be railroad tracks? Maybe we could just hop on a train."

"Nei, no rail lines dis far vest."

Spinning the map around in his direction, Toke swept his eyes over it. "So how about the Pony Express?"

With no clue of recognition, Jack gave a small shrug, so Dexter jumped in. "The Pony Express was pretty much invented for all the people that moved out here for the Gold Rush."

Every so often, they'd find Elizabeth hanging out by the table, drying a dish or doing some other household chore. This was Elizabeth's subtle reminder that there was still "women's work" to be done. But, her efforts were futile since Mae was *purposely* unaware of her presence.

Pulling the map closer, Dexter studied the details, following the route with his finger. "But," he began, tapping the area where Jack had drawn a familiar coastal inlet with Y.B. scrawled on the land, "wouldn't this be S.F. instead of Y.B.?"

"Nei. San Francisco is de water or radder de bay. Dis land here"—Jack circled the area with the tip of his pipe—"where dis harbor lay, *dat* dey call Yerba Buena."

"So, wait, the city of San Francisco doesn't exist yet? Holy crap." Toke smoothed a hand over his wispy blonde baby-fine hair that now covered his head.

Mae puzzled over the drawing and tapped her finger on the Yerba Buena Cove that ate into the city up to where Montgomery and Market would cross. "I'm sure that cove doesn't exist anymore in the future San Francisco we know. I wonder what happened to it."

Leaning over the map, Dexter asked, "So, how many people live in the city of Yerba Buena?"

"You can't really call it a city. Barely anyone is living dere 'cept de hide traders, mission Indians, an' a few Mexican military still at de Presidio." Jack leaned back in his chair and gazed up at the ceiling. "De last time I was dere, I saw maybe twenty foreigners, Germans, English, Swiss, French, all kinds. De rest were Mexicans or Californios an' not many of dem dere eider. Maybe a hundred or two total."

Jack packed his pipe with a fresh bowl of tobacco. "You might want to give a look at Yerba Buena forst. You vill find more interesting tings coming off de sheeps dere. Monterey is de government center, so dey heavily control wat comes in an' goes out. De sheeps dat dock dere tend to bring de type of cargo dat people of de government an' wealty ranchos are looking for. Fancy ladies' items, expensive liquors, ridiculous hats, less practical shoes an' finely made boots from Boston an' Europe."

"Is it even worth going all the way there when we can just go straight to Monterey?" Mae swiped her finger across the map, showing a much shorter direct route.

"It is your choice. At de ranchos along de way, you can find good animals an' small trades. Den outside de missions, some finely crafted tings like saddles an' moccasins. Bot anyting not born, grown or made here, you hef to get from de sheeps." Jack gestured at the "library" shelf. "Most of dese were banned from de Monterey docks, 'cept de Bibles an' de Almanac. Got dem all in Yerba Buena." Mae made a mental note to get Willie a bunch of new books since Jack was now using them as sketch paper.

"Basically, a more liberal choice," Dexter confirmed.

"Once you get here..." Their eyes followed Jack's finger. "Dat's Mission Dolores, den keep on going for a ways an' you vill get to de cove. I'm varning you now, de harbor is muddy. Real muddy. Bot it's de only place de water's calm enough an' deep enough for de sheeps to put anchor. Most of de coast op an' down California is much too rough an' dangerous for de sheeps to even get close to de land. Sheeps anchored in de Yerba Buena harbor might bring deir sopplies to shore or dey vill give you a ride to deir sheep so you can look at deir vares an' make dem a deal." Then Jack looked straight at Mae. "Many sailors hef not set deir eyes on a woman for a year. So, make shore you cover yoursef properly."

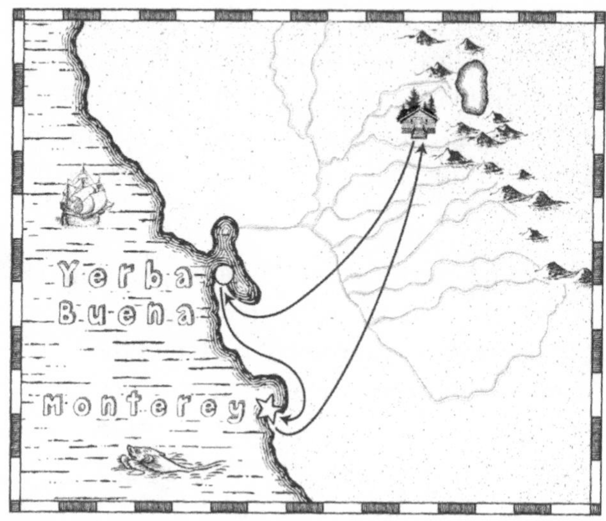

Mae preferred the much simpler route she drew in her head.

Elizabeth had appeared again, but this time to collect the breakfast dishes. And eavesdrop.

"An', as much as I would like to go wit you, I need to stay here." Jack reached his arm around his wife's back. "Nei, I'm not leaving Lizzie home alone wit people like dat man you killed running around dese mountains. Bot I'm letting my Villie go dere wit you. He's been down to de valley a few times an' vill be a big help in talking wit de many tribes you vill come across." Willie beamed, proud and confident.

"And, don't forget we even have our very own Indian maiden to parade and keep us safe." Toke gave a royal bow of his head toward Mae.

"Toke, just because I sort of look like a native does not mean all Indians will instantly like me. Tribes fight amongst themselves just as much. Depending on where we are, I'll probably be distrusted even *more* than you, white boy."

Jack continued, ignoring their conversation, "Maybe look for a few flat pine boards. Dat vill save me from shaving de logs down mysef. An' anoder ting. Don't get too close to anyone. Dey bring deir sicknesses wit dem off de sheeps."

Standing behind Willie now, Elizabeth rested her hands on his shoulders. "Please try to keep Willie away from as many people as you can." Mae hadn't given any thought to the illnesses and how dangerous being around new people could be. None of them had.

Dexter gave Elizabeth a reassuring nod, then turned to face Mae and Toke. "We're probably not immune to much here either like we were back home. For instance, tuberculosis. After countries wipe out a disease, doctors stop giving that particular vaccine. I'm pretty sure we got a polio vaccine but who knows what else we would need here in this time period."

"Like smallpox." A chill went through Mae. "That's *everywhere* here in these times."

"We might get lucky. They pack a hecka lot of crap in those boosters they shoot in our asses." Toke made a show of crossing his fingers.

"Let's not take any chances." Dexter tapped out the quill. "We'll need to be wary, as if we weren't vaccinated for anything."

"Mae, we will need to make you a bonnet." Elizabeth fingered through her pitiful pile of fabric. "Jack tells me you will also need to keep your skin as fair as possible to pass for a Spaniard. People down there aren't too eager to help anyone with Indian blood, I am sorry to say."

"And, she needs to fatten up. She's too thin to be wealthy enough to purchase land." Toke checked out Mae's figure like he was looking for drips to lick from his ice cream cone.

"He just wants me fat again."

"You weren't fat. You were voluptuous. All curves." Toke's hands shaped a woman's curvy body in the air and whistled.

This time Jack agreed, "Ja. Toke speaks de trute, or you'll need to admit you hef been sick. Den no one vill want to go near you."

Mae would really have to try hard to gain weight with all the exercise she was getting. She happily went to the kitchen and came back with a big slice of crusty bread piled with a thick layer of butter and preserves. Oh, but she did love bread…and patting her stomach, she noticed she had a good start with a little pooch there already.

Chapter Eighty-Eight

The countdown had begun. Jack did some trading on their behalf with the Ma'camo and got two old saddles and some braided horsehair rope. Mae's new bonnet, cut from her raggedy gold mining dress, sat finished and ironed. The women got busy mending durable clothing, baking, drying meat, and packing food away. And, even though it took her away from her house duties, Jack was willing to give Mae shooting lessons since one of the first things she'd be buying was a gun.

Toke checked over the horses thoroughly and fortified them with extra food in preparation for their long journey. They decided not to take the wagon going down, but get a new one for the way back. Just thinking about the luxury of buying new clothing not only excited Mae but Dexter and Toke as well. Shoes and boots that actually fit, with an entire bottom sole!

Willie put his mind to their biggest dilemma of trading with gold and came up with an excellent solution. He hammered out some of the gold into ten simple rings for them to barter with on their journey. "No one will question where you got the gold from if it's your grandfather's wedding band." Willie emptied the small pouch into Mae's hand. The rings were rough, but they'd have plenty of time to polish them along their way. She was so happy with Willie that she made him an entire pie. All for him.

At dinner, Toke picked up the pouch of rings from the center of the table. He placed one of the rings on his finger and studied it thoughtfully. "I want to tell you about the tragic adventures of my virile grandfather, who had been married ten times to ten beautiful women." He held the ring up to the candlelight. "This one was Annabelle. My grandfather asked her to marry him after only sharing their first soda. Unfortunately, she was hit by a bus crossing the street ten minutes later and spent the next two years in a coma. My grandfather sat by her bed every single day for hours until, one day, she miraculously awoke. They planned to wed on board an elegant passenger ship that would take them to Europe for a romantic six-month honeymoon. Right after the captain pronounced them husband and wife on their first day at sea, a great white shark sprung out of the water and yanked Annabelle off the ship and into the deep blue sea. She was never seen again." Toke wiped a dry tear from his eye.

The tragic adventures of Toke's virile grandfather entertained them around the fire at night in preparation for their journey as each ring got its own story.

The sunshine of the next day brought Yu'mi riding in followed by Milok and Willie's new horse. Mae ran over and threw her arms around Yu'mi, so happy to see him upright and with color in his face once again.

They walked into the house to a cheerful reception from Elizabeth. "Oh, my gosh, Yu'mi. It hurts my heart to know what you've been through. How are you feeling today?"

"I am very better." He leaned forward to show them the back of his head where it was healing nicely, but still had a lot more mending to do.

Before Yu'mi went home, they all gathered around and showed him the map with their list of things they planned to get. Yu'mi gave them some advice on the terrain, tribal territories and the rivers for horses to water. He made sure they knew which tribes they could trade with and what to do and not do if they came across any random, possibly hostile, Indians.

With all the prep work done, everyone relaxed around the fire, re-checking their list and maps and asking Jack last-minute questions. Dexter gave his full attention to the Fox farmstead map, busy adding extra details and trying to calculate distances. When he felt he could take it no further, he stretched and rubbed his tired eyes. "I think we should load the horses at dawn and plan to leave after an early breakfast."

"Time to hit the feathers then." Toke stood and fully gave in to a bestial yawn. "I've had a busy day of being awesome and need to do it all again tomorrow." Then, he disappeared into his room.

Only a minute passed when Toke began shouting from his room. "Spineless mother! Come here, you little bastard!"

Dexter looked at Mae, his brow raised in amused curiosity. They both stood and advanced toward the berated room. An excited Willie scooted past them and flung open the curtain. They were just in time to see Dexter's mattress airborne for a moment before Toke hammered it into the floor. Feathers and sawdust flew everywhere, causing an explosion of coughing while Toke kept pummeling the lifeless mattress.

"There it goes!" Willie scurried after something and then dove under Toke's bed. "Blazes! I missed it."

Suddenly a small rodent burst out of nowhere, landed on the annihilated mattress, then shot into the nearest hole. Toke tore the mattress open and plunged his arm in up to the shoulder, digging around impatiently.

"Don't hurt it!" Mae bounced nervously.

"Gotcha now. Ow! Sucker just bit me!" Toke yanked his arm out of the mattress, clutching the prisoner in his hands. "Okay, you little shit. You asked for it."

"It just wanted a warm place to sleep," Mae pleaded. Ignoring her, Toke pushed past everyone, through the curtain, and out the front door. She tried once more. "They don't understand property boundaries…"

Dexter sighed in despair as he knelt next to his near-empty mattress, and pitifully tried to re-stuff the flaccid bag. Elizabeth walked over, picked up a pile of the stuffing, and took a quick whiff. Her nose wrinkled in disgust. "We'll need to remake it with all-new stuffing. It is best if we don't let Jack know of this." She motioned them out of the room and slid closed the curtain. "He becomes quite passionate with vermin and could easily fill the room with buckshot."

"Dex," Mae offered. "You are most welcome to sleep in our room. Willie's bed is fairly large, anticipating his future bride, if you remember. Right, Willie?"

Willie blushed. He always got embarrassed whenever anyone talked about him and a girl. Dexter nodded and set about gathering some things before following Willie back to his room.

Toke sauntered back in, breathless, feeling like a hero. "Just in time. Damn thing looked pregnant. Dex can thank me later."

"Did you make it a nice new home safe from predators?" Mae asked, which sounded more like a demand. Toke just looked at her with tired amusement and ducked inside his room.

Mae marched over and threw open his curtain. "That's it? You're just going to sleep without wondering where Dexter's going to sleep now that you destroyed his bed?"

"Yeah, that kind of sucks," Toke said into his pillow with no sympathy in the least.

She crept over to his bedside and whispered in his ear, "Willie says there's more than one in here, and he thinks there's an entire family inside *your* mattress." With a pleased smile, she tiptoed back to her room, hearing a loud "Shit!" just before she shut the wooden door behind her.

Mae lay in bed, unable to sleep with all the anxiety about the trip flittering through her head. Propping herself up, she slid the room divider to the side and gazed out the window above the boys' bed.

Outside, the moon preened brightly, taking center stage in the entire night sky. Its promiscuous light explored every corner of their room, painting it passionately with beguiling shapes.

Mae lifted her face to the cool night breeze and smiled peacefully as it danced across her face. Her ears filled with the familiar hoot of an owl in the distance and a lone coyote howling its woeful story to whoever would listen.

She could feel her mind beginning to relax and closed her eyes, drawing in a long leisurely breath of the rich mountain air.

Her nose picked up another scent, one that didn't come from the outside. Something musty…and somehow…alluring. Masculine. Wanting more, she inhaled deeply, bathing her nostrils in the intoxicating scent of… Dexter.

She let her eyes wander down to the two forms slumbering peacefully on the bed across from her. Dexter's blanket was draped casually over his hips like a marble statue. The rest of his body lay exposed and vulnerable to the seductive sculpting of the moon's light.

Something inside of Mae stirred and she bit her lip softly. What if it were she who was lying next to him instead of Willie? Dexter's warm body pressed against hers…

Her eyes traced the contours of his muscular body, pausing on his powerful chest. She wanted to reach out, letting her fingertips tickle their way through the new little hairs curling on his chest…then moving up, up to his strong shoulders…dusting them with soft feathery kisses, teasing their way farther up…to his neck and then bury her face, taking in a deep breath…ohhh…his intoxicating pheromones…wanting so bad to steal a little bite…then letting her teeth drag, grazing their way up and over his perfectly sculpted jaw to his soft lips…devouring them in a passionate kiss, then reluctantly pulling her mouth away to dapple his cheek with small kisses…then breezing upward like a butterfly to tenderly kiss the lid of his eye—*which was staring right at her.*

Her mouth betrayed her with an audible gasp. In a tiny voice she squeaked out, "Can you…see me?"

His twinkling eyes held a studying look, then answered softly, "The moon is full tonight."

Suddenly self-conscious and completely mortified, she tugged her quilt to her chin. With an exaggerated yawn, she turned away to face the wall and feigned instant sleep. Tears of humiliation formed in her eyes, her shameful guilt now naked and exposed. She wondered if he was still watching her.

Chapter Eighty-Nine

Greg deliriously tugged at the arrow sticking out of his shoulder as he pushed his way through sharp branches and prickly bushes, trying to lose the person behind him. His body felt soaking wet and hurt like he'd been sprayed with a firehose. His head was floating away like it was filled with helium, he could feel his body wanting to follow…he heard men's voices… they were above him…

With a pounding head and aching bones from the bumpy ride, Greg forced his eyes open. Bound by his hands and feet and flung over a horse, unable to move anything. A splintering spasm shot through his leg as his mending bones separated with each jarring step of the animal. The pain was unbearable…and he was out again.

Bright sunlight burned through Greg's eyelids, waking him under the harsh afternoon sun. He forced his eyes as open as he could get them in the brightness, but they refused to give up their guard and remained tiny protective slits. Above him were branches of a tree that at one point, must have been his shade. Roosting in the overhead boughs were a grouping of buzzards that hungrily studied him, each laying claim to his choice body parts.

He lay on the side of a wide dirt path like discarded trash. In a mix of mental confusion and a cacophony of physical pain, Greg wracked his brain in a futile search for any fragments of memories he could stitch together.

He began to carefully trail his fingers up to his shoulder, in hopes the arrow was simply a dream. He was relieved not to find an arrow, but found it wasn't a dream either. A thick crusty mound covered the area that stung, so he began tearing it away, howling, and experiencing an all-new kind of hell. With great effort, he lifted his head and groaned when he saw a hole where the arrow had been and tried to put the gray covering back on. Excited flies frolicked in the pool of congealing blood, but he lacked the energy to swat them away.

He must have dozed off again because when he woke, his skin burned like fire. Heat rose from the dry ground in waves, and his teeth crunched on its dust. His tattered clothes and hair were damp from sweat, and it would be a while until he noticed his belt and shoes were missing.

With his good arm, he was able to pull himself back into the cool shade and lie back down. "Shoo," he said to the eager buzzards, letting them know he was still alive, and they should find their meal elsewhere.

Greg's entire body felt like it was baking in an oven, so he closed his eyes to quell the increasing nausea. He listened to the surrounding fields buzzing with insects and the vultures flapping their wings in irritation that they had to wait so long for him to die. Then, something rustled through the dry grass next to his head and he hoped more than anything it was a lizard, but it could just as easily be a rattlesnake. Sometimes it was just better to sleep…

Greg couldn't tell if he was hallucinating or if the talking man was real. He was forced to drink water and asked question after question that he didn't have enough energy to answer. His body had finally recovered from the paralysis of the arrow's venom, but it was now fighting the infection that was setting in. He wanted to feel the joy of being rescued and finally going home, but he just couldn't stay conscious long enough.

Waking to being dragged by his underarms, the stranger struggled to get him onto the horse's back with stubborn persistence, littering the air with torrents of butchered cursing. Greg wanted to help, if anything to stop the painful abuse to his tortured body, but felt like vomiting more, and maybe he did.

Greg listened to sounds floating around in his head somewhere. A crackling fire…hooting owl…trickling water…clanking metal…a snorting horse. Roasting meat filled his nostrils and he salivated, then his eyes flicked open for the first time in days. Where the hell *was* he? The last memory he had, he was sitting on top of a horse, tightly strapped to its back.

Seeing movement from Greg, a dog walked over and lay by his side. "That there's Buckeye." A rough but friendly sounding voice came, attached to a rugged, weather-beaten man somewhere in his late forties. The stranger walked over and then removed his cowboy hat, slicking back his graying, dirty blonde hair in its own grease. Squatting down next to him, the man put the back of his hand to Greg's forehead, then smiled, adding a whistle of relief. "I was worried there fer a few days when yeh was boilin' up. Yeh started shoutin' out all sorts of crazy things in yer sleep." Unsure what to think, Greg just looked at him skeptically, and for the first time in his life, felt speechless.

The man left his side and returned with a plate of food. "Be careful now. Yeh might wanna take it easy. Yeh been through a helluva lot."

Greg tried to pull himself up, biting back the searing pain in his shoulder. With help from the man, he was soon propped up against the log that lay by his side. He hungrily snatched up a sizable piece from the metal plate and gnawed on the chewy meat silently, while taking in his surroundings.

Miles of flat open land lay to his left, scattered with scrub brush and small trees as if someone sprayed them out of a hose. Walling it off from behind, far off hills busily tucked the sun to bed as it painted the sky a spectacular peachy orange in its wake. Greg picked up a new hunk of meat and tore into it. Just a few yards from their camp meandered a small creek that was being fed from the richly forested hills to the east. Then farther back, far behind the forest, he could barely make out tall rocky peaks jutting up sharply in the distance, peeking in and out of the hovering clouds. No matter which direction he looked, it was all empty country. Not one sign of human habitation anywhere. Except for them.

When he finished his second piece of meat, he dove into another, gulping down an entire cup of water in between. The dog waited eagerly for the bones and nudged Greg with his wet nose as a reminder. "Yeh can make a friend fer life," said the man, gesturing toward Buckeye.

But, with his thoughts entirely preoccupied by his new situation, Greg only responded with, "Where the hell *am* I?"

Buckeye whined and looked pleadingly at Greg until his owner finally took the plate from Greg and fed the dog the bones himself. With a grunt, he sat down on the rock across from Greg and pulled the cork off an unlabeled bottle of liquor.

"So." Greg felt his impatience growing. "Are you taking me to the hospital, or what?"

"No hospitals in these parts, son. Yeh was pretty bad off and gittin' worse. So, by the second day, I just fixed yeh up best I could. Had to cut out a good 'mount of yer skin and muscle to git all the 'fection out. Gonna hurt like hell fer a while yet. Never cut open nobody negra like yeh before. Wasn't sure what to 'spect inside." He took a swig from a bottle and wiped his mouth with his sleeve.

With the faint memory coming back of the arrow in his shoulder, Greg's hand shot up to feel his wound. Instead, he found a long cloth bandage that wrapped all the way around his chest and over his shoulder. "Uh, thank you…" he said apprehensively, as one would thank a person who thought they were doing you a favor by pre-chewing your food.

The man offered Greg his grimy bottle, but he declined, so the man took a swig himself saying, "We been ridin' for three days now. I know a squaw down a ways that'll bring yeh back to right and make sure yer leg is healin' the way it's s'pose to. Yer a damn lucky feller yer bones didn't break clear through the skin, or I'd a hadda take it off from the knee down. My knife needs a good sharpnin', so yeh wouldn't a liked that." He laughed, coughing through it, then spat.

Greg wasn't sure if he was hearing all this right. Was he being abducted by a lunatic? Not hiding his growing desperation, he pleaded, "Can't you just call an ambulance? They have helicopters that can be here in minutes."

Smiling and shaking his head as if Greg was just spouting off in his delirium again, the man said, "The name's Trigger. Been callin' yeh Jimi 'cause that's the name on yer shirt and the paintin' on it looks just like yeh." He motioned to the tattered t-shirt drying by the fire. Greg gave him an unreadable look. He didn't look anything like Jimi Hendrix, except that they were both black with a big fro. Trigger took another swig from the bottle, and in a kind, reassuring voice added, "Don't yeh worry. I got no plans to make money off yeh. Just wanna hep yeh out. Never saw any of yer kind way out here. I admire yer courage." He picked up Greg's empty plate and wiped it "clean" with his handkerchief.

Everything passing through Greg's brain was too surreal—vacuous like he had had a lobotomy. With a defeated sigh, he reached his arm out for the liquor bottle and Trigger eagerly obliged, desperate for a drinking companion.

Chapter Ninety

Mae woke to the hustle and bustle of the house already in motion. Today was the big day, their first glimpse into the world that they had never known. Jack had been up early, checking the horses and packing them with last-minute necessities, and Elizabeth had breakfast on the table.

This was their first trip without Yu'mi taking care of them and it would be brutally challenging, not to mention strange and emotional. They'd be passing the land they used to live on with their own families, pets, and friends. Was she ready? Were any of them? And would they even recognize it?

Blessed with cool and breezy weather, they couldn't have hoped for a more perfect day. Just a couple of things left to do, so she rolled up her bedding and then stuffed a change of clothing inside. She tied on the sunbonnet Elizabeth had made to keep her skin fair and—it went without saying—to hide her unfeminine short haircut. Dexter and Toke would have no trouble blending in with their already substantial beard growth and hair just long enough to peek out from under their hats.

Walking back into the room, Dexter picked up his pack and cinched the top shut. Most of the awkwardness between them from the night before had been replaced with new thoughts and concerns about their trip. But, she still could not look him in the eye and found herself tying far more knots in her sack than needed. Mae looked down and pressed her lips together. Just say something casual. Like nothing happened. "Dex, do you ever think about running into more people from the future where we're going?"

Toke yelled from the front porch, "Grab your grub! Let's get moving!" He spoke with such authority they almost believed he was in charge.

Waiting for a thoughtful answer from Dexter, he only said, "No, not really. We'd better get a move on. Need help?" All business this morning. Mae responded by flinging her entire bedroll over her shoulder and walking out first. Anyway, she shouldn't care nor have those wicked thoughts in the first place. She forcibly changed her focus to the future and quickly found her mood brightening.

The renewed hope of finding Greg on their journey now filled her thoughts and put a big smile on her face. She would not accept any other fact than he was alive and well. Greg was still so vibrant and animated in her memories, much like he was in reality—changing people's dark gloom into a bright and sunshiny day. He just had that insatiable optimism that was catchy and endearing. Still smiling, she put her foot in the leather stirrup and climbed atop Trixie.

Toke gave Mae a strange look as he tightened down her bedroll. "Wipe that creepy smile off your face."

Wrinkling her nose at him, she leaned forward and patted the side of Trixie's neck. Mae felt like a proud mom. The little horse was on her first big adventure, leaving the only mountains she'd ever known.

Checking one by one, Toke made sure they each still had their two pouches of gold nuggets stashed inside their clothes and a few of his grandfather's rings, conveniently located for quick trading. He felt for the small satchel of gold dust tucked under his saddle and then mounted his horse, joining the rest of them.

Once Elizabeth finished hugging Willie and warning him of anything and everything he had to watch out for, she stepped back to wipe her tears. With a quick nod from Jack, Toke snapped the reins. "Let's blow this goat farm. H'ya!"

The way Toke stepped up this time and took charge took Mae by surprise. She had more hope for him now as they entered this scary new world. Jack's rifle hung down his back, a sheathed knife on each side of his belt, as well as one secured to the brim of his hat. He was entirely in his element, taking full advantage of a land free from gun and weapon laws.

Two minutes into their ride, Yu'mi pulled up on his horse and rode alongside them for a while before saying goodbye. Mae never did get to have that talk about Greg with him, and, now that Waho knew the truth about her, maybe she never had to.

Yu'mi sat atop the hill, his hand raised in a frozen wave. Looking sad and dejected, he watched them blaze their own trail through the grasses. Toke glanced back and said, with a pained half-smile, "Sort of looks like a puppy being left home alone. I just hope someone remembers to feed him." Mae looked back for one final wave, but he was already gone.

By late afternoon the next day, they could see the side view of Sailor Rock peeking out above the trees on the small mountain to the left. It brought back a surge of emotional memories of the day they realized the truth of where they were.

As it came more into view, Toke shaded his eyes for a better look. "Aw. He looks so innocent, all clean like this. Not the dirty ol' sailor we've always known."

Dexter kept his eyes glued on the rock. "It's weird, and I'm sure my imagination's toying with me, but I can almost pick out two wolves up there, howling from the flames." His voice sagged a little. "Funny how the brain works." But, he slowed his horse anyway, and the others stopped to see for themselves.

"It's not weird, bud." Toke's voice grew with excitement. "Holy shit. There *are* two wolves in flames. No joke."

Willie chimed in, not quite understanding the significance. "Yeah. One's howling at the sun and the other at the moon."

Dexter's head snapped back around. "You're kidding," he said, but could tell in Toke's elated expression, he definitely wasn't.

Mae, afraid to get her hopes up simply to have them come crashing back down again, calmly shaded her eyes to get a clear view of Sailor Rock. Suddenly, her posture stiffened, and her heart began to pound so fiercely she thought it might crack through her ribcage. "Greg!" She turned Trixie sharply in the direction of the rock and raced through the trees, the rest following behind her.

Soon, they were right on her tail, shouting Greg's name the entire way. Baskets and sacks caught in the trees, but no one seemed to care except Willie, who stopped to collect them all. Once they reached the base of the big rock, they hastily tethered their horses and scrambled up the back of Sailor Rock.

They called his name constantly while searching every crevice of the rock formation. When they came to the small cave, they looked for any signs that Greg had slept there, but found nothing. "Wait, what the hell is that?" Toke reached his fingers over a small indentation in the back of the cave and with a quick tug to loosen it, brought out a dusty and corroded iPhone, looking as if it had been savagely tortured in a garbage disposal.

"Fender! That's Greg's!" Mae screamed, grabbing it from Toke and hastily pulled off the spider nests and slimy green coating. She started to cry and laugh and bounced up and down hugging Dexter, feeling intoxicated with hope.

"Okay, this is weird," Toke puzzled, taking the phone from Mae to examine it. "But, how did Greg have his cell phone when none of us even got to keep our fingernails?"

"He must not have had to swim through the blue water to get out," Mae squealed, still flying high.

Dexter scanned the surrounding landscape beyond Sailor Rock. "And, maybe we don't either if we find where that is." Then, he paused to assure Mae, "But, we're not leaving before we find Greg."

After one last inspection in the deep recesses of the cave, Toke recovered a stiff lumpy mass that was so rodent-chewed he could barely tell it was a leather wallet. He thumbed through the mildewed insides that nearly disintegrated in his fingers until he pulled out a nearly perfect plastic

California driver's license and a warped ATM card severely disfigured by bubbled lamination. "Yep. It's his," he said matter-of-factly, then stuffed the cards back inside and handed it all over to Mae.

She held it in her palm and eyed it warily as if she was waiting for it to breathe or bark. "But..." She felt her flurry of excitement spin itself down and become replaced by worry. "But, why would he leave his wallet behind? Especially with money and everything still in it?"

"He probably knew they'd be useless here, so why bother with it?" Dexter said.

"Yeah, you're right." She hit her forehead in a "duh" motion. Of course, Greg wouldn't want to risk being caught with things so dangerously unnerving to the times. A *United States* California driver's license with a *color* photo of his face, a *plastic* debit card, and money minted from some time in the *future*. Slowly, her mind relaxed, and her heart began to sing once again with anticipation.

For the next few minutes, they continued their hunt for clues and then called down to Willie waiting at the bottom that they would be right down. Dexter stopped in front of the substantial carving of their boyhood tattoo and traced his fingers along a wolf's back while thinking out loud, "He must be out there looking for us."

"He probably went down to the valley—*right where we're goingggg!*" Mae sang the last part, too giddy to contain herself.

Toke picked up a sharp-looking rock and tried scratching in today's date. October 5, 1840. "How the hell did he do this? I can barely make a scratch."

"He must have been up here this whole time just waiting for us." Dexter took off his glasses and leaned in for a closer look at Greg's carving. "Hmm. This doesn't look very fresh. It appears he's been gone for a while." Mae looked like he had just stabbed her in the heart with a knife. So he quickly added, "We're sure to catch up to him in no time."

But, Mae actually *did* feel like she'd been stabbed with a knife. Now that they had actual proof Greg was alive, a whole new crop of worries came up. Leaning heavily into the rock, she sighed. "You know, even though Jack says they outlawed African slaves in Mexico, what kind of place will this be for a black man? Not everyone follows the rules, and he could be worth a lot of money over in the U.S."

"Well, we've got the dough to buy him at *any* price," Toke assured her, then turned to climb down. "Let's haul some ass!"

The quiet solitude of their long ride let the enormity of what they were planning to do really sink in. Though overjoyed with the hope of finding Greg, they couldn't lose focus and become reckless. They were heading to a place where they could do some significant good, but, just as easily, irreversible damage, possibly preventing their *own* futures *and* the fates of people they loved from happening. Mae pictured her mom's face and what she remembered of her father's, then her friends, whom she loved like sisters. It was excruciating to think that she could be responsible for wiping out all of their innocent lives.

They were playing God with history and had barely started to make the changes they intended. This power the three of them held was enormous, and the task before them was utterly terrifying.

Chapter Ninety-One

Greg hadn't noticed when he fell asleep, but woke to Trigger mid-story. "There's beavers everywhere. I do most my tradin' in skins, mostly beaver, 'tween the Injins and the larger fur traders. Sometimes I go as far as to trade directly with the ships." He gave an exhausted chuckle. "It keeps me moving, and I leave a trail of happy squaws." He gave Greg a wink and chuckled again, then offered Greg another drink, which he took. "Learned me a few languages 'long the way, 'nough to get by at least. I don't get much trouble from no one. They leave me alone 'cuz they like what I bring, and my tradin' terms is generous. There's a helluva lotta competition out yonder, mostly tradin' otter skins, which are gettin' hard to find. But beaver, now, that's where it's going. Place is overflowin' with them, they'll be 'round forever."

To Greg's relief, Trigger stopped talking for a moment to spit in the bushes, then walked over to his saddle draped over the far end of the log. As he dug around his satchels for another bottle, Greg stared into the night sky, counting the stars, feeling helpless and completely dependent on this madman. He thought about escaping, but he was in no shape to go anywhere right now. Trigger said they'd been traveling for three days now… but, since it was by horse…and he stopped at one point to perform surgery on his shoulder, there was a chance they could be outside Sacramento somewhere. Except for those giant gray peaks, he couldn't remember seeing those anywhere near the city. "So, how long do you think before I'm healed up enough to walk?"

Plopping back down on the rock, Trigger offered Greg a drink from a new bottle. "Well, I'm guessing maybe Friday or Saturday yeh can be on yer feet again." Trigger cleared his throat. "So, now, where was I? Oh yeah, so the Injins been tradin'…"

"And what day's today?" Greg interrupted.

"Monday. No, Tuesday. Yes, Tuesday," Trigger hurriedly answered, eager to continue on with his endless story.

Greg impatiently groaned, "But what's the *date*?" He took a swig from the new bottle but immediately spat it out. That couldn't possibly be drinkable. It tasted like he had made the liquor himself. From his own urine.

Trigger frowned at the wasted booze at Greg's feet just soaking up the dirt. "The sixth of August." Then, for emphasis, showing that he was answering his question *completely*, and they could move on with his story, he restated, "Tuesday, August 6th, 1822."

END OF BOOK ONE

Note to You

My treasured reader, thank you so very much for reading the first book in my Tangle of Time saga. I've spent years doing extensive historical research to keep the facts and people as accurate as possible. The other characters are entirely fictional, as well as the tribe names: Ma'camo, Sekoma, Yiptuati, and their members.

My heart and soul have gone into writing this novel, and I truly hope you've come away with an enlightened perspective on the lesser known parts of history. Just wait until you read what happens in book two!

I would be forever grateful if you could leave a helpful review to aid others who may enjoy my book. Also, I'd really appreciate hearing from you and get your comments or criticisms—it's all constructive to me. You can reach me at ginwestcott@sonic.net, @ginwestcott, or through my website https://ginwestcott.com.

xoxo Gin

About the Author

GIN WESTCOTT is the author of the Historical Adventure/Time-Travel fiction TANGLE OF TIME and is currently writing the next book of the series. She comes from a creative world and spent years working in big Los Angeles advertising agencies as an award-winning art director and is currently a designer. Gin has an unlimited imagination bursting with ideas and found writing novels the perfect outlet. She is passionate about human rights, animal cruelty, gender equality, and injustice and finds these core values working their way into her fresh storylines. Having a dry, quirky sense of humor, she spawns unique, compelling characters that weave their way through exciting, yet often unsettling, situations. Gin is the mother of two great kids, two little dogs, and wife of the amazing Scott. When not writing or designing, she's either hiking in the lush mountains of Northern California or voice-acting for toys, commercials, and video games.

Acknowledgments

There are so many people I'd like to thank that helped me bring my story to print. My many beta readers who helped shape Tangle of Time with their excellent feedback: Scott Callow, Shelby Lestrange, Allison Callow, Hayley Westcott, Phoenix Eagleshadow of the Ohlone tribe, Sharon, Danielle, Brittany, Daniel Schafer-Dews, Georgina Dews, Sancy Beck Hilgenberg, Sharon Montooth, Betsy Fasbinder for her excellent coaching, Aaron Waugh, and my many insightful readers and editors from Entrada Publishing. Also a very special thank you goes to Valeska from Norway, who assisted me on Jack's Americanized Norse accent.

https://ginwestcott.com

CPSIA information can be obtained
at www.ICGtesting.com
Printed in the USA
LVHW091728270620
659154LV00001B/61